FURYSONG

FURYSONG

ROSARIA MUNDA

G. P. Putnam's Sons

G. P. PUTNAM'S SONS

An imprint of Penguin Random House LLC, New York

First published in the United States of America by G. P. Putnam's Sons,
an imprint of Penguin Random House LLC, 2022

Visit us online at penguinrandomhouse.com

Library of Congress Cataloging-in-Publication Data is available.

Printed in the United States of America
ISBN 9780525518273

1st Printing

LSCH

Design by Nicole Rheingans
Text set in Sabon LT Std

To my husband, Robert

PROLOGUE

The girl watched her father dig. The fields were quiet; Hettie and Lila were inside with the village women, preparing the body; Garet had wandered up the mountainside in the morning; and Rory worked on the opposite end of the grave, widening while their father deepened. The highlands in winter were cold and windy and slightly wet.

"Will Mumma go in there?" the girl asked.

Her father paused to wipe sweat from his neck. "Aye."

"And the baby will go here, if he dies?"

Da's pause was longer. "Aye."

"Go inside, Annie," her brother Rory said, his voice cracking. "Go inside with the women."

"Did the baby kill Mumma?"

"Da! Send her in!"

"Rory, take a break."

Rory threw down his shovel. The girl eyed the shovel as Rory stalked away across the field. "I can dig," she said.

The grave was already deep enough that it would swallow her if she climbed down into it, but she wasn't afraid. Her father, who could always tell when she was trying to understand, hoisted himself from the half-dug grave to sit beside her on the edge of it. He smelled of earth and sweat; his beard nuzzled her cheek when he drew her into his arms. The two spades were propped against his knee.

"The baby didn't kill your mother," he said. "The hunger killed your mother. The lords killed your mother when they took our food."

The girl thought the baby might still be to blame. The baby was what caused the pain and the blood. Not the lords. She didn't think Da wanted to hear that.

"You are very sad, Da?"

Rory would tell her to stop asking questions. But Rory was on the other end of the clearing, glaring at the valley below. And Da always answered her questions, even the ones that made him pause for a long time and close his eyes.

"Sad," Da said finally. "And angry."

"You're keeping it inside?"

"I'm keeping it inside."

This was the refrain they had, before collections. When our lord comes, whatever you're feeling, you keep it inside. You keep it inside because that's where it's safest.

Her father took her hand in his, so that it was her finger that he pointed at the unbroken ground next to them. "There's space beside this grave, for me. And beside that, for your brothers and sisters."

She did not cry. She kept it inside. "No," she said. "Not yet."

"Not yet," he agreed.

She heard how he said it, and changed her mind. "Never," she said.

His surprise rumbled through his belly. "My little skylark, my skysung queen," he said. "You are awfully young to be giving orders."

This was silly, because she wasn't a queen and couldn't give orders, but she curled closer and didn't laugh. When he ran a hand over her hair, his palm cupped her entire head.

"Did your mother ever tell you that you have her hair?"

The girl touched her fringe. "I have *my* hair," she said.

He smiled, lines splitting his face, beard rippling. It had been days since she'd seen him smile. "You have your hair, but it came from her," he said. "Brown as the earth, red as flame. You take her with you."

She tucked a finger into her hair and wrapped a curl around it, thinking: *I have a piece of my mother with me. A secret piece.* When he set her on her feet and told her to go inside and help prepare the body, she went.

Her father finished digging the grave alone. The baby, who died not long after, was buried alongside his mother.

As winter turned to spring, and spring to summer, her sister Lila took over her mother's chores, and she and her sister Hettie took over Lila's. Lila braided their hair as their mother used to do. In secret, out of earshot of Rory and Lila and Da, she and Hettie sometimes played the old game mumma-and-baby, but it took on a desperate edge. Like pretending had the power to bring her back.

"No, you have to say it like Mumma said it," Hettie said.

But she was starting to have trouble remembering how Mumma said it.

"I have Mumma's hair," she told Hettie, who did not.

Hettie burst into tears. She watched, keeping her feelings inside where they were safest. She asked Hettie if she wanted to play a *different game, and Hettie gulped and wiped her eyes and nodded. They played burn-down-the-village instead, and she let Hettie be the dragonlord.*

For a few warm months they had enough to eat—but not enough for the tax and the coming winter. The blight was back. In late summer, when the hair her mother gave her was streaked with gold from the sun, stormscourge dragons were seen in the sky again. The dragonlords had returned to their country estates for the season, and would soon begin harvest collections.

In the house of Don Macky, one of the village leaders, the men of Holbin added the crier's latest decree to the pile of notices delivered in the name of Leon Stormscourge and the Drakarchy of the Far Highlands. The girl, who had slipped in among the men unnoticed, studied this decree as she had studied the earlier ones, upright on her knees on the Mackys' long bench between her father and Rory. The men spoke of cellars and hiding and hoarding, and how much was too much to hide, but she didn't listen.

"Too risky," Don Macky said.

"So is another winter after blight," her father said.

"What does insuborbination *mean?" the girl asked.*

"Insubordination," her father corrected automatically. "It means when you disobey your lord."

"Silas," said Don Macky, nodding at her. "Look at your daughter."

The conversation paused as they looked at the girl, who was moving a finger along the writing of the decree, her lips forming silent syllables as she remembered the crier's words. She had been doing this at their meetings for months now, sandwiched unnoticed in her father's shadow. By now she understood enough of the words on the page to be able to take apart the symbols and turn them back into sounds.

"She isn't—?"

"I think she is."

Da placed a finger at the top of the page. "What does it say, Antigone?"

The girl moved his finger from the right side of the parchment to the left. "It starts here," she said.

Her father brought her to all the meetings after that on purpose. The men of Holbin welcomed her. Not because they had anything new for her to read: because she had become, in some small way, a talisman. This tiny girl, with her too-big name, who was as clever with letters as any lord. Sometimes they would have her read old decrees for their delight. Sometimes her father would lift her on his shoulders to carry her home, and she felt tall enough to touch the summer stars and pretended she was soaring overhead like the dragons that crossed their skies.

"You're faking it," Rory said. "Da only believes you can read because you're his favorite."

The first part hurt her the most, because it wasn't true, but she knew the second part was what hurt Rory. "I'm not," she said.

When she told Lila about it, Lila told her not to give Rory any mind. He was bitter because he had been Mumma's favorite, and now she was gone.

She noticed how Lila said it. "Whose favorite are you?" she asked Lila, who was plaiting her hair.

"No one's," said Lila, after a moment of thought.

"Then you'll be mine. And Hettie can be yours, and Garet can be Hettie's, so that it's fair."

She felt pleasure at working this solution out. It was like the scales the lord's secretary used on Collection Day, except she imagined not just two trays but five. Lila, Rory, Hettie, Garet, and her. All with someone who favored them, hanging in perfect balance.

"*You silly girl,*" Lila said with a smile in her voice, and tied off the braid. "*You can't make everything fair.*"

Collection Day approached. Cellars were dug and stocked and hidden. The men argued about how much was safe to set aside. Da made his cellar the largest of all and swore on his wife's grave that no child of his would go hungry again this winter. The boys practiced bowing, the girls practiced curtsying, and Da made sure they knew the Pleas by heart, just in case. In the past, this had been Mumma's lesson, and Da had resented it. This year, as it became his lesson, he drilled them until they knew the lines cold. Mumma had always assured them they would never be needed, but Da made no such promise. Instead, he added a lesson of his own.

"*They watch us kneel, they see the back of our heads, and they think we've given in. They don't realize you can think from your knees just as well as from your feet.*"

They were practicing in front of the house. The door to the hidden cellar was buried under reeds three meters away. The children were kneeling, their father standing in front of them, playing their lord. Up until this point, there had been a fair bit of giggling, as Hettie and Garet poked each other and attempted stiff faces. But at Da's last words, all poking ceased. They could feel the gravity of what they did rooting them to the earth.

"Rory," Da asked his kneeling son, "*what are you thinking of?*"

"*I'm thinking of the grain my lord doesn't know we've hidden safe,*" Rory told the ground.

Da went down the line, asking the same question of each child. When he asked Antigone, she said: "*I'm keeping what I'm feeling inside.*"

Looking at the ground, she couldn't see her father's expression.

"Good," he said.

On Collection Day, Da and Rory hauled the cart loaded with grain and other offerings down the path into the center of the village square. Lila carried the gift basket of bread, and the younger children trailed in a line behind. The dragon perch was already shadowed with its visitor, a stormscourge with red-tipped wings and a red crest. Lila told them it was bad luck to look, but when Lila wasn't looking, she risked a glance up at the great stormscourge and found slitted eyes staring back at her. She felt a pulse of fear, but also something else. Excitement.

The talons, the wings, the gleaming scales made the most beautiful animal she'd ever seen.

The queue moved slowly. Their lord took his time asking after each household, with a gracious smile and gently accented Callish. When the time came for her family, their cart was wheeled up for inspection while they made obeisance as they had practiced. She held her breath as numbers were murmured and shared with their lord. Would he notice that their offering represented only a fraction of what they had hidden in the cellar? The secretary frowned over the sums, and was about to bring a question to Leon when Leon's attention was caught by something else.

"Your wife," he said. "Why isn't she here?"

Silas laced his fingers across his waist. "She passed, Lord, in childbirth."

She noticed that he did not give the causes of death he'd given her. He didn't mention the hunger or the blight or Leon's taxes.

"I'm sorry to hear that, Silas," said Leon.

He did look it. He had very kind, gray eyes that turned on Silas's family arrayed behind him in concern. The secretary paused, lips pursed.

"She leaves behind a beautiful family," Leon said.

"Thank you, Lord."

"Have they all been presented to me? The youngest—?"

"Forgive me, I forget myself, Lord. This is Antigone, who only just attained the age of reason."

Lila applied pressure, unneeded, at her back, as she redoubled her curtsy under their lord's gray gaze.

"Antigone," Leon mused. "That's a Dragontongue name."

He sounded thoughtful, and as his interest was caught, so was the dragon's overhead. Its head perked, crest rising ever so slightly along its back as it swung round to observe its rider and the family he interviewed. Her neck prickled at the dragon's attention, but no smoke issued from the nostrils, no warning sign. A tremor was in her father's voice when he answered. "I heard it in a song. Beg pardon, my lord, I hope it does not offend."

"Not at all. I like to think proud names among my serfs only increases the pride of Stormscourge House."

Silas bowed. The dragon lowered its head and its eyes slid shut again. Leon told the girl: "I have a son a little older than you."

"Lord," she answered, keeping her eyes on his fine boots.

Leon Stormscourge nodded to his secretary, who rolled his eyes to the cloudless sky in exasperation. The secretary took two loaves from their family's gift basket, stacked them in Antigone's arms, and announced in reedy Palace-standard Callish, "A condolence for your family's loss."

She tightened her arms around the returned bread and curtsied to her lord, keeping her feelings inside. Silas growled, "May my lord accept the gratitude of his servant for kindness undeserving."

Glancing up at her father, bent double, she saw that his neck was bright red.

Leon flicked a wrist, and the secretary called: "Next!"

There was celebration in the village that night. The grain offerings had passed muster; the excuses had been bought; Leon's good temper had left the Holbiners' schemes successful. In Silas's house, the bread their lord had taken and then given back to them was torn and dipped in honey that had been hidden in the secret cellar, and turned into a feast. They toasted their lord for his mercy, and his stupidity. They toasted the mother he had killed.

The following morning, a shadow passed over their fields. A red-crested stormscourge landed in front of Silas's house. The soldiers, who came down from Harfast and the seat of the Western Triarchy, trickled into the village and surrounded Silas's yard.

Leon was just as mild-mannered today as he had been the day before. "I have spoken with my secretary. It seems there has been a mistake."

Silas didn't bow the way he bowed the day before, from the waist. He got to his knees and placed his hands in the mud. Behind him, his children did the same. It was what they had practiced, except this time, it was not pretend. He began to recite the Pleas he had taught his children, the ones used only at the end. Some soldiers stood between him and his family, surrounding the house, while others searched the yard. When the secret cellar was discovered, Silas ran out of Pleas.

"Your favorite," Leon said. It seemed to be a question, but Silas was unable to answer it.

As her father began to weep, she thought, *He needs to keep his feelings inside.*

She was so transfixed, watching her father, watching her lord and the dragon bearing down, that she did not notice Rory until he was pulling her to her feet. He rubbed two palms against his eyes. "Go to our lord," he said.

The last thing she wanted was to go closer to their lord or his dragon. "No."

"Annie, go," he said. His voice, which cracked and rose so often when it was used against her, was suddenly very calm. "You'll be all right."

Lila gave her a little push, and her feet began to walk.

She walked toward the dragonlord, and her father was led away from him. She tried to remember afterward how they had crossed paths in the space between the dragon and the house. Had he knelt to greet her, to ghost one last kiss on her forehead, as she walked away from death and he walked toward it? The truth was, she couldn't remember passing him at all. Only the dragon and the lord and her leaden steps toward them as they loomed over her. And then she turned to see her father behind her, his back to her, being led with her siblings into the house.

"Hello again, Antigone," said Leon kindly, as he saw who had been chosen. "Come here."

He set his hand on the back of her neck, as a father might a child he wanted to calm, or a rider with a restless dragon. The stormscourge beside him was alert, nostrils smoking. She no longer found it beautiful. Leon lifted his voice and pronounced his sentence in Dragontongue. She did not understand at the time, but years later, remembering the name of the punishment, she looked it up and read the words in a library far away, recognizing them for the first time.

"For he who earns the dragon's punishment, let his home be his tomb."

He gave the order to his dragon, and her home became a tomb.

When the fire started, she tried to keep her feelings inside. But they didn't stay. They spilled out, along with the Pleas she had been taught as she began to recite them. Leon ignored the feelings and he ignored the Pleas, too. He held her gently, but he did not let her look away.

"Yes," he said finally, "it is a terrible waste."

He turned her toward him and wiped her eyes with gloved thumbs. He stroked her hair the way her father had at her mother's graveside, and she was so distraught, she clung to him. "There, child. You've learned your lesson now, haven't you? You'll tell your father's friends down in the village?"

Leon settled her on her feet and took to one knee to meet her eyes, as if he were used to giving lessons in the way a child could understand.

"When you try to defy us, we take everything."

PART I

—

REVOLUTION

1

THE RECKONING

DELO

NEW PYTHOS

It's the eve of the Long-Awaited Return, and I'm about to lose everything.

Everything. That is what he's become for me, this boy who kneels beside me as I stare down my family, my court, as if I were alien to them. Griff Gareson, the humble-rider, the peasant, whom I never was supposed to love. I look down at his damp curls, at the burns that glaze the muscles of his neck, and wish we were alone so that I could kiss them one last time. I marvel at how steadily he holds his head.

Does he not realize what is happening?

"Why did you give it to him?" Lady Electra asks.

My crime: I gave Griff Gareson the key to his muzzled, chained dragon, which he used to find Antigone, Firstrider of the Callipolan Fleet, and turn spy against us.

Tonight, Griff's crimes have been uncovered even as our plan proceeds unfoiled. Ixion still sets out to bring Callipolis to its knees with the help of a foreign princess and a promise of bread. I'm closer to returning to my home now than I've been in these ten long years of exile. I should be glorying in our triumph.

But all I can think is that the one I love is about to be dropped.

The dragonborn exiles in this room look at me, look at him,

and make their assumptions. They assume I was a lovestruck fool, too smitten to ask what he did with that key.

I was smitten. I am smitten. But I was never a fool. I didn't ask what he did with that key, but I knew.

I let him.

Why? That is the question that turns over and over, like sea-smooth stones knocking in my hand. Why did I enable this treachery?

I have prepared for the Long-Awaited Return to Callipolis as eagerly as the rest of them. I long to go home. I feel the absence of the Skyfish Summer Palace like the ache of a missing limb, still waking up, ten years later, from dreams where I smell the Medean wafting through sunlit marble halls and hear the ghostly laugh of a mother the usurpers took from me.

"It's been a pleasure serving all of you," says Griff, bowing low, before he is dragged from the room.

Once he's gone, Father makes the one demand commensurate with my failure.

"You will be the one to drop him."

***

Hours later, in my chambers where I wait for dawn, a knock sounds on the door and my surroundings return to me. The tomes spread across my desk contain the old poems with their heroes; I've been staring at them, unseeing, since I lit the lamp and slumped in this chair hours ago. The childhood comforts have not worked tonight.

Outside the door, I find a young Norcian woman holding a note.

Mabalena, called Lena, was once a humble-rider, like Griff. Her limp, her strangely angled limbs, and her lopsided face are a reminder of the punishment she suffered six years ago. Found guilty of sedition and dropped, as Griff will be—though only an idiot would believe sweet, bumbling Mabalena capable of anything they accused her of. She's served in the citadel ever since. Her quarters are in the dungeons, in an unlocked cell; there's no point locking Lena in. She has nowhere left to go.

For her, the drop was a life sentence of pain. For Griff, it will be an execution.

"A message from Lord Rhode, my lord."

Rhode has written: *Do not despair so soon, brother. There are plenty more peasants to warm your bed.*

Moments like this, I strain to remember the childhood in which Rhode and I were friends.

I look over the letter at Mabalena, who waits with eyes downcast, her face placid, her usual matted hair limp as if a coarse brush had been recently forced through it. It's hard to believe, looking at this broken girl, that she ever rode on a dragon's back. The unasked questions shriveled on the vine years ago: *Do they touch you? Do they hurt you?* The same questions I learned not to ask Griff when Julia started summoning him and laughing about it afterward. What could I do with my knowledge? Nothing. And when nothing can be done, discretion is the last decency.

I used to wonder what was wrong with me, for *caring.* Whether it's me who is perverse, or my family, remains a matter of opinion. But with Griff about to drop, it's a little late for my cure. I take two steps to the fire and drop the note in it. Mabalena watches the parchment burn with flames reflected in her eyes.

"How is the Callipolan prisoner?"

Mabalena's eyes dart from the fire to my face. What tearstains she sees there, she doesn't linger on. "He struggles with sorrow spells still," she says. "Missing his skyfish. But he is kind. We speak a little Dragontongue. Daily he improves; his wounds heal."

All the prisoners are Mabalena's charges, but I noticed, when I surrendered Duck Sutter into her care two months ago after finding him improbably alive in the rubble of a blazesite, that she took particular interest in his rehabilitation. The Callipolan's sorrow at the loss of his dragon is something she understands, just as she knows what it is like to survive a fatal drop, and live with a shattered body, as Duck Sutter has had to do.

I hoped they would help each other. All the same, I'm not prepared for what Mabalena murmurs next. "The Callipolan has been . . . sunlight to my darkness, my lord."

She sounds as if she isn't sure it's a good thing. Her expression is, for a moment, so vulnerable it looks naked.

Sweet Mabalena, who fell so hard. Doesn't she know that happiness is something we're not allowed?

I gesture at the armchair between us, and Lena eases into it like a perching bird. I take the seat opposite. The expression on her scarred face grows all the more disconcerted as I pour wine into two goblets and offer her one. She drinks when I drink.

"Griff has been found guilty of treason."

Her fingers tighten on the goblet. Understanding, as only Mabalena could, what that word forebodes.

"Father has ordered me to do it."

"Then you should," she says.

Only when she says it, and I feel no surprise, do I realize this is what I needed her to say.

Because I've been thinking it, too.

Lena's eyes are ice gray. Like they've been drained of color.

"You can assure that it is done well, for the sake of his family. You can assure that his family is—spared."

Last time, Rhode did it. He was the one who decided to drop Lena's family and then her.

I've closed my eyes. A soft pressure cools my face: Mabalena has placed her fingers on my cheek. "Before Rhode gave me his message to deliver," she murmurs, "I saw your Griff, in the cell where they've put him. He had a message, too."

I look at her, and now my heart is racing. "What did he say?"

"He said to take Gephyra out before the drop. Take a long flight. Summon your courage, make your vigil, and when you come home—do your duty."

ANNIE

They intend to drop Griff at dawn, but we're ready long before that.

The pillars of karst surrounding New Pythos are black fingers against a gray sky when Aela and I leave the lairs of the ha'Aurelian citadel. On the crown of Thornrose Karst, among winter-dead brambles overgrowing their shrine of standing stones, Griff's sister, Agga, hides with her two children. They were moved here for their safety in the night. The three of them emerge when Aela lands, and the little boy, Garet, beckons me to a place on the edge of the cliff where I can watch for sunrise.

Garet. The same name, and nearly the same age, as my brother when he died. Our languages, Callish and Norish, share roots like they share damp winters and long hungers. I can't help feeling that I've got more in common with this peasant family on the other side of the sea than I do with the Callipolan elites who've been my classmates for the last ten years. Agga's barely older than me.

Her daughter, Becca, watches from a pace apart, her eyes traveling slowly from me to the dragon and back. She blinks very little, as if we might vanish if she doesn't keep her eyes wide open.

"It's done," I tell Agga.

Her voice is pitched low. "The poison?"

The lairs were still dark when Aela and I left them. The smell of smoked fish and charred leather was identical to that of the nests in Callipolis, though the murmured Norish of the squires, Griff's friends, was too quiet for a semester's worth of study to understand. I did not know these dragons, but they did, and they were the ones I gave the amphora of drachthanasia to and told to divvy it up.

"The squires did it. Aela and I took care of the muzzles."

With a squire named Fionna leading the way, Aela and I wormed our way down the damp corridor of the lairs, Aela taking each iron muzzle into her mouth, one by one, and breathing fire on it until the metal glowed and snapped. When we freed Fionna's, a tawny aurelian with deep black eyes, the woman's shoulders slumped in relief and the dragon whimpered.

Agga's eyes are rimmed white in the gray light. "They can fly free? They can fire?"

I nod. "The squire on duty will release them on our signal."

I ask Agga to show me where the drop will take place on the silhouette of the main island. Her trembling finger identifies Conqueror's Mound, a sloping hill at the center of the Norcian villages opposite the ha'Aurelian citadel, overshadowed by the statue of an invading lord. The Norcians will be summoned to witness and learn the lesson.

Griff Gareson, dropped for treason.

Griff Gareson, dropped for conspiring with the Callipolan First-rider.

Dropped for conspiring with me.

And we will turn this moment into the opportunity Griff needs to stage his revolution. Agga's grandfather Grady is rallying the four trusted clans now, waking village elders, and spreading word to prepare for war.

"I don't think you poisoned all of them," Agga says.

I'm about to ask her how she knows. There were empty stalls where some of the dragons should have been, leaving us all with a lingering unease. Ixion's stormscourge, Niter, was not among them, nor was the dragon that belongs to Freyda, the Bassilean princess he's courting. Her goliathan, a great breed from the continent, is rumored to be large enough to blot the sky. The squires filled the troughs of the missing dragons with poisoned feed anyway, assuring me that those absent must only be on patrol and would be back before dawn.

When I follow Agga's gaze now, I realize she means a specific dragon.

A skyfish has breached the clouds a few miles out, her slender silhouette a gray line against the wisps of fog hanging low in the morning, her narrow wings a crossbar as she glides. Her rider looks like a tiny toy soldier atop her back.

I stretch a hand toward Aela, stilling her. "Everyone get down."

We slide to our knees in the bracken as the skyfish streams overhead.

Garet's shrill voice hisses as his neck cranes for a glimpse of the dragon. "Isn't that Gephyra? It's Delo sur Gephyra. We don't have to fear Delo."

Agga forces Garet's head down and breathes her answer. "Today, we do."

I feel a small hand slip into mine, and find Becca crouched beside me. She looks up, not at the dragon, but at my face. Her tiny nails dig into my palm. Beside us, Aela's amber wings hug her sides and her neck twists so that one slitted pupil can take in the dragon passing overhead.

With a flick of her tail, Gephyra vanishes into the streaks of fog above us.

Becca's fingers untwine from mine. Garet shrugs off his mother's arm. We unfold from our crouches, and Agga's gaze lingers on the clouds into which Delo sur Gephyra vanished.

"Poor boy," she murmurs. "They'll make him do it."

I remember the way Griff's voice caught when I taught him how to write his family's names and he asked to add a single more. The way he carefully spelled *Delo Skyfish* in a practice notebook. I get to my feet, brushing twigs from my knees. "I thought the dragonborn were accustomed to taking peasants into their beds."

"Their beds, yes. Not their hearts."

So, less like the dragonlords of old and more like Lee and me. Or like we would have been if his father were still alive, and Lee's loyalty still to his people, when he learned to love me.

Come back to me, Lee said.

And I will, as soon as I get this job done.

"At least Griff will be the only one he'll have to drop."

The squires told me that the last time a Norcian rider was dropped in punishment, her family was dropped too. They whispered her name: *Mabalena.* The story, and their awed horror, was too familiar for comfort. Across miles, with a sea between us, with fire or without, the dragonlords punish families in the same way. I was my village's Mabalena.

So I was the one who insisted we move Agga and her children here, for their safety, until the plan is completed.

Because this has been my concern, I'm a little surprised at what Agga chooses to say next.

"I am grateful for your help today." Her children can't hear her low voice over the whistling wind. "But I want you to know, when I heard he had been meeting with you, I wept."

There is a fire in her eyes not unlike Griff's as she holds her son's shoulder and dares to look me in the eye. It has taken her courage to say this: I can see how her gaze darts to my dragon, then my face.

There must have been a moment when my father imagined the cellar he could dig and decided to make the gamble that would bring dragonfire down on our heads.

Agga knows, and I know, that I was that gamble for Griff.

I am the recourse to violence. I am the last resort. At best, I am the lesser evil.

I'm a dragonrider, and I'm here to do my job.

"You were right to weep."

I reach for Aela's saddlebag. I removed my flamesuit and armor under the cover of her wings in dunes far from here mere hours ago; Lee's trembling fingers unhooked the clasps. The dress and hair scarf I'm wearing are Agga's, borrowed by Griff, and I'm conscious of her stare as I unwrap them. Perhaps beneath these burn scars, she sees a peasant's body like hers. Or maybe she just sees a city girl raised in luxury, a lifetime of square meals making up for a childhood of famine, shaping me into something unrecognizable. Shivering, I strip and shimmy into my flamesuit. I fasten the clasps that Lee undid as brambles scrape the goose bumps on my bare skin.

When I reach for coolant, I find small hands holding up the saddlebag.

"I can help you."

Agga's arm jerks to restrain Becca. "Becca, don't get in her way—"

But Becca shies free, and I hear myself say, "It's okay."

Becca makes a very attentive assistant. She watches while I unscrew the suit's coolant valves, fit the canister to them, and top them off. When it's time to do the back of my suit, she steps closer still. "I can do it."

I take a knee so that I'm at her height. "Thank you."

I can feel small fingers twisting each valve along the shoulders of the back of the suit. "What's it for?"

"If I get burned, I flood the suit. Then it hurts less."

Agga's palm is rubbing so hard against her chin as she watches us, I think she might chafe it.

"I want to ride a dragon when I grow up. Like you. I'll be First-rider."

I'd almost forgotten, until she says it, that it's a title I once longed for, too. "It's not an easy job."

Becca shrugs. "I'm not scared." She sets the canister down. "Now the armor?"

"Now the armor."

I show her how to layer the plates, the cuirass, the pauldrons, the arm guards and leg guards. When it's time to arm Aela, I show her how the breastplate fastens across her soft underbelly to provide an extra layer of protection against javelins from below. Aela holds still, a single lidded eye following Becca's work as her tail twitches.

"She likes you."

Becca stares up at the dragon, and it's unclear whether her question is for Aela or me. "Are you going to save my uncle?"

Aela snorts a small puff of smoke. "Yes," I answer.

"Are you going to free Norcia?"

Agga, watching, looks stricken. Aela lowers her snout to

Becca's outstretched hand, and trembling fingers touch the flare of amber scales between her nostrils. "I hope so."

"I can help," Becca says.

I remember reaching for a shovel at the graveside, telling my father the same thing. I understand now why he put his arms around me instead of answering. I show her my arm guards.

"You have helped me. See?"

A sliver of pink shows along the horizon where the low clouds end. The bells of the citadel echo faintly across the water. The portcullis is opening, the procession about to begin. When I reach for my helmet, Agga is the one who holds it out to me.

"Shrines keep you," she says.

LEE
CALLIPOLIS

On the morning of the first People's Assembly, I wake to fears for Annie and the revolution she has gone to spark abroad. I don't think to be worried about what would happen today, at home, in Callipolis. Even when I'm warned by a ministry official that something might be afoot—a triarchist conspiracy to return my family to the throne—I dismiss it.

I dismiss it until the moment Ixion Stormscourge, my cousin, lands beside me in the center of the Eyrie at the opening of the Assembly.

Ixion has studied his Revolutionary history as well as I have. He knows how coups succeed and fail. He wastes no time informing me the gates to the dragons' nests have been closed, the senior officials of the Revolutionary regime are surrounded in the Palace box, and the Guardians are sequestered in the Cloister.

Then he offers the people Freyda's bread and credits me with it.

We stand shoulder to shoulder on the Eyrie, looking upon the first People's Assembly in a decade. Overhead, the goliathan and its princess circles under a bright sun and blue sky, casting a shadow of empire over the city-state of Callipolis.

"You have watched the Revolutionary regime fail you," Ixion tells the Assembly. "You have suffered because of Atreus Athanatos's incompetence. You have longed for a return to the rulers who were born to serve you."

He twists his arm with mine.

I could wrench it free and decry the maneuver. But already, I wonder how deep the plot goes. Directly before the Assembly, Miranda Hane warned of a shadow organization, a triarchist group that has been conspiring with Ixion from the inside—the Order of the Black Clover. Assuming Ixion has more backup than I realized, the Guardians and their dragons are in danger. And assuming he's not lying when he tells me Duck's alive and captive in New Pythos, he has the leverage of Annie's closest friend and Cor's brother.

I let my arm rise with his.

"Let us return to our roots," Ixion says. "To what is right. To what is *natural*. And let this hunger, this injustice, this scourge of ten years be forgotten."

The People's Assembly votes to reinstate the Triarchy as rightful rulers of Callipolis. They accept Freyda's offer of food aid from her empire.

So long have they suffered, and hungered, they don't even seem to remember that it was Ixion's air strikes that caused the food shortage in the first place.

Or perhaps, with the shadow of a goliathan circling, they're not keen to protest the point.

"And all because of my cousin, Leo Stormscourge, whose invitation made possible our return!" Ixion tells the Assembly.

It's bad enough to watch the reform I've fought for be subverted. It's worse by far to hear my name cheered in thanks for it. The nation whose aid we invited was Damos, a dragonless democracy. But it's too late to correct Ixion now.

The applause is deafening.

"You're an idiot," I tell Ixion, because I feel like the biggest idiot of all.

"Big talk from one who just got played as bad as you."

"I got played?" I jerk a thumb upward at the Bassilean princess circling on her goliathan, who just added another province to her empire.

"Do you refer to my future wife?"

I stare at him. Surely, he can't be that stupid. But he grins back, so it looks like he is.

"Anyway"—he waves at the populace—"I think we know who the real idiots are right now."

"They're *hungry*."

"Well, they won't be for much longer. Freyda's grain shipments are due to arrive within the week."

"Along with her troops?"

Ixion lifts a shoulder. A noncommittal confirmation.

So, we're to be occupied. Whatever deal he made was in exchange for Callipolan autonomy. The Assembly referendum in favor of it was just window dressing; Freyda's forces are going to arrive whether or not they are invited. The citizens at this Assembly who haven't surmised that yet will find out soon enough.

The slowly spiraling descent of Freyda's goliathan encompasses the whole of the Upper Bank, and we make our way down the ramp of the Eyrie in her shadow. At the Palace entrance to the arena, out of sight of the public, we are met by Lucian Orthos, General Holmes's chief of staff, and an aide. On Orthos's lapel, I see the black clover of the Triarchy-in-Exile.

"You?"

He always was intolerable—in class, and to Annie at meetings of the War Council—but this takes it to a different level. Lucian barely glances at me. "Holmes and the High Council have been contained along with Athanatos, my lord."

Atreus's less-commonly-used family name. "Good," says Ixion.

The aide's fingers are shaking as he pats down my Guardian uniform, but he does it anyway, not meeting my eyes. He retrieves the bootknives from my dragonriding boots and shows the inlay of one of them to Ixion.

The heather of Stormscourge House entwines with the initials my father and I share, L.S. The bootknife belonged to my father, but Ixion doesn't know that Annie was the one who found and gave it to me. He studies the heirloom and looks up.

"You," Ixion says, "are not the shit I was expecting."

"That's funny. I was going to say you're *exactly* the shit I was expecting."

Ixion lets out a bark of laughter.

He nods to Orthos's man. A fist pummels me in the stomach. I double over, gasping.

Here we go.

2

THE DROP

GRIFF

NEW PYTHOS

The only question in my head, as I'm led out of my cell, through the citadel, and down to Conqueror's Mound just before dawn, is what will happen to my family when I'm dropped. Mabalena's were rounded up when she was; I've no reason to expect anything different. I don't dare wonder whether Antigone sur Aela made it across the water from Callipolis, or the poison made it into the feeding troughs as planned. My thoughts are on my sister, her little ones, and Granda, who still waits for a lost son to return from the sea that swallowed him.

I promised Agga I'd protect them.

The world is still gray and colorless, dawn not yet on the faces of the ones gathered to watch our procession. The gulls are too sleepy to cry, and the salty air lies still and damp. It feels like the whole island waits, hushed.

"Griff, I begged a boon!"

A tiny voice splits the silence with Dragontongue, and I twist to take in the youngest ha'Aurelian, Astyanax. He's trotting alongside me as I'm led by my chained arms behind Sparker's cart. I can hear the boy's nurse hissing at him behind us, but he pays Shea no mind. He's Garet's age.

"My life?" I ask in surprise.

Astyanax beams and shakes his head. "Sparker's!"

He looks so proud of himself, my heart warms. Better Sparker than me.

"That'll do nicely, little lordling," I tell him.

He trots back to his glowering family, and I'm led to the top of the Mound.

It reminds me too much of Mabalena's drop: Sparker tied to the cart in front of me, his tail thrashing fruitlessly against the chains that bind him; the household turned out, squires and ha'Aurelians and dragonborn exiles to watch me take the fall; and surrounding us, a gray sea of pinched faces spread across the Mound, the Norcians who have been forced to attend. Astyanax swings nervously on his mother's arm beside the Greatlord Rhadamanthus.

I scan Clan Nag's turnout for my family, and find none of them. *Where are they?*

My panicked imagination invents reasons. They were taken. They're being held, ready to be dragged out in chains and dropped beside me—

Delo steps forward. His skyfish, Gephyra, waits behind him, and we are encircled by the remaining triarchal dragons and their riders: Phemi, Delo's sister, the long silvery-blue tail of her skyfish cutting a swath through the cringing villagers; Urianus and Orion, lesser ha'Aurelian cousins, side by side on their stump-necked aurelians, glaring down at us; and Roxana and Rhode, the Greatlord's eldest children, flanking their parents like an honor guard on dragonback.

Rhode winks at me. He's probably supposed to take over if Delo chickens out.

Which looks to be a near thing. Delo's skin, usually a warm

brown, has turned the color of ash. Sweat clings in droplets to his curls. His eyes dart to mine, then away. If he got my message about doing his duty, he's not looking thrilled about it.

But I have more important things to do now than worry about Delo Skyfish.

As soon as I'm untied from the cart, I hurl myself to my knees and say it.

"*Grant mercy, my lord, on your servant undeserving, let not his punishment duly owed be exacted on his family innocent—*"

I'm shouting the Plea with the hope the dragonborn will be satisfied by my humiliation. I'm surprised to hear my voice break, but I do not try to hide it. I can hear Rhode snickering.

Delo's voice is faint. "Your Plea is accepted by your lord. Rise."

I get to my feet, dizzy with a rush of relief. We stand a meter apart. Delo's glance flits past me, toward Clan Nag. "Griff," he breathes, "where *is* your family?"

That surprises me. "I thought you lot had them."

"No."

That's when I notice it.

Rhode's dragon, Ryla, is drooping. When she turns, I glimpse an eye crusty with mucus.

The other dragons are drooping, too, tails low on the ground, wings sagging. How have none of the dragonborn noticed? But then, I realize their riders don't look much better. The ha'Aurelians' usually olive skin is looking almost green; Phemi rubs the back of her neck like she's feeling something missing.

I've seen one other person do that in my life. Nestor. Their father, the sky-widower.

I look from those drooping dragons to the gray-faced dragonborn, and shrines help me, I feel the urge to shout the triumph aloud.

Antigone got here after all.

My family's missing because they're safe.

And these damned dragons aren't dead yet, but they sure as sparkfire have been poisoned. If I'm not mistaken, the drachthanasia's about to hit. These poor fools don't yet know what it is that's making them feel sick.

In fact, the only dragon who's *not* drooping is Delo's.

I think back to the instructions I gave Mabalena and nearly smile.

Looks like Delo sur Gephyra got my message, took a long flight, and skipped breakfast.

DELO

I thought I'd imagined it, this morning when Gephyra and I flew through Sailor's Folly before dawn. I thought I'd imagined a glimpse of amber scales glinting on Thornrose Karst.

Now, looking around the Mound, I'm not so sure. Where *are* Griff's family? And why do the rest of our dragons look like they're about to keel over?

He told me to tell you to take Gephyra out. Take a long flight.

What if there was more to that suggestion than a casual kindness? There was a moment weeks ago, when Griff and I gripped each other in the darkness of the lairs and I asked him like a fool to spare the twins and my dragon, whatever he was planning.

Amber scales on Thornrose Karst. I know I saw them.

I'm pretty sure Griff's not meeting my eyes. But I hardly know what to think of him either. With balled fists, I turn and approach the Greatlord Rhadamanthus. He stands with his family in the space set apart for their officiating. Little Astyanax bounces at

Lady Xanthe's elbow; their elder children, Rhode and Roxana, flank them on dragonback, looking green and sweaty enough to vomit.

"I think we should call it off."

"Delo's getting cold feet? What a surprise," Roxana mutters. She wipes a sweating forehead.

"It's not cold feet. Something's up. His family's missing—"

"So we drop them later," growls Father, from the Skyfish section.

"That wasn't what I meant—"

The rest of it's on the tip of my tongue: the amber scales, these green-faced riders. Do none of them see the drooping dragons? But then a treacherous thought occurs, and even though I should be worried about what this plot might mean for my people, I find myself thinking of what it might mean, instead, for a single person.

Because all else aside, if I *did* see amber scales, Griff might still have a chance.

Father steps forward. "Either you do drop him," he says, "or Rhode will."

From his tone, he makes no mystery of what he'll think of me if I don't.

The familiar sound of his disappointment triggers my perverseness like clockwork. Whatever argument I had thought to make, I know my father will take it as one more proof that I am *weak*. My jaw clamps shut. I turn on my heel, return to Gephyra, and kick a foot into the stirrup.

On our own heads be it.

Once in the air, I guide us down. Griff, the conspiring sweating bastard, disappears under our wing. I feel Geph's instinctive satisfaction, like a hawk trapping its prey, as she hooks talons into his shoulders. Because unlike these wilting dragons around us, my Geph is flying just fine. Spared, it seems, by a tip-off from my traitor lover.

I don't know whether I'm more furious with Griff, in this moment, or myself.

I hear, or perhaps only imagine, his grunt of pain.

We rise up.

And I scan the horizon. The villages, speckling the hillside. The shoreline, dipping down to the sea. The clan-karsts, the nearest perimeter of Sailor's Folly. With Griff's life dangling from Geph's talons, I feel the desire through my fury as clearly as light piercing a blanket of northern clouds. *I can't save you. But maybe someone else can.*

And of course I want them to.

We rise higher. Scanning, waiting.

Come on.

We pass the point of a survivable drop. Still higher. Conqueror's Mound shrinks below us. The wind picks up. Gephyra circles on the updraft, fighting to hold her position. If we drift, the fall drifts. The drop will land in the wrong place. The spectacle will be diminished.

But I will have a different kind of spectacle.

Come on. Come on already.

Come while this faint heart still has the wrong kind of courage.

Griff shouts from below. "I think we're high enough."

The wind curls over us both. "Not quite."

"Delo, get it over with!"

His voice cracks.

At last I see it, the flash of amber, and I dig my heels into Gephyra's flank below her wings.

Now.

Griff drops.

Antigone sur Aela bursts through the cloud cover and dives.

GRIFF

It's madness that this is how it ends, in the air, when the air was always my best escape. How different it feels to fly when there's nothing between you and the ground but your own two dangling feet.

I have never loved nor hated Delo sur Gephyra so much as in these stretching moments.

And then I feel Delo's heels send the jolt through her.

Geph's talons release my shoulders.

The wind rips the yell from my lungs. My insides somersault. The ground rises up—

Death hurtles to meet me, hard as stone and as unforgiving—

And I'm knocked sideways. Another set of talons hook my tunic and the belt at my waist. I'm staring up at the amber membrane of an aurelian's wings.

"Hang on!" Antigone shouts.

My lungs are full and I am laughing with the shock of it. We're diving. Antigone strains her voice over the whistling wind. "Agga and the little ones are safe. Hiding on Thornrose Karst. Your grandfather's got the weapons ready in the villages. We've done the rest."

She means the drachthanasia and the muzzles. Through the haze of relief I latch on to the only thing that matters now. "Get me to Sparker."

"On it."

Conqueror's Mound rushes toward us. Norcians and dragon-born are scattering, and the highborn riders attempt with little luck to get their sodden, poisoned dragons airborne. Antigone aims for the manacled black hulk that is my beautiful Sparker, pride of the fleet. I can *feel* him bucking his chains, and I urge him on with my heart swelling.

Fight them. Break them. Come to me.

Iron screws burst from their bolts. Metal screams. Sparker rears, the broken chains of his neck collar flailing. He uses the leverage to slam his muzzle against the wooden pilings of the cart.

The muzzle shatters. I feel the relief of our freedom separate my own jaws.

And then I remember what I've got to tell Antigone. There's good news, and there's bad news, but I've got about two seconds to say anything, so I pick the good.

Because right now, good is all I feel.

"Antigone, your friend—he's alive!"

"What?"

"Duck's *alive*." Sparker's just below us, and I bellow the cue. "He's in the citadel dungeon. Drop NOW!"

Aela releases me. I plummet the last ten feet and slam onto Sparker's bucking back.

For a moment I lie flat, winded. Then the joy of our reunion gives Sparker the last burst of strength needed. He rears, chains bursting, and I cling to his bare back with knees hooked over his wing joints. The air rattles back into my lungs.

All I need.

Sparker arches his back and bellows stormscourge fire, in all its glory, into the sky. I feel I could bellow fire, too. We're surrounded by the stunned audience that came to watch our drop. Norcians, shifting weight. Dragonborn, staring. All, momentarily, stunned into silence.

"What will it be, Norcia?" I roar.

Leary Thornrose, puppet king of the Norcians, steps forward to face me, his face a painted mockery. Beside him, Rhode and his mucus-encrusted aurelian lurch like a swaying ship as the dragon growls at me. *Good luck getting that one airborne,* I think, but she doesn't need to be airborne to stick her maw in Bran's face and threaten fire. They've corralled the Norcian squires, dragonless, in the center of the Mound, and their empty hands are raised over their heads.

But the squires' eyes are on the horizon. And I know what they're waiting for.

"We will take no part in this treachery," the puppet king Leary spits.

Someone points at the sky and screams it.

Dragons incoming.

I turn and take in the most beautiful sight of my life.

Norcian dragons are streaming out of the citadel lairs. Under their wings—I hear myself laugh aloud—are painted the Norcian clan stars. The squires have done it in woad, the blue battle-paint of Norcia from a time before her conquering. Today, the woad is worn again, in a new way.

On our dragons.

The Norcian screams of fear turn to recognition. *Woad,* someone shouts. *They're painted with woad. They're ours.*

And they're unmuzzled, bellowing fire.

The Norcian riders use the moment of distraction to spring for the dragonborn surrounding them. Bran launches for Rhode, tears him from the saddle of his whining aurelian, and at first I think he's throttling him until he snaps a chain from Rhode's neck. His summoner was kept by Rhode, the lord he serves.

Until now. Bran brings his summoning whistle to his lips and blows into it like he's expelling a lifetime of held breath. He's not the only one. Fionna scrabbles with Roxana; Moira claws at the chain still twisted round Phemi's neck—

And our summoned dragons are dropping from the sky like pellets of hail. Norcians and dragonborn alike shriek and cower at their fiery ascent—

"Get him," Rhode screams, but even as his dragon turns her mucus-encrusted gaze on Bran and lurches toward him with fangs bared, Bran's aurelian, Beria, lands between them. She seizes the other dragon's throat, sets her fangs into the soft scales, and brings them together with a crunch.

Rhode doubles over and screams.

At the sound of his scream, the realization spreads.

Rhode, the Greatlord's firstborn son and scion of New Pythos, has been widowed.

One down, the rest of the fleet to go.

Rhode is crawling away on all fours. The Greatlord Rhadamanthus, standing with his wife and younger son, looks as though all speech has stuck in his throat. The rims of his black eyes are white. Roxana, seeing what has happened, begins to scream like her brother. Her summoner has been snatched by Fionna; her dragon thrashes, unable to get airborne, as the Norcians tighten ranks.

Our puppet king backs away as if to fade into the chaos unnoticed—but not fast enough. Sparker pounces. His jaws close over Leary's head.

When he's done, the Norcians have no more puppet king.

Bran throws himself barebacked onto his aurelian and lifts a fist. At their feet lies the dead dragon of the lord he used to serve.

Norcia! Bran sur Beria bellows. *Norcia!*

The chant rings out, taken up by his clan, Turret; then mine, the Nag; spreading as Fionna takes it to Knoll; and is joined by

Colleen from Kraken. The Norcians that surround me on the ground reach into their tunics and produce knives and cleavers that will not be used for kitchen work today.

The roar of Norcian dragons shakes the earth.

And the dragonborn run.

3

THE MISSING

LEE
CALLIPOLIS

When they lead me into the courtyard of the Cloister, the Palace residence of the Guardians, we find the entrances guarded by Pythian dragonriders. A rider who looks to be in his mid-twenties greets us in the main courtyard. His hair is fair as flax, his body built like a farmer's, but his silver eyes look oddly familiar. The Stormscourge crest on his armor is done in gray.

"This him?"

"Leo, meet Edmund Grayheather," says Ixion, his tone bored. "Captain of the Bastard Grayriders and your half brother."

Of all the events so far, this is the first to stop me dead.

"My father didn't have—"

Edmund's laugh is booming. "It always does come as a shock. We'll have more time to share family history later."

"Edmund's been promised Farhall and its lands in the Restoration," Ixion informs me, like this is supposed to land a blow. "No hard feelings, I hope. Since you seemed so bent on giving up your inheritance. And killing my sister."

He smiles pleasantly at me.

"Shall I collect wristbands, my lord?" Edmund asks.

For Guardians, wristbands are both the designation of their elite class-metal status as Silver and Gold, and their means of summoning. The whistle pitched to a frequency for dragon ears is built into the band.

Taking them means they're cutting us off from our dragons.

Ixion jerks a thumb at me. "Let him do it."

A bag is shoved into my hand. "Go on," Edmund says, pointing at the solarium entrance. I can see Guardians waiting inside, their faces blurred circles of pink and brown through the glass as they peer at the courtyard.

I shove the bag back. "I'm not taking their wristbands."

Ixion, leaving the courtyard with a fist raised to his own summoner for Niter, turns back.

"Leo, we've got two dozen Guardians to deal with, plus their dragons. We don't really *need* to keep all of them alive. So choose your battles, hmm?"

The bag remains in my hand, which has begun to shake. I reach for my own wristband, to unclasp it first, but Edmund notices. "Keep yours on."

He shoves me toward the door, smirking.

ANNIE
NEW PYTHOS

"Your friend," Griff tells me, as the island explodes around us. "He's alive! He's in the citadel dungeon—"

Aela's talons release him onto Sparker's back, and for a moment all we can do is drift on the wind.

When Duck fell during the air strike, we were so high above the ground I heard no sound on impact. He was lost in a burning building. All I ever saw of his remains was a bit of his cuirass that Griff took from the rubble afterward.

So when Griff tells me he's alive, I don't believe it.

Don't believe it, as we race to the citadel, leaving the erupting battle behind.

Don't believe it, as Aela scuttles down the side of the fortress, searching for the lowest windows, the ones with bars that betray a dungeon.

We find the bars, a row of them. We call Duck's name through them. There's no answer.

It's not true, it's not true, *it can't be*—

At the end of the row of barred windows is a single door that opens as a sluice gate. The cliff wall is stained with trails of waste below it. The door has no handle from the outside, so Aela sinks her talons into the old wood and yanks. It breaks from the wall with a soft crunch. We peek into an unlit corridor that smells of mold and human waste.

It's not true, it's not true, it can't be true—

I'll keep the mantra up, to ward myself, protect myself from the disappointment that waits at the end of this corridor when I learn Griff is, *must be*, mistaken.

I scramble off Aela's back and into the stinking corridor, not believing.

Don't believe, as I hammer my way down the row calling Duck's name. A lifetime of training has taught me that to call the names of the dead, to wake from dreams they were alive still hoping, leads only to more heartbreak.

I don't believe until I hear Duck's shaking voice in return.

LEE

I enter the Cloister solarium with the bag to collect wristbands and find frightened faces turned up to me from every corner of the room. The Guardians are still in the ceremonial armor that they were planning to wear to the Assembly this morning; the Pythians must have corralled them here right before it began. Apart from a handful of riders recovering from the last air battle in the infirmary and the few with outstanding missions that kept them from today's obligations, most of the corps are in this room. Rock sweats in a corner beside Lotus. Cor is on his feet with his arms folded over fists.

Power alone acts relaxed, his legs crossed on an empty chair, seated in a circle with Darius and a few other patrician riders. But the fingers he drums on the arm of his uniform betray his nerves.

The door hasn't swung shut behind me: Edmund Grayheather stands watching from the threshold.

I can feel my fingers sweating on the bag. "I'm collecting wristbands."

I watch their expressions shift from relief at the sight of me to something else. Glances begin to fire. Doubts ripple across faces. I feel my own silver-and-gold wristband, still on my wrist, attracting their gazes.

"Is that a joke?" Cor says.

For a second, I think my mouth is too dry for speech. "Duck is being held captive in New Pythos."

It was what Ixion told me, when he landed on the Eyrie and surprised the people with bread.

"No talking!" Edmund barks.

But it's enough. Cor's eyes widen. He looks from Grayheather waiting behind us, to me and the bag, and gets to his feet. "Right," he says, his mouth a line, and drops his wristband in.

It seems to take an interminably long time for all of them to hand their wristbands over, and afterward, I have a hard time remembering what their expressions were. I can't remember if it's because I was avoiding their eyes or they were avoiding mine. When it's done, I hand the bag to Edmund Grayheather.

"Thanks, ha'brother," he says brightly.

Dragontongue isn't a strong language for many of the Guardians, but the term *half brother* is elementary enough. I watch Rock's brows knit together at the address.

Edmund remains standing in the doorway, preventing further conversation.

A thump rattles the windows of the solarium and makes us all look up. Through the rippled glass, we can make out the outline of a second stormscourge settling in the courtyard. Edmund steps outside, closing the door after him, to confer with the new arrival. In the split second that it leaves us, I turn to the corps.

"Antigone, Crissa, and anyone else absent from this room are on patrol."

Deirdre looks puzzled. "But I thought Crissa was—"

On a mission to Damos, the neighboring democracy. Bryce elbows her, and Deirdre's eyes widen. "Oh," she says.

As to what Annie's really up to, Power's the only one besides me with any idea. But when I search his expression for indication of what he plans to do with that information, I find his black eyes as unreadable as ever.

The door bursts open. Ixion and Edmund stand framed in it. Ixion lifts his voice.

"Good morning, Guardians. I am Ixion sur Niter, your restored lord, and I am not unmerciful. Not all of you will be executed. You won't even all be widowed. *But.* I require loyalty. To that end, I will be conducting private interviews. Proceed, Edmund."

Edmund, a cheery smile plastered on his face, now holds a scroll in one hand and an empty grain sack in the other.

"Darius sur Myra?" he calls, like a nurse in a hospital waiting room.

The room seems to hold its breath. Darius looks at his hands.

Beside him, Power looks at nothing at all. They are childhood friends.

"I'll remind you that your exits are blocked by dragons on all ends," Ixion says. "We can just as easily smoke you out."

Power shifts in his chair. Darius pushes himself to his feet with shaking wrists. He's pale beneath golden hair, his usually proud posture diminished as he makes his way across the solarium to Edmund and Ixion.

"Thank you for your cooperation," says Ixion.

Edmund pulls the bag over Darius's head.

He lets out a choked cry of surprise. Deirdre shrieks. Edmund yanks Darius over the threshold and slams the door shut behind him.

The sound echoes in the still room.

Edmund returns a quarter of an hour later and calls another name. He produces another bag. There's no more talking after that. The ones who are taken don't return. Bryce, an aurelian rider of the Thirty-Second Order, vomits into the fireplace. Deirdre curls her face into her knees.

The room slowly dwindles of occupants. Until only members of the Eighth Order are left—Rock, Cor, Power, and I—and one lower-ranked exception, Lotus.

"Where is Crissa Ward?" Edmund asks.

"On patrol."

Too many of us say it at once. Edmund's brow raises, and his lip curls, as he consults his list again. "Antigone, I take it, is also *on patrol*?"

This time, the group overcorrects to silence and halting nods.

"Well, there will be plenty of time in the dungeons to straighten those stories out," Edmund says, rolling his eyes. "Cor Sutter?"

Cor gets to his feet. "I want to see my brother."

Edmund chuckles. "That will depend on you."

He hands Cor the bag. Cor looks down at it, his face contorting. Then he places the bag over his head himself. He allows himself to be steered from the room.

Power, chin resting on a cupped hand, snorts softly. Lotus's fingers clutch at his curly hair where he waits beside Rock, who is shock white beneath his freckles. I stand, arms folded, with my heart in my throat.

The door opens, and Edmund consults the scroll.

"Parcival Graylily?"

There is no one by such name in the corps, let alone in this room. The surname, Graylily, is the bastard assignation of Skyfish House. Rock lifts his head, frowning. Lotus removes his hands from his hair and studies them. Then he turns to look at Power.

Power does not move.

"Parcival," Edmund repeats. "Parcival Graylily, bastard son of the triarch Kit Skyfish, fostered by Hesperides House. Rides a—it says here, *stormscourge*?" Edmund's voice lifts with incredulity.

Power twitches, rolls his eyes to the ceiling with an air of great inconvenience, and flows to his feet. "I go by Power."

Rock stares at him. "You're a bastard?"

"I think we all knew *that*," says Power with a twisted smile. In Dragontongue, he asks Edmund, "Trust we don't need to bother with a bag?"

"Depends on if you can help us find the peasant Firstrider."

Power offers his most menacing grin. "That bitch? I can try."

No bag is placed over Power's head. He follows Edmund out of the solarium.

Rock swears under his breath. Lotus closes his eyes.

"You don't seem very surprised," I observe.

"Nor do you," Lotus answers.

No. Now that I consider it, it's the first thing I've learned about

Power that makes sense. For all the ways he's looked down on people of low birth like Annie and Rock, the loathing I saw in his eyes when he learned I was dragonborn was something more. Power was the son of a Janiculum housekeeper who had been abandoned, by her baby's father, to die in a poorhouse. Now I know that father was a Skyfish lord. No wonder he's borne a grudge against people like me.

Though not enough to stop him from leveraging the connection now.

"In grammar school," Lotus murmurs, "he went by *Parry*."

Rock looks up at me, the whites of his eyes visible and bloodshot.

"Lee, that Stormscourge—Ixion—his father's Crethon, isn't it?"

I nod. "Triarch of the West, lord of Nearhall."

Rock's fingers clench. "That means he's—I'm—"

"I know."

As Annie remembers my father, Rock remembers Crethon; and where my father was known for being harsh, Crethon was known for being cruel. Rock's village was in the Near Highlands, under his domain. All evidence points to Ixion's having inherited his father's tendencies, and if Griff is any indication, Ixion will find the idea of one of his family's serfs riding a stormscourge just as abominable as his father would.

"Rock," says Lotus, laying a hand on Rock's thick one. "You will be fine. I swear it—"

The door opens once more. This time, Ixion stands beside Edmund again, and Ixion is the one who speaks. His tone is playful and triumphant.

"Richard Nearhallserf."

Rock flinches.

It's a feudal nomenclature I haven't heard since before the

Revolution. I step between Rock and Ixion. But before I can speak, Lotus gets to his feet. "His name is Richard sur Bast."

At the sound of the drakonym, Ixion's gaze travels from Rock to Lotus. "You're Teiran's son?"

Lotus nods. He rolls his sleeve to reveal a clover-shaped cuff link.

The Order of the Black Clover. The counterrevolutionary group that's been passing information to New Pythos with the help of informants on the inside of our ministry and, it appears, even inside the Guardian corps.

The dots fire, connecting. Richard Tyndale, the poetry professor who wanted me to reunite with my family last summer. Lo Teiran, renowned poet laureate and Tyndale's friend, fiddling with a clover cuff link in a bathroom mirror as he asked for my help with a poem to honor the dragonborn dead. And now Teiran's son, addressing Ixion as if they know each other.

"We made a deal," Lotus says. "Richard won't be harmed."

Ixion smiles. "He won't," he agrees, "if he obeys his lord."

"That wasn't—"

"Bloody sparkfire," Rock snarls, rounding on Lotus, his voice rising. "Deal? *Deal?*"

Lotus lifts his hands. "Rock, I can explain—"

"I'll give you two a minute," Ixion says. "Come out when you're ready."

He slams the door shut on us.

But the other two hardly notice as their voices rise and clash. Lotus is talking about his father, about Dean Orthos and the Lyceum, about literary censorship and eroding values under Atreus, and Rock is shouting over him—*How could you do this?*—with tears streaking down his face.

"It was you," I realize, in a pause where Rock catches his breath. "Leaving information for the Pythians on the Island of the Dead."

Lotus nods.

"How long have you been working with them?"

Lotus answers faintly. "Not long. Only once it became inevitable. I knew I had to protect the ones I loved." His glance darts at Rock, who's glaring at the ceiling. "The patricians are sick of Atreus. They want their libraries back."

The literary censorship and purges of the Revolutionary regime came as an unpleasant surprise to the elites who backed it and have been a source of discontent for years. But all the same—

Rock slams a fist into the table. "My freedom for a *library*?"

I'm having the same thought.

Lotus waves an arm. "Oh, don't be so dramatic—"

That's when the roof creaks. A shadow lowers outside the glazed glass window. It presses against the panes. They shatter like spun sugar—and we find ourselves staring at the snout of a dragon nosing through the full-sized window like it's a dog door.

Freyda's goliathan has landed on the roof of the Cloister.

Lotus, Rock, and I back away from the intruding snout. Shards of glass still clinging to the frame curl away from the heat of the dragon's scales like peeling paper. Smoke issues from nostrils the size of a tree hollow, billowing into the Cloister.

"A few of them are still in there," Ixion says, outside.

A woman's voice joins Ixion's in the courtyard. "Perhaps they could use a little encouragement?"

ANNIE

I must have imagined I heard Duck's voice. I'm racing down a single long prison corridor that slopes up to a guardroom. The smell of human waste, of decay, of mold makes the air heavy. My voice sounds raw, strained in my ears.

"*Duck*?"

"Annie?"

Can I have dreamed it? I round the corner and skid to a halt. The darkness is complete save for the light from the disposal chute whose door Aela tore off. Cells that yawn into blackness are lined with bars on either side—except for one, whose grille swings on its hinges as if it had just burst open.

And in front of me, in the middle of the corridor, silhouetted by the faint light of the open chute, stands Duck.

He's gripped from behind by Rhode ha'Aurelian, who holds my gaze and a knife to Duck's throat. Sweat makes his face gleam.

If I doubted for an instant that it's really *him*, my Duck, saved by some miracle, his effort at assurance convinces me. Sweating, shaking, he gasps, "Annie, it's okay—"

My sweet Duck is alive.

And he's about to get killed.

"*Shut up.*" Rhode shakes him. He looks feral. He stinks faintly of vomit. His breath is elevated as if he ran the whole way here.

He is, I realize, freshly widowed.

"I knew you'd come to save him," he says. Every word seems to cost him effort. "This is only fair, isn't it? Fire for fire. You take from me, I take from you. Ixion was planning to make you watch this, anyway."

I feel the hair on the back of my neck rise. A second thought blooms like darkness in my vision: Where *is* Ixion?

Why haven't I seen him at all today?

Not to mention the goliathan whose princess he was purported to be courting—

The squires assured me he and Freyda would be back in time for the drop, but they were nowhere to be seen—

"We figured we'd drop this one again, *properly*, for your benefit. But this will do."

I can see blood beading on Duck's throat where the knife presses.

This cannot be how I find him, how I lose him *twice*—

Seeing my panic, Duck starts comforting me again. "Annie, it's okay, it's okay—"

And then he grunts.

The screaming in my ears is my own—

Rhode slumps backward on the floor as a third figure mounts him and stabs. She is screaming, too.

Duck steps free, massaging his throat, and turns slowly.

A young woman closer to Duck's size than Rhode's straddles the dragonlord, a knife in her hand that she drives over and over into his chest as she sobs. Blood is on her hands and in Rhode's mouth. The woman's hair is long, matted, her limbs oddly crooked.

I can only just understand the Norish that she pants.

"For my brothers. For my sisters. For my mother. For my father." And then, with a choke, "For *me*."

Duck kneels beside her to pull her off him.

"It's over," he says, speaking Norish he didn't used to know, "it's done, Lena."

And then he looks up at me as he holds her. His face is splattered with blood, gaunt in a way it was not when I left him, burn scars I don't recognize swirling up his neck beneath overgrown hair. But those kind eyes that I remember are the same.

And the tentative smile he offers at the sight of me melts me with relief.

He bends down, with tenderness that I remember from the days when I was the one who needed his comfort, and lifts the woman's chin to look at him. His lips brush her cheek.

"Hey," he says, smiling. "There's someone I'd like you to meet."

They get to their feet and I notice then how Duck, too, moves crookedly, how they are both angled like people who broke and healed wrong. Duck, his arm around her the whole time, introduces me to Mabalena, the girl the dragonborn once dropped.

Her face is shining as she looks at him.

"We knew you'd come," she tells me.

LEE

Smoke seeps into the Cloister solarium, gushing from the Great Dragon's nostril and smelling of sulfur. The trunk-sized tail swishes idly against the glass. Every time the goliathan shifts above us, the roof creaks.

"They're smoking us out," Rock realizes, his voice faint. "Classic. Straight out of the dragonborn feudal handbook—"

Lotus is breathing through his sleeve. "I was trying to protect you," he tells Rock, but I hear the uncertainty growing in his voice.

A smoke-out probably wasn't part of whatever bargain he struck with Ixion.

The smoke is thick in our nostrils now. We're all coughing. Rock palms at his streaming eyes. "You don't understand. There is only one way someone like Ixion will ever see someone like me."

He reaches for the handle of the solarium door and curses as his palm burns.

"Rock," I say, and he turns.

Numb horror has been replaced by a desire for something else.

"I'll stay in here, with you. If you want it."

Rock inhales a shuddering breath. His bloodshot eyes fix on me, bright in his ruddy face, and I know he understands me and that, for a moment, he is tempted.

Let this dragonborn blood fizzle and dry up in my veins, in the kindling of our Guardian training center as it burns, in our hopes for this nation as it falls apart.

Let me die with you.

Rock shakes his head. "Not today, Lee."

He uses the sleeve of his uniform to turn the handle.

Ixion and Edmund wait outside in the courtyard, accompanied by Lucian Orthos, the general's chief of staff, and half the Protector's Guard. Dwarfing all of them is the goliathan, whose body folds over the Cloister roof, scales glinting like tiles. A single lidless eye follows us like a lamp. The Bassilean princess stands on the roof ledge beside it, her bronze helmet still covering her face, a full-length mantle shimmering over her shoulder. Perched on our roof, looking down on us, motionless, she might as well be a statue of a long-dead god, a queen from the Golden Age.

Rock, who stumbled out of the Cloister first, cranes his neck to look at the dragon overshadowing us before turning to Ixion.

"Richard Nearhallserf?" Ixion says again.

Rock screws up his face. "My lord," he answers.

"Better," says Ixion, smiling.

4

TO HOPE FOR NO SAFETY

DELO

NEW PYTHOS

As soon as I see the dragons streaming out of the citadel lairs with woad on their wings, I know that in helping Griff, I've cemented the end of dragonborn rule on New Pythos. For a moment, high above, level with the wisps of breaking fog, Geph and I watch our world crumble: Antigone sur Aela dropping Griff onto Sparker's back, the woad-blue dragons swarming over the Mound, our people cowering, fleeing, as dragonfire rains down—and then we snap to our senses.

Phemi. Ethelo. Father.

We dive after them.

It's such a mad scramble on the ground that it takes us a moment to even find Phemi or her skyfish in the fray. They're under Moira's aurelian.

Moira. Phemi's squire, until today a gentle, unobtrusive presence I barely thought once about—

Gephyra's blast sends Moira and her aurelian sideways.

"Get off her!"

Moira's laughing as her dragon frees itself and kicks off from the ground. Phemi's got blood dripping from her temple but looks otherwise unharmed as she scrambles to her feet.

"Where are Father and Ethelo?"

Ethelo, Phemi's twin, is a *passus*—forsaken by dragons, never Chosen. He'll be on foot with Father. Phemi scrambles onto the back of her skyfish and jams her heels into her sides. "They're heading for the *Invicturi*. Come—*on*—"

Her skyfish, Hecate, whimpers and kicks at the ground as if it were holding her down. The sight of her skyfish hatchmate circling above her gets her off the ground with trembling wings. She joins us fifteen feet above the fray, where we find one other dragonborn in the air: Roxana ha'Aurelian.

"What the hell's gotten into them? Rora feels like she's drunk."

"So does Hecky," says Phemi, with a palm to her skyfish's slender, trembling neck.

They're doing better than anyone on the ground. Rhode's dead dragon is being gutted by the mob; as we watch, a woad-painted stormscourge pounces like a mountain cat on a fleeing ha'Aurelian uncle. When the dragon turns, I see the rider on his back. Griff's face is smeared with blood, his grin a streak of white.

Griff will have the retribution he has waited for today. They will sing about him like warrior kings of old. I will be a footnote, the failed executioner who set the stage for his triumph.

But even knowing my own ignominy, I have a moment watching Griff glory in his bloodlust where all I can think is he was born for this moment, and he's beautiful.

I tear my gaze away. "They were poisoned. Drachthanasia."

"We don't stock drachthanasia," Phemi says.

"They probably got it from the Callipolan Firstrider. I saw amber scales on Thornrose Karst this morning. I think she's been here for a while."

For a moment, Phemi's cool gaze on me makes me hear the unasked question loud and clear: *Why didn't you say anything?* But I don't have time for it. "We need to get to the *Invicturi*."

The line from the *Aurelian Cycle* is loud in my ears. *Our last hope for safety is to hope for no safety.* The ha'Aurelian tradition has been to plan for just such an eventuality, with a clipper ship designed for a speedy departure at the ready in the citadel's private harbor.

And that's where our families are fleeing now.

"Really?" Roxana sounds pretty drunk herself. "I was thinking of making a stand."

I'm about to say that's a terrible idea when Phemi gets there first. "We're outnumbered three to one. Eventually, they're going to run out of fun down there." She gestures at the carnage on the ground; even slumped with the effects of drachthanasia, she's doing math. "We should get out while we still can. The mainland has always been the plan."

And it's our luck that Ixion's already there, waiting for us.

Roxana shakes her head. Her eyes are streaming as she looks down on Norcia. "For you, maybe," she says. "My family has ruled this island for generations."

Phemi's glazed eyes focus on her.

"The firepowder?" she says, her voice cooler than I've ever heard before. "Why not."

Roxana's jaw clenches. She turns to me. "You said Thornrose Karst?"

I have no idea what they're talking about. "I—what?"

But Roxana and her aurelian are already peeling away from us.

Phemi's skyfish has begun to lose altitude with every hacking cough. I'm not sure how much longer they'll be able to stay air-borne.

"Delo," says Phemi, and I hear the fear in her voice.

"She'll make it. Come on."

Phemi sur Hecate can't get up to more than a coasting speed, so we drift toward the citadel and the private harbor inside its walls, sheltered by the nearest looming karst—Thornrose, whose clan we favor and recruit for our staff. The same karst I saw amber scales hiding on this morning. Why, I wonder again, was Roxana asking about it?

The screams of the dragonborn fleeing, being routed by Griff and the rest of the Norcians, are distant below, and I have the briefest hope that when we clear the citadel walls, we'll find an end to the carnage.

Instead, we find the private harbor in flames. The *Invicturi* is lost in smoke.

The Norcians have cut off our escape.

At the sight, the last of Phemi sur Hecate's strength gives out. The two of them drift and falter: They need shelter. I guide them onto the ramparts of the citadel's outer wall, deserted in the fray. Phemi slides from her dragon's back, and I dismount from Geph to hold her. I can see the burning harbor from where we're perched, the Norcians dragging dragonborn royals away from their attempted escape in triumph. Ethelo and Father are stumbling as they're led, shocks of brown skin among the olive tones of the Norcians. There's no sign of the Greatlord Rhadamanthus or Lady Xanthe.

As her dragon gasps its last, Phemi lowers her face into the sky-fish's side and sobs.

"It's your fault," she tells me. "You and your Griff. He did this. And you let him."

I hold her on the ramparts as our world burns and know she's right.

GRIFF

The ha'Aurelian clipper ship we set afire in their harbor is sleek, light, nothing but sails and Damian anti-air harpoons, and they go up like dry leaves. The painted wings of Aron, the dragon that flew Uriel to safety in the Aurelians' first exile, peel hissing from the sides. Along the prow is carved the name that—thanks to Antigone—I can now read: INVICTURI. *They who shall not be conquered.*

But now it's lost in flames.

Bran and his aurelian begin ushering the dragonborn who would have fled off the burning ship and onto the docks where the Norcians wait to serve them justice. Delo's brother, Ethelo, a *passus* who rides no dragon, emerges supporting old Lady Electra's arm. The Stormscourge widow glares at me; Ethelo just stares blankly.

"Griff?" he says. Blood runs down his temple.

I give a jaunty salute from Sparker's back. "Good to see you, my lord."

And then a voice speaks in Norish, and I find Astyanax's nurse, Shea, clutching my sleeve with fire-blistered fingers. "The boy's still down there. Please—Griff."

The other Thornrose servants are being rounded up with about as much sympathy as the lords they betrayed the clans for, but Shea's plea plucks at me. I look from her to the burning clipper ship and think of the little ha'Aurelian lordling, who so kindly thought to spare Sparker. I try to tell myself the heir to the ha'Aurelian line should by rights be exterminated along with the whole lot of them, for good measure—

But it's no good. Shrines take all of them and my confounded heart.

"Keep the dragonborn in your sights," I tell Bran, as Sparker leaps over the heads of the crowd and onto the deck of the burning clipper.

I'm coughing from the smoke as soon as I dismount. Bodies are everywhere, some of them stirring, others still. Thornrose bodies, Norcian bodies, dragonborn bodies: the remains of bloody strife. I scramble down the ladder into the hull two rungs at a time and find flames illuminating the Greatlord Rhadamanthus's bloodied, crumpled head and his wife's blood-matted hair at the foot of it. Their eyes stare glassily at the ceiling. Each breath brings the smell of smoke and blood and salt water; I breathe through my mouth until I hear what I'm listening for.

A child's weeping.

I find Astyanax hiding in the privy three feet from the bodies of his parents.

"Griff?"

"Little lordling. You must look at me and only me."

When I lift him into my arms, he clings.

I stumble up the stairs and out, coughing, to Sparker where he waits, and then we are up in the air and swooping across the distance to join the Norcians and their corralled dragonborn on the docks. "You've got to be kidding," Bran says, when he sees who I've got in my arms.

"He's a child, Bran—"

"He's their heir, and he's better off dead."

Good thing Astyanax doesn't know a word of Norish. There are gasps around us; people start to scream. For a moment I think they're still fussing about the kid when I see fingers pointing toward Thornrose Karst.

Roxana ha'Aurelian is streaking toward it. For a moment I watch, unconcerned, as Roxana's dragon prepares to fire on the clan-karst, because serves Thornrose right for their traitorous backing of the ha'Aurelians—

And then I remember what Antigone said.

Agga and the little ones are in hiding on that karst.

5

THORNROSE KARST

ANNIE

We've only just cleared the dungeon, stepped onto the ramparts, and Duck taken in his first full breath of fresh air, when I see it. A single triarchal dragon, conspicuous for her lack of woad, streaking away from the citadel—away from the harbor—and toward the nearest karst of Sailor's Folly.

Toward Thornrose Karst.

I'm on Aela's back, in the air, without a second thought.

From the corner of my eye, I see Griff sur Sparker burst from the citadel's burning harbor at full speed, straining for the same interception.

We race them toward Thornrose.

As we gain on the aurelian rider, I recognize her. A streak of deep red hair flows down the rider's back in a braid. She has no armor, no flamesuit; the dress she no doubt wore to Griff's drop is hitched around her knees. Less than twenty-four hours ago, I wrestled with her in the Driftless Dunes before her kinsmen dragged Griff away.

Roxana ha'Aurelian. Now making a beeline, on dragonback, for the karst where Griff's family is hiding.

The bracken that provided such good coverage will also make fast kindling.

Her fires start before I get there, lit from the base of the karst. The vines are brown, dried from winter, and catch quickly. The fires lick the side of the outcropping and climb. Agga will be hidden with the children at the top, among the standing stones of the shrine, surrounded by brittle undergrowth.

Sparker dives into the bracken on the crown as Griff shouts his sister's name. I go after Roxana.

Aela catches the aurelian's tail in her fangs and *yanks*.

Roxana's dragon jerks to a halt in midair.

We slam the dragon and rider into the burning bracken, smothering it. They crash into the wall of sheer rock beneath with a *crack*, and we pin them there like a squashed dragonfly.

I have them, and I will suffocate this girl on the karst that she and her dragon set afire.

But between gasps, Roxana is laughing.

"Such a little heroine. You're missing the *bigger picture*, peasant."

She has to wheeze her words. I'm close to laughing, too. Broken, pinned between her dragon and the rock, Roxana wants to trade insults? Even her final attempt at sabotage will be foiled by Griff, rescuing his family now from the top of the karst. "Your people are routed. Your family is dead, your line with it. Your rule is over."

Between pained gasps, Roxana just keeps laughing.

"When you and your peasant friends crept into our lairs this morning," she says, "did you not notice that dragons were missing?"

My fingers clench white on Aela's reins. Her whole being is tensed to fire and waits for my wish. I won't even have to make the order aloud.

And yet. What Roxana says nudges my lingering doubts.

Dragons *were* missing. Dragons whose troughs we poisoned anyway, assuming they'd be back in time for their feeding before Griff's drop. But they still haven't shown up.

She names them for me, sneering. "Ixion Stormscourge. The Bastards. And most important, a whalefin from Bassilea. Or did you forget about Princess Freyda's goliathan?"

For a moment all I can hear is the crackling of the fires creeping up the vines.

I haven't seen any of them today. I should have seen them.

"They're coming?"

"Hardly." Roxana leans forward and speaks between gasps. "They're *waiting*. In the Great Palace that you left behind, in the halls that had been taken from them, on the thrones from which they were once deposed. And I'm sure the absence of the Callipolan Firstrider at the time of countercoup was particularly appreciated."

Countercoup?

Atop the karst, the shrine is almost entirely engulfed. Sparker's wings are black silhouettes as Griff rises from the flames with figures huddled in his arms—

"That's not possible."

Roxana's laugh is wheezing. "Like I said, Antigone, you're missing the bigger picture. You're so focused on winning this battle, you lost the war."

I open my mouth to answer—and the wall of rock beneath us crumbles.

GRIFF

Agga's lungs have always been weak. Weak lungs like our mother's, that one day refused air for long enough that she fell asleep and didn't wake up. Lungs that ginger calms, but never quite eases. That can barely tolerate mists from the seas, let alone smoke.

Her lungs are all I think of as Sparker scrambles through the burning bracken. I've got no flamesuit; the tunic I'm wearing will be burned off by the time we're out. But I don't stop calling her name.

And then she's there, pressed against a standing stone, thrusting Garet up to me over Sparker's wing, then Becca.

"You too—"

"Them first—"

Her lungs. But also, the way she looked at me when she said: *This is a fantasy that will get my children killed.*

I take the babes into my arms. "I'll come right back for—"

And then my ears shatter, and the world goes black.

DELO

The sound of the explosion ripples through the air and under our feet. For a moment the scene above it is frozen: Griff sur Sparker above the flames, two small figures suspended in his arms as he lifts them from the burning bracken, held up to him by hands belonging to a body I cannot see. The two aurelians frozen, one pinning the other against the side of the karst. Crouched on the citadel walls beside Phemi, I can see all of it. I can see for miles.

Thornrose Karst mushrooms like a shattering glass.

Norcians on the ground below begin to scream.

I hurl myself over Phemi, and Gephyra flicks her wing over us, growling, as the debris flies. Limestone chunks the size of cannonballs thud into the water. When the sounds of impact are over, and Geph rolls back her wing, I risk lifting my head.

The karst is cracked open like a broken flowerpot.

And when the flames, and steam, and dust settles, the air has cleared of dragons. Phemi is leaning against the ramparts, weeping. I think of the knowing way she and Roxana conferred—*The firepowder, why not?*—and round on her. "What just happened?"

Tears are streaming anew down my sister's face. She saw the woman and children atop Thornrose, too. "We rigged the clankarsts. Ethelo and I. We're good with firepowder. After that debacle with the Callipolan air strike, the Greatlord wanted a reserve means of cowing the natives—"

Phemi and Ethelo have always been the arithmetical ones, but this takes it further than I could have imagined. "Why didn't I know?"

"Because you're the peasant lover!" Phemi shouts.

And the Triarchy-in-Exile guessed I might consider rigging the Norcians' sacred shrines with firepowder as a trick too dirty to contemplate. I'm shouting, too, my finger jabbing at the smoking ruins where Agga, Becca, and Garet were silhouetted moments ago. We're alone on this stretch of wall, with no need left for discretion if I still cared for it. "There were *children* on that karst!"

I expect her to say *Stop being such a peasant lover* at that, and my fists are balled with such fury I can feel Gephyra summoning fire.

But my little sister only lowers her face into her hands. "I'm sorry," she says. "I'm so sorry."

GRIFF

I come to with my ears ringing, the world still churning. I'm on a slab of stone that once made up the trunk of Thornrose Karst, which now lies sideways in the water, raw and dark where it cracked open. Sparker leans over me, snorting ash into my eyes. I roll onto my side, coughing seawater, to find Antigone beside me, weeping.

"Where's my sister?" I ask. "Where are the little ones?"

The babes were in my arms when the explosion went off. But now my arms are empty.

"Griff, I'm sorry—"

"Oh, thank the shrines."

Antigone's beside my sister. My sister's lying next to her, safe, and so is Garet. But Antigone won't stop crying.

Which is stupid, because they're fine. All we've got to do is find Becca, and then they're all going to be fine—

I crawl to Agga, to shake her awake, and that's when I see that what I thought was water pooling under her head is crimson.

"Griff, I'm sorry—"

"Stop saying that! Agga, wake up!"

Garet's not moving, either.

"Aela got them as quickly as she could—she's still looking—"

Screams come from the shore, distant and tinny as gulls' cries, but here on the smoking, exploded karst, as I stare into my sister's face and will her to open her eyes, it is too quiet.

"Griff," Antigone says, her voice wobbling, "where's Ixion?"

"How should I know where Ixion is?" I snap.

She is sobbing, hugging herself, blood running down her wet forehead, diluted by salt water.

"Did he go to Callipolis, with Freyda?"

I feel like she's a gnat, flitting at my forehead, as I kneel over my sister and try to shake her awake.

And then I remember that I know he did. I was at the council when they brought me in from the Driftless Dunes, where they said Ixion's plan was proceeding as desired with Freyda. I was in the air when I saw Ixion and the Bastards making for Callipolis.

"Yeah," I say, and then begin to pump my sister's heart.

Antigone lowers her face to her knees, digs her nails into her hair, and screams.

"Agga, *wake up*!"

But for all I try to force those stupid lungs to do their work again, she lies still. *"Stop crying,"* I tell Antigone, but it only makes her cry harder as I pump, and break—pump, and break—pump, and break—and when I stop to catch my breath the third time, Agga's head lolls in that crimson pool and she's still wretchedly, horribly still.

"Please, no."

I feel like a storm wave is rising over my head, about to drown me. *Don't think it. It can't have done, she can't be*—

She's not even warm.

Neither is Garet.

"I'm sorry. I'm so sorry—"

This time, it's me saying it, as if it's a Plea with the shrines, as if I can barter guilt for mercy like I might groveling before a lord, but the shrines are as silent as my sister and her son. For what have the shrines ever done besides witness our sorrow? As now I hold the cold body of a sister who told me this dream would get her babes killed, and instead it killed—

My thoughts circle the offending sentence as if walling it off can prevent it getting in. But the wave still looms. Whatever walls I raise, it will soon crash over.

"It's not your fault," Annie says, reaching out a hand.

I knock it away.

She's wrong. She has no idea how wrong she is.

I can't breathe with the weight of how wrong she is.

But then the screams trill again from the island, and as I lift my head and take in the shore, the corralled dragonborn, our oppressors rounded up like cattle for their crimes, I realize there is one very specific way Antigone is right.

It's my fault. But it's their fault, *more*.

I reach for Sparker.

Mercy be damned. They deserve to pay.

6

MERCY UNDESERVING

DELO

For a moment, I stand frozen beside Phemi on the citadel ramparts, taking in the sight at the harbor below: my kinsmen, cornered on the docks around the burning clipper ship, surrounded on all sides by Norcians. At the sight of the exploding clan-karst, even the servants of Thornrose have turned on us.

What was a surrender is about to become something else.

All eyes are on the single stormscourge making its way from the remains of Thornrose Karst.

Griff lands on the dock in the space between his kinsmen and mine, and the wooden planks creak under Sparker's great weight. Even from a distance I can see Griff's face twisted in naked rage the likes of which I've never seen upon it. Sparker's fangs are bared, flames licking white hot within them.

There have been times when, across distances, I could feel Gephyra's emotions as if they were my own. But today, I feel as if I've spilled over, not with my dragon, but with another person.

Griff wants murder. Not the glorious rampage of this morning but the cold obscenity of total death. Every single dragonborn on this rock, my father, my brother, the ha'Aurelians who've sheltered us, the exiles with whom we've taken refuge—

All of us are about to be slaughtered.

I move without conscious thought, rising from Phemi's side, launching onto Gephyra's back, and kicking off from the ramparts with an arm round my dragon's neck. It takes two beats of her wings to descend to the harbor and land us between Griff and my people. Gephyra is the only dragon left to defend us.

Outnumbered seven to one.

I release my grip on Gephyra's neck, and my boots slide onto the creaking dock.

It goes against bone-deep instincts to walk toward a dragon whose fangs are bared and flames are summoned. But I force one foot after another forward, not looking at the roaring Norcians, not looking at my watching family, not looking even at Sparker.

I keep my eyes locked on Griff's rage-stricken face.

At firing range, I lower to my knees and place two palms flat on the planks.

I've seen Griff kneel like this more times than I like to think. To his lords in the Glass Hall, on all fours like a dog. In front of me, as he wept to thank me for saving family that never should have been in danger.

And now, for all my peasant-loving, they're gone.

I stare at my hands and recite the Plea in Norish, as Griff's people have been taught to say to mine.

Grant mercy, my lord, on your servant undeserving.

GRIFF

When I land, I mean to kill all of them. Even Astyanax. I mean to make them *hurt*. But when Delo starts reciting, I can't look away.

Delo knows every single Plea by heart, and he seems intent on saying all of them. He's on to the third before I think to stop him.

Not a soul speaks as we watch a young dragonlord on his knees reciting Pleas like a peasant. His accent in our language is good. Better than most of our lords'. After avoiding attention for as long as I can remember, Delo's making a scene like his life depends on it.

It's so strange, neither the Norcians nor the dragonborn can look away. On the ramparts above us, Phemi Skyfish looks on from the side of her unmoving dragon. It's plain from her tearstained face and her vacant stare that she's been widowed. When I glance past Delo at his huddling family, I see his father's lip twisted in fury.

But we all watch, equally transfixed.

"Stop," I hear myself say.

Delo hears me, falters, and keeps going, shouting the Norish at the ground.

". . . *grant that my punishment duly owed not be given to my family blameless . . .*"

I dismount from Sparker.

"Griff," Bran hisses from behind me. "What the hell is this—"

"Hold."

I approach where Delo kneels. When I'm level with him, he gives a rattling sob and lowers his lips to my boot. Behind him, Nestor makes a choking noise. But my heart is pierced with the memory.

Delo stooping to my level as I knelt in my own home with my lips pressed to his boots, his fingers lifting my chin, his hand on mine to give me Sparker's key. *Do what you need to do.*

And now I've done it, and lost everything.

"Enough."

Finally, Delo stops his recitation and looks up at me. His face is drenched.

"Your family are not blameless," I tell him. "They do not deserve our mercy."

The shattered clan-karst smoking into the sky is proof of that.

"No," Delo says, "they don't. But you need to think strategically."

We're speaking in Dragontongue.

"Strategically?"

A flash of the old Delo appears in the line between his fine brows, the usual impatience at my stupidity. He's still kneeling, but he eases back onto his heels. "Notice who's missing," he says, gesturing behind him at his cowering family. "Half the fleet is *absent*. Ixion's taken Callipolis and he will not be pleased."

For the first time, the import of Antigone's tears hits home.

Our uprising will be futile. Ixion and Freyda will make his Long-Awaited Return on the mainland, and then the Bastards will return and make us pay.

But even as I realize it, I find I couldn't care less.

When it's all been for nothing, what's a little more reason to despair?

"So?"

"*So you need to let the majority of us go,*" Delo pants. "Keep a few as hostages, treated well enough that Ixion is kept at bay. Send the rest of us to the mainland in one piece. Give Ixion no cause to seek retribution."

It's like I'm hearing him through an earful of water. I can't make sense of it.

I'm doing this for them. I'm doing this for you. That was what I told Agga, when she wept, when I told her we would have revolution. I close my eyes at the memory.

This is a fantasy that will get my children killed.

What was it all for if they don't live to see it?

I hear a soft rustle and open streaming eyes. Between us has landed Aela, Antigone's aurelian. Her fangs are hooked on a single small and sodden tunic, and hanging in it is a soaked girl, who's coughing up seawater and wiping her eyes.

"Uncle?"

Aela releases Becca into my arms as gently as a mother cat depositing a kitten.

"Uncle, why are you crying? Where's Mumma?"

I pull her against my chest, and the fire in Sparker's maw finally flickers out.

7

HOSTAGES

DELO

A few hours later, after the Norcians have established control of
the citadel and cleanup has begun, Griff receives me in the Greatlord's parlor. He's throwing the sigils of the ha'Aurelians and the
Triarchy-in-Exile into a roaring fire when I enter. The sigil of Norcia, with its five clan stars, has been moved to the center position
on the wall. The crumpled remains of Thornrose Karst are visible
through the window.

His face has dried. The open rage that he demonstrated on the
pier has been replaced by a cold distance. I learned from Bran,
who escorted me to this meeting, that Griff's grandfather's body
was found among the dead on Conqueror's Mound, a fishing spear
in hand and woad on his cheeks.

Griff has lost his grandfather, his sister, and his nephew in
one day.

And my own sister was widowed by poison his conspiracy
brought.

Now that our grief has had time to cool, it stands between us
like a wall. I stand, Griff sits, and he does not invite me to do the
same. I've been sent as the dragonborn delegate to finalize the
hostage arrangement.

"I'll keep Electra," Griff says.

It's a good choice. Electra is a widowed Stormscourge, an aunt Ixion is fond of but not passionate about. He won't feel hard pressed to rescue her. I incline my head; Griff blinks at the hint of obeisance. He otherwise acts as though our new dynamic, with me as his suppliant, is not remarkable.

"Lady Xanthe for House Aurelian?" I suggest.

For this conversation, we speak in Norish. It's not the language we used in bed; it's the language of his people, and it feels like a layer of armor placed over the moment, to keep each other at arm's length. It helps that Norish contains no distinction between formal and informal, superior and servant. I don't like to wonder what forms we would use right now if we spoke in Dragontongue.

Griff shakes his head. "Dead. Along with Rhadamanthus."

He says this as remorselessly as if he were talking about strangers, not the family whose son he trained with, whose parents he frequently served at table.

But why should Rhode, who bullied him, or Rhadamanthus, who was dismissive toward him at best, be deaths Griff mourns? I, on the other hand, who found in them a kind of extended, imperfect family, feel my throat close.

Griff kicks back in the Greatlord's chair like he's sat in it his whole life and announces, with mock casualness, "I'll take Astyanax. He survived."

The youngest son of the Greatlord is barely older than Becca. "He was just orphaned."

Griff lifts a shoulder, indifferent. "He likes me. He could have worse fates. He could, for instance, take a fall off the citadel walls for being the Greatlord's only surviving heir."

This is bluster and I know it; Griff's fond of Sty. I am gripped with the sudden urge to shake him, to shout at him, to set aside this mask of triumph he has worn ever since I took to my knees. It's not like I can't see the grief beneath it.

"For Skyfish House," Griff goes on, with the determination of a battering ram, "I would take Phemi."

"Griff, for the love of the dragon," I say in Dragontongue.

Griff's brow lifts. "We will speak in Norish," he says. "Phemi is my choice."

"Why?"

He enunciates each word. "Because she is your father's favorite."

Griff served as my squire for nearly ten years. He knows, more intimately than most, the hierarchy of my father's preferences among his children. And now he brandishes his knowledge like a cudgel.

Why are you being so cruel?

"She was just widowed. By your *friend's* poison."

Griff lifts a shoulder. He holds my gaze. He does not blink.

"You promised," I hear my own voice break, "you said you wouldn't hurt them—"

It is the first time I've ever referenced the pleas I made for the twins, half at wits' end, kissing him as I admitted to myself for the first time what he must be doing with that key. When I could have reported him, and didn't.

And now I've lived to rue it.

Griff cuts me off. "I didn't hurt them. The twins are safe and sound. Which is more than can be said for my sister and her son. Phemi was also the one who rigged the karsts with black powder, was she not?"

The words are uttered softly, but I know they are themselves explosive. A fuse presented that requires just one spark to light. He saved my sister, as I asked him once to do, but I didn't save his. For a moment, the only sound is of the dragonborn sigil crackling in

Griff's fire and the carousing, in the distance, of his people looting the homes of mine.

I can't wallow in guilt over what happened to Griff's family when mine is still in danger. My heart is a thudding weight. "Let me stay in Phemi's stead."

He blinks.

"Please. Keep me as your secretary, your servant, your—whatever you want—"

It's a half-formed thought, but it is there. Griff's lip curls as he understands.

"There is an art," he says delicately, "to what you are attempting to do, which you are lacking."

I feel the heat in my face. "Forgive me if I don't have your practice."

Griff's brows are level with his curling hair. It is unnerving to stand while he sits, to *wait* like this. He gives me long enough to remember that I would do best not to insult him as I seek to curry favor. I have the sudden feeling that I don't know what to do with my hands.

I backtrack slowly, forcing them not to ball. "I would be powerful leverage."

Griff snorts. "As my—what—concubine? I'm pretty sure you wouldn't be."

"As my father's heir."

That, I still am. Whomever Father favors.

Griff studies me. I know he is, despite himself, intrigued. Or maybe just amused. "I don't have interest in a concubine," he says, inspecting his nails, "though I'm flattered. Could use a lairhand, though."

He is absolutely, undeniably, toying with me now. But I'm too desperate to care. "I could run your lairs."

"I didn't say run them."

He wants me to muck shit? Fine.

I will do whatever it takes to repay the debt I owe my family for betraying them.

At my silence, Griff snorts. "Sure," he says, getting to his feet. "But your dragon gets on that boat."

8

TILL DEATH RELEASE ME

ANNIE

In the wake of the destruction of Clan Thornrose's karst and shrine, Griff calls off all violence toward the fifth clan—except for a display of their puppet king, whose body is hung from the citadel walls. The fallen dragonborn, at Delo's request, are allowed a burial pyre, and the rowboats the Three Families will take into exile are prepared on the shore beside it. Their manors have been sacked, their storerooms emptied, and by midday, feasts spring up across the island. Norcian pipes fill the air with melodies that sound so like the ones I knew as a child, I wonder if they're descended from the same ancient songs.

Duck and I do not participate in this gory revelry. We have nothing to celebrate.

Instead, perched on the cliff that overlooks the dragonborn pyre, we piece together the evidence and weigh our odds. Ixion gone. Freyda also, with her Great Dragon. A third of the fleet, made up of illegitimate dragonborn known as the Bastard Gray-riders, all missing. A plan that Roxana gloated about to me, and before that, Ixion and Rhode gloated about to Duck in prison when they tormented him.

A countercoup.

Duck's company keeps the immensity of my failure at bay, but at intervals it swells again: I swore to protect Callipolis, and then I left her defenseless. I broke my vows as a Guardian and failed as Firstrider. And I got Griff's family killed in a revolution that will, for all I know, come to nothing.

My whole body itches with impatience for flight, and it ripples into Aela, curled in the seagrass beside me. I've failed, but I'll finish what I've started. We need to go home.

First, there's something I have to tell him. "Duck, during the air raid—"

Attempting to say it makes me feel cold. He'll return alive to his family, but he'll find a sister missing.

"I know what happened to Ana."

Aela's been grooming the scales left itchy after a day in armor, but looks up when she feels my surprise. Duck's staring hard at the line where the gray sea meets the sky. "You remember, Ixion's been smuggling Callipolan papers out. Cor's article—he and Rhode read it to me."

During the Bunker Riots, Cor penned an article describing how his sister's iron wristband prevented her from finding a place in a bunker during the air strikes, all because she tested poorly. The article was understated but the heartbreak unmistakable. I imagine Cor's words being read to me, about my own sister, by a sneering Ixion. When I look at Duck's face, carefully emotionless, I think: *I will kill them all.*

Aela's growl is low and rumbling beside us.

I search for the thread of argument to move past my horror and Duck's dead stare. But he speaks first. "I know there was unrest. I know the plan was for Ixion to try to hijack the Assembly with some sort of offer of food aid from Bassilea. But I don't believe it would work. Accepting aid from Bassilea would mean vassalage. Callipolan citizens are smarter than that."

Where did Duck get this doe-eyed optimism, and how is it that even after months in prison he still has it?

"Callipolan citizens are like anyone else when they're starving. Desperate."

And with Freyda Bassileon, her goliathan, and her troops—how much choice would they have?

Duck hugs his knees tighter and into them, he murmurs, "You're going back?"

It's not the question I'm expecting. "Of course."

"I thought of . . . staying." Duck studies his knees. "Lena asked me to stay with her."

This, I think, like Becca's emerging from the water spluttering and alive, is a fresh shoot of green in a bed of dead leaves. "You're happy, with her."

Duck nods. "When I was widowed," he says, his head bent so far over his knees I can only see his nape, "it was horrible. I missed Certa so much." I'm frozen, suddenly conscious of the hand I've absentmindedly got scratching Aela's crest, of the way he hasn't looked at her once, since we joined him on this hillside. But then he lifts his head. "It was also a relief. I felt like I'd been set free of something."

It takes me a moment to understand. "The vows?"

Our lives sworn to the City's protection, no family or future aside from it, till death release us.

Duck nods. "We took them so *young*, Annie. Do you ever won-der what it would've been like if we hadn't . . ."

I consider carefully before answering. The what-ifs I can make of my own life's alternatives are mostly dismal. I remember the girls I knew in the orphanage, with prospects of workhouses at best, at worst the street; my mother, beset by mouths she couldn't feed and pregnancies she couldn't prevent. Was she happy, before she bled out on a birthing bed? I don't remember her well enough to know. Even if she was, it's a life I can't imagine wanting.

It's my turn to avoid looking at him. Aela's got a line of dead scales worn off by the saddle that I'm scraping with a thumbnail. "I think, for me, most of the alternatives would have been worse."

Duck doesn't argue that. But I know from his silence he's noticing how I said it. Maybe as a child, I could be bright-eyed about the glamour of dragonriding. But I know differently now. Becca wants to be me when she grows up, but I'm not sure she's right to.

I used to imagine we would be heroes. Today's attempt at heroism led to the greatest failure of my career.

If I could go back, make the choice to take the vows again, would I?

Aela twists round, blinking a single amber eye at me. I wonder if I'm imagining that her glare is a little accusatory, as if she knows exactly what I'm second-guessing and takes insult. I have the urge, which would feel unseemly in front of Duck, to bury my face in her warm neck. Instead, I force myself to smile at him.

"I'm happy for you," I tell him, and tell myself I mean it. "I'm happy you're happy."

A line wrinkles his brow as I get to my feet. "You're allowed to be happy, too," he says.

I'm not so sure I am. Aela vaults onto her haunches, shaking her wings with a smart rattle, already eager for flight. She leaves a dragon-size imprint of wilted, charred grass behind her. I touch Duck's shoulder. "Stay here, stay with Lena, prepare a refuge that we may need."

Have happiness for us both.

Aela and I make our way down to the beach to gather a final piece of information before we depart. Dragons are what I need, a whole fleet of them, but I know the Norcians can't spare that right now. They have an island to stabilize and, hopefully, defend. So instead, I'll ask for what Griff can give: information.

I find him watching the dragonborn prepare for departure from the edge of the shoreline. His gaze lingers not on the pyres or the rowboats but on a single slender figure, entwined in a skyfish's embrace like a coiled python, his palms cupping her long face. Delo, parting with his dragon. At my approach, Griff turns a stiff face toward mine.

"I need you to tell me everything you know about Freyda."

He grunts. "I know she got me locked in that prison. She was the one who wrote the note calling for the squires' arrest. And then she must have told on me for reading it."

A voice speaks so quietly from behind me, I don't at first hear it. "She didn't." Delo has extricated himself from Gephyra's embrace, though his fingers remained curled into her iridescent crest. The dragon's tail streams in the wind, listless. "We only found out she'd given you a note after Scully reported your dragon missing. Ixion was furious with her for handing you the edict. I was there."

Griff's head tilts at the sound of Delo's voice, but he doesn't turn.

"And her response?" I ask.

Delo lifts a shoulder. His voice remains even, distantly ironic. "Freyda can be . . . hard to read. She seemed more amused than anything. Said she admired Griff's pluck."

Griff's jaw juts, as if his pluck is the last thing he wants to be reminded of now. For a moment, the fraught silence hums. Delo seems to have had enough of it. The dragonborn are struggling to light the pyre; their dead tower over us, propped on driftwood. Delo clucks, and Gephyra ripples toward them to offer flame. Griff speaks to me.

"Ixion will want your blood. Now more than ever."

I show Aela her saddle, and she lowers herself to take it with a grumpy huff. "I know."

Griff pulls, seemingly unconsciously, at his sleeve. "Do you?"

The first time we met, Ixion called me a *peasant bitch* and told me that one day, he'd make me and my stinking kind remember that he owned us. I've seen what that ownership looks like on Griff's scarred arms. The beatings and burns that Ixion reserves for peasants who defy him.

Griff thinks I don't understand what I'll be facing. But he doesn't understand that I don't have a choice. I tighten Aela's girth with two swift yanks. After a day of hard riding, I know it chafes her, but my good girl makes no complaint. "Will he be more merciful to Lee, who killed his sister? With my riders, who are also lowborn?"

Griff has no answer to that.

I climb into the saddle already saddle-sore, and Aela's wings snap open.

It's time to find out what mess I've made at home, coming here to play the hero.

9

ATREUS ATHANATOS

LEE

CALLIPOLIS

My wristband is removed only after the rest of the Guardians are gone. No bag is placed over my head, so as we make our way from the Outer Palace courtyards to the Inner, I'm able to see the sigil of the Triarchy rising to replace the Revolutionary flags on the battlements. Ixion keeps pace with me, and Edmund's grip on my arm steers the way. My wrist feels bare, too light, without means of summoning Pallor.

"The dragon's fine," Edmund says, noticing my glance down, "for the time being."

We enter a disused corridor of the Inner Palace that I recognize at once. In the anteroom of what was once the Stormscourge wing, I stop dead.

"There a problem, cousin?"

Ixion knows exactly what the problem is. When I don't answer, Edmund tugs me over the lintel. "So these are the ancestral halls about which I've heard so much . . ."

Ixion smiles, unamused. "Would you like to hear some cherished memories?" Ixion points down the main corridor, disappearing in the unlit gloom, toward what were formerly the apartments of the Triarch of the West. Since the Revolution, it's served as a clerical space. "Down there was where Julia and I hid in a cupboard on Palace Day. They marked my mother with a cattle brand, you know. A tribute to my father, who they then murdered. I still remember the sound . . ."

He imitates the hissing of hot iron on skin as he lays a finger on my arm. Edmund laughs nervously.

"What are they serving as now, our old apartments?" Ixion squints at a directory on the wall. "Sub-offices of the Censorship Committee. Charming."

I start fighting in earnest as Edmund hauls me to a halt in front of the door I've known, since we entered this wing, would be coming.

"And this is the . . . *Palace Revolutionary Collection*," Ixion reads the plaque on the door. "So I'm paperwork and you're storage. Bureaucracy!"

He kicks in the door to what were my family's apartments.

"Grandmother's old vases!" He glances around the converted storage room and rotates on his heel to face me. "Parlor, wasn't it?"

I can feel cold sweat breaking out along my back.

The truth is, I've avoided this part of the Palace ever since I was admitted into the Guardian program. The one time I came close to stepping into these chambers, I bolted. Even here, on the threshold, I'm so aware of *that room*, it might as well be emanating the whispers of the dead.

"Leo?" Ixion prompts, smiling. "Lead the way."

I yank my arm free of Edmund's grasp and wind my way through the dusty, decaying piles of my family's old things. My mother's faded dresses peeking from a wardrobe. Larissa's hair combs, lost in cobwebs on Laertes's dusty writing desk . . .

He wants you to see these things. He wants you to remember it. He wants you to feel it.

And it's working.

I stop in front of the parlor door. The whispering in my ears is deafening. I barely hear what Ixion says as he places something in my hand. I look down and find my father's bootknife in it. The one that was confiscated this morning. Annie found it in this room, not days ago, when she was looking for drachthanasia.

When you look at this knife, I want you to remember that it belonged to a father who loved you. And I want you to remember that I was the one who gave it to you.

Annie's still out there. *Annie.* Her name is like an incantation, returning me to myself. To the person I chose to be.

"What am I supposed to do with this?"

Ixion smiles. "I think you'll find your task self-explanatory. We'll collect you at sundown."

Edmund turns the handle and pushes me through the door.

The parlor is poorly lit. Floor-length drapes, now moth-eaten, are pulled over windows overlooking the Firemouth. A chandelier hangs crookedly from a cracked ceiling. A single folding card table has been placed in the center of the room between two straight-backed chairs, as if for interrogation. All original furnishings have been removed save the rug, which is stained rust brown in exactly the places I remember blood.

Father where he knelt. Mother where she begged. Larissa struggling; Penelope promising she wouldn't. Laertes gasping, dying. Laughter.

The door closes behind me, and I'm left to steep in it.

As the shadows lengthen and fill the room, like ghosts rising from the dust, I wonder if I'm supposed to use the knife in hand to kill myself.

Stop this foolishness at once.

Please, Atreus. My son.

The Callish I didn't know then but know now: *Take the boy into the hallway, and slit his throat.*

The memories close over my head like rising waters and I am under them, in the dark.

When the door opens again, and a voice speaks, I find I am kneeling alone in the center of the stained rug that once contained the bodies, and I am staring at the silhouette of a figure with hands bound who has been shoved into the room with me. A transom window high above us illuminates a long face already swelling with bruises, but the eyes pierce with the same steel they always have.

"Hello, Lee," says Atreus Athanatos.

I scramble to my feet, my father's knife unsteady in my hand. Atreus's mouth has curved into a smile. Blood trickles down his forehead. His arms bound behind him, he has no free hand to wipe his face.

"I suppose it's only fitting," he says.

I'm shaking so badly, it extends to my jaw. The words are bitten out. "What is fitting?"

"This room. That knife. You."

He looks so calm, so unsurprised, that if it weren't for the fact that his hands are bound, and I stand opposite him holding a boot-knife, I could mistake this for class.

He assumes I'll kill him.

Ixion, Edmund, and Atreus all assume that if they put me in a room with the man responsible for my family's murders and hand me a knife, I'll do the execution myself.

Blood on my hands as a baptism out of one regime and into the next.

What if I don't want that baptism?

I've had the chance to kill Atreus before. I refused it. I can refuse it again. Even if the ghosts in this room are whispering that they want it.

I set the knife, with a shaking hand, on the card table.

Atreus looks as if this amuses him most of all.

"Lee," he says, "my time is up. Spare me or don't, I remain a dead man. You, on the other hand, have a chance to walk out of this room with hands unbound."

"They could give you a trial."

Atreus's laugh is soft. "A trial with only one possible outcome. All considered, I'd prefer *this* to a long drop and a short stop, or any of the imaginative variations your cousin might devise in the arena."

I take this in with some surprise. "You want me to do it?"

Atreus's chin dips slowly. "I think it's time for you to avenge your family. But before you do, I would like to discuss what you'll do after."

***

I untie Atreus's hands. We take chairs opposite each other at the lone table, my father's knife between us, the stained rug beneath our feet. The shadows lengthen as the day grows long. Atreus's voice, disembodied, floats like it belongs to one more ghost of my past.

But the other ghosts have gone quiet. The room is still except for us.

"You told me that my vision of justice was a perversion," Atreus says, with the equanimity of a teacher in review, and not as if he's recounting something I shouted at him while Pallor bore down and prepared to fire. "Very well. How would you improve it?"

This is the discussion Annie suggested, a few months ago, that

I have with Atreus. Such was my anger with him then that I wouldn't consider it. That anger is gone now. I find I want Atreus, mentor and teacher, to check my reasoning, as he has always done.

"It starts with all of us being equally deserving."

As soon as I say it, I find myself stopping short. This was how I thought when I first began to pen articles advocating for democratic reforms in the lead-up to the Bunker Riots, but now I know more. It starts with democratic reforms, maybe, but it doesn't end there. Now I've seen what happens next.

I've seen the hijacked Assembly.

At my silence, Atreus says gently: "Every solution is imperfect."

I wonder aloud, with desperation: "Then what's even the point—"

"—of trying? I would say, the point *is* trying. You will be surrounded, when you leave this room, by people who care not a jot about doing good in this world. I was once so surrounded. Believe you me, you will feel the difference."

In the early days of his career, Atreus was advisor to Arcturus Aurelian, the triarch whose regime was so corrupt, Atreus eventually rose in revolution against it. All these years later, the memory of it still evokes a note of fury in Atreus's voice.

"These mere words, these stupid ideals: Those who don't have them, underestimate them. They can't imagine that your tiny flame of purpose could turn into a fire to burn down a world. They can't imagine that such featherlight words will give you strength to endure the harshest pain. They can't imagine ideas could be more powerful than dragonfire.

"But you, Lee, are in on the secret.

"You will have a candle in hand. A flame guttering in the wind. You will have to protect it. For a time, you may have to take it underground. And then you will have to decide how to use it. Will you make a conflagration, and build in the ashes? Will you light a lantern and climb, hoping that your light will be enough for those below? Or will you choose to light the way for someone else?"

I think of Atreus's *Revolutionary Manifesto*, its first draft penned when he was not much older than I. "You decided to make a conflagration."

Atreus nods slowly. "Power was always my lure and my weakness. Just as it is for you."

I could try to deny it; but in this room, with no witness but the dead, I don't dare. It's a certain relief to be able to point out, "I won't have much hope of power now. Even if they let me out, after—this. I'll be hamstrung under the Restoration, at best a figurehead."

At worst, dead on Ixion's orders, to avenge Julia.

Atreus says, "I think you are about to face the greatest temptation to power that you have ever known."

I feel a chill that has nothing to do with the winter cold.

At a knock on the door, I jump.

I almost forgot what comes next.

"I believe that's your cue," Atreus says, and this time, his small smile is visible in the waning light, twisted with the particular irony that is his signature. "I'd like to listen to the evening gulls, if you don't mind. I've always found the City loveliest at dusk."

I part the curtains, unlatch the cobwebbed window, and the sound of seabirds fills the room that was my family's parlor.

Then I take my father's knife in hand and approach the First Protector.

"Lee?"

The name he anointed me with, on Pytho's Keep, after I killed my kin and forsook my family's name. Affirming my vows as a

Guardian to serve the Revolution because I believed—naïvely, perhaps, but so gladly—in the vision this man promised.

"Yes?"

"You were my greatest mistake."

My vision blurs. I grip the knife. And then I plunge it down.

* * *

I open the door on the second knock, the handle sticking red to my palm. Atreus slumps, unmoving, behind me.

"Good," says my half brother, looking from my wet face to my stained hands. "I see you'll be attending Ixion's first Privy Council."

PART II

—

RESTORATION

10

—

AN OLD FRIEND

ANNIE
CALLIPOLIS

It's dusk on the evening of the Liberation of Norcia when Aela and I make our return flight. Long before we reach the coast of the Callipolan mainland, we see the flotilla pulling into the harbor at Fort Aron bearing the yellow whalefin of Bassilea. No cannons fire, no attempt is made to close the port. Their arrival is welcomed.

I nudge a boot into Aela's side and we drift upward, into the stratus, out of sight.

We breach at intervals as we coast south, above to scout, below to orient ourselves, until the tendrils of sun-laced clouds tear away and we look down upon the rolling hills of the lowlands, the city and Pytho's Keep rising in the distance. A dragon the size of a whale circles the Keep lazily, dwarfing it. Her shadow across the city is as long as the karst's.

My first glimpse of Freyda's goliathan.

After that, there's no point getting close enough to see what banners are flying. I already know.

We're about to rise out of sight when we spot a patrol pair.

Two stormscourges, but their armor is not the Revolutionary red. It's gray, with the Triarchy's three dragons circling a black clover. White is for legitimate triarchal bloodlines; these, wearing gray, must be the Bastards I've heard about.

Pythian sigils are patrolling above *my city*.

And one of the dragons, I recognize.

Power sur Eater is outfitted in gray armor, patrolling alongside the enemy.

They spot me a heartbeat after I spot them. For a moment the three of us sit frozen, a mile apart, separated in the golden light in the space between two layers of stratus. Eater's tail stiffens on the wind. Aela, who knows Eater as a sparring partner, twitches and snorts beneath me, sensing something is not quite right.

The two stormscourges swerve toward us, and Aela dives. We burrow back into the stratus and begin to cut a wide weave through it. The setting sun diffuses the mist with golden light.

Wham.

A hulking black shape materializes out of the golden brightness and slams into Aela. She shrieks. We spiral, losing altitude. I can hear Power cursing. Eater's talons clamp onto Aela's wings, flattening me into the saddle.

"You got her?" a voice calls in Dragontongue through the mist.

Aela flails, attempting to free herself, and I'm sobbing in frustration. *"You traitorous bastard—"*

Power lets out a raw, wild laugh. Aela twists and bites Eater's talon. Eater screeches, but doesn't let go. Power kicks his flank. He mutters a command to the dragon that I can't hear.

Eater releases.

"Nearly," he calls through the mist.

My heels drive needlessly into Aela's side: She's already bolting.

After, in the cloud-refracted sunset, with wind biting through my flamesuit and rime ice turning to icicles in my hair, I bury my face in Aela's crest and weep.

Power has removed all doubt: Callipolis has fallen. I left my city unguarded when it needed me most. And now I can only imagine what's happening to the Guardians who weren't willing—as Power seems to have been—to switch sides.

I can feel Aela's ache for her nest, for the Palace caves where she thinks Pallor's waiting. I have no way of conveying that it may never be her nest again.

Is Pallor even there? Is he all right?

And Lee—?

I hardly dare think of it.

"Not yet, darling."

It's dark when Aela dares to nudge her head out of the cloud-bank again. We survey Callipolis spread below us, dark and twinkling. Aela tosses her head, resisting my tug on the reins, straining for the Firemouth. Instead, I steer us to the far side of Pytho's Keep, where a virgin cedar grove carpets the base of the karst.

We plummet through soft branches and thump onto the bed of fallen needles, and when that stills, we hear burbling. Parron's Spring is close. I haven't visited it since a Guardian field trip when I was a child, but I remember the lesson: It was here, they told us, that Pytho the Unifier hatched Parron before building his Keep on the karst above and ushering in a Callipolan golden age. What matters to me now is that the spring is deserted and protected by dense woodland. The overcast sky paints the cedars black.

I unstrap my boots and slide from Aela's back. My thighs are aching; it's a relief for my feet to find solid ground. No sooner have I straightened than Aela begins to furrow through the darkness like a dog on the hunt.

"Aela, *stop*—"

The branches whip against my face as I race blindly after her.

I find her at the base of the karst, in front of an opening visible in the darkness only as a greater gash of black. Her nostrils flare as she sniffs the cold air pooling at the cave mouth, and as an image of Pallor materializes in my vision, I understand.

It's an entrance to the dragon nests. The underground network of cave tunnels below the Palace is expansive and labyrinthine, and its lowest levels are said to connect with the city drainage system. Years making my way down to the aurelian cave corridor and Aela's nest only exposed me to a fraction of the tunnel system. I knew there were other entrances, but until now, I'd never seen one.

Close by, the River Fer roars at the base of the cedar grove and Parron's Spring. The entrance to the nests yawns before us. Aela strains, sniffing, and her hackles rise. Her alarm spills into me: Pallor's scent is there, but it mingles with other dragons' she doesn't know. Unfamiliar dragons, in our caves.

Ours are there, too. Frightened—the tunnel reeks of fear even from here—but so far, still in one piece.

Including Pallor.

She launches into the yawning mouth with a growl—and before I can so much as hiss at her to heel, her snout butts against something hard and cold.

An iron grate bars the passage, each bar as thick as my wrist. When she starts to summon flame, I stop her. "If we break in now, we give away our position. There has to be a plan."

She swings her head round to glare at me in the dark, as if to say, *Then make one.*

A mirage of Pallor, silver and slender and alluring, clouds my vision again. I swat at the back of my neck, pushing Aela's thoughts out. *Alluring?* Ugh. "Keep those thoughts to yourself. He's in there. Safe for now."

But for how long?

I need answers. Answers I can't get as a dragonrider.

"Lie low during the day," I tell Aela. "If you hunt, go at night."

Aela leans forward, her snout in my face, and huffs hot air. This seems to signal approval, because she begins winding in obliging circles, smoking the needle-covered earth into a make-shift nest. Her wings fold to her sides as she settles, and her tail curls round them.

I shoulder my saddlebag, rub Aela's chin beneath her already-closing eyes, and make my way on foot to the bank of the Fer, my dragonriding boots slurping in the hard-packed mud. The Island of the Dead looms in the middle of the river, its ancient dragon-born tombs rising in black silhouettes that were cracked and ruined by the Revolution. The water roars louder than my thoughts as I trace the bank downstream around the base of Pytho's Keep. The arena rises over me first, then the Outer Walls of the Palace, and finally Highmarket Bridge. Vagrants gather by a barrel fire under the stone pillars. Before leaving the bank behind, I step into shadow and rummage in my saddlebag. The dress I have is Agga's. My throat tight, I pull it once more over my flamesuit and wrap her scarf round my hair.

Then I climb up the narrow utility stairs onto the Riverwalk, and cross the bridge into Highmarket.

My first stop is based on a single remembered conversation. *Annie, I need to talk to you . . . something's going on.*

She's not the help I would have wanted; she's not even someone I like. In our longest conversation, I threatened her family with dragonfire, and days later she splashed the story of that exchange on the front page of the *People's Paper*. But whatever reform she wanted, I'm pretty sure *this* wasn't it. And I think she was try-ing to tell me about it the last time we spoke, when I shrugged her off.

Thanks to the file I reviewed before interrogating her in the Vault, I know exactly where to find Megara Roper.

My tired feet carry me across the People's Square, down the Triumphal Way, and into Southside, to the inn known as the Misanthrope. The bar on the ground floor is open despite the late hour; Val Lazare, Megara's uncle and leader of the Passi, lounges against the counter and glances my way without interest when I enter. "Wipe those boots," he calls.

I kick river mud from my boots and ask a serving boy stoking the fire for directions. "Megara?" he asks in surprise. "That's my sister. What d'you want with her?"

So this must be Lex. I last encountered his name on a list of relatives I threatened Megara with. "I'm one of her friends from the Lyceum."

Lex's face sours, as if the elite school his sister attends is not something he likes hearing mention of. He directs me up uneven stairs to the second floor of the inn, points to a door with peeling paint at the far end of the hall, and hurries back downstairs. A middle-aged woman with wispy, peppered hair answers my knock, smiling at me with vacant and slightly crossed eyes. "You're not Val," she says.

"Mum, I told you I'd—"

Megara Roper appears beside her mother. She freezes at the sight of me. Her black hair, shorn during her arrest at the Vault, spikes around her face, her bright green eyes matched by the scarf wound tight around her neck.

"You've got to be kidding."

"I'm sorry, I didn't know where else to—"

Megara looks down the deserted hallway with wide eyes, then reaches for my arm and yanks. *"Get inside."*

Megara drags me to her table, stuffs me on a stool, and serves me soup—all the while, glaring at me. The cluttered room is lit by a single oil lamp and smells of musty bedclothes. Her mother, Katarina, remains aloof by the door. Megara gives me a pewter spoon, but I'm in no state to use it. I slurp the soup directly from the bowl. I can feel its warmth pooling in my empty stomach.

"You've got a lot of nerve."

Megara stands opposite me, as if unwilling to commit to conversation by taking the stool opposite. I lower the nearly empty bowl and wipe my mouth. "I've got nowhere else to go. There's been some sort of—coup—"

"You mean a change of government by order of the reinstated People's Assembly?"

I feel my heart sinking to my toes. "So it was a legitimate transfer of power."

Megara lifts a shoulder. "As legitimate as it can be, with a goliathan circling overhead while you take the vote. Though, honestly, most people seemed more excited by the spectacle than frightened by it."

"Why would they be excited by a goliathan circling over their heads?"

Megara hesitates. Her face puckers, like she's on the verge of laughing or maybe crying. "Some princess was . . . throwing bread from its back."

And that was all it took.

Megara seems not to notice herself sinking into the stool. She stares down at her own hands unseeing, as if the horror of the memory has momentarily taken her somewhere else.

For the first time in my life, I think I might just be sharing an emotion with Megara Roper. After centuries of dragonborn oppression, after only ten years' freedom from it, the people chose dragonlords. All it took was a bit of a performance and some loaves of bread.

And even though I know this Assembly would have been filled by the urban poor, who suffered less under the dragonlords and were most affected by Atreus's rationing program, the ease of the Revolution's fall is still a testament to the ways the regime I served failed its people.

By the door, Megara's mother lets out an unexpected staccato laugh, still staring at shadows.

"Ignore her," Megara mutters, her mouth twisting.

Katarina was arrested for protesting the new regime's dissolution of its first democratic Assembly, years ago. She emerged from prison unrecognizable. I know this from my interrogation of Megara during her own stint in the Vault.

Failure, failure, failure. My failures blur with Atreus's. His regime ruined Katarina and then I threatened to use dragonfire on Megara in that regime's name. Innocent victims, mistakes that litter this city and leave it open to the first voice raised to offer an alternative.

Ixion Stormscourge, come to rebuild his dynasty in the rubble.

I look at the dregs of the soup and find I no longer have any appetite. "Tyndale was in on it, wasn't he? And Lo Teiran. Your Passi friends. That's what you were trying to tell me, the other day."

Megara nods. "They call them Clovers. After the Triarchy's sigil of exile. I didn't realize until the plan was already—in motion. My uncle had no idea, either."

"And now you're going along with it?"

Megara grimaces. She runs a finger along a grain of wood. Her table, I realize, isn't a table at all, but a door spread across two barrels. "Tyndale says they'll let the *People's Paper* print freely. The Bassilean grain shipments will feed our hungry. My uncle's been invited to represent the Lower Bank at the first Privy Council, and the rumor is they'll allow the Assembly to stand. So . . . I've got what I wanted, haven't I?"

"You sound uncertain."

Megara lifts a palm, and fingers clench and unclench in her shorn hair as she thinks through it. "The Lyceum's closed," she says. "They're saying it's temporary. But there's talk of reopening it with different admission standards, now that the metals test has been eliminated." She pauses, leaving me to imagine with perfect ease the kind of admission standards Ixion and his ilk might put in place. "Whatever," she adds bitterly, "it was only ever rich kids there, anyway."

But she and I, both students of the Lyceum, are evidence that wasn't true.

The faults of Atreus's regime were gaping; Katarina stands evidence of that. But the Lyceum he established let in—albeit grudgingly and rarely—commoners and girls. A triarchist Restoration, backed by patrician conspiracy and an occupying empire, has every reason to discontinue such reforms. The one sputtering spigot of social advancement that Atreus's regime offered to its poor, its lowborn, its women, to lift themselves from the stations they were born to will be cut off.

The metals test unfairly favored the privileged, but with Ixion at the helm, its elimination will be an excuse to rewind the clock ten years.

"Then what will you . . ."

"I'm already on Tyndale's staff at the *People's Paper*. I don't need to finish school."

Megara's emotionless tone doesn't fool me for an instant.

"Going to try your hand at making change from within?" I ask.

It was the strategy she used to mock me for. She matches my sarcasm with a scowl. "I assume *you're* here to start a counter-countercoup? Assassinate the dragonborn and every one of their Clovers, put Atreus back in office? All it would take is a little massacre—"

I shake my head. "No point. We're occupied. I saw the Bassilean reinforcements on their way here."

I can't fight an empire. Not with one dragon—not even with every Guardian—against a dragon the size of Freyda's. Perhaps we could make a valiant last stand, but I'm not interested in that.

Callipolis has had enough bloodshed.

What I can help are my friends. Locked away in the Palace, for all I know already suffering torture and death. Callipolis has fallen, but the Guardians remain my responsibility.

I set the bowl I've drained on Megara's stained and crumb-strewn table.

"Have you had any sight of Cor or Lee since the Triarchy was reinstated?"

Megara shakes her head. "But Lee seemed chummy enough with his cousin at the Assembly."

I feel a prickling along my neck at this idea, which I suppress. The idea of Lee being friendly with his family feels like a recurring nightmare, its fear well forgotten. I remind myself that whatever Megara thought she saw at the Assembly, I know Lee, and I know Ixion. I know their history.

"The chumminess you thought you saw was a ruse. Lee killed Ixion's sister. And if you haven't seen Cor, he's under arrest."

I know she considers Lee a close friend; and Cor, whom she's known since grade school, more than that. Megara's fingers drum against her folded arms; she has paled. "What do you need?"

"Get me into the Palace. I'll do the rest."

11

THE PRIVY COUNCIL

LEE

The morning of the second day of the Clover Restoration, I attend Ixion Stormscourge's first Privy Council as Protector of Callipolis in Atreus's stead. I rinse my hands of his blood in the washroom on the way. Civil servants dangle by their necks in the courtyards I pass through; they were all high-ranking officials, all Gold, most lowborn. One of them, a straw-haired young highlander named Declan, once danced with Annie at a feast. His face is blotched and bloated in the dawn light.

Either he failed a loyalty test or finishing him was a loyalty test someone else passed. The message is clear enough: The Restoration has no need for lowborn blights who rose so high.

My empty stomach churns as I make my way into the Council Room. Ixion greets me on the threshold. "Cousin. I'm glad you could make it. How was your visit with the Protector?"

"Edifying."

"I thought it might be." Ixion opens his arm to the woman standing at his side, a veil folded back over her long hair. "May I present Her Divine Highness, Freyda Bassileon."

The court etiquette I'd been taught by the time of the Revolution was not extensive, and much of it I've since forgotten. When I straighten from the full-courtesy bow I guess is due, the Bassilean princess's smile seems more amused than anything. The young woman who has come to make Callipolis a vassal state does not have particularly commanding features—a heart-shaped face, warm brown hair pulled into a long braid, and smiling eyes—but she moves with the poise of someone used to being obeyed. It's impossible to forget that she brings a goliathan and an empire with her smile. "Leo sur Pallor," she says, in guttural Dragontongue. "The one about whom we've heard so much."

"Your—Divine Highness." The Bassilean honorific, at stark contrast with the Callipolan tradition of gods long-dead, chafes on its way out. Freyda's lips remain curved.

Ixion takes Atreus's habitual seat at the head of the table, Freyda to his right, and gestures for me to take the seat to his left. The room has been minimally modified, with the sigil of the Restoration, three circling dragons containing the black clover, replacing the Revolutionary dragon on the high wall. A single great stormscourge with a silver-tipped crest lounges outside on the Firemouth balcony: Ixion's stormscourge, Niter.

My wrist is still lacking a wristband or summoner, Pallor still cut off from me.

Ixion's freshly composed Privy Council begins to file in. Some are clearly longstanding members of the Order of the Black Clover, like Richard Tyndale and Lucian Orthos. I'm more surprised when we're joined by those who look less eager: General Holmes glances at the altered wall hangings in consternation before taking a seat; Miranda Hane, the Minister of Propaganda, sports a bruise on the side of her brown face and hides trembling hands in her lap; Dora Mithrides, one of the chief constituents of the Janiculum, offers Ixion a creaking curtsy though her lips remain pursed. Val Lazare, the leader of the Passi and Megara Roper's uncle, sinks heavily into a seat beside Dora, who eyes him with distaste and scoots sideways.

Were they threatened, I wonder, or bribed? Or did they only touch a finger to the changing winds and adjust course?

Do they hope, as I do, that some good can still be wrought from within?

Power sur Eater comes in last of all, laughing loudly at something Edmund Grayheather just said. He catches sight of me and cocks a brow. Unlike me, he has been permitted his summoner.

When all are gathered, Ixion speaks. "The First Protector has taken ill. In his absence, Leo and I will provide guidance, Leo as your interim Protector and I as your new Firstrider."

Holmes's reaction is automatic and incredulous. "*You* are not our—"

But then he remembers himself and blanches. Too late. Ixion's smile is curdling. "Remind me again, what class-metal was your son's test result going to be? Iron, or was it at least Bronze? Lucian told me you were quite *surprised* with that news yesterday." When Holmes doesn't answer, Ixion's fingers lace themselves and flatten on the table. "But yes. You have introduced our first item on the agenda. The so-called Firstrider of the Callipolan Fleet, Antigone Farhallserf, who seems to have . . . fled in the night."

Ixion uses the feudal designation, just as he did with Rock. Except now the drakarchy named is not his father's, but mine. Antigone's pre-Revolutionary status, belonging to us like the land she was born on.

Antigone sur Aela. The drakonym feels like a ward against evil. *Her name is Antigone sur Aela.*

"We had an encounter," Edmund Grayheather says. "Parcival even got talons in her. Over the Ferrish Plain."

Outside, Niter's tail swishes, and the glass rattles. Ixion says, "And you let her go?"

Power shrugs, though his gaze flicks to Niter's swishing tail. "She tore free. But she can't have gone far. We'll find her."

So Annie's come back from New Pythos. Which leaves the question, what did she leave behind? And when will Ixion find out?

"See that you do. I would like to put an end to any confusion about my title."

The other outstanding question is about the whereabouts of Crissa sur Phaedra, whom Ixion refers to as Crissa Ward. By now the patterns of his nomenclature are clear: Patrician riders alone retain the drakonyms we took when we became Guardians. Commoners like Crissa and Cor are referred to by their family names. And Annie and Rock by less than that.

"Titus is on it," Edmund says. "Lucian informed us Ward was on a diplomatic trip to Damos and should be on her way back shortly."

Ixion moves on to the needs of his constituents next, represented by Val Lazare for the Lower Bank and Dora for the Upper. For the Lower Bank, Ixion is willing to leave the *People's Paper* autonomous, *within reason*, and more than willing to approve the suspension of the metals laws as the People's Assembly decided in its referendum. At this allowance, Miranda Hane stirs.

"Miranda?" Ixion invites warmly.

From my angle, the bruise blooming down the side of Hane's cheek is clearly visible. Her voice is reed-thin. "There have been questions about plans to reopen the Lyceum, and . . . criteria for admission, now that the metals test has been retired."

Ixion smiles. "Well, we have a good deal of debt to pay off to our generous benefactors," he says, with a nod to Freyda Bassileon. "I was thinking education might be an immediate source of revenue. State expenditures in that department have been wildly bloated by Athanatos's public scholarship funds, an unnecessary luxury in these trying times. Let the Lyceum be open to all. All who can pay for it."

Miranda's swallow is loud. Lazare's eyes have narrowed. It escapes no one that *those who can pay for it* will be, almost exclusively, of patrician birth; at the least, from families of already minted elites. Power is the one who speaks first. "Clever, my lord."

He hasn't looked so viciously amused since the day Atreus introduced a stratified rationing program.

"Thank you, Parcival. That brings us to . . . the Janiculum."

The Janiculum is the neighborhood on the Upper Bank, at the foot of Pytho's Keep, where most patrician families keep their manors. Many of the wealthiest, like Dora, retained their status after the Revolution by being helpful to Atreus during it. Dora Mithrides, caught off guard pulling at the neck of her sweater as if it circles too tightly around her throat, lifts her chin and returns Ixion's stare. "I think you will find the Janiculum cooperative, sire."

"Oh? Good. Because while the Palace is being restored to its original grandeur, the dragonborn will require quartering. I was hoping your manor, and others, might be available for our use."

Dora's eyes widen. "It would be my pleasure, my lord."

"My family would be honored to host as well," Power says. "My foster family, I mean. Hesperides House."

"My wife would love to have you, my lord," Lo Teiran adds.

Ixion smiles. "Perhaps we should spread the word," he says, "and see which noble patrician houses are most eager. The most eager should be willing to provide names of those who are less so. Particular favor will be given to those who can name Palace Day perpetrators for whom justice remains to be served."

Dora's chin wobbles slightly as she inclines it.

The international situation is reviewed next. Freyda reports that her grain shipments are on their way, on schedule, via canals that connect the port at Fort Aron with the Fer. Bassilean warships will bring with them her household and her personal army, a division of the Imperial guard dedicated to the princess-heir and known as the Little Immortals. When Ixion compliments her willingness to buck the custom of servants preparing the way for the lady, she says, "You will find I'm full of surprises."

Ixion laughs, charmed. Freyda smiles back. General Holmes's brows are level with his hairline.

So I'm not the only one thinking Ixion is an idiot.

"And the dragon?" Holmes asks.

No one has to ask which dragon. Freyda says, "Obizuth has been nesting atop Pytho's Keep. She likes a high perch."

Not to mention, a vantage point out of range of our cannons, from which a goliathan could set the greater part of the city on fire with a single long breath. Holmes folds his arms and expels air. "Does she."

Two skyfish Grayriders have been sent as messengers to New Pythos, informing the dragonborn waiting there that the way has been prepared for the Long-Awaited Return.

"And the plucky Norcian humble-riders?" Freyda asks.

This comment seems to touch a sore point; Ixion's smile has tightened. "As discussed. They have been disposed of."

Unless Annie has a big surprise for you.

Freyda only seems more amused. "Very good, my lord," she says.

"What about my riders?" I ask.

Ixion looks at me for the first time. "You mean *my* riders?"

Hane has actually braced her palms against the edge of the

table, as if to push herself out of the way of our crossfire. I can hear Atreus's voice in my ears, challenging and cool. *It's time to discuss what you'll do when you leave this room.*

"I mean the Guardians."

"I think, between the goliathan and the dragonborn, we don't really have need for *more* riders, do we?"

In its way, this veiled threat is the news I'm looking for. It means Ixion's reserving the Guardians for leverage. Means they are still alive. Means that somewhere, down in some dungeon, they're awaiting his verdict.

Outside, Niter's wings ruffle and the glass creaks. My wrist itches for its wristband, for Pallor. I force myself to look not at the stormscourge but at Ixion. "The Guardians are celebrities in Callipolis. Children know them by name on the street. They will not be so easily forgotten, and if you want your—our—Restoration to be a success, we will need them."

"I'm prepared to keep the patrician Guardians. We can discard the rest."

Discard. As if he were clearing a pantry of spoiled goods. Patricians make up perhaps a third of the Revolutionary fleet. Their families are reputed to have diluted dragonborn blood, from occasional intermarrying with the Three Families; it's a point of pride that I've heard Dora mention before.

"Works for me," says Power.

I've seen Power snarl that his mother was a Cheapsider. But no such outburst seems forthcoming today. Which is hardly surprising, because if one thing can always be relied upon, it's that Power can't be. My fingers are curling on my knees. "Some of our most popular riders are lowborn. Not to mention highest ranked. Cor sur Maurana, Richard sur Bast—"

And Crissa sur Phaedra and Antigone sur Aela, except the last thing I want to do is remind him of them now.

"But that's the thing," Ixion says. "*That* seems like it could be confusing to the people. Much like Antigone Farhallserf at large, a rival claimant to the title of Firstrider, these suspiciously high-ranked riders of low birth make it look as though any commoner can fly as well as a dragonborn. Which, we all know, is not true."

There is a moment where Ixion waits to see if anyone will contradict him, and everyone else makes a point not to meet anyone's eyes. Freyda is smirking, though it's unclear at what.

"You see the difficulty," Ixion goes on, once he's satisfied with our silence. "There cannot be two Firstriders, two Alterni, two Tertii, and so on. It would be terribly confusing for everybody."

My heart is hammering in my ears. "Then let them prove themselves."

Ixion cocks his head.

"You've got two claimants for Quarti, let them face off. Set Cor Sutter against Edmund Grayheather in the arena."

Edmund lets out a single barking laugh, as though I've made a joke.

To my surprise and immediate foreboding, Ixion smiles, too. "You know, cousin," he says, "I rather like that idea."

12

THE INTERVIEW

ANNIE

When I wake, I find the soreness left over from the work in Norcia and the flight afterward has stiffened my limbs like concrete. It takes a moment to remember that it isn't a nightmare I've woken from but *to*: I'm home, and home is flying the yellow banners of Bassilea. My friends are locked inside a palace now controlled by Ixion. And I'm sleeping on a pile of sour-smelling laundry in the apartment of a girl who was, until recently, probably my least-favorite person in Callipolis. When she shakes me, roaches scatter.

"What time is it?"

"Past noon. You looked like you needed the sleep."

Megara sets a bottle of vinegar beside a pot of steaming black tea her mother, Katarina, is stirring. Their makeshift table is one of the few excuses for furniture in the room; most of the Roper family's possessions, laundry and kitchenware, are stacked in piles directly on the floor. Her brother Lex snores from another pile of clothes. I have the groggy thought that for all the time Megara and I spent circling each other, resentful of the other's supposed privilege, her family's home is almost as humble as mine was, and more neglected.

"You're in luck," Megara says, and hands me the proof of an article slated to run in the afternoon edition of the *People's Paper*.

IXION SUR NITER,
FIRSTRIDER OF CALLIPOLIS,
CHALLENGES
ANTIGONE FARHALLSERF
TO PROVE HERSELF IN THE ARENA

"Farhallserf?"

Megara nods. "The style guides have been updated."

That was fast. I skim the rest of the article: Each ranked position in the fleet will be competed for publicly by any Guardian who wishes to challenge a dragonborn for the slot in what is being called a Winnowing; the dates of the competitions will soon be announced. Anyone who knows the whereabouts of Antigone Farhallserf should come forward for a reward.

"Well?"

"Well what?" I ask, passing the paper back to her.

"*Well*, shouldn't you face him?"

"And accomplish what?"

Megara stares at me. She slaps the paper on the floor, where we're sitting, and a roach crunches. "You think it's a trap."

I nearly laugh. Obviously it's a trap. "Not the problem. You might want to ask after that reward, though."

Megara rolls her eyes. "If you don't show, people will say you ran. That you're a coward."

"People say a lot of things about me already."

Her lips tighten. The things they say about me—that I'm a heartless and cruel leader, that I slept my way to the top of the corps leveraging Lee's affection—are narratives she helped create in the *People's Paper* during the Bunker Riots. After *bitch commander* and *dragonlord's whore*, why not add *coward* to the list?

"I know," she says slowly, "that Ixion might be a challenge for you."

"I could wipe the floor with him." I say this with such surety that Megara's chin goes back. But why demure? Aela and I have met Ixion sur Niter in the air before. We know our abilities against his. "That wouldn't help my friends get out of prison, or to safety, and that's what I'm here to do."

"You're Firstrider," Megara says. "Don't you have any desire to defend the title?"

Why won't she drop it? "It's not my mission."

Megara puffs air from her cheeks. "Fine," she says. "Then we do plan B."

Plan B is the tea and vinegar. The Palace, undergoing renovations for the Restoration while the dragonborn quarter in estates of the Janiculum, is on a hiring spree as a part of a new loyalty initiative; Megara intends to dye my hair so I can interview disguised. "Word from the Clovers is the transition team's taken special interest in getting some highlanders on the staff," Megara says. "Can you still do the brogue?"

"I—don't know."

"But it's easy, lass."

"Please stop."

A half a bottle of vinegar and a cup of black tea later, I stare at my reflection in a dirty tin mirror, and a dark-haired young woman stares back at me. Dressed in Agga's patched dress, I look more like a peasant woman from my home village than the Guardian whose flamesuit I've folded in a corner. I'm vaguely unsettled by the sight.

Now that Megara's dropped it, the goad lingers. *You're Firstrider. Don't you have any desire to defend the title?*

I think of the moment Roxana told me I'd won a battle and lost a war, that while helping Griff, my own city had fallen. The snapping point after weeks and months spent bending to serve a city that painted insults about my incompetence on its walls.

In the end, the insults were right.

I can wipe the floor with Ixion. But that doesn't make me deserving of a title as Callipolis's defender. Not anymore. Defeating him wouldn't change that a goliathan perches on Pytho's Keep or that our streets swarm with Bassilean soldiers. If the uncomfortable truth is that I feel safer rescuing my friends wearing a peasant's dress than my flamesuit, that doesn't mean it's not the best way to get the job done.

It's blisteringly cold, sunlight glaring from a dry blue sky, when I leave the Roper apartment for the first time. Mrs. Roper's thin brown mantle is wound tight around Agga's dress for warmth, and my Guardian wristband, with its summoner for Aela, is tucked inside my brassiere on the same chain as my mother's pendant. It seems like a lifetime since Lee gave it to me.

As I trudge through the city, I take in the changes since I last walked these streets: the yellow whalefin of Bassilea emblazoned on the breasts of the soldiers overseeing ration distribution; the triarchal banner of the Restoration fluttering on the Palace walls; and unfamiliar dragonriders silhouetted overhead. The only dragon I recognize is Eater.

Aela has sensed no violence from the lairs, only fear. I know instinctively, through our connection resting dormant at this distance, that I would feel if she had cause for greater alarm.

They're all in there. I just have to get to them.

On the way, I leave a letter from Duck to his family on their back step, informing them he's alive.

After crossing Highmarket Bridge, I follow the slow trickle of citizens making their way through security at a side gate of the Outer Palace. The job applicants let in by the guard gawp at the grand courtyards with open mouths. Nine years ago, I gawped, too.

A porter directs me to the interview queue at a side hall, and as I recognize it, I suppress a horrible laugh. It's the hall where students made eligible by the metals test once had our Choosing Ceremony. This is where Aela Chose me, and I became a Guardian.

No dragons wait for me inside today. Instead, three chairs are clumped in the otherwise deserted room, and a plump, middle-aged woman with a round, pink face invites me to sit in Callish accented with Bassilic.

Beside her sits our old drillmaster, Wes Goran. A clover adorns his lapels.

It's all I can do to keep myself from stopping dead. Last I heard, he was dismissed from Atreus's administration for his bigotry toward those of birth like mine. It looks like he has found an employer more tolerant of it.

And now my short ruse is up.

For a frozen moment, as I look at my drillmaster, I consider running.

But then his glance flicks from the clipboard to my face, and he doesn't so much as blink.

"Abigael Nearhallserf?" he asks, sounding bored.

The hall's not particularly well lit; my tea-stained hair and commoner garb little resemble the commander he should recognize; but more than that, I suspect Wes Goran does not know me because, for most of my life, I was an abomination he avoided letting his eyes linger on.

And now, it seems a bit of black tea in my hair is enough for him not to see me at all.

I nod shakily.

"Please, sit," the pink-faced woman says warmly, in her rippling Bassilic accent, and I do. "I'm Betsuna, mistress of Freyda's household. This is Wes Goran, High Steward of the Clover Restoration."

I compose my expression into something that I hope approximates awed intimidation.

"You're from the highlands?" Betsuna asks, checking her roster.

The brogue that used to be mine had to be regained with practice, in a mirror, alongside Megara. At least mine, unlike Megara's, sounds natural. "Yes, my lady."

"How did you come to be in the capital?"

"Looking for work, my lady. The Usurper's rationing ran our village dry."

Goran's vaguely bored gaze fixes on my face for a breath longer than I'd like it to.

"You highlanders really do look alike," he comments. "Inbreeding," he grunts to Betsuna in Dragontongue. "You think your royalty is bad."

She lifts her hand to cup a startled, tinkling laugh. I keep my expression slack and still, the way I learned to when this man was my drillmaster and insulted me to my face. "Do I resemble someone you know, my lord?" I ask in Callish.

Goran grunts and does not correct the title he isn't owed. "But *that* highlander did not know her place."

Betsuna glances between us, surprised by the challenge in his tone. I incline my head, feeling a flush creep up my neck. Then I take a breath and make the speech that I drafted in Megara's living room and practiced with her until the words made my face burn.

"No one would say this," she told me at the time.

"My father would have said it."

"Was your father a groveling dog?"

I looked up at her. "When he needed to be."

Now I think of my father. I keep my feelings inside. And I say what Wes Goran wants to hear. They want loyalty? I'll give them loyalty.

"Your servant knows who is her lord. Her family thanks the long-dead gods that Lord Ixion has ousted the Usurper and regained his rightful seat. To serve in a dragonborn house would be the highest honor and the greatest privilege this humble one could hope for."

I stare down at my lap and feel my own furious pulse. The skin of my exposed neck prickles as if it senses Goran's gaze. For as long as I can remember, when Goran did trouble himself to look at me, I knew he saw a peasant girl who had forgotten her place.

Now let him see one who has remembered it.

He speaks to Betsuna in Dragontongue. "She's easy on the eyes, at least."

***

Back in Megara's flat, I sink shaking onto the stool, lower my face into my knees, and burst into panicked, sticky tears. I've been holding them in for the whole walk back.

"What happened?" Megara asks, abandoning the proofs of a weekend edition, which are spread across their cluttered table. "Were you recognized?"

I take the handkerchief she presses into my hand and clean my face. I'm breathing as hard as if I'd returned from the Palace at a run. "I got the job. Palace staff. Specific appointments will be made after the renovations are complete."

"That's good, isn't it?" Megara asks, bewildered. She sinks to her knees beside me. "Did someone hurt you?"

She's lowered her voice. I shake my head.

No one hurt me. But I'd forgotten, until that interview, what it was like to be so *vulnerable*. To be talked about as if you're not there. The child being held down and beaten, the surviving witness being forced to watch. And now to be a *woman*, whose attractiveness is commented on with candid disinterest by superiors—

And I've got what I've wanted, which is the chance to go back for more.

My tears are drying, but Megara continues to stare at me. I grasp at an explanation. "My old drillmaster interviewed me. He didn't recognize me."

"Well that's good," Megara says. "Tea stain did the trick."

13

—

THE PRINCESS'S SUIT

LEE

Dora Mithrides's manor is overrun by House Stormscourge. Dora herself evacuates to her coach house. Her servants are left to manage the Bastards getting drunk from her liquor cabinet and their dragons overflowing in her gardens. Watching the gardener dart around the grounds putting out small fires makes me aware as never before of the reasons the Palace was built from stone. It's strange to imagine that one of these stormscourges, simmering perpetually with the rage of their breed, should have been mine. I still haven't been allowed to see Pallor.

To Ixion's consternation, Annie remains nowhere to be found. Her dragon hasn't been spotted again. Even his challenge in the *People's Paper* hasn't been enough to goad her into the light.

"Your whore is a coward," he tells me at breakfast, as we eat Dora's toast.

I smile back at him.

Denied my wings, and under what is pretty transparently house arrest, I have ample time to get to know my half brother and the other Grayriders while Ixion attends to business in the Inner Palace. The Bastards breakfast late, with heavy helpings of champagne in their juice. Despite the efforts of a put-upon staff to contain it, their gatherings have the feeling of a student party. Many of the Grayriders, like Edmund, are in their mid-twenties.

"Ha'brother!" says Edmund jovially, from the settee where he sprawls in the sunroom. "Drink with us?"

It's ten in the morning. "I'm good, thanks."

The glass doors to the balcony overlooking the gardens have been thrown open; a stormscourge with nostrils smoking like twin cigars lounges halfway into the breakfast room. Edmund tells me to take a seat beside him—it's somewhere between a jocular invitation and an order—and waves a hand carelessly toward the other two Grayriders drinking with him, who have the characteristic Stormscourge black hair, though theirs is curly. All the Grayriders are male and unmarried; in the evening, the Janiculum has begun throwing dinner parties in their honor that swarm with eligible patrician daughters. "May I present Titus, Angelo . . . our cousins by not-marriage. Ixion's ha'brothers. The dragon's Wrath. We coordinated names around the vices."

At the sound of his name, Wrath nickers sparks onto the carpet. Titus and Edmund throw back their heads, laughing like baying dogs, as flames begin to curl round the edge of the carpet. Angelo, Titus's scrawny younger brother, scoots his chair out of the way with a curse. "Oy, we talked about this!"

"A little help here?" Titus calls to the maids frozen in the act of clearing empty champagne flutes.

They scurry around the dragon and, absent footwear durable enough to stomp the flames, attempt to smother them with Dora's throw pillows, yelping as their fingers burn and their caps slip sideways. The boys watch, laughing, not bothering to get up. The parties of young dragonlords have always had a reputation, but this is the first time I get the sense of what they must have looked like. I seize the nearest pitcher of wine-spiked orange juice, overturn it, and watch the carpet fire hiss out. The maids stop hopping and yelping, the boys stop laughing, and Edmund scowls at me.

"We were going to drink that."

"You should douse your dragons if you let them in the house."

Edmund rises. I set down the pitcher. My fists are curling—preparing for it to come to blows, eager for it—when a shout goes up in the central courtyard of Dora's manor.

"I do believe that's your ha'brother screaming," Edmund says to Titus and Angelo.

"Well," says Titus, stretching as he vaults to his feet, "you can't choose family."

We find Ixion in the center of the courtyard, tearing at his hair. The reason for his distress is a message borne by skyfish Grayriders who've just returned from New Pythos.

Or from as close to the former New Pythos as they could get. They could go no farther than the edge of Sailor's Folly, where Norcian dragonriders led by Griff Gareson formed a perimeter. There they found rowboats bearing the surviving dragonborn and the ashes of their dead. The survivors are on their way to Fort Aron; from there they will be ferried to the capital by barge.

Griff and the other riders—once squires but now styling themselves as the Woad-riders—sent Ixion's messengers home with word that New Pythos is now Norcia, and that while they want no quarrel with the Restored Triarchy, they have taken hostages to ensure the peace.

How was the uprising brought about? I hear a quick whisper of her name and feel a chill down my spine. These messengers forget to use the new styling. They tell us that Antigone sur Aela came with drachthanasia, she broke the muzzles, and the ha'Aurelian citadel burned.

It's all I can do to keep my face still.

She did it.

Ixion rages like a toddler in a tantrum, heedless of the audience of dragonborn surrounding him in the courtyard, of Dora's servants pursing their lips. When he learns of the death of the ruling ha'Aurelian family and of his friends Rhode and Roxana, he tears his hair and screams. I'm relishing the sight until I distinguish the words in his sobbing rage.

"I will butcher them. I will scorch them from the earth—"

Niter is roaring at his side, ash and sparks spewing from his mouth.

"You will not."

Phemi Skyfish rode as a passenger with one of the messengers and has dismounted his skyfish. She stands in front of Ixion, alone. Rather than the blue of her House, she wears the sackcloth of a sky-widow. She's smeared ash across her lids and her cheeks, and that ash has run with dried tears. Slender and tall, the brown skin of her head visible beneath clumps of roughly shorn hair, she looks like a walking ghost.

Ixion, on his knees, goes silent as he looks up at her.

"You will not attack Norcia," she tells him, speaking in the meter of an old oath. "You will leave my brother, who has sacrificed everything to protect me, in safety where he now lives as hostage. You will give the Norcians no cause to harm Astyanax ha'Aurelian, last surviving heir of Rhadamanthus's house, or Electra Stormscourge, the great-aunt who raised you."

"Those ungrateful animals deserve to be massacred, Phemi," Ixion says, his voice raw.

Phemi goes to one knee in front of Ixion, to meet his eyes.

"You will have mercy, for the sake of my brother. You will hear this boon of me, freshly sky-widowed. Swear it on the death of your sister."

Ixion wipes tears from his cheeks, drags wet fingers down hers, and she touches her hands to his, affirming the vow.

"I swear it."

Then Ixion gets to his feet and turns to Power, who has landed, with Eater, at his right. *"Find her."*

The cold I feel is nothing compared with the expression on Power's face as he nods.

But come evening, when Power returns yet again empty-handed, Ixion improvises. Two figures, hands bound, bags over their heads, are carted into Dora's courtyard and deposited onto their knees in front of Ixion. Angelo and Titus Grayheather restrain me on the opposite side of the yard. The bags are removed to reveal two Guardians: Rock, sprawling, white-faced, and gagged; and the aurelian rider Bryce. Bryce is a commoner from Southside, unskilled in the air despite the remedial drills I've run for him as long I've been squadron leader. When they take off his gag, he begins pleading for his life in Callish; then he sees me and begins pleading to me.

"You want to know how we teach lessons in *Norcia*?" Ixion asks me, and I know then that I am the nearest proxy for his rage, the closest he can get to Annie and Griff Gareson. "The Norcians call it *being put in the pen*."

He nods to Edmund, who summons his own hulking storm-scourge: Envy. I'm straining so hard against the Grayheathers, one of the skyfish Grayriders has to join in to hold me back. "You said you'd let them prove themselves—"

"I'll let *some* of them prove themselves, Lee. Others are perfectly expendable."

"They—are—innocent—"

But that seems to be the point.

Phemi Skyfish and the princess Freyda Bassileon watch from the far side of the courtyard, Phemi's expression a wall of stone,

Freyda's unreadable behind a veil. Envy alternates between fire and fang. He works over Bryce slowly, with relish, until Bryce stops moving and I've stopped screaming. And then Ixion yanks the gag off Rock and cuts the ropes binding his hands. He points at the smoking corpse beside him while Rock kneels on all fours shaking.

"Clean it up."

* * *

The room I'm staying in stinks of my own vomit, but I can't bring myself to open the window. Skipping dinner wasn't an option, which meant I had to watch Rock serve Ixion, had to let Rock serve me, and the only thought that got me through it was that whatever hell this was for me, it was worse for Rock. We couldn't look at each other. Freyda Bassileon, who dined with us, asked more than once if I felt all right.

I stop vomiting when there's a knock on the door.

"My . . . lord."

It's Rock, not meeting my eyes.

"Don't call me that."

Rock pinches the bridge of his nose. He looks both ways down the corridor, then shakes his head slowly. His face is wiped empty of emotion as if he'd run out.

"I think it's going to be easier for both of us," he says, "if I do."

It's just a word. It's not a battle worth fighting. But I still feel like tearing this house down over our heads before I let it happen. Rock has been a comrade in arms, a loyal subordinate, a good friend. He was the one who once taught me how to do collections like a dragonlord, before he knew that I was one.

"I was sent to prepare your room," Rock says. "My. Lord."

He brought a fresh chamber pot and leaves with the one that has my vomit in it.

I lie in the too-soft bed and stare at the filigreed ceiling of Dora's guest room through the night. I did not have the heart to ask Rock what *clean it up* meant for the body, so I lie there wondering. I think of Atreus's words, which seem meaningless now, asking what I'll do with this guttering flame, professing faith in the importance of *trying*.

What can I do with this guttering flame? I think bitterly. *Nothing. I can watch my riders be humiliated and butchered, and know it's wrong.*

Such intoxicating power.

It's just after dawn when a rap on the door rouses me from my stupor.

"My lord?"

Not Rock, this time: The voice is female. The language is Dragontongue. But the accent is—unfamiliar.

I open the door and find myself face-to-face with Princess Freyda Bassileon. She has dispensed with her veil.

"Your Divine Highness," I say, making the most flourishing bow I can physically manage, because at this point, the lack of sleep and the excess of horror leaves me feeling a bit drunk. "What an unexpected and glorious surprise."

Freyda huffs through pursed lips. "Walk with me," she says.

14

—

NEW HIRES

DELO

NORCIA

I hope the twins and my father have arrived safely in Callipolis and are enjoying their return to luxury. My first week working in the Norcian lairs, my hands are so unused to manual labor that they blister and bleed.

There's an etiquette to the hosting of dragonborn hostages, Electra will inform you, but these barbarians respect none of it. She's invited to join the Norcian women at the looms but refuses, taking this as an effrontery rather than an offer of paid work. The result is that my employment in the lairs provides for our total board. I'm determined not to complain about any of it: the long hours; the pain or exhaustion; the lightheadedness that I eventually realize is caused by hunger. I'm unused to the rations of commoners.

For his part, Griff seems determined not to spare me. More accurately, he seems determined to act as though he's forgotten I exist.

This new life divides into parts I can control and parts I can't. I can't control the hunger, the blistering hands, the fact that Electra's breakdowns prevent her from continuing Sty's education as I'd hoped or that Sty avoids leaving the house for fear of Norcian children beating him in the street. I can't control that Griff's eyes slide over me as if he were confusing me with a piece of furniture whenever we run into each other.

How had I pictured it, life as a hostage among the people I betrayed my family for? A string of blissful days with a lover, our history forgotten?

Not exactly, but I still want to kick him when he looks through me like that.

I didn't kill your stupid sister, I imagine telling him, in my most furious, blistering moments.

But even the imagined protest I amend. Poor, sweet Agga was clever beyond her education, a loving mother, a loyal sister, with a son who deserved to live and a daughter who should not have been orphaned. Griff should not have had to find Agga dead when he was so close to saving her forever. How can I blame him for avoiding me? I'm a walking reminder of my sister's devices, and of the long scourge my family has been for his.

I wonder, instead, as I pop blisters and pull splinters, how it is that even with splitting palms, with an aching back, with a gnawing stomach, I still am able to empathize so easily with the enemy.

But even the old self-loathing wears out when you're tired enough.

Parts I can control: getting up; planting two feet on the ground; and making my way through this damp island in the dark to the lairs before dawn, to begin a day that will end after dusk.

ANNIE
CALLIPOLIS

The servants hired to facilitate the Restoration of dragonborn rule are quartered on the arena side of the Outer Palace. My first thought is that this assignment must be a mistake, because the only residential quarters in that section of the Palace are in the Cloister, where the Guardians live. Then I realize that they *do* mean the quarters in the Cloister. I'm installed with the other maids in my old dorm room.

I shouldn't be so surprised. The Cloister was originally servants' quarters; the Guardians' humble living situation was a celebrated feature of Atreus's program, highlighted often in propaganda.

And now the rooms have reverted to their original purpose.

I tell myself, as I shove my new work clothes with shaking hands into drawers that once held a Guardian's uniform, that this is good news. The rumor is that permanent work assignments will be made with reference to our backgrounds: Recruits from the city will be preferred for household staff; those from the countryside for stable work. I can't very well advertise my past ten years' experience qualifying me for dragonkeeping, but I can hope my restored highland accent leads them to give it to me out of sheer prejudice. With luck, I'll keep my bed in these quarters, which will become those of the keepers, with easy access to the nests, which I'll need to get the Guardians and their dragons out.

This is good.

But it's hard to remember that, looking around at my dorm room stripped. The desks where we once studied have been removed and replaced with still more beds. The laurel I pinned to the wall after winning my first public tournament against Darius sur Myra has vanished. The sense of purpose that used to hum palpably in the air as Callipolis's best and brightest trained to be its first generation of lowborn leaders is gone.

It's replaced by the tired bustle of servants trying to rebuild the past.

I bed beside two sisters from Cheapside. Vicky and Verra were present, along with their family, at the Assembly that welcomed Ixion. The one time I forgo better judgment to ask them about it, they both exclaim about the excitement.

"It was like something out of a fairy tale. Like the Skysung Queen, descending to rescue us!" Verra says. She's a bit younger than me, Vicky a bit older. They share wispy blond hair and the thick, hearty accents of Cheapside that I associate with caretakers from the orphanage. We're in the washroom, scrubbing off the day's grime; I'm taking care not to wet my tea-stained hair, though it's overdue for a wash.

"The Skysung . . . ?" For a moment I don't know why it jogs my memory; I didn't grow up with books of fairy tales, like Duck did.

Then I hear his voice. *My little skylark, my skysung queen, you are awfully young to be giving orders.*

I know the name because it was something my father used to call me.

And now Callipolans are using it to describe Freyda Bassileon, our invading princess. I reach for the soap and dig my dirty nails into it.

"Papa caught one of her loaves," Verra adds. "The princess had them in a great sack tied to her goliathan. It was—godlike, Abbie, you'd have to see it. Made our little fleet look like swallows to a hawk."

"And then everyone voted to bring the dragonlords back, just like that?"

"Well," says Verra, "better than Atreus and his bitch commander. Too little too late, that's what Papa says."

My smarting fingers have frozen in the washbasin. I earned the nickname *bitch commander* on the streets of Callipolis, enforcing Atreus's rationing policies. Somehow, even after hearing it shouted at me by rioting crowds, this casual mention by a perfectly nice coworker still feels like a gut punch.

I begin scrubbing the soap from my raw skin with fury. Would they like to stand for hours in restless squares, trying to keep food in the same people's mouths who curse everything you do? We didn't have a foreign princess with a great sack of loaves, miraculous and godlike, to toss to the hungry. We had waning food supplies because Pythians had destroyed our trade fleet and tipped us into famine. And we didn't sell Callipolis into vassalage to solve the problem.

But what seems to matter to most Callipolans is that they were hungry before, and aren't now.

To my surprise, the older sister, Vicky, speaks up. Her voice is soft but severe. "Papa doesn't know everything."

Later that night, lying in bed staring at the ceiling, I feel it: Aela within my range, listening to our dragons within the tunnels, smelling their fear, and then the spike and the cry.

A dragon's widow-cry.

One of ours.

That's how I know Ixion has killed his first Guardian.

LEE

Freyda's early-morning visit to my chamber is followed by a walk through Dora's gardens, a carriage ride to the base of Pytho's Keep, and an unexpected proposal. She asks the question almost absentmindedly as she descends from the carriage on my arm. Still feeling a bit waterlogged after the punishment of Bryce and Rock, I nearly laugh.

Marriage. Not to Ixion. I don't know whether to be more flattered or alarmed.

"I assumed you didn't really intend to marry anyone."

Freyda seems as surprised by my candor as I am by hers. "Why shouldn't I? I'd prefer not to be a despot, but I intend to stay in Callipolis. I am looking for a husband whose bloodline and position in this country will secure the legitimacy of my reign."

"And that's not Ixion?"

We stand at the foot of the winding stair that leads to her dragon's nest, preparing to leave the carriage behind and climb. Freyda removes a bucket of sudsy water and a tack bag, then strips from her fine dress. Underneath, she wears a work skirt and saddle boots. "Ixion is a sadist. I do not wish to marry a sadist."

She hoists the sudsy bucket and begins to climb, leaving me speechless at the base with the tack bag at my feet. Of all the ways my father could have hoped I'd make a good match, this was not one I think even he could have imagined: on a walk up Pytho's Keep with an occupying Bassilean princess, discussing marriage amid a counterrevolutionary Restoration.

To be fair, I wouldn't want to marry a sadist, either.

But there are a host of reasons I can't consider her offer, I remind myself, as I hoist the tack bag and hurry up the stairs after her. An obvious one is the vow I took at nine, forswearing family and children to become a Guardian, but that's not my first thought. My first thought is of Annie.

I join her side and attempt to relieve her of the bucket. "I'm sort of . . ."

Freyda doesn't hand it over. "In love with someone else?"

When I'm too startled to reply, she reaches for the tack bag on my shoulder, and trades me. The bucket is surprisingly heavy. "Do not deceive yourself"—she turns to lead the way up the stairs at a brisk pace—"I have no wish for romance. You're welcome to carry on with your peasant paramour. I shall have my own affairs."

I have to jog up the stairs after her to keep up, sudsy water sloshing my arm. "My peasant paramour commands the Callipolan aerial fleet."

"Well, at the moment she's missing—she doesn't command anything."

Freyda doesn't have to add that most of the Callipolan aerial fleet is also under arrest.

I had assumed the princess's lifestyle to be numbingly inactive, but she makes the climb with surprising ease. I'm the one who's out of breath by the time we reach the summit. Atop the karst, lounging across the Sky Court, roosts a dragon the length of the Inner Palace, great wings draped like a leathery wedding tent. The goliathan opens one lid slowly to look at us; its eye is the size of my head.

"It is customary in the presence of a Great Dragon to make obeisance."

I don't need urging. The sheer scale of the dragon inspires awe. After I drop to my knees, Freyda taps my shoulder and I resume my feet. At her invitation, I approach, but it's with the same foreboding I've seen in children summoning up the courage to pet Pallor. I lay a shaking palm on the hide of the dragon's great maw. I could climb inside its nostril.

"What's his name?"

"*Her* name," says Freyda, with a ghostly smile, "is Obizuth. Will you help me scrub her down? I like to do her keeping myself."

It takes two hours to groom the Great Dragon. Her scales must be washed individually like great plates, the dirt-caked cracks between them wide enough to unclog with a finger. In those two hours, as Freyda's arms go gray with muck and her long hair starts to fall in wisps from the braid, I begin to glimpse—or wonder if I glimpse—the person beneath. She murmurs to her dragon in Bassilic, and Obizuth rumbles happily back to her, vibrating the stone under my feet. At the end, dirt smudged on her face, twisting to relieve a sore back, Freyda tells me the Great Dragon likes me.

"Next time, I could introduce you to Pallor."

Freyda smiles, like she sees through that. "Not yet, Leo."

15

—

OLD FRIENDS

DELO

NORCIA

In the second week, Griff shows up on my stoop—which used to be his stoop—drunk. Until this moment, I'd disregarded the rumors he wasn't himself: He had withstood so many small tragedies and hardships throughout our childhoods, day in and day out with head unbowed, that I didn't believe he had a breaking point.

When he appears drunk on my doorstep, I realize his breaking point was Agga.

My first feeling, a selfish one, is frustration. How is it that, after a lifetime of cleaning up after one broken drunkard, finally free of him, I've found myself another? I said goodbye to my father two weeks ago.

"Oh. I don't live here anymore," Griff realizes.

"No. You don't."

"*You* live here," Griff says, and starts laughing like this is the funniest thought in the world.

After the Liberation, the Woad-riders moved into the vacated ha'Aurelian manors, keeping the citadel apartments free until the kingsmoot. The Norcians' fast adoption of dragonborn housing hierarchies is an irony no one seems to appreciate but me. I appreciate it from Griff's shack, where the three political hostages have been installed.

Lady Electra's habitual seat in this shack is the chair Griff's grandfather used to occupy by the fire, embroidery in hand that she's been picking at listlessly since the move. At the sight of Griff's indecency darkening our doorstep, she rises with a huff and retires to the back room. Astyanax, on the other hand, creeps closer.

"Griff?"

I find it hard to take that Sty still hero-worships Griff even after his revolution put him in a hovel.

"Little lordling," Griff hiccups. "Who gave you that shiner?"

Sty lifts a shoulder. *Who do you think?* I consider asking Griff, but I'm not sure Griff is sober enough to catch the sarcasm. Though Sty's mute about his injuries, it's apparent enough they're gifts from Norcian children who come across an orphaned ha'Aurelian on their streets.

Griff sways, casts around for conversation, and says: "Just dropping by to see if you need anything."

I'm two weeks into my new life of dawn-to-dusk manual labor by this point, and the blisters that have turned bloody are not yet calluses. The rations provided by a commoner's day wage leave Sty asking for seconds that don't exist. The few books I've been allowed to take with me from the Greatlord's library lie unopened, possibly never to be read again, in the corner of the shack. I consider answering: *You could get off my stoop and go home.*

"No, we're good, thanks."

Griff's grin has a mischievous glint now. "Really? Sure you aren't hungry? Medicines? *Maybe the boy needs new shoes?*"

It's my own words parroted back to me: a conversation I had, in this home, after Julia died. I surmised correctly that their relationship entailed a certain kind of exchange, and that Griff's family had certain needs unmet. Two weeks into my sojourn as hostage-turned-lairhand, I'm pretty good at being angry at Griff, a low-humming fury that fuels me when I'm tired, for his not looking at me, for leaving us in squalor at the mercy of his people. But even so, this mockery of old kindnesses hurts. My fists tighten on the doorframe.

"Go home, Griff."

"I could send for you," Griff gloats suddenly. "I could have you *sent for.*"

So that's where this was going. Drunk Griff wants to talk about Julia. The parts he wasn't willing to discuss even at our most intimate when we shared a bed. Which means grief must have brought him low indeed, tonight.

And then I feel my treacherous heart melting.

"How about instead of you sending for me, I walk you home?"

He lets me sling one of his arms over my shoulder like an injured foot soldier and push him out the door, into the alleyway. Norcians peep through slats in their shutters as we pass—though it's unclear whether they're more intrigued by the sight of their war hero drunk, or my helping him. It's the first time we've touched since the days when I was his lord and we weren't supposed to.

"Agga thought it was really romantic," Griff says, as we begin to trudge up the hill, lopsided. The ha'Aurelian manor Griff moved into overlooks Clan Nag. He killed its occupants during the uprising.

"You and Julia?"

"Me and you."

It's the first time my eyes have so much as prickled since the Liberation, though there have been plenty of better reasons to weep than Agga's kind heart. I keep my voice light. "Well, that was very open-minded of her."

"If I sent for you, what would you do?"

"I don't know. What did you do?"

"I told her Agga needed medicine," Griff says.

I've never been able to imagine Julia's affair with Griff without my skin crawling. Griff doesn't have much more to say about it than that. "Well, she did need it," I say finally.

"Now she doesn't need anything." This seems to depress him most of all.

"What about Becca?"

"What about Becca?"

"Becca needs things."

"Becca needs her mam."

"Becca needs *you*."

I swing open the gate to the manor and lead Griff through it, into the opulent but deserted hall that he conquered but now lives in surrounded by ghosts. Becca's nowhere to be seen, but in Griff's current state, that's a mercy. "I could make you do things you didn't want to do," Griff says, as I lead him into the master bedroom and help him into the dark, grand, empty bed. "And afterward you'd say you liked it because you'd worry what would happen if you didn't."

It's too dark for him to see me wipe my face. I always weep for the wrong things.

"She said it would get her babes killed," he says, "and she was right."

"Do you want me to stay?"

I can make out very little of him, only the glint of his eyes reflecting the moonlight from the window, but it's enough to see the question sobering him as he understands.

"No," he says.

He sounds surprised, as if his own answer comes with a

realization about himself. Like he wasn't sure this was what he'd find until he checked.

I, on the other hand, am not surprised at all.

"Good night, Griff."

"Good night, Delo."

ANNIE
CALLIPOLIS

In the renovation period leading up to the Long-Awaited Return, there is not a spare moment to look for Guardians or dragons in the Palace. From waking to bed, we are worked. Inch by inch, with suds and scrub brushes, mops and polishing cloths, the Restoration's new fleet of servants undo Atreus's work and replace it with the world Lee's family lost. Ornate ministry offices that began as dragonborn residences are returned to their original purpose; the more austere archival rooms on the lower levels are reverted to kitchens and still more servants' quarters.

Ten years are erased in a matter of weeks.

I had forgotten, in the many years of well-rounded study since I scrubbed orphanage floors, what it is like for my whole body to ache for bed. My hands blister, my knees scrape and scab, my clothes stiffen from sweat. I scrub until my blisters bleed and tell myself that when the work of preparing the way for the Long-Awaited Return ends, I'll find my Guardians.

Except then I'll have dragonborn here, lords to serve, new humiliations and insults to stomach, and when will I ever have time to roam—

I begin to hear whispers of coming trials: trials for members of Atreus's regime who could not, or would not, be repurposed by the Restoration; trials for those who received commendations for their services in the Revolution. I hear about hangings in the People's Square, and for the highest-profile cases, execution in the arena by the dragon's punishment.

Atreus himself remains, officially, ill. But the rumor circulating is that the Revolution's Son was locked with him in the room where his family died and drove a knife through the Protector's heart.

It doesn't sound like the Lee I know.

The Clover fleet, as Callipolis's new dragonriding corps is called, will have its first Winnowing Tournament the day the dragonborn are restored to the Great Palace, in celebration of the Long-Awaited Return. Cor sur Maurana will face Edmund sur Envy. I've seen no sign of him, or any other Guardian, since I arrived here. The lower levels, where the stockade gives way to dungeons and the dungeons give way to the tunnels to the nests, are monitored by the Little Immortals.

It feels as if the Guardians have vanished—until I run into one by accident.

Two days before the Restoration goes into full effect and the dragonborn return to the halls we have prepared for them, I'm gathering plates to be sorted from the Palace Revolutionary Collection when I hear a familiar voice.

"Sorry, can you direct me to the rolls of Stormscourge tapestries? Lord Ixion's a man obsessed—"

I turn on my heel and blurt, *"Rock?"*

Rock stares at me. He's dressed in servant attire, as am I. A flush creeps up his pale and freckled neck.

Verra and Vicky, the sisters whose father caught one of Freyda's loaves, look up from the piles of plates we're sorting. "You two know each other?" Verra asks, intrigued, with a glance between Rock and me. She lingers on his muscled shoulders.

The question snaps me to my senses. "Of course he does. Remember me? Abigael, from Harfast Primary?"

Rock blinks slowly and then nods.

"Harfast—Primary—Abigael—yeah."

Vicky makes a sudden gasp of recognition. She turns to Verra and whispers in her ear, a tarnish-blackened finger poking out of her cupped hands toward Rock. I'm pretty sure she's just realized she's in the presence of a Guardian, and judging by her embarrassed giggle, it's not escaped her that he's in serving attire. His face is the color of a tomato.

"I can show you where the tapestries are being kept."

"Yeah—good—"

We leave Verra and Vicky giggling behind. Around the corner, in a side room where rolled tapestries are piled to the ceiling, I ease the door shut and let out a breath.

"Bloody—sparkfire—" Rock splutters, doubling over. His wheezing makes dust billow from the faded weave. "What are you doing here?"

"What are *you* doing here?"

Rock is the last one I've been expecting to run into, roaming freely about the Palace and turning the staff who recognize him starstruck.

"Ixion's got me serving as his valet."

"What? *Why?*"

Rock's jaw unhooks, and then he presses the line of it with his thumb. "When he realized you'd . . . liberated Norcia, there was a bit of a—retribution."

"He punished you?"

Rock shakes his head. His face is screwing up so hard, it looks like he's smiling. "Bryce," he manages. "He made me—clean it up afterward."

Aela felt it. The widowed dragon. *Bryce's* widowed dragon. My shoulders rise in horror. "Where are they?"

"The rest of the Guardians?" Rock wipes a hand across his eyes. "Guarded to the gills. I was with them until recently. It was hell, but Cor and I were sort of—keeping everyone calm. Dunno how they're faring now. Lee's loose; Ixion seems to think it's funny to drag him along for the ride. Power too, because it turns out he's the natural son of Kit Skyfish—"

"*What?*"

I knew he was adopted, but I'd thought his birth father was unknown. No wonder he's always been so prickly about his parentage—and no wonder he was so readily absorbed into the Clover fleet. Though it doesn't undo the fact that I'm pretty sure he pulled Eater off me in the mist.

"—and Lotus, otherwise known as the world's biggest ass."

Lotus had been Rock's closest friend. He closes his eyes and rubs his jaw again. This time, I recognize the gesture. When Griff and I studied together, on the Driftless Dunes, he rubbed his jaw, too.

"And . . . Bast?" I venture.

Rock has been keeping his composure, barely, until now. But at mention of his dragon, he starts to say it and then can't. I'm gripping his shoulder so hard, my knuckles are turning white beneath a coating of grime. Rock even looks a little like Griff—pale complexion aside—stocky, square-jawed, with a stubbornly provincial accent that comes out in moments of pressure; and like Griff, he rides a stormscourge. I say it for him. "They muzzled him."

Rock's voice breaks. "I can feel it. All the time, I can *feel* it—" He swipes at the phantom cage on his jaw again. "Ixion looks at me and I know he knows I'm feeling it."

Ixion left Griff and Sparker behind in New Pythos and replacements in Callipolis.

For a moment, fury leaves us both quiet.

But noticing my hand on him, it's like Rock wakes up. He sets both hands on my shoulders and pushes me back from him. "You need to get out of here. Ixion wants your head on a platter. All the Guardians who are missing, but yours and Crissa's most of all. He talks about it constantly, about—about what he'll do when he catches you—"

Panic enters his voice. But rather than fear, this news gives me the first real satisfaction I've had in days.

I'm stuck in Ixion's craw? Good.

"I'm not leaving until I get you out. All of you. The Guardians and the dragons."

Rock's shaking his head, palms waving me back. "Annie, even if you did," his voice rises wildly, "we have nowhere to go—"

But here, at last, I have an answer. The one way my mission to help Griff wasn't a mistake at all: the refuge that awaits.

"We'll go to Norcia. As soon as I figure out a way down to the stockade."

"Annie," says Rock in a strangled voice, "they're not in the stockade. They're not in the *Palace*. They're holding them in the Vault."

LEE

Freyda and I continue our walks and carriage rides without Ixion's knowledge. It goes without saying that the possibility we discuss would work around him, against him. And it feels blasphemous in ways beside that. Every glance at the sky makes me wonder, for the hundredth time, where Annie is and how long it will take for Power to find her.

What would Annie say if she knew I was entertaining Freyda's proposition?

Our final carriage ride, the day before the Long-Awaited Return, Freyda takes me into the city. When I last walked the streets, they were littered with the devastation of air strikes and riots. Now we find Freyda's Little Immortals working alongside the city guard, plowing snow into heaps on the sides of the People's Square, carting debris from the riots away to dump into the river, and working with citizens at the sites of greatest destruction to repair their homes and shops.

The city bustles to rebuild.

Freyda and I make our way along the Triumphal Way, observing this bustle, from inside our usual covered, unmarked carriage. I'm in Stormscourge livery, the only kind of clothing I've been provided since the coup. Freyda's mantle is lined with white fur today, a veil folded back over a brown braid done prettily down her shoulder.

"You will find," she says, as her carriage trundles through my city, "that your and my politics are not so different. Our parents' obsession with bloodlines is not one I share. I am happy to give the common people a voice, as you seem so interested in doing."

What does a voice matter in vassalage? "You're happy to absorb Callipolis into one more tax-paying province for your empire."

"A formality," says Freyda, waving a hand.

"Maybe to you."

"Everyone pays taxes to someone. Why not pay them to someone whose grain stores are gathered from a whole continent? While you concern yourself with high ideals of sovereignty, your people starve."

"That's why you're here, then? Kindness."

Freyda's chin goes up. "If I stayed in Vask, my fate would be to marry my brother and my dragon would be offered up in sacrifice after serving her function as a broodmare. As is required by our laws for the ascension of the male heir."

My jaw has separated, and as she sees it, she smiles thinly.

"You would have no reason to know," she says, "that your cousin was why I sought to defy the traditional fate and bond with a dragon doomed to death."

"Ixion?"

"Julia. The one you killed."

Freyda holds my gaze with a cool disinterest that, I think, is feigned. She draws thin fingers across the condensation on the window beside her, the better to see Highmarket's shopfronts beyond. "Julia is gone. I will not squander her legacy with mourning or with grudges. I will take what chance I have at freedom, far from dear brother Froydrich and the God-throne that awaits him. Yes, I intend to use Callipolis as my bargaining chip. But that does not need to be a hard yoke for your country, unless you make it so."

Seeing my lingering hesitation, she laughs. "You are still hoping your peasant Firstrider will swoop in and save you?"

"Maybe."

Freyda waves an arm, as if to brush aside this delusion like a cobweb. "You and I could do good together. More good than ever will be done with Ixion at the helm."

When I don't argue it, Freyda adds the point that tugs the hardest, as if she hears what I've begun, against all resolve, to wonder.

"I could also help your friends."

16

THE WINNOWING TOURNAMENT

ANNIE

I haven't got a hope of getting into the Vault without dragons. I haven't got much of a hope of getting into the Vault *with* dragons, but that's a problem for after I've got them. Work assignments are made the afternoon before the Long-Awaited Return, and I need to be given stable work.

"You," Betsuna says, reviewing her notes in her small study, which is off the Aurelian wing repurposed for Freyda and her household, "work harder than any of the other girls, and I'm told you hardly speak at all. Are you stupid?"

Fleeting memories cross my vision: teachers swatting me with homework they believed I cheated on, the metals test open on my desk and the world glitteringly clear as I moved the pen. The results in my hand, my name at the top of a letter sealed with the Revolutionary crest, a door opening into a new life.

All of that life, scrubbed away now by my hands.

Stable work. I need to be assigned *stable work*.

"I have little to say, ma'am."

Betsuna studies me, her pink lips pursed. I personally wiped cobwebs from the upholstered chair she sits in two days ago. "You know what I think? I think you're not stupid. I think you're clever.

And cleverness with reserve is a commodity to be valued in a servant. I know there have been motions to keep the provincial girls out of the household, but I'd like to try you out as a parlor maid."

"I'd really be more comfortable in the—"

Betsuna's eyes narrow instantly at the impertinence, and my mouth closes. I curtsy the way my mother taught me and correct course. "It would be an honor, ma'am."

I don't even know what a parlor maid is until I ask another girl afterward. This, too, is a body of knowledge I'm slowly absorbing: the intricate domestic hierarchies that Betsuna and Wes Goran are carefully reconstructing in the image of the past. It's explained to me that where chambermaids stay out of sight, parlor maids interact directly with their masters.

Worthless. I don't need to be pouring tea. I need to be shoveling dragon dung.

I have half a mind to quit the job and run. Two things keep me in place: that Cor's tournament is something I don't intend to miss; and that Betsuna has placed me on Freyda's personal staff.

I am, I'll admit, curious about the Bassilean princess. Her dragon flattens the bracken atop Pytho's Keep, a daily reminder of her dominance, but the story relayed by Delo leaves me curious about the girl herself. What sort of royal would bother to tell an incensed Ixion that she admired the pluck of his errant serf? It can't hurt, I tell myself, to see if some missing piece to the puzzle might be discovered in her service that I'd miss in the bowels of the Firemouth.

Vicky is promoted alongside me; Verra is assigned the work I wanted, in the stables. She's so disappointed, she cries.

In our new quarters in the Inner Palace, level with the kitchens, the new recruits are provided with the morning and evening dress appropriate for the position, white caps for our hair and a bib and apron for our frocks. Vicky looks in the tin mirror with a palm against her cheek at the sight of her uniform. Her brow is furrowed. I think she's pondering the fit of her cap until she speaks.

"Cheapside Grammar reopened today."

Vicky has not, so far, shown any inclination to speak of education. I hadn't realized until she says this that she'd be of age to attend. Cheapside Grammar is the school I went to with Lee, before we took the metals test. "You go there?"

"Used to. My brother's the only one going back. It's too expensive for Verra and me to go too, with the new fees." She straightens her cap, eyes on her reflection in the mirror. "The funny thing is, I was the one who tested Gold, so next year I could have . . . Are you all right, Abbie?"

I don't realize until she asks that I've pressed my hands against my face. My heart feels sticky in my chest.

Of course. I was so naïve as to wonder if Ixion would revert to birth-based-admission practices, but he knew better than to bother. I've heard Duck's father complain about the wasted outcome of his daughter's education, for whom he could have otherwise *found a suitable match* the old-fashioned way. How many more fathers have made the same calculation when faced with schooling that went from free and mandatory to optional and fee-based?

Most lowborn families won't continue school at all. Those who can scrape together the tuition will use it on their sons. My education was a blip in a long history of women who will enter this world and die without reading a book or hoping for a future besides what their families choose for them.

And now, for all my education, I'm scrubbing floors just like my mother did before me.

I tighten the parlor maid's cap over my stained hair and set my jaw.

Get the Guardians, and get out.

LEE

The morning of the Long-Awaited Return, before we install ourselves in the renovated Palace, Stormscourge House empties what is left of Dora Mithrides's larder for a luncheon celebrating her hospitality. Dora, little better than a prisoner in her own dining room, has long stopped making an effort to smile.

"The pleasure was mine," she tells Ixion.

The light at the end of my tunnel—slim though it is—is Cor's match, scheduled for noon today, that the dragonborn will attend and the public are invited to. Apart from Rock, Power, and the other patrician riders who have been out of prison forsworn, this will be the first Guardian I've seen since the coup. I keep telling myself Cor's odds are good. Grayheather's decent, but not unbeatable. Cor can earn his slot back.

Maybe they can all earn their slots back.

A cool hand settles on my arm. "Dear boy? Open it later. Privately."

Dora Mithrides sets a folded document in my hand and moves on. From a glance as I tuck it in my breast pocket, I gather it's some sort of public record.

Ixion, finishing up an uproarious speech, notices nothing. He stands on Dora's table. "Tonight, we will dine in the Hall of Plenty for the first time since it was wrongly taken from us!"

Cheers around the room, wolf whistles. Fists beat Dora's tables. The morning sun glints on Ixion's black hair as he drains his glass and hurls it at the floor, where it shatters.

"To the Long-Awaited Return!"

Stormscourge House makes its boozy way out Dora's hall and onto her front drive. The servants are arrayed to pay their respects, along with a purse-lipped Dora. Our belongings will be transported from the Janiculum to the Palace by her carriages while we attend Cor's match. The turnaround is teeming with saddled stormscourges, smoldering and awaiting their lords.

As well as a single white aurelian.

"Pal!"

Pallor closes the distance to me in two bounds.

He's unharmed, and I don't know if it's his relief or mine that spills over first. I press my palms against the warm silver scales of his neck and rest my forehead against his. He's snorting with delight, wings rippling, unconcerned with the stormscourges that dwarf him on all sides. Images flicker in my head, scents: Aela. There's a desperation to the way he's shoving the thoughts of her forward, as if he wants to tell me something by them.

"I know. I miss them, too."

But I can tell by how he tosses his head with sudden excitement that that's not it.

"It was thought," Ixion says, appearing at my side, "that questions might be asked if you were seen publicly without your dragon. We took the liberty of dousing him. You have my betrothed to thank for this consideration."

Yesterday I was in Freyda's carriage, riding through the city in secret and entertaining conspiracy against Ixion. "I'll remember to thank her at tonight's feast."

Ixion nods to Edmund. "One last thing before we go."

Edmund takes Dora's arms in a tight grip. Her lips thin.

"Oh," she says. "Already?"

"I believe you've served your purpose, you traitorous bitch," says Ixion, "and we like your house."

Edmund yanks her head back by its silver hair and exposes her throat. Ixion opens it with his bootknife.

"To the Palace!" he roars.

He leaves Dora Mithrides bleeding out across her drive.

ANNIE

Freyda arrives at the Palace with her luggage and retinue an hour before the tournament. Her small household is composed of an array of advisors and companions, all elite female slaves like Betsuna, who settle into their dedicated apartments with a flurry of disgruntled Bassilic. Even the slaves are skeptical, we are told, of Callipolan standards of luxury. When Betsuna introduces the princess to her Callipolan staff, Freyda casts an uncaring glance down the row of maids and the apartments we have scrubbed and polished for her till our fingers bled. Her trunks, delivered by barge, make a mountainous pile in the center of her drawing room.

"I'll be having a guest for coffee after the tournament. The parlor will be ready by then?"

"Of course, Your Divine Highness. I'll send one of the girls to serve you." Betsuna opens a hand to indicate me. "May I recommend Abigael Nearhallserf, a native of Lord Ixion's land holdings. Her discretion is assured and her language is limited to the Callipolan commoners' tongue."

Freyda gives me a swift, uninterested glance as I dip into a curtsy. "Very good."

Between the Restoration Feast planned for tonight, the transfer of personal effects from the Janiculum to the Palace apartments, and the arrival of the remaining dragonborn exiles from Norcia due by a barge this afternoon, I think Betsuna would prefer the household skip the Winnowing Tournament. But Ixion wants everyone to be present—especially his staff. Our frantic preparations are made even more frantic by a pause at noon to find hasty seats at the back of the arena for Cor sur Maurana's match.

It's the first time I've ever attended a dragonriding competition as a civilian. The audience's murmurs of recognition, the squeals from girls like Verra and Vicky, I've only ever heard as an indistinct murmur. Now I'm privy to their every exclamation as the dragons descend in the opening ceremony, and I'm surprised to feel the excitement of the crowd infect me with a sudden lightness. The blue sky overhead is the first I've spared eyes for in a week. The air smells earthy, like spring training. Like flying.

It fills me with sudden, baseless hope.

The court that returns to the Palace today makes their grand arrival on dragonback. They descend two by two to the Palace Box like an image from the glittering tapestries I've spent the last weeks laundering, but amid the spectacle my eyes are drawn to a single figure. Lee sur Pallor is outfitted in Stormscourge regalia. A white mantle flows over a silver breastplate, the heather adorning it a glimmer of violet beneath; his hair, slicked against his forehead, is as dark as his armor is bright, and on Pallor's silver back the brightness is blinding. He looks like something unleashed.

It's easy to imagine *this* Lee driving a knife through Atreus's heart. Harder to imagine him kissing me. Or holding me, tenderly, as he did when we last parted, his lips fitting to mine . . .

How do I look?

Like someone I was taught to ignore.

My collar has grown hot remembering it.

Verra seems to be having a similar reaction. "Lee sur Pallor is looking *good* today."

"Cor for me," says Vicky. "Like them a bit more rugged."

I should have known this was the kind of conversation going on in the stands while we competed. The thought of considering Cor's handsomeness feels wrong, like ogling my own brother, and comparing him with Lee laughable—but I'm not surprised Cor has a popular following, especially among Cheapsiders. He led the protests with them during the Bunker Riots.

"Preference, Abbie?"

"I thought you decided I'm having a torrid affair with Richard Nearhallserf."

They titter.

After the dragons have been dismissed to their caves, Lee takes a seat beside Ixion in the front row of the Palace Box, surrounded by dragonborn. I can make out his head tilting toward Ixion's as they hold conversation. I remember how Megara described it: *chummy*. It was easier to assure her it was an act when I wasn't watching it.

But then I remember how Rock put it: *He likes to drag Lee along for the ride.*

Lee may look like he's enjoying himself, swathed in all that bright glamour. But he's just as much a prisoner as Rock or Cor.

I'll get them out. I'll get them all out.

How?

On the other side of Ixion sits Freyda Bassileon, Ixion's betrothed and my new mistress, her face hidden from the public by a veil. Her dragon perches above us, curled atop Pytho's Keep like a whale-size cat on a sleeping stand. Obizuth sleeps so deeply, it's almost possible to forget a Great Dragon looms over us.

Vicky clutches Verra's arm. "There's my man!"

Cor sur Maurana and Edmund Grayheather have mounted the Eyrie. The applause for Cor is roaring; for Edmund, tepid. Apart from his being Lee's natural-born brother, not much is known about him. The real star here is Cor.

He blinks in the bright sun as if it blinds him. But then, I realize it probably does. He's been in a cell, unable to train, unable to so much as see the light of day until this moment—

And now he has this chance for freedom.

After they've summoned, but before they launch, Ixion makes his speech. His lungs, like Atreus's, are more than a match for the acoustics of the arena.

"Citizens of Callipolis, welcome to the first match of the Winnowing Tournaments. Today we will cull the weak from the strong. We will create a better, more valiant dragonriding fleet than this city has yet known. The Winnowings will celebrate one of the great values of the Revolution: merit-based advancement."

I can hear the laughter in his voice. I'm primed to hear it: Ixion has mocked me every time we've spoken.

"Cor Sutter, a commoner's son, will compete against Edmund ha'Stormscourge, a dragonlord's. They each, in the Callipolan fleet that was previously divided, ranked at the position of Quartus—the fourth highest in their fleet. Today, only one will continue in that role.

"May the best dragonrider be found worthy."

Until now, I hadn't spared much thought to these tournaments—whatever they were going to be, it was a sideshow to the fact that my friends have been imprisoned by the enemy. But now, Ixion confirms what I'd have guessed from the start.

This is a setup. Which begs the question: What ruses will be used to ensure the desired result?

As the bell rings, and the stormscourges charge and veer, I clutch my knees and watch with narrowed eyes. Ash spews from two maws: Both dragons have been doused, which answers my first suspicion—whether Cor would have to face sparked dragonfire on a doused dragon.

No. Nothing so crude as that.

They go for each other again, this time in a contact charge, and Vicky shrieks and cheers beside me as Cor's dragon gets the upper hand, clawing his way up—

Ash spews from Maurana as Envy bucks away. The bell rings: Cor earned a penalty hit.

"That's right, Cor."

My voice is only one of many; the crowd is full of people calling out their support. The riders separate for the reset, and Edmund opens the coolant valves in his suit to relieve the burn.

Then the bell, and they slam together again.

It's not until Edmund lands a penalty hit that I guess it. He's already taken his position at reset distance; the bell waits for Cor.

And Cor keeps fumbling with his coolant valve.

"Let's go, Cor!" Vicky's shouting. She isn't the only one. "Why won't he reset?"

"His suit doesn't have coolant."

"Doesn't have what?"

She's too riveted to attend my answer. Cor fumbles a little longer, and then his shoulders settle: He's realized the ruse, too.

This wasn't ever meant to be a fair fight. After languishing in a cell, in fear, with this one hope on the horizon—it's going to be taken from him.

I see the realization in his sagging shoulders.

He assumes position. But now, he's hunching close to his

dragon. Stiff in the saddle. The penalty hit got his right side and dominant arm; he grips the reins with his left hand because it's the only one he can still use.

I only realize I've lifted my fingers to cover my face when Verra tugs at them.

"He'll be okay, it's only a tournament, Abbie!"

But by the end, even she's crying. The roast is slow. Unable to relieve the pain, Cor curls closer and closer to his dragon's back. He manages to get another penalty hit on Edmund, but Edmund's coolant works just fine, and he recovers as if he didn't feel the burn at all. After Cor takes another penalty, he stops really guiding his dragon at all. Maurana takes over, screeching at her rider's anguish, attempting to keep him safe from the blasts. But eventually she tires. For the final blow, though it need only be a penalty hit, Edmund's dragon performs a full-heat blast that blankets them.

What's called a kill shot.

They have to carry Cor off his dragon.

"Do you think he'll be all right?" Verra asks, as she rubs Vicky's back.

"Doused hits aren't fatal," I say, "if he receives medical attention."

If.

A terrible thought grips me: *What if they want it to be fatal?*

"I had only thought," Vicky says, wiping her eyes, "that he'd be good enough. But I suppose that new one is dragonborn."

I turn to look at her. "You think that's why Cor lost?"

Vicky lifts a shoulder, looking ashamed and bewildered. "Cor lost to Leo last time, didn't he?"

In semifinals for the Firstrider tournament, when I beat Power,

Cor was the one Lee eliminated to become a finalist. Callipolans now know, as they didn't then, Lee's parentage.

Ixion steps forward. "People of Callipolis," he says, "you asked for democratic reforms, so now I give them to you. You have seen the outcome of this match; but far be it from me to dictate who will fly for your fleet. Today, the choice is yours. Do you give Edmund the laurel for Quartus? Do you give an *aye*?"

My fingers curl into fists on my apron as I understand. It isn't enough to humiliate a lowborn rider in front of the whole city: Ixion will use the apparatus of democracy to ensure it is the people themselves who find him less worthy. I squeeze my eyes shut, to block out the sight of the hands lifting into the air in confirmation, but I still hear it. The swelling of the *ayes*, quiet and first, growing louder. Until finally it is a chant that fills the arena, and even Vicky whispers it beside me.

"Aye."

I blink burning eyes open. Edmund ha'Stormscourge, Lee's bastard brother, lifts a fist in the air from the Palace Box where he's landed to receive his laurel from Freyda, his wispy white-blond hair glinting in the sun. A frightened kind of cheering answers his crowning.

Lee alone of the dragonborn seems to have forgotten to clap.

"May I present Edmund ha'Stormscourge," Ixion proclaims, "your new Quartus!"

As we exit the arena, I listen to the murmurs from others, like Vicky, who watched their champion lose. *Maybe the next Guardian will make his slot,* someone says, but I already know that's a fool's hope. Ixion will drive any lingering doubt about dragonborn supremacy into the ground, one sabotaged flamesuit at a time.

I follow numb steps back into the Palace, and then remembering my duty to serve Freyda's coffee, I take off for her apartments at a jog.

LEE

I'm prepared to raise the roof if they don't let me see Cor, but Ixion seems to think it's funnier to allow it.

I find him on a stretcher, in a covered cart, on his way out of the Cloister courtyard to the nearest side gate in the Outer Walls. They intend to return him to the Vault. He smells of burns.

"Cor!"

"Lee—"

The helmet protected most of his face, but even here the lines of skin rippling, bubbling, are visible. No physician has been called: The men in charge of the cart are military. Cor's eyes close after they find me. I have no bootknife myself, so I turn to his guard.

"Cut him out of his flamesuit."

"My lord, we have orders to take him directly—"

I hold eye contact, and the soldier, who recognizes me, loses nerve. At any rate my status as both dragonborn and Guardian leaves my rank in the chain of command negotiable. I have cold water sent for, rags, and whatever ointments that can be found: coolant or aloe or, that failing, honey from the kitchens. I have to hope that after he's returned to his cell in the Vault, no one follows up to make sure he died from this. What care I can give him now will have to be enough. I'm siphoning cold water over the worst of the burns along his side, sopping up pus-soiled water with a rag, when he finally croaks words out.

"Really thought we had that one in the bag."

I motion for another bucket of cold water. "It was my fault. I told Ixion to give you a chance."

Cor laughs hoarsely. "I'm flattered by your . . . faith in me."

When I've done everything I can think of, Cor grips my hand with his raw-red one. "Don't let them hurt Maurana."

As they roll him away, I wonder whether I'll ever see him again.

I'm almost back to the Cloister before I remember I don't live there anymore. I rotate on my heel and make my way to what once was—and now is again—the Stormscourge entrance to the Inner Palace.

In the time it's taken me to tend Cor, the Bastards have made themselves at home in my family's restored apartments. I find Edmund, still wearing the laurel, lounging in the parlor on what was once my mother's favorite settee, since reupholstered. The Bastards surround him, toasting his name; his stormscourge, Envy, spreads ash across the freshly laundered rug.

Edmund glances at the pus on my hands and the ash on my arms when I enter. "You look like shit."

I lunge for him.

"You—cheating—coward—"

I don't get halfway across the room before the other Bastards restrain me, and then Envy lifts his head and hisses. Ash stings my eyes and chokes my breath. As I cough, Titus and Angelo force me to my knees.

"He's the cheat," Edmund says coolly. "I've got no obligation to play fair against a commoner who stole one of my family's dragons."

The hypocrisy of this makes me burst out laughing as my eyes stream. "Your *mother* was a commoner."

She must have been. Edmund is built too much like a highland peasant for her to have been anyone else. It fits my father's profile: a considerate father, a loving husband, the sort of man who'd never be unfaithful to his wife with anyone he considered her equal. It would have been an abuse of power, the kind he never thought about afterward except to pay the father for the inconvenience of a ruined, pregnant daughter.

Edmund hears the appeal to his decency as an insult. His dragon's fangs bare and its hackles rise. Edmund gets to his feet. "Yeah? And apparently you share *our father's* proclivity for serfs. Get him out of my sight."

Titus and Angelo throw me from the drawing room.

Outside, a valet scurries to my side, helps me to my feet, and brushes off my sooty uniform. I miss his name completely and hear hardly a word of his nervous chatter as he leads me down the corridor. I come to my senses when he directs me into a bed-chamber I have not set foot in since I was eight.

"Lord Edmund claimed the master suite, so we've prepared the room that—was yours before, my lord."

The bed, which was child-size, has been replaced with an adult frame. The door that led into my nurse's chambers has been shut. The curtains and the bedclothes have been replaced, though they still have the heather embroidery, now also embellished with black clovers. The painting over the mantel is the same: a clutch of storm-scourge eggs, with a single slitted eye peering out the first one cracking. I used to bob my head to create the illusion it was moving.

I turn to the valet and realize, for the first time, that I know him.

"Bart. You worked at the Lyceum Club."

Bart bows. "Aye, my lord. But before that, I served like this."

His lined face betrays no emotions, though I wonder how he survived, one regime to another, and what he saw or did. Some of the household turned on their lords. Others were punished for serving them in the first place.

"My lord? Her Divine Highness sends this with her regards."

He holds out Pallor's summoner. It's been snapped free from the Guardian wristband that once contained it and is strung on a chain as my father's once was. The arched window that looks out over the balcony and the Firemouth has been cracked to let in a chill breeze that battles with the flaming hearth.

One day, Leo, a dragon of your own will be yours to summon from this perch.

Stinking of Cor's pain, numb with my failure, I suddenly crave Pallor's presence so strongly that even the misgiving of my father's memory isn't enough to stop me.

I take two steps to the glass door, throw it open, and lean over the balcony. The whistle sounds a blast too high for human ears to hear into the Firemouth looming below. I don't have long to wonder if Pallor can hear it: Within a minute he emerges from the caves, spiraling on an updraft, to land lightly on the dragon perch of my childhood bedchamber. I lean against him, inhaling the familiar smell of his ash. He's been scrubbed down by a keeper, his saddle removed.

Inside, I find Bart waiting stiffly on the side of the room farthest from the dragon perch. "The princess also invites you to coffee, if you are available before the feast."

One look down makes me realize how unfit I am for polite society in this state. "I don't think I'm—"

"I've prepared a basin for your ablutions, and can be of assistance."

"I'll do it myself."

"I insist, my lord," Bart says.

He sounds like the servants I remember. Proficient in his Dragontongue, with just a hint of the Lower Bank stopping his words, roughening them. I look at him and though he flinches, he doesn't back down. Ordered, perhaps, by someone who outranks me—Ixion, or Freyda.

I can feel tiredness sinking into my bones. I reek of ash, of the smell of burned flesh. And on the edge of my mind, the thought that Cor's burns were my fault sits waiting.

After everything else that's happened, resisting the motions of aristocratic toilette feels like dying on a molehill.

I ease into the nearest chair, and Bart rolls over the basin of warm water.

"That's it, my lord."

I let him wash me.

And though there are reasons why it should feel strange—to let a servant tend to me like this, to have Pallor just outside, basking in the sunlight of a dragon perch from the life before—there are reasons why it feels right, too.

And I'm too tired to fight the feeling of its rightness.

Shadows have lengthened on the walls of the Inner Palace, glowing warm and golden in the winter afternoon light, when Bart finishes toweling my hair dry. Only when I reach down to unclasp my flamesuit do I remember the letter tucked inside it from Dora Mithrides.

I open it, and the words swim before my eyes.

It's a deed to a highland estate registered to Dora's name. A small sketch of the house and its floor plan leave no doubt which it is. I read the listed assets numbly: Stripped of its feudal land holding, the property is reduced to the manor and its immediately surrounding acres of vineyards, orchards, and thermal springs for dragon hatching. A single groundskeeper and dog come with the property. Dora's purchase receipt is dated to a post-Revolutionary auction.

A codicil to the deed stipulates that upon the death of its owner, the estate should return to its original heir, Leo Stormscourge.

Clipped to the rider, in what must be Dora's spindly hand, is a note. *You remember when I once told you we had more to discuss than a tapestry? This was it.*

Bart speaks, and he has to say it twice for me to hear him.

He's asked if I'll be visiting Freyda the old-fashioned way. I thumb my eyes dry before I answer. "I might as well."

Dora Mithrides was no-nonsense to the end, and I think she'd want me to be, too.

Bart nods. "Then I'll prepare him, my lord."

The *old-fashioned way* means by dragonback. Bart removes a small court saddle from its mount by the balcony door. Little more than a thick rug, it's used for traversing the Inner Palace via the Firemouth. It seems that dragonkeeping, too, is a skill set Bart claims with traditional competence. He approaches Pallor with a jerking bow. Pallor's tail flicks. He eyes Bart coolly and then lowers his head in return.

Bart lays the court saddle over his haunches.

"That will do, my lord and dragon. She's in the Aurelian wing."

It's the first time I've heard the apartments that became the Offices of the First Protector so named in a decade. "In the Rose Parlor?"

"Indeed, my lord."

I mount Pallor and we hop into the air of the Firemouth. The windows and dragon perches of the Inner Palace spin around us, some of them dark, others glowing as the evening lamps are lit. For a moment the memories layer over again: my father on dragonback, making his way from one social hour to another in a Firemouth bustling with the transit of dragonlords. Years later, poised like this with Annie, I located Atreus's office from memories of the old regime when we first reported the sighting of a Pythian fleet.

That's the memory that feels distant, right now, and the memory of my father close enough to touch.

Pallor and I cross the Firemouth in the long light and land on the perch outside Freyda's apartments. The Rose Parlor is where Atreus entertained dignitaries and high-ranking officials. Before that, it was Arcturus Aurelian's most intimate receiving room. It's been refurbished in the traditional style and is brightly lit; inside, Freyda is visible sitting alone at her sofa as a maid strains the coffee, and when we land, she looks up and her smile shows through the rippled glass.

I dismount Pallor and go to the glass door, which the maid opens.

Freyda has risen to her feet. A smile transforms her face, melting its coldness and crinkling her eyes with warmth. "I see you got your summoner."

"I did. Thank you. I hope you don't mind that I brought Pallor along."

"Not at all," Freyda says. "I had heard this was a tradition of your court. It is *clever.*"

"But surely your great goliathans must make a court far grander," I answer, as the maid takes my mantle.

"Perhaps where size makes for grander courts, cleverness is encouraged by fleets of great number."

I feel like we are tossing a ball back and forth in a way I haven't done in years, but it comes so easily I hardly know what I say. Between the return to my family's old apartments, Pallor's summoner in my hand, and the profound sense of futility left after Cor's match, it's as though I've been unlocked. What comes out is—court banter.

I'm done fighting this.

"And now with your Great Dragon and our numerous fleet, our court will be both grand and clever."

Freyda lets out a tinkling laugh. The maid approaches with the coffee service.

"I am sorry for what happened to your friend today." Freyda's tone sobers as she receives her coffee. The cups are half as large as Callipolan teacups, and the steaming Bassilean coffee, even strained, looks mudlike. "I had my suspicions, but hoped they would be wrong. Do you know if he—"

"He'll be fine. Thank you."

Her sympathy is as unwanted as her mention of Cor. After going to the effort of scrubbing the day's failure off me, I have no interest in being reminded of it. Coffee, even the Bassilean variety, isn't strong enough.

Freyda nods. She drums her fingers lightly on the table and lifts the tiny cup to her lips. "And my proposal? Have you given it more thought today?"

"How could I not?"

"I was hoping that might be the case. Please," she adds, with a hint of impatience, snapping the maid forward to fill my cup, because she's been standing frozen by my chair.

The maid steps forward, bends to pour my coffee, and sloshes it. I glance at her.

It's Annie.

17

A POLITICAL ARRANGEMENT

ANNIE

I should have seen this coming. Freyda having a guest for coffee:
How many possible options could there be? How did it not occur
to me that working as a parlor maid for Freyda Bassileon would
put me in the presence not just of the princess, but of the rest of the
court?

Of *Lee?*

My stomach goes into my mouth at the sight of Pallor silhouetted in the glass. Even though reconnecting with the Guardians is
what I've been working toward since I returned, this isn't how I
want to do it. I don't want Lee to recognize me in front of Freyda,
dressed up like a maid serving coffee in a stupid cap and frock—

But when he doesn't so much as notice me, that's a hundred
times worse.

It's not that I wanted to find him miserable and distressed after
weeks locked away with the family he betrayed. But instead to find
him carefree, happy, and—flirting?

And discussing a proposal. It doesn't take a genius to guess
what kind.

If I were Freyda, I wouldn't want to marry Ixion, either.

He's speaking in a way I've never heard before, jaunty, bantering, his Dragontongue mellifluous and luxuriant. At ease and

pleased with himself, handsome and conscious of it, an ankle propped across a knee, fingers idly tracing the embroidery of the chair he lounges in.

When Freyda snaps her fingers, I come to my senses.

He doesn't so much as look at me even as I approach his chair with the coffeepot.

How do I look?

Like someone I was taught to ignore.

It's less charming now.

I could touch that hair, I could slap that face. I could tear this maid's cap off and hit him with it—

Only when my shaking fingers lift the spout of the pot too jerkily, and a bit of coffee splatters on the tiny saucer, does Lee glance up. His expression vaguely bored, a little curious, as if a servant's mistake doesn't bother or interest him but does, slightly, surprise him—

And then our eyes meet.

This is the moment I'd been anticipating and dreading in equal measure since I embarked on this fool's mission of infiltrating the Clover Restoration. I had not anticipated it happening in front of Freyda Bassileon.

But Lee has had many years of practicing a straight face. After the flash of recognition, his expression smooths. Exactly the way I've seen it do in classes, for the last ten years, when teachers talked about Palace Day and Lee pretended to be no one and feel nothing.

"I'm sorry," says Freyda in Dragontongue, "the staff is still in training. Much of my household had to be left in Vask."

Evidently, she attributed our pause to the spilled coffee. Her gaze has narrowed as she looks not at me, but at Lee. As if she were using this moment of perturbation to evaluate him.

Lee smiles at her, a flash of white teeth. I feel a swoop in my stomach at the sight; we still stand close enough to touch. "Oh, don't apologize," he tells Freyda, waving a hand. "You're fine," he adds to me, in courteous and slightly disinterested Callish. "What do they call you?"

It's precisely the tone his father used speaking to villagers of Holbin during collections.

I'm so flustered, I seize upon the familiar script as well. It's not ill-suited to giving Lee the information he needs. "Abigael, my lord," I answer, balancing the pot as I curtsy.

Lee's still smiling, but he blinks at the curtsy. "Pleasure to meet you, Abigael. Is that a highland accent I hear?"

"Yes, my lord, I'm from Thornham."

Lee lifts his cup to toast me. "To Abigael of Thornham," he murmurs, "from the highlands."

A blush creeps up my neck as I curtsy again and remove myself to the doorway. From this vantage point, I can easily observe Freyda, studying Lee over the lip of her cup with a small measure of appreciation, and Lee, oddly pale in the face as he turns back to her with his brightest smile.

"Where were we?" he says, with a gesture as if to wave away everything in the room but Freyda.

But where they were, neither has a chance to recall. The door to the parlor is opened by Betsuna, her nose in the air. "Your Divine Highness has a second visitor for coffee."

Freyda twists, her mouth puckering. "Betsuna, I told you I would be undisturbed—"

Betsuna lifts a significant brow. Ixion steps around her, grinning jauntily.

"My lord Ixion," says Freyda. Lee has stiffened.

"I didn't realize you wished to be undisturbed with cousin Leo," says Ixion, with a curious glance between Freyda and Lee.

"Not at all," says Freyda. "In truth, we were discussing—your upcoming Triumph."

Ixion's strange smile relaxes. "You don't want me to help plan it?"

"One should never have to plan one's own party," says Freyda.

Ixion moves to kiss Freyda, and the princess, smiling, turns her head so that the kiss lands on her cheek. "My betrothed is so bashful," he tells Lee, with a show of humor that sounds strained.

"When will this betrothal be announced?" Lee asks, brows together as he watches the two of them.

Freyda says, "We were thinking at the Triumph. It would be good to have everything tied up in time for the next League summit."

She must mean the Medean League. The talk of the spring summit will, without a doubt, be Bassilea's expansion into Callipolis, and it would help Freyda's case if she achieves legitimacy before then. Amid all else, I find myself impressed with her head for strategy.

Ixion tosses himself into the chair beside Lee. "Quite a disappointment from your Highmarket friend."

Lee's lips form a line.

"I'm thinking I'll save all the defeated Guardians for the Triumph. I'd like a procession of them as tributes—and then, maybe, a sacrifice? Or they can be handed out as prizes. I haven't decided yet. The dragons, naturally, will be disposed of once they breed."

Lee's back is rigid, his knuckles white on his saucer. Freyda clears her throat. "I hear the dragonborn from New Pythos have arrived safely on the river barges, and will be attending tonight's feast."

Ixion ignores her attempt at a change of subject. "Ideally, we'd have the Firstrider captured by then. Prize of honor. Parcival says he has a lead, so perhaps he'll deliver in time—"

He twists in his chair and stares directly at me.

"Are you going to just stand there?" he asks in Callish.

My hands shaking again, I take a step forward. Lee squints down at his coffee. Freyda studies Ixion with a line forming above her brow. I pour with the distinct feeling that Ixion is eyeing me.

Is he staring because I look familiar?

We've seen each other face-to-face, helmets off, exactly once before on Wayfarer's Arch when I returned Julia's body. But it was at a distance. After Goran's failure to recognize me at the interview, I felt confident gambling Ixion wouldn't, either. Now I wonder whether I misjudged.

"Is this the Nearhall serf?" Ixion asks Freyda.

"She is my parlor maid," Freyda answers curtly.

Ixion laughs. "Right," he says. "But she's still, you know, mine."

He glances over at Lee with a lifted brow as if to include him in a joke that he doesn't expect Freyda to appreciate, but Lee's jaw only twitches. Ixion heaves a sigh.

"No one around here has a sense of humor. What's your name?" he asks me in Callish.

My face has begun to burn with a muddle of shame and fury; for a moment the panicked thought occurs that the blush will give away my understanding of their Dragontongue. But it seems Ixion's tone is suggestive enough that no one questions my discomfort. Lee's face is now as white as the china cup he holds, which rests still in his frozen hand. Freyda gets to her feet.

"Please excuse us," she tells Lee, and then snaps her fingers at Ixion as she did at me a moment earlier.

Ixion rises, smirking like a student who's been caught at mischief by an overbearing teacher, and follows Freyda out of the room with a wink at me as he passes. I'm shorter than either of them by a head. Freyda closes the door behind them, but it only muffles the severity of her lowered voice.

Lee remains sitting with his back turned, staring at the cup in his hands. I do not move from my position by the door. A pulse pounds in my ears and heats my face.

"What are you doing here?" he asks.

"I was trying to"—my voice is faint, laughter at my own idiocy breaking it—"rescue you."

Lee stares into the dregs of his coffee. Then he lifts the cup to his lips, drains it, and sets the empty cup on the table in front of him.

It takes me a moment to understand. I reach for the coffeepot and cross the room. As I refill his cup, Lee's fingers take those of my free hand, which is shaking, and press them in his.

The pressure of his hand on mine makes my knees go weak.

I want to crawl into his arms. I want him to take me miles away from this nightmare, from those monsters on the other side of the door—

Or maybe just one monster. Surrounded by so many worse alternatives, I can find little fault with Freyda—even if I suspect her argument with Ixion is more about her own honor than her staff's. Given a choice between despots, I'd rather have one who admires a peasant's pluck and stands up for her maids than one who doesn't.

The cup fills too quickly. Too soon, Lee releases my hand and I back away from him.

"You should do it," I tell him, as I arrange the tray of honey biscuits.

His back is still turned. He has not looked at me once since we were left alone. I think if he does, it will undo me. "Do what?"

My vision burns, and I stare down at the biscuits, counting breaths. "Marry her."

"Annie—" he says at once.

"I'm not saying it out of spite. I mean, my feelings aside. It would be good for Callipolis. Far better than Ixion. If we're going to bear the Bassilean yoke either way—"

"Annie, *I don't love her.*"

Outside in the corridor, Ixion's voice cuts off Freyda's, rich with sarcasm. For a moment I let the word *love* wrap around me like an embrace, feeling its warmth release the tension in every muscle in my body. Then I set that aside.

"That's not what these kinds of marriages are about."

"Will you"—Lee finally turns his head, to glare at me—"stop thinking like a Guardian for one minute?"

I glare back at him.

But even this can't be sustained. His gaze softens. "You changed your hair," he murmurs.

"I did."

"And you liberated New Pythos."

"Well—I helped."

Lee's lips curve in a smile, and I feel a faltering smile hitch itself back on my face.

For a breath it's enough to forget Ixion, that imbecile. To forget this city and my many failures. I've found Lee again, and his smile is every bit as beautiful as I remember it.

But that's not enough.

"If Freyda makes a gambit to establish you as her partner rather than Ixion, she'll need to do it publicly. Probably at the Triumph. Which could be my opportunity to move, if he's got the conquered Guardians in the procession."

Lee hesitates, as if he isn't sure he wants to tell me what he says next. "She's suggested making a deal with her."

"Your hand for the Guardians?"

He nods.

"Well, that's perfect."

This is an opportunity, and it should not be squandered. Whatever my heart says. But Lee shakes his head bleakly. "It wouldn't free the dragons, Annie. So long as Ixion has them, he's got a direct line to every Guardian's nerve center even if he doesn't have them in his prison."

But for the first time in a long time, I'm smiling. Lee's just cut my job in half.

"That's fine. You take care of the Guardians, and I'll take care of the dragons."

We have a time, a place, a chance. Aela and I will figure out the rest.

LEE

I attend the evening's feast in a daze. I haven't been in the Hall of Plenty since the Lycean Ball, and after a winter of famine, the bounty provided to welcome the dragonborn feels obscene. But it seems Freyda's allowance from Bassilea has been sufficient to resupply our stores—or at least, it is for the time being. Someone found a pig to roast, in whose mouth could be stuffed an apple.

I sit at Ixion's left, across from Freyda, at the head of the table. Farther down, Lotus and Power sit among the Clover riders. In my father's time, the dragons of honored guests were invited to lounge along the skirts of the hall, which means that tonight Pallor glints in the shadow of the columns, curled at an uneasy distance from Niter. Freyda's goliathan, as large as one of the Palace courtyards alone, remains roosting atop Pytho's Keep.

Rock serves at our table. Annie is nowhere to be seen.

But the reunion with her earlier, and the prospect of Freyda's proposal, seem to cancel each other out. One reality cannot be true without the other. Can Annie really have suggested such a thing, accepting *this*—

One second, she spoke of rescuing me, the next of making this my final future. Letting a servant wash me, bantering with a princess, barely glancing twice at the maid who takes my coat: I feel like I'm succumbing to the decadence of my father like a slowly boiling frog.

I can run and run and run, and still the blood catches up with me.

I don't want this to be how I lose Annie for good.

Will you climb, Atreus asked, *and hope your light shines brightly enough to light the way for others?*

Would it be selfish not to?

After dinner, I extend a hand to Freyda Bassileon after she has opened the first dance with Ixion. The Medean waltz, the same that I once danced with Annie, turns us on the flagstones of the cleared hall. Freyda's waist is narrow and warm in my hand, her button nose a shadow beneath a sheer veil. She is, I notice perhaps for the first time, and without enthusiasm, pretty.

We could make this work. Eventually, I might even forget the girl I love and find a kind of happiness with this one, for whom I have growing respect.

And one day, I might even talk her into resuming the Revolutionary reforms that Ixion has been so keen to discontinue.

I could do good with this.

I speak in her ear. "I want pardons. For every single one of the Guardians."

Freyda's smile is visible through her veil. "That can be arranged."

"I want their safe passage ensured to Norcia." My fingers are shaking so badly as I hold her waist, Freyda shifts in my grip.

"Of course," she says. She presses her lips together, studying the room, at the turn. Some watch us, but none can hear. "We'll announce the engagement at the Triumph. Until then, we'll need to be discreet. How do I reach you?"

The answer is obvious, even if giving it has the feeling of stepping into my own grave. "Send messages through the girl."

Freyda doesn't ask which one.

ANNIE

I lie awake the night of the Long-Awaited Return with my stomach twisting. I'm quartered in the lower levels of Freyda's wing of the Inner Palace, across a courtyard from the Hall of Plenty, and the sounds of revelry vibrate through the stone. I can just make out the high notes of their violins. The dragonborn are feasting, and their parlor maids are not required. I'm free to stew in my own thoughts.

I've found Lee at last, and I face losing him permanently.

Every way I look at it, it's the best way: If Freyda's here to stay, let her share her rule with one worthy of it. If I'm to free the conquered Guardians, let me do it with the least bloodshed. If Ixion is to have his Restoration, let him be outsmarted.

All these calculations add up to one solution. And yet it feels that my aching heart outweighs them all.

It takes me an hour to realize the writhing of my stomach, the insistent turbulence, is not mine alone. I'm feeling Aela.

She's so distant, her feelings are barely a pulse, a whisper almost out of earshot. But as I still myself, quieting my own thoughts, hers come free like shells revealed by a tide.

She's not alone. She's with—

A mother-of-pearl sheen of scales. Golden hair.

I sit bolt upright.

I know my way to the Cloister courtyard so well that I can find it in the dark. Inside, I shuffle into what was my old dorm room, where Verra still sleeps with the other keepers-in-training. I shake her awake, and in the hallway outside, I make a hasty excuse.

"Richard Nearhallserf really misses his dragon. I was hoping to go give it an apple."

Verra inhales with excitement. "We *knew* you two had a thing! But—I don't think dragons eat apples, Abbie."

She sounds like she is not one hundred percent certain about this.

"Please, Verra? I know where he's stabled and everything."

Young love wins. She lends me her key to the armory.

Inside, I swap my slippers for a keeper's cave boots and throw a protective leather mantle over my shoulders. This close to her, I can feel Aela's mind tethering mine like a cable wire. I make my way through the next door, down the stairs, and into the caves with a lantern tapered low.

Another night, I'll need to map out exactly where our dragons are and theirs. But tonight, I only need to follow the connection to Aela without blowing my cover. The keeper's gear will smell familiar to the dragons, and between that and a soft tread I wend deeper without incident. I hear deep, slow breathing and smell sulfur. But no dragon stirs from sleep.

The line of our connection clarifies the deeper down I go. Pretty soon I've left the known networks of caves and am making my way out of the Palace entirely, into tunnels that lead to the city sewers in one direction, the drainage systems of Pytho's Keep in the other.

I make my way along the main tunnel that burrows under Pytho's Keep.

After what must be an hour, when my toes have grown cold

and damp in the keeper's boots, I find myself staring up at a grating that crisscrosses the deep blue of a night sky beyond.

Silhouetted on the other side waits Aela. She snorts with pleasure as I reach through the partition to lay a hand on her snout.

"Annie?"

A second dragon's head rears beside Aela's, this one slenderer and paler. And beside her stands—

"Crissa."

Crissa reaches through the grating to take my hand. Her blond hair is silver in the moonlight filtering through cypress boughs.

"Hang on," Crissa says, reaching for the dead bolt holding the metal partition shut. She twists, and it snaps off like a dead branch. "Didn't want to risk dragonfire drawing unwanted attention," she says, holding up a hacksaw. "We've been working on that all evening."

I swing the grating open. Crissa pulls me up and over the threshold, embraces me, and Aela's forehead nudges mine, her crest flattened. She's purring.

"Come on," Crissa says, "they're waiting for us."

At the foot of Parron's Spring, looking out over the moonlit river and the spires of the Island of the Dead, sit a ring of dragons and their riders.

My Guardians.

"Annie!"

I'm blinking around at them as my eyes adjust. "What are you—where did you—?"

"Not all of us were in the Cloister the day of the coup," says Alexa, smiling.

As I warm myself by the spring, they share how they escaped the coup. Some were on patrol; some were in the Palace infirmary, recovering from injuries sustained in the air strikes, and snuck out when they realized something was wrong. Crissa, on her mission with another skyfish rider named Warren, found them one by one when she returned from Damos, after she saw the changed flags on the ramparts.

"And then when Aela found us, and led us here—you know the rest."

The feeling of being surrounded by so many familiar faces, as friendly and relieved by the sight of me as I am by them, warms me as much as the steam off the hot spring. The quiet night, the whispering cypresses, seem to curl around us as if Pytho's Keep and the river herself protect us.

Of course, now that I'm surrounded by them, it occurs to me that I myself should have tracked down the Guardians still at large when I got back. Crissa acted as a commander should have. My first impulse was to put on an apron and apply for a job as a maid.

"And you?" Crissa asks. "What have you been doing in the Palace?"

Scrubbing floors.

"I've been undercover. I made contact with Rock and Lee."

"Ooh," says Crissa warmly, "well done. How?"

I find I don't want to tell her exactly how. "They were hiring new staff; I took a job." Crissa makes a noise of appreciation at this contrivance, but there is a pause, as she studies me, where I'm pretty sure she's able to figure out what kind of uniform I'm wearing.

"Well, that's great, Annie," she says. "I saw that challenge Ixion put out. I'm glad you didn't fall for it."

Her tone is light, encouraging, a bit of a squadron-leader voice, but underneath I can hear her hesitation. What I can't tell is why. Because she thinks I've messed up? Or because she can sense the shame that I feel radiating from my own face in the dark?

Why am I so ashamed?

"Yeah, well. That was a trap."

"Obviously." Crissa shudders. "We all saw what happened to Cor."

Crissa and Cor were always close—Lee's inner circle—and I realize that whatever she saw of the tournament today must have been even more excruciating for her than it was for me.

"He's fine. They're saving him for the Triumph."

Crissa lets out a slow breath. "And Lee?"

"He's courting Freyda."

"*What?*" Crissa's squadron-leader tone vanishes with her squawk of indignation.

"He's going to negotiate a pardon of the Guardians as a part of the engagement. I just have to get the dragons out; we're thinking at the Triumph—"

"Annie!"

"What?"

Alexa giggles. I can see Crissa's eye-roll in the moonlight. "Sometimes you terrify me."

I feel a certain exasperation, tinged with fondness, as I understand. Crissa and I have our own history of romantic rivalry, and I appreciate her skepticism about a new arrival—but really? In the middle of a counterrevolution, with friends in danger, she wants me to prioritize my feelings? "Political marriages aren't romantic."

Crissa throws up her hands. "So, what? He marries this princess, we retreat to Norcia? And that's it?"

I'm not sure what she's getting at. "Yeah, *that's it*. What else is there?"

Crissa exhales through her nose. "I don't know, revolt?"

For a second, I think she's joking. Then I realize she's staring at me, wide-eyed. As are the rest of the Guardians. I think I just snorted.

"I'm serious," Crissa says. "The Bassileans haven't taken the southern coast yet. With enough rogue Guardians and a good jailbreak of dragons, we could stage a resistance from Harbortown. I've got friends in the garrison there. Damos wasn't interested in offering food aid to Callipolis, they've got a new administration that's on an isolationist streak. But with Bassilea's occupation, I'm willing to bet they'd pay attention now—"

The scale of what she suggests is dizzying. Another Bassilean War. Haven't we read enough about the carnage the first two wrought?

"The Bassilean occupation was voted in by a legitimate Assembly, Crissa."

"Which was stupid—" Alexa protests.

"No one's denying that."

"If you lead the resistance, you'd lend us legitimacy," Crissa insists. "Firstrider, Commander of the Aerial Fleet. And if we got Lee, we'd have the Protector-designate, too. Against what, a half-vacant Triarchy and a foreign princess? We could push them out of the capital."

"Until Freyda's goliathan lays waste to the Ferrish Plain with half a breath and her reinforcements arrive from Vask. She has an *empire* at her back."

The other riders are watching our argument like it's an exchange of dragonfire. Crissa says, "If we could get Damos to turn up, so would we."

Aela's hackles are rising as I lose my temper, but none of them can see her in the dark. "And turn this into a proxy war? Our citizens dying, our villages turned to battlefields, so two empires can play capture the flag over our dead? How would that be *better*?"

Alexa speaks up, her voice hardening. "Anything's better than vassalage to the dragonborn."

Really? Alexa, from her cushy house on the Janiculum, wants to lecture me on what it's like to bear the yoke? I round on her. "You speaking from personal authority on that point, Alexa?"

Aela lets out a growl. Alexa takes a quick step backward. Somebody lets out a nervous titter at my comeback that sounds birdlike in the dark. I have the suspicion Crissa's eyeing my clothes again, and I want to snap: *What are you looking at?* But when her skyfish whimpers, she loosens her folded arms to place a gentle palm on Phaedra's glimmering side. Her voice is clipped with exhaustion.

"Annie's right. Damos can't save us. And this isn't a war we can undertake until it's one we know how to win."

She still doesn't quite see it. "If Lee has Freyda's ear, we won't need a war at all."

For a moment after I say it, the only sound is Parron's Spring burbling in the dark. All at once I hear myself. I remember Leon meeting my eyes: *You'll tell your father's friends down in the village?* A hand stroking my hair so gently as he said it. *When you try to defy us, we take everything.*

Same old message, and I'm still delivering it, just like Leon wanted me to.

"Either way," I say, my throat tight, Aela's muzzle against my curled palm, "we've got to get the Guardians out."

Crissa's nodding. "Tell us what you need."

18

—

IXION'S TRIUMPH

DELO

NORCIA

After his first drunk visit, Griff comes by again. He talks about Julia, he talks about Agga, and sometimes I have trouble keeping track of who is who. When he needs it, I walk him home. We never touch more than that. He continues ignoring me during the day.

Why am I putting up with it? I suppose I've begun to think I deserve what this island gives me.

He visits so often that word gets out, and then the rumors start.

I first get wind of it in conversation with Seanan of Clan Kraken, a hero from the Liberation, who oversees harbor transition and is my chief contact for procuring the day's catch to feed the Norcian fleet. Evidently, he takes an interest in my romantic life.

"Is it true you're Griff Gareson's—"

It's an anatomical slur, set in the passive voice, that I have to parse to make sense of: There are limits to my Norish. And then a widening vista of new hells present themselves as I understand. This is a form of targeting I'm not prepared for; such labels are considered, among dragonborn, hickish.

"We take turns," I tell him, which makes Seanan laugh, but he still grins at me in a way I don't like, in a way that makes me calculate my size and weight against his. I'm glad when I have the cart filled and can wheel it away from the docks.

The next day, Fionna, Roxana's former squire, joins my side as I make my way from one lair to the next with the morning feed. Aside from the greedy snorts of dragons roasting their breakfast, the only other sounds are Duck's and Lena's laughter as they prep fish in the workroom at the far end of the corridor. "You give it to them like that, you'll lose a hand," Fionna warns.

"Show me, if you're so good at it."

She takes the bucket and turns it, protecting her hand, before emptying fish into a salivating aurelian's trough. "Are they always so insufferable?"

It takes me a moment to realize she means Duck and Lena, not the dragons guzzling fish. Lena's snort carries down the corridor. I shrug. "Young love, all that." At Fionna's disgusted noise, I smile.

"Speaking of young love"—she passes the pail back to me and catches her breath with a hand to her hip—"I hear Griff's been visiting you at night."

"Seems like the whole island's heard."

Still, I'm relieved to hear none of Seanan's salacious curiosity in her voice, and it confirms my guess that the squires knew something about our tryst even before the Liberation.

"I'm worried about him," Fionna says. "All the squires are."

"You mean the Woad-riders?" I tease gently.

Fionna blushes at her slip, and the burn scar across the side of her face becomes a streak of white. She follows me as I make my way down to the stalls. "He sleeps all day. He doesn't speak. You're the only one he's been known to seek out in weeks. Do you think you could—"

"Talk sense into him?"

Fionna grimaces, as if even she hears how *talking sense* into

Griff Gareson sounds ludicrous when said aloud. Griff's never let himself be talked into sense. It's his defining feature.

Her hand is on her waist again, bracing it. I've been at parties where Roxana joked about cutting the pregnancy out of Fionna herself. *Slut thinks we don't know.* Today she makes no effort to disguise how her belly strains against her flamesuit. "The Woadriders have been delaying the kingsmoot as long as we can," she says, "to put Griff forward for it. But the other clans are getting restless, and the elders will call it with or without him. Bran said Seanan's likely to be put forward for Kraken."

"The one who runs the docks transition?" Griff in line to become the first High King of Free Norcia is not as hard to imagine as it should be, given he was once my servant. Seanan, on the other hand . . . I rotate buckets and reach for the next mackerel. "He's a bully."

"Exactly. But the story goes he slit the Greatlord's throat during the Liberation, and he survived the pen before that. Not to mention, he's sober. Griff's not . . ."

Here. I wonder if that's the word she gropes for.

We've come to the last stall, the empty one I choose on most days not to look at, but today I make myself see it. Gephyra's stall. She's so far away now, stabled in Callipolis, I can't feel her at all. Whenever I think I've stopped missing her, the ache rises again.

"I'm not here to involve myself in Norcian politics," I tell Fionna.

That night, anonymous Norcians give me the jumping I've been waiting for.

I'd been expecting it since I heard Seanan say that slur, and it unfolds as predictably as the second act of a Silver Age penny drama: They put a bag over my head, haul me off the main thoroughfare of Clan Nag, land blows with kicks and what I guess are a bag of oyster shells, and ask me if I'll get my boyfriend to save me. *Heard he was Gareson's even before the Liberation,* someone says. *Where's your dragon now, Skyfish?* another asks in broken Dragontongue.

I stagger home and lean into Griff's foggy excuse for a mirror to inspect the visible damage. There's little. I suspect broken ribs but can't find more than a bloody nose, though it now hurts to move. The most infuriating thing is my own relief it wasn't worse. Though I suspect the mildness of the beating means it was designed to be repeated.

Going to tell your boyfriend?

Approaching Griff with the problem is unthinkable. I didn't see their faces; I'd have to repeat that stupid, hickish passive participle; and anyway—Griff doesn't deserve to be asked for help. Not when he hasn't bothered speaking to me sober in weeks. Despite what my anonymous friends down the alley might think, I still have self-respect.

In any case, Griff would just as likely laugh. I can imagine what he'd think of it. *What's the matter, dragonlord doesn't know how to take a beating? Toughen up.*

"Uncle?" Sty's crawled out of bed to find me.

"You should be in bed."

"I miss Mother," he says.

His lip's trembling. It's been freshly busted. I look at him and think: We make quite the pair.

The next morning, in a terrifically bad mood, aching all over, I make my way to the lairs to find Duck excavating the storerooms in their entirety. He sticks his head out and beams at the sight of me.

"Just in time," he says. "Some of this stuff is too heavy for me and Lena."

We're in a sorry state if I'm the fit one. "What's going on?"

Duck looks surprised at the question. "We're opening more stalls. Antigone will be bringing dragons with her."

So far, to my knowledge, there has been total silence from our contacts over on the mainland. Duck's optimism is hard to handle on the best of mornings, but with bruised ribs it's nearly intolerable. "Has there been any indication that's likely?"

Duck just shrugs. "She said she was going to do it."

Evidently, that's enough for him.

LEE
CALLIPOLIS

Ixion plans to announce the Triarchal Ascension in the People's Square at the end of the procession. What he doesn't know is that he's not the only one planning to make an announcement. Freyda does, as well. With our engagement, Ixion's status as triarch will be reduced to that of a figurehead and from there, neutralized.

And I'll be—engaged.

It's not a prospect I've ever had to contemplate; the Guardian vows eliminated marriage as a possibility when I was nine. But now, grasping to comprehend it for the first time, my thoughts go, inexorably, to the man I'm usually so good at not thinking about. Facing the roles I knew my father in—with a family, a wife, *children*—imagining myself stepping into such roles myself—it's all I can do not to recoil. The rot extends like a network of fungus underfoot: not just to my memories of my father and my family but to the prospect of any future where I follow in his footsteps.

The truth about my father taints this future just as much as it taints the past.

I find myself turning instead to obsessive, blasphemous thoughts of Annie. When I dare to imagine it—the wrong girl replaced by the right one, Annie with stars in her eyes spread across a bed that is ours—even the hint of rot isn't enough to make me recoil.

Instead, I feel like kicking something.

That's when I remember all the ways Callipolis will be served by a match with Freyda.

One of the few things I'm allowed to do freely is roam ministry corridors, which have been relocated to buildings in the Outer Palace. What's left of the government is in shambles. Departments have been gutted, their staff have been fired or worse, replaced by Clover men and talentless hacks whose chief recommendation is loyalty to the Triarchy; it does not seem to be a coincidence that none of them are lowborn.

Lo Teiran, the Callipolan poet laureate who conspired with the Order of the Black Clover, has replaced Miranda Hane as Minister of Propaganda. He has undertaken a dramatic reversal of policy where—instead of banning Dragontongue literature that contains triarchist and blood-determinative sympathies—the previously censored texts are translated into Callish and distributed in libraries and bookstores on the Lower Bank. The *Aurelian Cycle* goes from being banned to bestselling overnight, and promoted alongside it are books celebrating a mythical conqueror known as the Skysung Queen. New editions of the fairy tales are released where the Queen on the cover is depicted with a veiled face, a long brown braid, and an oversized dragon.

Among the other departments, the few officials who remain from the last regime remember Guardians doing rounds and invite me into their spaces with welcome. But even the best intentioned of these seem overworked and overwhelmed. Freyda and the

Bassileans bring grain, but her satraps in Vask are already beginning to needle Callipolis for payment, and even with the revenue of Ixion's fee-based school model, we are ill-equipped to answer them.

This ship of state is leaking, drifting with a faulty rudder toward shallow ground, and it will only be a matter of time before it begins to sink.

In a particularly torturous twist, Freyda's and my agreement is arrived at with Annie as our messenger. Freyda's final decision comes two days before the Triumph: *The riders can be sentenced to exile. But their dragons are forfeit.* Annie delivers it to my bedchamber.

"Well, I'd have been surprised if she agreed to let a hostile fleet fly off. Lee, are you listening?"

She's caught me staring at her face.

"Yeah, your . . . hair's lightening up. You should redo it."

A blush spreads up her neck, burying freckles, disappearing into her hair. I want to trace the heat with my fingers. There are so many reasons to move forward with this plan, but alone in a room with Annie, the single reason not to overshadows them all. It overshadows them so much that I have trouble remembering what we're talking about.

"I'll redo it when I visit Megara." Annie adjusts the cap, businesslike despite her blush. "Aela and I can take care of the dragons. She's been figuring out the tunnel systems connecting the nests to the drainage canals. If she can get them to the gate under Pytho's Keep, Crissa and the others can escort them from there."

Stop staring at her. I reach for parchment, pen, and any comment that will make me not sound like an idiot. "I didn't realize you could feel Aela from here."

Annie waves a hand with a grimace. "A bit? Sometimes. When I really . . . concentrate."

I scribble out an answer to Freyda and stamp it with one of my father's old seals. Annie steps closer to take the note. I am aware of the space between us as if it were radiating heat.

"I'll just take this back to her, then."

The sounds of the Stormscourge Bastards' laughter filters through the closed door from the parlor: masculine, loud, inebriated. Annie scowls at the sound; it's not hard for me to imagine why. "Do you want me to escort you out?"

"I think that would draw more attention to this meeting than either of us wants."

But still she hesitates. I think it's out of reluctance to run the gantlet of the Bastards' party until she says, "I'll go straight to the nests after the announcement is made."

So this is goodbye.

She seems unwilling to step closer, and words have failed me. I reach for her hand, and as she realizes I want to reel her in, she breathes, "Freyda?"

It takes me a blank heartbeat to understand her. First, with tenderness, the realization: Annie's thinking about the other girl. And then, the horribleness of it. Already, she thinks of me as belonging to someone else.

From now on.

"She said we would both be free to conduct our own affairs."

Little consolation in our case, with Annie's best hope for survival to go on the run, but for these few stolen minutes—?

"Well, in that case," says Annie faintly, and kisses me.

For a moment there is nothing but this: her tea-stained hair clumping in my hands, the chill of her fingers pulling at my shirt, the taste of her lips on mine. But at the moment where I pull her closer, I feel her sigh on my cheek. She steps back and straightens her cap without meeting my eyes. I have the impression she's trying not to blink.

"I should go," she says.

I'm left staring at a closed door.

ANNIE

The preparations for the Triumph absorb my attention in the days leading up to our escape, which is a merciful distraction from the fact that I'm about to break my own heart.

Really, Crissa's right. I've outdone myself.

My every waking minute is spent on errands. Betsuna sends me to the Palace kitchens to finalize a program for the feast that will follow the procession; into Highmarket, to check on banners and florals commissioned for the occasion; and between these, to serve Freyda as she hosts meeting after meeting in her parlor.

I also squeeze in final arrangements of my own. On my way back from a Highmarket seamstress, I leave a note for Megara Roper to pass to Crissa sur Phaedra. Megara heaves a sigh at the inconvenience when I ask her to re-dye my hair, but seems happy enough to gossip while she does it. When asked about the Winnowing Tournaments, she flutters her hand like a faltering scale. "Some are whispering foul play. Others remember that Lee shot to the top of the Firstrider Tournaments we had, too. Technically, Callipolis has never seen a dragonborn defeated in the arena."

"I beat Parcival," I point out. Power and I faced off during semifinals.

"But Lee sur Power destroyed you after that."

"Because during our match, they *sparked*."

"That doesn't help your argument."

Sparking is one of the legendary proofs of dragonborn supremacy, rooted in the persistent myth that only dragonborn blood can spark a fleet. I wrinkle my nose at the smell of vinegar and reflect that many would be surprised to learn Griff Gareson sparked first in his fleet among dragonborn like Ixion and Julia.

They also might be surprised to find out that Ixion's sparkforsaken.

But that particular discovery—made sparring him during the Midwinter Attack—seems to be one Ixion keeps very close to the vest.

"Annie," says Megara seriously, "you should challenge him."

I passed a dozen pictures of my own face on my way here. Rewards of increasingly high numbers are being offered in the *People's Paper* broadsheets and on posters plastered on city walls: Ixion will do anything to have me in hand for the Triumph. I would be his crowning trophy.

"Do you want me to get your boyfriend out of that cell or not?"

At the mention of Cor, Megara's lips thin to a line and she drops the subject. When the time comes, her job will be to help refugees, including the Sutter family and her own, flee north to safety. When I ask her if she wants to get out as well, she shakes her head.

"I've got work to do here."

Her old self-importance inspires the familiar urge to strangle her. "Running puff pieces on Freyda Bassileon must be pretty fulfilling work."

I've been skimming a proof of the *People's Paper* as my hair dries. It's full of character assassinations of Guardians; sympathetic portraits of dragonborn, whom we've apparently misunderstood all along; and lengthy meditations on the reasons Atreus's regime failed.

Megara snaps the paper from my hands. "More fulfilling than firing on civilians? You can go now."

I drape the damp towel on her stool and leave with still-wet hair. But the headline FIVE WAYS FREYDA BASSILEON RESEMBLES THE SKYSUNG QUEEN remains stuck in my head, unwanted.

Every time I see mention of the mythical queen, my heart twists with thoughts of my father. They've taken so much from me, I think, do they have to take this, too? A sneaking voice answers: *As if a queen's story were one you had any right to.*

Who brought bread to the people? Freyda. Who will marry the dragonlord I love? Freyda. If there's a heroine in this story, it isn't me. My days as Firstrider of Callipolis are over; the brief history I made will be erased; and most of the time, when I consider it, fading from the spotlight is something I long for.

Most of the time. Every once in a while, I imagine what my father would say if I told him that I failed so badly as Firstrider of Callipolis, I ran away.

You and me, Dad, we do what it takes to protect the ones we love.

During the night, I lie awake, stretching out my senses to feel Aela slithering through the tunnels below me, learning their routes. I wake with headaches and blood dried down my cheeks: It seems that the strain of finding her, over such a distance, makes my nose bleed.

"Ew," Vicky says as she hands me a handkerchief.

One day before the Triumph, I find her sister, Verra, in what was the refectory of the Guardians' quarters but is now a mess hall for the new dragonkeepers. I tell myself this will be the final fool's mission.

Assuming the Guardians get the amnesty Lee's requested, and Aela successfully frees the dragons she's searching for, the reunion between the two parties will be aided significantly by a certain piece of hardware that each rider has had confiscated.

"Richard really wants his summoner."

Verra chokes on her tea. "Abbie, I don't think he's allowed that."

"He doesn't mean to use it! Just, you know, have it as a souvenir."

Verra makes a sympathetic noise, like she's contemplating a sad puppy. "I heard Lord Edmund keeps the Guardians' summoners. Maybe you could ask someone on his staff?"

Lord Edmund. I could gag.

I wait until the dragonborn dinner hour before letting myself into the master suite of the Stormscourge wing. Edmund's chambers are a disarray of stinking armor, recovered treasures from patrician estates he's been dragooning, and half-filled glasses of alcohol and cigar butts. Either the staff in charge of tidying gave up, or Edmund prefers it this way.

I've just begun rifling through his cluttered drawers when a noise from the dragon perch outside makes me jump.

I left the door to the apartments ajar, but forgot the Firemouth balcony.

The glass door swings open to let in Edmund, followed by Power. For a moment I think they've been drinking: Both are a little heavy-footed, and their laughter's slurred. Then I see the dilated pupils and hear the whoosh of dragons taking off for the nests. They're spilled over.

"Bloody sparkfire," Edmund says, gripping the back of his neck and rolling his eyes back.

Are they drunk, too? From the smell of them, they might be both spilled over *and* inebriated. I suppose there's no reason not to combine the activities, though we hardly had the opportunity in Guardian training.

As Edmund's pupils contract, they find me. He emits an obscenity.

Power turns and stills. "Oh," he says. "You."

"You know her?"

Power leers at me. "In a manner of speaking." He starts laughing, like a joke's only now making sense to him. "Are *you* the one
they're saying is Richard Nearhallserf's girl?"

"They don't speak Dragontongue. She's Richard's? I keep seeing her go into Leo's rooms."

Power is swaying as he grips the door handle. He lifts his eyes
to the ceiling like he's willing the brocade to stop spinning. Then
he looks at me and smiles. "Yeah, well, these highland girls really
get around."

Power knows I understand his Dragontongue perfectly. I blink,
willing my fists not to curl, willing neither fear nor fury to show in
my face.

You want to rat me out, get it over with.

Power lunges forward, surprisingly fast for his sloppy movements, and seizes the back of my neck before I have a chance to
move. I've been manhandled by Power once before. He's so much
stronger that he barely feels me struggle, and when his fingers
tighten on my neck, I stop trying. He bends me over, his weight
blanketing my back, and growls in Callish in my ear.

"What are you doing?"

My eyes are watering from lack of air. Edmund chuckles. I hear
a cork being pulled from a bottle and liquor poured into a glass.

The last time Power and I stood this close, he confessed feelings
for me, and when I rebuffed him, he told me to go back to Lee like
the *good little peasant I was.* I'm acutely aware of Power's hand on
my hip. Holding me against him, making a show of violation with
deliberate, clumsy fingers.

But Edmund's watching, drinking steadily, and Power hasn't ratted me out yet.

Which means, in his own twisted way, he's covering for me. He doesn't seem to mind that it comes with an excuse to be insulting, but then, when has Power ever passed up a chance for that? He's got his own reasons to cozy up to the dragonborn, no doubt starting with saving his own skin—but he's also got friends in the Guardian corps, just like I do. We don't have to be on speaking terms for him to help me.

"I'm looking for the summoners."

"Oh, I see." Power's sarcasm tickles the hair in my ear. "On whose orders?"

Mine, you imbecile, I want to snap, and then I understand what he might just be getting at. "Freyda's."

Power shoves me from him. He translates what I just said to Edmund in Dragontongue. Edmund's face sours. "Freyda's got no right to send a maid snooping round my room."

"Pretty sure Freyda's goliathan gives her the right to do whatever the hell she wants."

Edmund jerks a thumb at a drawer to the left of the one I was going through when they arrived. "In there."

I push aside tangled socks with shaking fingers, retrieve the locked box, and then dare to push my luck. "The key, my lords?"

For a second, as Power blinks at me, I think he might hit me. Then he translates for Edmund, and Edmund slaps the key in my hand with a slur that wasn't covered in ten years' study of literary Dragontongue, but is clear enough from context. Power snorts. He's already turned away to fill a second tumbler.

Outside, I make my way, as quickly as possible, to the maids' washroom. There I slump inside the stall, massage my neck until my hands stop shaking, and when my breathing has calmed, I fit the key in the lock and peel open the box. Silver and gold glints inside, the wristbands of Guardians and the summoners of a fleet.

So much power contained so easily in one safe.

I wrap the box in my apron to hide the fine inlay and make my way to the menservants' quarters, where they're changing from day to evening uniform. "From home," I tell Rock, pressing the box into his surprised arms when he comes to the door. "A gift from my mam."

"But your mam's—oh."

He stows it, then accompanies me up the servants' stairs into the courtyard above. We can hear strings tuning in the Hall of Plenty. "I'm on cleanup," I tell him, and he walks me down the colonnade to the servants' entrance to the hall. Neither of us looks at the main doors, through which we once walked in state. "Everything's in order. Freyda's set to pardon at the Triumph; don't summon until she puts you on the road. Crissa and I should have the dragons loose by then, your summoners will help us find you. Once we're in the air, we'll cross to Norcia."

Rock squints past me, biting his lip. "And my family?"

Rock's family live in Thornham, in the Near Highlands. "We're sending word to all of the Guardian families to get out. You'll see them there."

Rock's smile, caught in the torchlight of the spring evening, brightens his face like sunlight.

The following morning before sunrise, I'm helping Freyda dress for the Triumph when she jerks round and stares at me. The layers of buttons and underlayers a royal is subjected to are interminable and confusing, even more so for high ceremony, and I'm at first worried I've pinned her instead of her sarafan.

"What happened there?" she asks. In her mirror, I'm able to

make out the marks from Power's fingers on my neck. They turned yellow overnight.

The question is in Dragontongue; I'm not expected to understand it. Betsuna, reading over the day's agenda, gives me a once-over glance and, judging by her scowl, finds the bruises leave me lacking. "I'll have an alternate maid brought in—"

"No need." Freyda waves at me to continue. "Tell the girl she can help herself to my powder once she's done."

Betsuna translates, and I make full obeisance in thanks. It's cover enough to hide my surprise. Freyda snaps her fingers to bring me back to my feet while murmuring to herself, "*Un*believable."

The Triumph's procession arranges itself at noon, outside the Triumphal Gate of the Aurelian Wall. Freyda and Ixion proceed in a chariot drawn by Ixion's dragon, Niter. I am one of the maidservants following Freyda on foot, a veil over my sarafan according to the practices of her court; we are followed by the cavalry of Freyda's Little Immortals, armed in leather brigandine and longbows. Their technology would seem charmingly outdated were it not being sported by an occupying army. After these, the dragons: Obizuth, like a skulking whale, her wings arched to avoid toppling roofs; the rest of the Clover fleet, led by Lee and Power; and finally, on foot, come the conquered Guardians.

In the earliest days, the conquered dragonriders of the Stormscourge and Skyfish clans were the chief spectacle of Triumphs, a custom brought by our Aurelian invaders; later, after Unification, tributes came from conquests in the Bassilean Wars and the vassal islands the Three Families acquired. Today, the tributes are my riders.

They're led stumbling in chains behind the Bastards who defeated them in the Winnowing Tournaments, and they're heckled. Lotus, among the forsworn patricians, sweats visibly and turns, more than once, to crane his neck for a glimpse of Rock's slow steps. But Rock doesn't look at him.

By the end of the procession the Guardians are dripping with bits of tomato that vendors, positioned on Ixion's orders, sold to the crowd. Actors have been hired to infiltrate the crowd and guarantee the mood. Only a few citizens contradict the vitriol that prevails on the streets, racing up to wipe a Guardian's forehead or offer water. But those who are caught by Ixion's soldiers are led away.

The spectacle is shameful, but perhaps most shameful of all is that I'm safe, veiled, unknown, while my riders suffer.

A taste that isn't my own fills my mouth: the crunch, the tang, of hot iron breaking in my jaws. I feel wetness above my lip and reach under the veil to touch it. My fingers come away red: My nose is bleeding.

Somewhere far away, inside the Firemouth, with none of Ixion's dragons there to find her or obstruct her, Aela has begun to break the chains of the Guardians' dragons.

All that's left is to lead them out, tonight.

LEE

The procession I've grown up watching is the Palace Day Parade. But it's only now, seeing this full splendor, that I understand how pale a comparison that parade was to the Triumphs, and how inspired by them. Our procession stretches for miles. The Triumphal Way, the main thoroughfare that leads from the main gate of the Aurelian Walls to the People's Square in Highmarket and across the Fer into the Palace, was built for this. I have the unwanted thought, which I resist, that Atreus's regime was the aberration, and this is how it's meant to be. This is what this city was made for.

For the first time in my life, the crowds swell with the name my father gave me, and a small part of me finds this change to be— tolerable.

The procession lasts the day. By the time we're led up onto the dais of the People's Square, it's dusk. The platform on which Ixion stands is the same one from which Atreus delivered speeches glorifying his Revolution. Where my father's dragon, ten years ago, was beheaded.

Today, Ixion speaks instead. Freyda and I take either side, Niter and Pallor behind us. Annie stands in Freyda's household train, indistinguishable among the many veils; the conquered Guardians wait in supplication at the base of the dais. My palms are slick with sweat: The scene is something from my father's life, not mine, the luster and grandeur of the old order, and I am one more set piece in it. The Guardians, transformed in their humiliation, complete the picture.

Atreus may not be officially dead. But with this scene, he is erased.

For a time, the flame you carry may have to go underground.

Can I appreciate this return to glory, and still carry that flame?

Ixion speaks of the Triumphal Return. Of a new era that Freyda's partnership brings. Of the retribution he is owed. Of the lone duty he takes, as Firstrider and, soon, as Triarch.

To do that, he says, he must have loyalty.

He lifts an arm into the air and Obizuth spreads her wings. They shadow the People's Square, blot the sun, as she arches her back. Citizens are screaming, pointing up at her as they shrink like field mice before a cat. When she rears and kicks from the ground, we feel the drumbeat of her launch under our feet.

As she circles overhead, her fire fills the sky. The clouds found by it turn to shimmering rain, wetting the neighborhoods one by one: the Janiculum, Highmarket, Scholars Row, Cheapside and Southside, the Manufacturing District. Citizens are laughing, stretching their hands up to feel the Great Dragon make the sky weep.

Like the Skysung Queen! they shout.

Beside me, Freyda sways. Beneath the veil, her pupils are so full with spillover, the whites are no longer visible. She's black-eyed.

Tethering. I've heard it described in history books. Goliathans are so large a breed that flying at full speed, they could suffocate their rider. Thus in war, and in training, they are rarely ridden. Their movements in the air are controlled by their rider on the ground, through a spillover connection—a tether.

But the history books never described these black eyes or the way Freyda's fingers, when they reach up to massage her neck, come away to reveal a spreading web of veins where she has rubbed away concealer from her nape.

The way her lips have parted in a silent scream while she works.

Ixion, busy bestowing titles to the Bastard Grayriders, does not notice Freyda's transformation. "And to you, Edmund Grayheather, we dub Edmund Stormscourge and bestow Farhall and its lands, equal in honor to any heir by marriage . . ."

The mention of my own house passes through my numb ears, barely enough to distract me from the princess and her goliathan. As Obizuth completes her circuit and descends on Pytho's Keep, I reach out a steadying hand to Freyda. She is resplendent in yellow, the color of the Bassilean royal family, like a glowing orb of light. She blinks, her eyes slowly regaining the white rims, her gaze finding mine.

I push aside my growing doubts.

"We need to do it now."

After the recognition of the Grayriders comes the loyalty trials of the Guardians, where they will be asked to bend the knee to the dragonlords and agree to become servants of the Restoration—muzzled as Griff and the humble-riders were—or refuse and face the dragons' firing squad.

They have been arranged in a row before the dais, with the Grayriders facing them.

We can't let it come to that.

Freyda steps forward, laurels on both arms.

"To the victorious in the Long-Awaited Return!"

She crowns first Ixion, then me, with a laurel, and then the Bastards. When they are adorned, she turns back to the square, and folds back her veil to let her smile be seen by the people. For most, it is their first time seeing her face.

"In victory there is life, and in life there is hope for a future for Callipolis. Men and women of this great island, it is my honor today to announce a future sealed today for our two nations."

Ixion turns, preparing to accept her hand.

"Let Bassilea and Callipolis join their greatness together in this union between myself and the Protector-designate, now full Protector of Callipolis."

I extend my hand on Freyda's other side and she takes it. Cheering erupts. Ixion's smile freezes. Freyda turns to me and lifts her chin. Her pupils are still a little too dilated.

It takes a strangled instant to understand what she expects.

I set my lips on hers and taste cool, smooth lips. Their chill makes me think of death. When I lift fingers to touch her nape, I feel her flinch as if I've touched something tender.

She turns back to the crowd, quelling their rising cheers with a lifted arm. Beside us, a sneer curdles Ixion's face. Freyda ignores him.

"In a gesture of goodwill, to honor new beginnings," she goes on, "my betrothed has requested a boon. Those whom you called Guardians kneel now before us, humiliated in their demeaned status. They chose this life of service as children, before they could know the great failings of the man or regime they served. We have no more need of their ineptitude on dragonback. But that does not mean they deserve death. Today, I offer them a new life: one of exile."

Freyda looks upon Rock and Cor and the rest of the conquered Guardians standing chained.

"My guards will escort you, your families, and your friends, to whatever port city you ask, from which you will leave our land and never return."

19

—

SHATTERED GLASS

ANNIE

After the procession, back in the Palace, the dragonborn change into their dinner clothes and freshen up for a banquet that will last the night. Vicky is among the maids filing into Freyda's chambers to help her prepare; I tell her I'll be there directly and then head in the opposite direction.

It's time to go.

The caves below, the cover of darkness: Now is the only chance I'll have to lead the Guardians' dragons to freedom. Even from here, distantly, I can feel Aela's anticipation. She broke the muzzles during the Triumph. She led the dragons down the tunnel to the entrance to Parron's Spring, where Crissa waits. They're ready to go.

All they're waiting for is Rock's summoning from the road and for me.

"Going somewhere?"

A hand grips my arm so tightly, I feel the blood cut off. I look up into the face of Ixion.

"Abigael?" Ixion asks. He's smiling strangely.

"I was just going to—help—the princess—"

"I'm sure she'll understand if I borrow you. I would like to entertain, and my manservant was just sent into exile."

He leads me, fingers manacling my arm, down the corridor. Servants bustling on their own errands glance at us curiously and then avert their eyes.

Back in the Stormscourge wing, he leads me into his parlor.

Lee sits to one side of a table in the center of the room, pale and sweating, still in ceremonial armor. On the other side of the glass wall, Pallor and Niter take up opposite ends of the dragon perch, glaring at each other. At the sight of me, Lee half rises, freezes, and then eases back down into his chair.

"You see?" Ixion tells Lee brightly, shoving me in the direction of the bar. "You can't expect me to celebrate your engagement without proper service. Whiskey for us both, Abigael," he adds in Callish. "Bassilea's finest."

Lee's gaze tracks me beneath knitted brows as I uncork the only bottle whose label is written in Bassilic and fill two tumblers. I approach the table where Lee and Ixion sit facing each other. Lee sits as far back in his chair as his body will allow without tilting it.

"Thank you, Abigael," says Ixion.

He holds his glass up, clinks Lee's, and as Lee lifts his to his lips, Ixion says, "To peasant lovers."

Lee's glass freezes at his lips. Ixion, on the other hand, drains his completely. I stand frozen, halfway between them. Ixion lowers his glass and then, in a swift motion, dashes it to the floor.

It shatters.

Ixion smiles up at me.

"Pick it up," he says.

I look from him to Lee. Lee is sheet-white. I drop to my knees. Ixion laughs softly. Neither boy speaks as I gather shards of broken glass into a shaking hand. When I rise, Ixion's hand darts out again. It takes mine, the one holding the shards.

That's when I realize my mistake. *Pick it up.*

He was speaking in Dragontongue.

Ixion's hand, holding mine holding the shards, starts to squeeze. Glass begins to puncture my palm and fingers. At the same time, I feel something cool against my throat.

Ixion's bootknife presses under my chin.

Lee says, "Ixion."

Ixion says, "Good to see you again, Antigone."

Blood drips down my wrist. Lee is on his feet. "Let go of her."

"Your little ruse was *so close* to working." Ixion tightens his grip on my hand as he speaks, wringing it over the glass like a drying rag. The cool line of the knife is steady on my throat. "If it hadn't been for Freyda taking me to task at breakfast for throttling one of her maids—which most regrettably I *hadn't done*—Edmund would've never told me about little Abigael of Thornham on an errand for summoners Freyda never sent her to fetch, not to mention visits to Leo and to Richard—you *bitch*!"

So preoccupied was he turning my right hand into raw meat, he neglected to restrain the left. In a split second, before he can react, I've plunged it down the collar of my dress, retrieved my Guardian wristband, and lifted it around the knife at my throat to blow into Aela's summoner.

Ixion yanks the summoner away, but too late: From deep below, I can feel her rising to the call.

And I can smell the fading scent of Crissa sur Phaedra and the others vanishing out the tunnel and into the open night.

They're out.

Inside the room, Lee lunges. Ixion is knocked sideways—the bootknife spills out of his hand and he shouts *Guards*—Pallor and Niter slam against each other and a stray tail slings sideways, leveling the glass of the balcony door like a sheet of water—Clover men stream into the room, pulling Lee off Ixion—

We are surrounded, dragons behind me on the balustrade, guards in front of me and on either side.

Last of all comes Power, hauled in by one of Freyda's Immortals with his arms pinned behind his back. "Come to think of it," he says at the sight of me, "she does look familiar."

Ixion rounds on him. "I will have that *tramp* you call a mother strung up—"

Power's eyes bug from his head. His voice goes raw. "She's usually *ginger*! I'm loyal, I can *prove* I'm loyal—"

"Enough."

Freyda Bassileon has entered the room. Her hair half undone, wearing nothing but her dressing-room gown, she still manages to sweep into the room with such authority that our attention is immediate. For the first time since I've entered her employ, she looks at me as though she sees me. "Antigone."

The sound of my name rings like a challenge. I dispense with titles or obeisance as I straighten.

"Freyda."

Freyda's lip turns up in wry acknowledgment. She looks past me to Ixion. "While you were so busy doing *this*"—she casts a disinterested, disgusted glance at my bleeding hand—"I hope someone was sent to prevent the dragons escaping, or to delay the caravan of departing Guardians so they don't have a chance to *reunite*."

Lucian Orthos steps forward with a bow. "The Grayriders are on it, Your Divine Highness. The caravan's already past the Aurelian Walls, but it's been recalled. And we're blocking off the Firemouth and the arena gate."

Freyda looks once again at me, and whatever she sees in my carefully blank expression makes her exhale through pursed lips.

She asks with the air of a teacher drilling a slow student: "And are those the only exits from the dragon nests?"

Orthos blinks. Ixion's jaw loosens.

Freyda says, "Will someone please sound the alarm."

Lee bursts out laughing. Outside, Pallor and Niter still tussle, but Pallor's made a show of tiring. Niter has him on his back. Lee looks up at me, eyes wet from mirth and more than that.

"Do it now," he says in Callish.

As Freyda's commandeered the room, I've backed slowly toward the balustrade, glass crunching beneath my feet. My dripping hand leaves a trail of blood across the floor.

Aela is right below us.

"Are you—?"

"I'll be fine. *Now.*"

As Pallor rolls over, pinning Niter under him in a surprise recovery, I turn and make a running leap. Over their entwined tails, onto the balustrade railing—and fall.

For a moment, light spins around me as the interior windows of the Inner Palace stream past and the darkness of the nests rises to meet me.

And then I slam onto Aela's back. Crissa has her saddled. My helmet, flamesuit, and gear are tucked in her saddlebag. She purrs with pleasure at my weight as I gasp for breath.

"You did it, Aela."

The Guardians and their dragons are free. With any luck, they'll be streaming toward Norcia within the hour.

But we're not done yet.

As the alarm bells finally sound, as we rise from the Firemouth into the sight of Grayriders waiting to trap the Guardians they thought would flee through the front door, Aela and I gain speed. I tear off the maid's uniform with clumsy, blood-sticky fingers and pull one limb at a time through the legs of the flamesuit as we leave the Great Palace behind. Last of all I yank on dragonriding boots and hook them in the stirrups.

We won't try to find Crissa and the others with the Bastards on our tail. But we can buy our riders time.

LEE

As soon as Annie throws herself off the balustrade, Pallor's jaws close on Niter's jugular. Ixion reaches for his own throat as he feels it.

Freyda's hand grips my arm. "Call your dragon off Niter."

Her eyes have turned black. The lines are spreading from her nape to her jawline, climbing like tendrils, as her veins darken. Her voice rattles like it comes from the bottom of a well. Somewhere above us, nesting on Pytho's Keep, a goliathan is stirring.

Pallor releases Niter, who slumps, rasping.

Her black eyes on me, Freyda lifts fingers and snaps them. "Leave us," she says to her guards. The Little Immortals bow stiffly, their leather brigandines doubling tubelike from the waist, before backing from the room.

Ixion gets to his feet, still fingering his throat. He jerks a thumb at me. "We should *off* him."

Freyda's voice regains human timbre. "You have other matters to attend to, my lord Ixion."

Ixion shoves Power. "You want to prove your loyalty? Find me the caravan."

"At once, my lord," says Power, scrambling to the balustrade to summon Eater.

He and Ixion disappear on dragonback into the night, leaving

Pallor panting in the broken glass outside, and Freyda and I alone within. The black tendrils slowly retreat down her neck. For a moment, the only sound is the alarm bells tolling, vibrating under my feet.

The sound of our triumph.

We did it. We got them out.

And I'm staring into the black eyes of a woman I'm pretty sure is about to set her goliathan on me.

"This was not our deal," Freyda says. "I hoped to have you at my side, ruling this city together. I can't if you're undermining my politics with subterfuge."

"I understand that," I say through gritted teeth.

In the original plan, my connection to Annie would not have been revealed. The fact that this conversation is taking place at all feels like a slow and unnecessary punishment. *Just finish me.*

"Do you?" Freyda lifts an arm and points toward the balcony where Pallor waits. "Let me make the choice clear. If I don't take Callipolis by right of marriage with its Protector, then I will claim it with Ixion and his lackeys as my viceroys. This is the last chance I give you to change that course, Leo. This is your last chance to choose me, *this*."

It takes slow heartbeats to understand her.

Freyda will still have me, is willing to continue this engagement, even with this compromising scene on my record.

I still have the choice.

If it can be called a choice, when for once the stars align: For once duty and ambition are the same; I can be a dragonlord's son and the next Protector both, carry the flame of my father and Atreus at once and walk side by side with a princess into the future.

This is a chance I'd be mad to turn my back on.

Except—

Except Annie just flew the coop with half of Ixion's Grayriders on her tail.

And Freyda hasn't sent Pallor from the balustrade. He waits, saddled from the Triumph, not armed for war—but ready for flight.

"Or?"

"Or you can take your chances with your dragon." Freyda indicates Pallor and speaks through thin lips. "I like you, Leo. I was prepared to risk a great deal on liking you. But I have my limits. Either you leave your peasant paramour to her fate and go with me to our feast *now*, to celebrate our engagement—or you get on the dragon, go after that girl, and hope our shots miss. There will be no coming back."

I feel sweat on my fingers.

She'll have backup, I tell myself.

Except I know as soon as I think it that she won't. With the Bastards on her tail, Annie won't try to reunite with Crissa and the others. She'll head as far away from them as she can. Her dominant hand was bleeding, making flying difficult, and if the loss of blood is sustained, she'll be weakened when she is outnumbered.

She'll sacrifice herself for her riders, as a commander should.

And suddenly no ambition to lead, no duty to my city, no length of Guardian training matters like the plight of a single girl.

Atreus's final conversation returns to me in its entirety: *Will you light a lantern and climb, hoping that your light will be enough for those below?* he asked. *Or will you choose to light the way for someone else?*

I told myself for a while, cornered and in desperation, that climb I must. But now I remember I was never supposed to climb. The way was always for Annie, for the first lowborn Firstrider of

Callipolis, who now flees routed, hunted, and condemned by the regime her people died to overthrow.

The light was always meant to shine for her.

I have the feeling, for the first time in a very long time, that I know exactly where I'm supposed to be. And it's not at a betrothal dinner.

Freyda's eyes glint, like she sees the answer in my face. Something like amusement, or maybe disappointment, that she masks almost at once. For the first time I glimpse the wound she hides at the root of it all: loneliness.

"I thought not," she says.

"I'm sorry—"

But Freyda lifts a hand, disinterested.

"Good luck getting past Obizuth."

20

—

FLIGHT

ANNIE

There are five Grayriders on our tail.

Two stormscourge and, in advance of them, three skyfish. They will be the Skyfish Bastards: Ariel, Bardolph, Cadwal—nicknamed the ABCs by the staff—natural sons by the same father as Power. One of the Stormscourge riders, I recognize by his dragon's girth, will be Edmund, Lee's half brother. The other Stormscourge is either Titus or Angelo, their curly-haired cousins.

Five Grayriders on our tail means five fewer on Crissa's.

It's an overcast night and usually we'd go high, bury Aela in the cloud cover and hope to lose them in the darkness. But tonight, I'm not trying to lose them.

So we ride low. Skimming over the Aurelian Walls, the shanty-towns that sprawl from the gates and give way to fields and villages. We skim low enough to see our rippling reflection in the canals that cut straight lines across the farmland between northern port towns and the gushing Fer. Snows have already begun to melt, leaving the river swollen, a black ribbon winding toward the highlands.

Crissa planned to steer the Guardians east, to find the North Sea by way of the Driftless Dunes. So I'll go west by way of the Fer, for as long as I can keep up the ruse.

I have the thought, as I slam a heel into Aela's side and lead the

Grayriders away, that in the air again, dodging enemy dragonfire, I'm finally doing what I'm good at.

I'm going to miss this.

The skyfish gain on us first. Aurelians are fast, and Aela's one of the fastest, but skyfish are always faster. One from above, one coming in from behind to my left, the other to my right. They're pushing us to maximum speed, which prevents Aela from getting a good weave. As they close range, I open every coolant valve in my flamesuit. Crissa's stocked it.

The firing starts.

We're close enough for a flick roll. As heat erupts over my shoulder, Aela's wings contract and we curl under the other dragon. I didn't have a chance to properly tether my boots; I have to hope they stay hooked in the stirrups. We pass so close over fields of the Ferrish Plain that I make out individual tilled rows—and then we come up from behind the leader, only to find the other two looping back behind us again. We fire, they fire, and I feel the first burn go down my back. I smell burning leather, but the coolant prevents the worst of the damage on my skin. The leader screams: Bardolph. My aim was true, and he was knocked back with the force of the blast, careening sideways and down toward the fields below.

One down, four to go.

And we're fine. We just have to outlast them long enough for them to run out—

But I know the odds of my surviving longer than it takes two skyfish to run out is unlikely.

And after that, the two stormscourge riders following behind will be there to clean up what's left as we tire.

The point isn't to survive. The point is to lead them away.

So I hug Aela's back, close my eyes, and dig my heels into her side.

"Just keep going."

We don't bother with manuevers after that. We take hits once, twice more on our backs as the flat farmland gives way to hills—

My suit disintegrates to the point that my burning back feels the breeze. When I reach for the reserve coolant bottle, I find my glass-ground hand no longer works, the fingers cannot grip the cap to turn it—

The sky bursts into light in the east. Clouds pop with gold and violet and red. Dragonfire.

Somewhere over the Driftless Dunes, Crissa's party has been intercepted at last.

"Shit," Cadwal says to Ariel, in Dragontongue. "Shit, we're in the wrong—"

The skyfish peel off me one by one, signaling with horns to the stormscourge pair behind. Calling them off my tail as they turn east.

I should follow them, try to detain them, but I can barely see for pain. I remind myself they're miles behind and their likelihood of catching up with Crissa's group is low—

Aela is slowing, gasping, allowing herself to coast for the first time since we took flight—

But then light explodes behind, and we turn to see a single black dragon still on our tail.

The rest of the Grayriders peeled off. But Edmund Grayheather and his great stormscourge Envy are closing in.

LEE

No sooner have we cleared the highest turrets of the Firemouth than the stars go out. We hear a growl so deep and loud it sounds like it comes from the bowels of the earth. Obizuth expands from Pytho's Keep with a darkness that envelops half the sky.

And then we collide with a moving wall.

Wham. Pallor spins off course like a bird hitting a window. Obizuth's tail, slinging through the dark, catches him on the stomach. We're spinning, losing altitude.

Wham, a second time. I feel it wind him, wind us.

The third swing, Pallor just manages to roll out of the way, hammering the wind with his wings to steady himself. He fires. But he might as well be firing at the karst itself for all Obizuth feels it.

How did they ever bring these monsters down?

My ancestors did it, during the Bassilean Wars. But as we dodge this moving mountain, the idea of subduing her is unimaginable.

"Don't bother attacking. We just have to get past her."

The next time the Great Dragon's tail swings, whistling in the dark, we dive. We race along her back, following the crest of her scales through the hollow between her wings, over her horned crown, and into the dark. A *snap* behind us, too close: a great maw closing on air, fangs gnashing in the dark.

We hear her roar behind us as we leave Obizuth and Freyda behind.

And then we race north, following the trail of flares Annie sur Aela leaves in the wake of her flight.

ANNIE

At the sight of Edmund behind us, I dig my knees into Aela's flanks. We shouldn't have slowed.

"Go, go—"

But Edmund's dragon lunges. Aela shrieks as his talons hook into her wings. They pull. Edmund's distinctive, hair-raising belly laugh is disembodied in the darkness.

We both scream as her wings puncture. Aela twists, her sharp fangs piercing the shoulder of the overbearing stormscourge, and as he yelps, she kicks free and sets off again.

But now it's not just me suffering injuries. Aela's wings are cut open.

I can feel her tiring, her agony spilling into me as our pain ricochets. We try rising into the cloudy night, then fluking into the cover of the sloping forest, but no matter how hard she pummels the air with her punctured, bleeding wings, the stormscourge is always just a little closer behind—

Running us down.

Aela's beginning to hack from exhaustion as her wings falter. Branches pummel our faces, disturbed snow exploding in white bursts around us, as we sink lower.

Her strength is giving out.

I lay a hand on her flank. "It's all right, Aela. Find us a defensive position."

She skids down a gorge and splashes under a rocky overhang where a brook turns. The stirrups snap like dried twigs as I slide from her back. Stars peep beneath fir boughs where here and there the clouds have parted. Low on the horizon, growing steadily larger, loom the black wings of the stormscourge still tracking us.

Edmund saw our descent. Aela's wings tremble with the effort of lifting to mantle me; it takes equal effort to rise to my feet beside her.

"Steady," I say, for myself as much as for her. The wet stone is cold under my boots' charred soles. Highland air, fresher than anything I've breathed in weeks, fills my lungs. It smells like home.

Edmund sur Envy dives, and Aela fires everything she has left. I can feel it leaving us, the last burst of energy, draining us down to the tips of our talons and the ends of our toes.

And then she's done, she's run out, and Edmund is still there, chuckling.

Aela takes a step forward, spreading her wings between me and our attackers. The stormscourge is so much bigger than her, we can still see Edmund's white slash of a grin.

"Get them," Edmund says.

His dragon lunges.

LEE

We hear them before we find them. Aela snarling, Annie screaming, Edmund's terrible laugh. His stormscourge, twice the size of Aela, has thrown her to the ground. Edmund hasn't bothered to dismount; he clings to his dragon's back, relishing the mauling, as Aela squirms beneath them. Pallor can smell her blood and her fear.

And even my human ears can hear the *ripping*.

Envy has Aela pinned in his talons. The only reason I'm not too late is that he's decided to take his time. Instead of going for her jugular, he's shredding her wings with his teeth. Annie's shrieks mingle with Aela's and reverberate on the stones. I can just barely see her shadowed form, doubled over at the back of the cave, clutching her arms where Aela's wings tear. But Edmund's saving the rider for last. I can hear him egging his dragon on.

They're taking their time with Aela because they want to enjoy it.

Fury rises in me such as I have never known. A dragon's fury. Pallor's rage engulfs mine.

So consumed are they with their sport that they don't hear the soft thump of our landing behind them. Pallor pounces, a silver snake in the dark, and his jaws close over my half brother's head.

It crushes like a melon.

Before Envy has time to register what has happened, Pallor tears his rider from the back of his dragon by the head and hurls him against the rocks like a rag doll. The sickening crunch of a body on impact sounds *good*. The sharp, fresh scent of human blood bursts in the air. Envy goes rigid at the sound, then rears.

He screams.

I've heard the widow-cry before. Then, as now, it was from a dragon that belonged to kin. When it was Julia's dragon, it gutted me.

Today I feel nothing but visceral satisfaction.

The stormscourge rounds on us, turning his back on Aela's crumpled form, and Pallor bares his fangs. Though he's larger than Aela, he's still outsized by Edmund's stormscourge. I've no doubt we'd be their equal in a tournament, even a duel, but in this scrabble on the rocks any skill in the air is lost advantage. Envy spreads his wings to show their full span, and Pallor's crest flattens as he goes low to the ground, taking the defensive position. I clamp my knees against the saddle and reach for both bootknives.

"Steady."

Envy pounces. Pallor and I launch under and up. Pallor's fangs spread wide and dart for Envy's protruding neck, puncturing it; as his maw summons flame, I dodge the heat and jam my bootknives under his chin. I yank them together. The scales tear open like plates of rusted metal. A hot rush of blood drenches my face, my chest, my shoulders.

The fiery glow in Envy's maw goes out. He sways. Then he topples, with a colossal *smack*, into the blackness of the flowing brook.

I slice the straps that hold my boots in their stirrups, slide from

Pallor's back, and scramble toward Annie and Aela, wiping dragons-blood from my face as I go.

We find them curled together under the rock overhang, two meters away, a shadowy huddle in the moonlight. Aela whimpers from a bed of blood-black snow, where her wings lie shredded and inert. Annie's hand is a bloody pulp that she cradles; the back of her suit is mostly burned away.

"I'm here, I'm here—"

I hardly know who I'm speaking to or who is speaking as I take Annie into my arms. Pallor goes to Aela. He nuzzles her and she whimpers. Annie stares back at me with spillover-wide pupils, shuddering. It's so cold, our breath rises in steam.

"Hi, Lee."

She's in shock. I think they both are. "Hey."

"That's a lot of blood."

"Not mine."

"Do you think they made it?"

I realize she's talking about the Guardians. The coup, the politics, the war all feel distant like a dream I fled. What's real is the girl in my arms and the bloody dragon beside her. They're my responsibility now.

My only responsibility.

"You had half the Grayriders on your tail. Crissa and the others would have been more than capable of throwing off the rest of them. They made it."

Annie closes her eyes.

I take stock of our situation as my heartbeats slow. The sky, a gash of starry blue, shows no sign of aerial battles taking place to the east. We've crash-landed in a shallow gorge between two ridgelines, cutting off a view of the lowlands. If we can't see their fire, they couldn't see ours.

We're safe here, for the time being. If nobody freezes, bleeds out, or dies from infected burns.

The principles of first aid return to me from distant memories of basic training: Stabilize the injuries. Control the environment. Find help.

The rock overhang that Annie and Aela have backed into becomes a shallow cave, the stones dry, a few feet deeper in. It'll have to do. After a quick rinse in the stream, I pile winter-dry vines, torn from the rocks, on the dry stones, which Pallor lights. Beside the fire, I lay out the once-white ceremonial mantle I've still got pinned to my shoulders and help Annie lower herself onto it. It's stiff with dragonsblood.

"Aela's—worse off than me."

The dragon's wings have been torn from the dactyl down. Pallor, curled around her, is licking them carefully. She'll need stitches before she flies again, but she's already stopped bleeding. Annie's the one at greatest risk for infection. "I'm more worried about you, honestly. Can you extricate?"

Annie shakes her head.

So that's how much pain they're in. "Okay. That's okay."

I rummage in her saddlebag. When I find honey preserved in a heat-resistant scale tin, I let out a slow exhale of relief. A painkiller and a disinfecting agent, honey is a rider's best friend for burns on the road. Annie sees it and lets out a rattling laugh. "Crissa always knew how to pack a bag."

I use my father's bootknife to cut what remains of her flamesuit off her back and rub honey on the burns. Annie is too tired to think of modesty, though when I strip off my ceremonial armor and pull the outer tunic over my head, she reaches for it. I help her cover herself. Last of all, I take her hand and pluck out the shards of Ixion's whiskey tumbler, silently cursing him, cursing my family, cursing my blood. We rinse her hand in the brook and I wrap the wound in strips of fabric torn from the lining of my mantle. I have her drink more water from my cupped hands.

That's when I notice that this brook, though fresh and flowing merrily, is warm.

It's the first time I have an inkling of where we might be.

Pallor curls round Aela at the entrance to the cave, making a wall of warmth that cocoons us. I smother the fire, lie down beside Annie, and wrap the mantle over us. No sooner has she begun to relax than she stiffens again.

"The engagement," she realizes, sitting up. "Oh dragons—the engagement—Lee, you have to go back—"

"It's off."

"Oh," says Annie. For the entirety of my ministrations she has remained calm, dry-faced, cool-voiced, but now I hear it wobble for the first time. "But that was the plan."

Is she so disappointed I'm not getting married to someone else? "I figured I was more needed here."

To my exasperation, her shoulders have started to heave. She's crying.

"Look," I say, preparing to explain what I think should be pretty damn obvious, but then she says, "I'm really glad you're not marrying her."

She's full-on sobbing now.

As I understand, my eyes grow hot. Her back is turned to me, her movements too slow and stiff for her to do much more than lean a bit against me as her shoulders shake, but I bend over to kiss her forehead.

"I'm glad I'm not marrying her, too."

For a moment the only sound is the brook rushing away in the night.

"What do we do now?" Annie murmurs.

"We sleep. Tomorrow we find someone who can stitch a dragon's wing."

"In the highlands?" I hear her skepticism.

I'll have to wait for dawn to know for sure, but I'd guess we're close; if I'm not mistaken, the warm brook puts us closer than I could have hoped. The Riversource, which marks the boundary between the Near and Far Highlands, must be just upstream, and from there I'll know the way. Whether it's passable on foot is another question.

"I've got a place in mind."

PART III

—

EXILE

21

—

THE REFUGE THAT AWAITS

GRIFF

NORCIA

It's got to be a sin to hammer on a bedroom door this early in the morning. The sun probably isn't even up yet. Dragonborn blankets are unbelievably soft and I've got three all to myself, a cocoon that beckons me back to nothingness. When I dream these days, my dreams are of the sea, of Da's ship sailing through parting storms as if he were not—like Agga, like Granda, like Garet—*gone*. It was a good dream, and I'd like to go back to it.

Every knock on that door pulses directly into my skull.

"Go away."

But whoever knocks doesn't go away. The door creaks, and the curtains rattle as they're drawn back. An unseemly amount of sunlight pours into the room. When I pull the bedclothes farther up my face, they're yanked back by small hands. "Wake up, Uncle!" Becca's beaming, her face inches from mine. "Antigone's coming! Antigone's coming with *ten dragons*!"

"What madness is this—"

"Not madness," Bran's voice says. "I was on watch when we sighted them. Too far to make out the call markings yet, but they're definitely Guardians. They'll be here within the hour."

"Antigone!" Becca repeats, bouncing on her feet. "It has to be Antigone!"

Looks like little blustering Duck was right after all.

I sit up, palming my eyes open. I didn't know light came this bright in Norcia. Whatever is coming from the windows might actually be slicing my head in two. Bran's standing by the opened curtains, his arms folded. "You should put clothes on. And maybe . . . wash."

Becca giggles. Bran winks at her. I kick them out.

Ten minutes later, I step out the manor door, dressed and bathed, to find Sparker saddled and waiting for me, courtesy of Becca and Bran. That's when I realize it's been over a week since I last rode him. Not just that—it's been a week since I've seen the sun.

Shrines. What've I been doing with myself?

"Beds need to be prepared, and stalls for their dragons—"

"Fionna's got them preparing guest rooms in the Provisional Palace. Duck and Delo have been working on the stalls for the last week."

At his mention, I have the flashing image of Delo's face in shadow, a single eyebrow lifted. Have I seen him recently? That doesn't add up. I've got nothing to say to Delo. But then—there are whole swaths of the last few days I find I can't remember. Nag Manor's liquor cabinet must be pretty close to empty by now.

"You get a sense of the shape their riders are in?"

Bran shakes his head. "Too far off."

I reach for the flamesuit that's suddenly within arm's reach. Becca's beneath it. "Pretty sure Ixion wouldn't let ten dragons fly off without a fight."

Ixion's not *that* stupid. Or blind. It probably got hot. Antigone likely started out with more riders, and these are the ones who made it.

Still, ten dragons to fortify our fleet isn't half bad. And it'll be good to see the little Firstrider again. The day of the Liberation, we hardly said goodbye. I remember how I found her on that collapsed karst after the explosion, tearing her hair at our failure as in my arms I held—

Not that.

Suddenly I'm itching for the saddle.

"I'll ride out to meet them," I tell Bran, as I shrug on the flamesuit. "Make sure healers are ready at the balustrades for when we arrive."

"Can I come, too, Uncle?" Becca asks.

"Not this time, love."

Her hair's not been brushed in what looks like days. Who's in charge of her hair? Am *I* in charge of her hair? How do I not even know?

"Who brushes your hair?"

"Lena," says Becca.

Lena? She's not even our kin. She doesn't even live here. Though come to think of it, I don't know where she lives, now that she's no longer obliged to live in an unlocked prison cell. Somewhere in the citadel with Duck, maybe?

"Well—go ask Lena to brush it, then."

My head's still splitting, but kicking off from the ground leaves some of the pain behind.

***

We meet the incoming dragonriders midway over Sailor's Folly. The North Sea has gifted them with a glorious blue-sky welcome that's so unlike any weather they're going to see in Norcia hereafter, it feels like a bad joke. At the head of the Callipolan party, I find not the little amber aurelian I'm expecting but a skyfish, who pulls ahead of her riders to join my wing. When she takes off her helmet, I recognize her with some foreboding as the fair-haired scout I once mauled. Her long blond braid gleams in the uncannily bright sun.

"Hello again, Griff," she says, in decent school-Dragontongue. "I hope you will be more willing to talk this time than last?"

It takes me a second to realize she's teasing. "Ah—yeah."

Her laugh is breezy. "Good. I'm Crissa sur Phaedra, skyfish squadron leader, and this is Cor sur Maurana, stormscourge squadron leader."

A second dragon has joined us. Cor removes his helmet, revealing dark wavy hair and a square jaw I recognize. "You're Dorian's brother."

"It's true he's alive, then?" Cor asks eagerly.

"Alive and well. Got himself a Norcian girlfriend, even."

Cor goggles. "Duck's got a *girlfriend*?"

I can't help laughing at his incredulity. His back's a web of burns, some older and some fresh, no flamesuit to be seen. I glance back at the group behind them. All are in various states of burned tatters, few flamesuits between them.

So it did get hot.

"We had to get out in a hurry," Crissa says. "Full gear wasn't possible."

"Any losses?"

Crissa swallows. "Some," she says.

"Where's the Firstrider?"

Crissa looks at Cor, who shakes his head. "She was supposed to join us on the way. We don't know what happened to her."

22

—

THE OLD ROAD

LEE

THE HIGHLANDS

I get us moving a few hours before dawn, determined to be miles away before anyone comes looking for Edmund. Annie lets out a slow groan in my arms when I say her name. My shoulder's so stiff from her using it as a pillow, it's lost feeling. I haven't slept myself.

"Already?"

"I'm sorry."

The night lends itself to whispering, though there's little need for it. Pallor nudges Aela, who growls at him. Annie gets to her feet slowly and sluggishly. "Buck up, Aela."

Aela struggles to her feet.

They're both in a pitiful state. Annie's riding boots are torn to tatters, Aela's wings limp and stringy. We cut the leather straps from the girth of Aela's no-longer-needed saddle and use them to bind her wings, hoisting them from the ground to keep them clean and safe from dragging.

"Pallor would let you ride him," I tell Annie.

She shakes her head. "If Aela walks, I walk."

So we bind her boots together, too.

The night sky has cleared, and the moon is close enough to full that it casts shadows on the hulking carcass of the stormscourge and his rider half submerged in the brook. Annie waits while I carry Edmund's remains to the shore. If he's found, they'll be able to provide him a proper burial. I'm surprised by how little beyond that I care.

After killing a cousin I loved, what remorse is left for killing a half brother I hated? The emotions are already cut away like dried vines.

We make our way upstream on the sodden, moonlit banks. I lead the way, testing the mossy stones for smooth and solid footing, gripping Annie's arm to support her. Aela follows behind, and Pallor takes up the rear, prompting her when she falters. Compared with the ease of flight, it's painfully slow going. Every time we stop, I make Annie drink water; her burns will be dehydrating her.

Gradually the banks rise and the sky lightens. Annie's slow steps grow slower, but she makes no complaint except to ask: "You're sure this is the way?"

"The water's warm. It's got to be a distributary of the River-source." The hot springs that feed the Fer, where my oldest Storm-scourge ancestors hatched their first dragon eggs. "The rim of the Riversource connects to the Robber Road, which will take us the rest of the way."

"The Robber Road?"

I've translated it uncomfortably into Callish. After a floundering description, Annie hums with sudden understanding. "The Old Road," she corrects softly. "We called it the Old Road."

I know it by the Dragontongue, as my father called it. Before early Aurelian settlers carved roads into the highlands to make them passable for their horses and carriages, a footpath linked the cliff towns of the northern coast. *The way of thieves and brigands,* my father would muse as he studied the map. But Annie's *we* refers to the highlands she's from, to the peasants who worked this land but were not allowed to call its fruits their own. They would have had their own reasons for needing a secret road to pass undetected. I don't call it the Robber Road again.

We find the rim of the Riversource at sunrise. The dragons wait hidden beneath low boughs of fir trees as we scramble to the barren ridge and look down.

"That's where I killed Julia."

The Riversource steams and overflows from the depths of the fissure, a black pool of heat. No evidence is left of the duel: The body of Julia's stormscourge, Erinys, was long ago retrieved for processing as armor, and Julia's returned to her people. I'm surprised to find, looking down on the place, that I feel none of the original agony. Instead, I have the thought that I'm looking on the place that made me.

This is where I became the Revolution's Son, of no father and no house.

The sun lights the ridgelines of the highlands, gilding peaks still white with snow and accenting firs so dark a green they look black. Slender blankets of fog creep slowly over the hills, but the skies are clear. A patrolling pair of dragons skims a ridgeline some miles away. Annie shields her eyes to study them. "One of those is Power sur Eater."

With vindictive satisfaction, I mutter, "Traitor."

Annie's voice is quiet. "I don't think so. He recognized me, in the Palace. He kept my cover. And he's very close to his mum—he must be terrified for her."

I don't want to know how Annie knows this. *I* don't want to know this. Power's much easier to despise, and I've got more practice doing it. I'm glad when she changes the subject.

"Do you think they'll look for us after they find Edmund?"

"Not here. They won't know he shredded Aela's wings, they've got no reason to think we're on foot."

Still, we leave the dragons in the cover of the firs while we search the rim for signs of a trail. Annie's the one who finally notices the small stone marker half submerged in snow, and a little farther past it the narrow stone stairs leading down from the ridge in two directions. To the east, just visible poking above the tree-tops, are the crenellated towers of the great House of Nearhall, seat of the Stormscourge Triarch. The Riversource served as the estate's breeding spring. To the west, the Old Road continues into the Far Highlands, and would take us all the way to Dragon's End, if we wanted it to. But our destination lies closer than that.

We return to the dragons to find a mountain hare dangling limply from Pallor's maw. We don't usually let the dragons out from the Great Palace to hunt—farmers don't appreciate it—but that doesn't mean they can't. He looks terribly pleased with him-self, and I'm flooded with relief myself. I'd been wondering all morning how we would find food.

"Well done, you."

He smokes the little body, fur and all, and then tears it into strips, feeding us one by one: Aela, Annie, me. The meat is a per-fect medium-rare; Annie scarfs it down and says solemnly, with juice dripping down her chin, "This is the best breakfast I've ever had."

Her eyes are black with spillover. I try not to laugh. "I think you might be channeling Aela."

Personally, I'm craving bread, but I have a feeling we won't be seeing any for a while.

When fog rolls over our ridge, we make our way down the westward fork of the Old Road in its cover, and cross into the Far Highlands. I'm surprised how passable the path remains centuries later, even in winter. Though we glimpse occasional villages and hamlets through patches in the woodlands, we see no other travelers. False forks every few miles along the trail lead to shallow caves, called cavates, that have been carved out of the limestone and can be used as shelter.

"For smugglers to hide in?" I wonder.

Annie hums again. "Older than that, I think. Dad said they were built to hide from dragons, back when they roamed wild."

By midafternoon, her bandages are seeping blood and pus through the back of her tunic, and she's shivering beneath the mantle I've wrapped round her. Aela's tail droops so badly it drags on the ground. The road opens out at the base of a hill whose sheep-dotted ridgeline I recognize at once. Now that we see it, I can't believe I didn't realize we would pass it.

Of course. We're close enough now that we've entered the old feudal land holdings, and that village is Holbin Hill.

The village where Annie was born. The village my father burned down. Right now, all I can think about is their larders.

"Annie," I say, slowing. Smoke rises from the chimneys of the collection of squat houses at the top of the hill, inviting, the afternoon quiet. We haven't seen any patrolling dragonriders for hours. I imagine warming my numb, cold hands by a fireplace.

Annie looks up at Holbin, and her shoulders draw up to her ears. They're stained brown from the tea she's been sweating from her hair. "No," she says, like she knows exactly what I'm about to propose.

"They could help us."

"No," Annie says again.

The thought of bread is making my mouth water. "We wouldn't even need to take the dragons—we could just go ask—"

"Do you know what happened the last time I *went home*?"

Annie turns to glare at me. "I was spat on. They hate me. Just like everyone on this whole island, they hate me. They won't help us."

Annie's bald assessment of her status gives me whiplash. It's too enormous to argue with. I feel desperation rising. "Maybe I could—"

"*You?*" She's stopped; for a brief glare she takes in the length of me, and then she actually laughs. "I can promise your popularity with the commoners of Callipolis will not extend to Holbin Hill, *Leo*."

My face heats as if it'd been slapped.

"Come on," she says, turning.

Fury fuels her steps with renewed vigor. She leads us away from Holbin without looking back.

***

We don't speak again until dusk. The trail has begun to climb steadily, more often stairs than not, and the ridgeline that will face us tomorrow is the sheerest yet.

"It's up there."

Annie cranes her neck to take in the steep wall rising, blotting the sky above us. At the base, a seamless snowdrift buries trees for miles and the Old Road disappears entirely. "It's passable on foot?"

She's not wrong to ask: I remember arriving by dragonback with my father. But Mother and the servants took a different path, a fork from the Aurelian Way that led to a stair, and I just have to find it.

"There's a way. We'll look for it in the morning."

We take shelter in one of the cavates off the Old Road next to a fall of melting snow-water. Pallor starts a fire from damp wood he bullies into sparking; Aela lowers herself into the ice-cold pool with a groan. Our backs warming from the fire, Annie and I remove our boots and place blistered feet in the water beside her. At my asking, Annie rolls up her tunic for me to check the dressings on her back.

"This whole island doesn't hate you," I tell her.

Her back is turned, the nubs of her spine poking from angry red skin. She shakes her head. "There were these girls I worked with in the Palace—lovely girls, Cheapsiders—they told me everything they thought of the bitch commander."

I cup water to run over the burns. "You're *not*"—the city's slur sticks on my tongue like old porridge—"a bitch commander."

She closes her eyes, and wetness leaks from beneath the closed lids. "It doesn't matter anymore."

I can't think how it doesn't. But she sounds almost relieved.

"Ixion's Firstrider now, and they can forget all about me. I'm—retired."

That's the first time I realize Annie thinks she's done with Callipolis for good. I reach for her hand to unwrap the bindings. "You don't think the people deserve better than that?"

Annie lifts a shoulder. "At least with Freyda, they're not starving."

"Annie. Spare me the class-iron propaganda sheets."

It's a retort from our classroom days as Guardians-in-training. Her eyes flare open. "*You* left them to Ixion and Freyda, too."

No. I came to save their Firstrider. I'm trying to get Aela's wings stitched so they can return to our fleet, in Norcia, and from there—

Annie sees the answer in my eyes and pulls her hand from mine. "I'm done, Lee. *I failed.*"

So that's what she thinks of it? That *she* failed?

"*How*—?"

Annie's chest is heaving, her breathing labored, her eyes bright. "Did you know that in Norcia, peasant girls pretended to be me? It was considered such a dangerous sign of rebellion that their parents had to ban them from it for fear of crackdowns by the dragonborn."

I didn't know that. I can only imagine how it felt for Annie, water on parched earth, to be a symbol of hope. The laurel I've borne easily for as long as I can remember that she's never been fitted with. When Callipolans weren't too bigoted to believe a lowborn girl was worthy, they were mad at her for doing a terrible job well. "But that must have felt *good*—"

Annie shakes her head forcefully. "It did feel good. That's what I'm trying to say. It was the only thing I'd ever *felt* good at, helping Griff and the Norcians. I was finally the hero, not the bitch commander. And I helped, it's true. I helped liberate a people. But in doing so I forsook my vows. All those times Holmes told me to stop fraternizing with Norcian peasants and do my job? *He was right.* Ixion slipped in while my back was turned. I was in Norcia playing the hero when our Revolution was defeated. I didn't defend my city, as I'd sworn to do. I left it in its hour of need. And Callipolis *fell*. So don't—tell me—I didn't fail."

She is shaking with suppressed sobs, gripping her knees as she hunches over. The moment is broken by the thump of another dead hare landing at her feet. Pallor peers into her face. When she opens her eyes, she lets out a faint laugh.

"Well, at least the dragons like me," she says, opening her palm to him.

We chew our way through more game in silence, and though I sense she's glad for the conversation to be finished, I can't stop myself saying it. "It's the Alternus's job to defend."

The Firstrider's job to attack, the Alternus's job to defend.

She wasn't the one who failed. I was.

Annie blinks at me. She sets aside bones she's stripped clean and wipes her mouth with the back of her hand.

"Where we're going," she says, "will its new owner mind we're dropping in?"

"I don't think so."

"Really?" Her voice becomes hesitant. "Who is the new owner?"

"I think . . . I am."

For a moment Annie stares at me. Then her voice becomes cautious indeed. "Lee . . ."

She's looking like she worries I'm delusional. I hasten to tell her about Dora Mithrides's inheritance clause. "Edmund Grayheather was supposed to take it from her, but obviously he now can't. I'm sure they'll change the paperwork when they bother to look at it, but I don't think they will for a while yet. The estate's been stripped of its holdings, and what's left is too remote to be valuable."

Annie's lip is quirking. "So you're the lord of Farhall, after all that?"

"Yeah," I say, reddening.

"Well, my lord," she says tartly, lying back on the mossy bank, "I hope your house has very soft beds."

I stretch out beside her. A handful of stars have already winked to life, brushed by the swaying fingers of the fir trees. The fire warms our faces as the pool relieves our aching feet. I know we should move into the cavate to take shelter and attempt to sleep, but neither of us seems able to summon up the energy to move from the pool's edge. There's a splash as Aela climbs from the water, shakes like a dog, and nuzzles into Pallor's side.

Annie speaks to the stars above us, her voice barely louder than the falls. "Is it true you killed Atreus?"

I keep my eyes on the swaying branches. "Yeah. But not like they said."

"You made your peace with him?"

Only Annie could guess such a thing. "He told me . . . to take care of you."

Annie turns to look at me. "Really," she deadpans. "He said those words *exactly*."

"Well. Maybe not exactly."

Annie snorts. She rolls over and kisses me on the nose.

"You rogue," she says.

***

Annie and Aela have both taken a turn for the worse by the following morning. Aela's spilling over into Annie again, the rips in her wings have reopened and are bleeding, and neither of them has an appetite for the game Pallor rattles in front of us. He has to masticate and feed Aela like a hatchling, and then he begins licking her wings while she whimpers. Annie's curled into her knees, gray-faced.

"How much farther?"

"A half day, tops. We just have to find the entrance to the stairs and climb—that."

Annie's gaze travels slowly up the cliff that rises over us. Her laugh is faint.

I leave her with the dragons and search alone, suppressing growing panic. I know the ridge, and even the ravine that connects to the stair to the Old Road and the Aurelian Way, which continues to Dragon's End. But the private stair is deliberately camouflaged, and what I remember of it, I saw after spring thaws. This far north, the snowdrifts have accumulated in meters, rendering the landscape I remember unrecognizable.

Not to mention, I never knew it from the ground.

Finally, I make my way back to Annie and the dragons. She and Aela are slumped, Pallor alone awake, his wing mantling Aela. "I need to see it from dragonback."

It's late morning, and the sun is already high on the steepled horizon. Annie stirs and blinks the light from her eyes. "You'll be seen."

"Pallor's snow-colored. He'll camouflage."

We risk a brief flight. At once, as the ground falls away and the ridges around us shift apart, the world turns from foreign to familiar: This is how I knew the Far Highlands as a child. On dragonback with my father, we'd rise to the summit and catch first glimpse of the North Sea peeping between cracks in the cliffs as the servants trailed up the stair below bearing our luggage and the family's litters. We made the journey in late summer, when the hills rippled with heather.

It takes surprising force of will to resist taking Pallor all the way up. Instead, we glide low, skimming the snowbanks that climb the cliffs, until we spot the switchbacking stair emerging from them.

Pallor drops his tail into the snow and drags it all the way back to the overhang where Annie and Aela wait, leaving a trail in the snow behind him. On the ground, we retrace it on foot. Pallor clears the snow by burrowing into it; the panic we're both feeling about Annie's and Aela's worsening state renews our vigor. But even the trail he clears is tough walking, and Annie and Aela begin to stop for longer and longer periods to pant, knee-deep in snow. Aela's wings leave bloody streaks in the white that Pallor flicks his tail over to hide.

"We're nearly there."

"You mean we're nearly to the *stair*," Annie corrects faintly, "that we've got to *climb*."

The steps are steep but well insulated from the wind, cut so deep into the escarpment that they're more like a shallow tunnel zigzagging through the limestone. The steps were designed for horses; the dragons will have to go on their bellies—it's lucky that they're aurelians, because it wouldn't be passable for a stormscourge. I fasten the sling containing Aela's torn wings closer to her side and Pallor nudges her up after us as we begin our ascent.

"I can't believe your family climbed this every year," Annie says, panting.

"I can carry you."

"You will not," Annie says.

But by midafternoon, halfway up, her legs give out and I hoist her onto my back. "Truth be told, they had litters."

Her voice is faint in my ear. "Oh, so people like me carried people like you?"

I shift her legs more securely around my waist. "Yep."

"Tell me about your house."

My house? The truth is, I'm frightened to see it again for how beautiful I remember it being, and more frightened at the idea of showing it to Annie. I keep imagining I'll either find it burned down, or worse, in perfectly good repair only to have Annie look upon it in horror. She wouldn't without reason. *This was what you lived in while we starved?* "It's obscenely grand," I tell her recklessly. "A whole room just for china. Chandeliers with crystals the size of your fist. The walls are covered in wolf heads—"

"You're joking."

"No, we hunt them. It's our service to the local peasantry."

"Oh, I see. Thank you, that's too kind."

I wonder whether we're both delirious. Annie hums into my shoulder. She's still for so long I think she might have fallen asleep. Eventually all I can feel is the burning in my calves and Pallor's panic. It's started to spill over at a rate I don't try to manage. Aela's tail drags on the stairs; when she slows, he nips gently at her haunches, and she shuffles on. Until finally she doesn't.

"Annie?"

Annie stirs and answers the unspoken question. "She needs to rest."

I let Aela rest for a half hour, then Pallor forces her to her feet. We filled our canteens with melting snow before mounting the stairs, and I've not spared any for myself or Pallor. Aela takes the last of it. Pallor fairly goads her the final few switchbacks, up toward the light growing at the end of the tunnel, and we spill out onto the cliffwalk to a sudden smell of salt.

The North Sea spreads below. The water has turned silver flecked with the gold of a setting sun; cloud tendrils caress the cliff face and refract the rich light. Sailor's Folly is stubble on the eastern horizon; level with us, a line of pelicans flows high over the churning waves.

"See? We've made it, we're here," I say. "Farhall's just around the—"

I turn to find Aela collapsed on the stairs, her eyes closed, her breath faint. Her wings ripple loosely in the wind. The sling's come undone.

"Annie?"

But she's out, too.

I lower Annie to the ground beside her dragon and tell Pallor, "Wait with them here." Pallor claws at the stone, snorting and glaring at me as if to say, *Hurry.*

I take off up the cliffwalk at a run. The salt breeze fills my lungs, the surf crashing far below pounds in my ears. The sun is dipping into the waves, the sky full of fire, when the cliff wall to my left finally opens into green pasture sheltered on all sides by snow-capped escarpments.

On the far side of the pasture, looking out over the North Sea, is Farhall.

I have a few gasping breaths as I bolt up the drive to confirm that it's exactly as I remember it: the gardens, the vineyard, the brook a black ribbon through the green; the Big House, built to withstand winds and to keep out long winters with thick stone walls and narrow windows. Its roof is so weathered and mossy, it looks like a second garden. By the standards of the Skyfish Summer Palace or the Great Palace in the capital, or even of Nearhall in the middle highlands, this house is humble.

But to me it looks like home.

The grouting's recently been retouched and the vines that cling to the windows look no more than a season old, but the shutters are drawn. It seems the manor has been maintained under Dora's ownership, but not inhabited. I don't stop to inspect further; I dash past it to the groundskeeper's cottage buttressed against the near escarpment and hammer on the bolted door.

"Mr. Garth! Mr. Garth, please open up!"

I haven't got anything to go by more than a hunch that the servant listed on the deed is the same one I knew as a child; or even that Nigel Garth will be glad to see Leon's youngest son. But I remember my father's groundskeeper as a man who liked dragons better than people; if he's still here and it's dragons he's loyal to, I've got dragons for him. There's smoke rising from the chimney, but the door doesn't open.

And then comes his voice from behind me, ten years older than I remember.

"Turn around slowly, boy, I don't like unplanned visitors."

I rotate on my heel. Nigel Garth has a weathered face where it once was smooth, his brown hair now peppered with gray, and his long, narrow frame is even more wiry than I remember. He's pointing a crossbow at my chest. As he sees my face, his eyes widen.

I don't hear what he says next because I am bowled over by a gray blur.

Enormous paws are planted over my chest, a gray muzzle lowers to look at me with fogging eyes, and then Argos, whom I remember as a yearling wolfhound, begins to lick my face as his whole body wags with his tail. I reach up to scratch him beneath the fuzzy ears and the corners of my eyes prickle.

"Argos. You and me both, huh?"

When I'd read on the deed *groundskeeper and dog*, it had been too strange to think of. That I wasn't the only one who survived; that maybe that dog was *this* dog, the one I remembered. Now I rub Argos's scruff the way my father did as my vision blurs. Larissa and I used to take rides on his back.

Nigel sets aside the crossbow. "My lord. I'd heard rumors but didn't dare believe. Argos, get off him."

I roll out from under Argos and onto my feet, wiping slobber that hasn't changed in ten years from my face. And suddenly, despite the desperation, despite my fear for Annie and Aela, my heart is light because I'm *home*. This tiny corner of the world is still, in some small way, mine.

I didn't lose everything after all.

"Mr. Garth, there's a downed dragon—at the cliffwalk—she's wounded, she needs help."

"Yours?"

"Not mine. But mine's with her. It's a—friend's—"

I remember Garth as being supremely calm in a crisis and always up to any task my father had for him. Today is no different. He asks no more questions, only steps inside to find the gear he needs, and emerges two minutes later with a medical kit and water.

"Lead the way."

23

—

A NORCIAN WELCOME

GRIFF
NORCIA

On the citadel balustrades, the Callipolan riders are greeted by their lost comrade, Dorian Sutter. Cor grips his brother's face in both hands and kisses his forehead and cheeks ferociously while Duck laughs. They're speaking in a torrent of Callish while Lena waits to be introduced. I wonder if she's imagining, like I am, finding out a lost loved one wasn't really gone for good.

Delo waits in the shadow, watching me, like he doesn't get that the whole point is we pretend the other doesn't exist now.

Or at least, I think we don't. Again, I can't shake the feeling we've been spending a lot of time in each other's company at that particular stage of the night where I've started doing everything I can to make the world go dark. In the blurry memories of that darkness, Delo remains silhouetted and clear.

When Fionna taps my shoulder, I'm glad for the excuse to turn from him. She's got a hand up under her belly like she's propping it, the other braced on her dragon's crest. When did the child get so *big*?

"We've got a flotilla of small craft entering Sailor's Folly from the south," she says.

"Military?"

"Refugees, I think. Crissa sur Phaedra was saying some of the

Guardians' families were attempting to get out during an amnesty window." Fionna has lowered her voice, though none but Duck would be able to understand her Norish. We watch the Guardians dismounting, greeting their comrades, being welcomed by Lena and the clan healers who've been summoned to assist the wounded. Crissa has wrapped her arms around Duck, slapping his spotty beard with a watery laugh while he stutters sheepishly. Pretty sure the word for *straggly* is the same in Callish as Norish. When he presents Lena to them, Crissa hugs Lena like a long-lost sister and Cor kisses her face, too.

"You and my brother?" he shouts in terrible Dragontongue, gesturing between them with waving arms. Lena covers her mouth as she giggles.

"Cor, she's Norcian, not deaf," Duck says, rolling his eyes.

And then as the questions continue, the smiles start to fade and heads start to shake. Duck's asking after Guardians he was expecting to see. I hear names I know: Lee, Annie. And then more I don't. Lotus, Deirdre, Alexa.

And then when he says *Rock*, Crissa sur Phaedra begins to weep.

Grayriders, Cor is saying, his voice hoarse. And then, *Power sur Eater*.

I know that one. That was Antigone's friend, the one who came to the Driftless Dunes with us when she was teaching me to read Dragontongue.

"What are they saying?"

Delo starts, not expecting me to have joined his side, not expecting me to talk to him. I've asked him before I had time to stop to think I shouldn't. The thing is, I know he must know Callish; even if he grew up speaking Dragontongue in Callipolis, this is the language his servants would have spoken.

Delo's always been good at learning the languages of servants.

Now, of course, he looks as servile as the rest of us. It's still odd to see him in commoners' clothing—an undyed tunic, sweat-stained and soiled from working in the lairs—but I find I don't mind the sight. He seems determined to move nothing but his eyes, which flick to the group of Callipolan exiles as if, now that I'm talking to him, he'd prefer not to look at me.

"They're . . . talking about the flight here. There was a pursuit. A compromised Guardian named Power sur Eater brought down someone named Rock. Killed the dragon, possibly Rock, too, they're not sure."

That can't be right. "But I know Power. Decent fellow. He's friends with Antigone."

Delo's lips thin. "Well, it's what they're saying."

At his cold tone, I turn to look fully at him. He continues to stare straight ahead.

I'll be damned if there isn't a bit of a bruise coming out from under his collar.

"You get into a fistfight with a feeding trough?"

"Pretty much," says Delo.

He moves away from me without looking back, finger digging at the hair by his ear.

Shrines. It was a *joke*.

No sooner am I wondering who Delo must have gotten into a fight with than a thought occurs that leaves me cold.

What if the person he got in a fight with was *me*? What if the drunk thing I've been forgetting doing with Delo over the past few weeks is taking the stuffing out of him? Shrines know there've been days where I wanted to slam a fist in that handsome mug. It's not like he'd be much good in a fight—I'd have beaten him easy—and if I had done, what recourse would he have? He's a political hostage I agreed to keep. The only person on this island who might care about his well-being is *me*.

"Griff," Fionna reminds me quietly. I'd forgotten her waiting behind me. "The flotilla in the Folly. What do we do about the civilian refugees?"

I'm still staring after Delo. "We help them," I say, tearing my eyes from what I think might be a second bruise on the back of his neck.

Fionna frowns. "Without approval from the clan elders? Where are we going to put—not to mention *feed*—?"

"We'll feed the extra mouths it takes to gain ten dragons." The elders might not get the value of doubling our fleet size when Ixion's at large with a goliathan on his side, but that's an error I'll disabuse them of when I've got this tied down. None of these riders will be any use to us worrying about their families. "We can ask for forgiveness after."

Fionna's lips purse. Then, to my surprise, she says, "It's good to have you back, Griff."

Shrines on the karst above, they're all infuriating. "I wasn't *gone*."

I rally the mounted Woad-riders with a lifted arm. "I want everyone in armor, skyfish with rescue gear to help the small craft navigate the karst forest—ropes, buoys, oars. Aurelian and storm-scourge riders should be carrying pikes and shields."

I'm not putting it past Ixion's Clovers to try to interfere.

"Dragontongue!" one of the Guardians shouts. The language we all have in common, thanks to our former lords and the Calli-polans' spiffy education. I say it again in Dragontongue, watching the Callipolans' faces light up at mention of their families so close.

Cor lifts a hand like I've been giving him briefings my whole life. "Do you have spare gear? We can help."

Duck steps forward. "I've got flamesuits and armor ready for those fit for duty, with your permission, Commander."

Commander. He's talking to me, and I don't mind it.

Crissa and Cor take charge, hooking lines to the small craft—a collection of dinghies and rafts full of dissidents and family members that got out in time—and hauling them through the karst pillars toward Norcia. Cor greets his family with a whoop from dragonback on our way to the perimeter we're setting up on the outer edge of the karst. It's pure heaven to have so many riders at my disposal: For the first time, I feel like I can get a proper defensive line around this rock.

And I'm not wrong to think we need it. The flotilla doesn't arrive an hour too soon. By afternoon, Bran and I are able to see a Callipolan blockade forming from Wayfarer's Arch, the southernmost karst pillar off Sailor's Folly. A combination of the Clover fleet and Freyda's Bassilean warships form a line that expands by the mile, by the hour, facing northward. Preventing anyone crossing from their shore to ours, or ours to theirs.

Except, of course, by dragon.

If more Callipolans hoped to flee the Restoration by boat, they're out of luck.

"Just so long as they don't try to encircle us," Bran says, handing me the spyglass.

If the blockade forms a chokehold on Sailor's Folly, their navy will cut off our ore trade with Damos and the Medean archipelagos—shipping routes we depend on to compensate for our small island's lack of farmland. "We can fish."

"We can't fish grain." I know Bran's thinking of the Callipolans being hauled into our harbor, a hundred-odd more mouths to feed. "You don't think taking them in might be perceived as an escalation?"

Privately, I think there's no sweeter joy than escalating with Ixion, but I don't think Bran wants to hear that. "It's always better to be able to defend ourselves."

Bran scowls, like he suspects my innocent tone.

With the glass to my eye, I can make out Ixion sur Niter among the stormscourges doing laps over the masts of the blockade, Niter's hulking black form distinguishable from the others by a silver crest that, at this distance, shines like a line of light. Freyda's goliathan, the shape and size of an airborne whale, is easy to identify even with the naked eye.

You want us? Come and take us.

I've got seventeen dragons in my fleet.

Though I do wish it weren't missing the little amber aurelian and her Firstrider.

I collapse the spyglass and pocket it. "Shrines, but I don't like to think what they'll do to her if they've got her."

Bran doesn't have to ask who I'm talking about.

DELO

The Greatlord's Hall, which is being rebuilt without the Greatlord or his decorations by Thornrose Clan in atonement for its treachery, has yet to be renamed. So it is to his father's hall that Astyanax receives an invitation, when he opens the door the afternoon of the Callipolan refugees' arrival and finds a messenger from the clan elders. It seems the Norcian love of hospitality, for now at least, outweighs their anxiety about additional mouths to feed: Tonight, they will welcome their guests in style.

I hide my misgivings about our invitation from Astyanax, who is giddy at the prospect of a feast, and perhaps a little too sweetened by the sound of the phrase *Greatlord's Hall*, as if it had the power to bring his father back for the night. Electra frets about what we will wear, choosing between the three dresses she was allowed to take with her from her apartments in the Provisional Palace, none suitably formal. She insists I bathe—ten extra dragons' worth of sweat and soil scrub off with some effort, especially given our lack of soap—and lays out the single tunic I still possess dyed blue in the color of my House.

"I think it might be better to go unadorned."

"Don't be silly. We're still *dragonborn*."

That, I consider saying, is the problem. But Electra looks so imperious that I decide I'll take my chances with the Norcians and put on the tunic without further protest.

Sty enthuses giddily about what longed-after dishes we might sample again tonight as we make our way up the hill to the citadel. *Do you think the dogs will be there?* Sty misses the citadel dogs, whom he enjoyed feeding scraps at feasts. *My father's dogs,* he keeps calling them. Electra leans heavily on my arm for the uphill walk. I am weighing, with a kind of detached curiosity, the odds that the humiliation will be to serve at table: Sty is too small and Electra too doddering, but they might ask it of me.

Naturally, I'm being too optimistic.

At the door, a man I recognize as one of Seanan's friends stops us.

"And look at you three, in the tricolor!" he says with a delighted laugh, at the sight of Electra's black, my blue, and Sty's red, and I know at once it was a mistake not to put my foot down with Electra about our clothing. Sty smiles nervously at him. "Wait here. Want to give you the proper entrance."

"What did he say?" Electra's Norish is minimal. I translate, and she looks pleased. "Ah yes, it will be fitting to announce us."

The doors burst open, and more of Seanan's friends usher us

through. The hall is warmly lit, and though the lumber is fresh and unstained, the long tables are arranged in the usual rows. Tonight, instead of the Triarchy-in-Exile at the high table, it's Woad-riders and Guardians. Sty has an instant to take in the changed decorations, his face falling, before Seanan's friend pushes us forward. Though Electra's Norish might not be good enough to understand the introduction he makes of her, she's more than capable of understanding its intent when she's escorted down the main aisle and then, instead of being seated at the high table, she's led to the side of the hall and pushed to the ground among the dogs.

Sty shrinks against me, as if to back out the door. But more Norcians are there to keep us in place. Some of the Callipolans' brows are raised, as if they find this entertainment a little too rustic for their tastes; the blond rider, Crissa, actually gets to her feet and begins to argue with a Norcian elder near her, gesticulating fiercely as he scowls. But some of the Callipolans look gratified. Especially the riders who have the pale, emaciated look of freshly freed prisoners. They look like the sight of a dragonborn being humiliated is the sweetest thing they've seen in weeks.

I find myself searching for Griff, hating myself for doing it, and unsure whether I'm relieved I can't find him or more frustrated by it.

My procession comes next. I smile at Sty and keep my tone light, as if by force of pretense I could make him experience this as a fun game, not a degradation in the hall where he was once princeling. "Aunt Electra and I will be waiting for you on the other side, okay?"

They have to pry his fingers from my hand.

It's over fast enough: the mock title announced, the hurried walk, the stare that avoids the catcalls and the jeers on either side. Then I'm on the ground beside Electra, surrounded by the dogs Sty missed so much, watching him be dragged toward us. There are cheers; at the invitation of Seanan's friends, scraps start flying our way. A chicken bone hits Electra in the eye. She is silent and shaking, backed against the wall as if hoping to press herself through it. Sty is red-faced, fists balling as he curls into my side. I lift his chin to look at me and shake my head.

"Do not cry."

The last encouragement this hall needs is the sight of the Greatlord's son breaking down.

I watch him focus on this single imperative, and his breath seizing.

Gradually they lose interest in us. I ask Sty about the dogs, once he's regained his voice, and he scratches the chin of the one closest to us, telling me about him. The dog's hungry, but remembers Sty. Sty feeds him the chicken bone. At some point, a small girl from the Clan Knoll table scurries from her mother's side and sets her full plate in my hands.

"What's this?"

"You saved us," she says, "in the air strikes. Lord Delo."

Just when I might have thought to regret it.

She curtsies and backs away as if I were still her lord.

"You saved her?" Sty asks curiously, lifting his head from where it slumps on my shoulder.

"There were children locked in this hall, during the Callipolan air strike. I helped them out."

"Norcian children," Electra spits, stirring. *"Peasant lover."*

It's like she hopes the acid in her words will open holes in my skin. But Sty's fingers are tightening on my arm at the sound of her vitriol rather than recoiling from me. Salmon lies steaming in a bed of cream and potatoes on the plate in my hands. Lacking any appetite, I proffer it to Electra. "Do you want—"

"No," hisses Electra, white-faced. She pants as if she might faint.

So I pass it to Sty, who feeds the girl's donation to the dogs around us. At this point, they are happy for our company indeed.

He's beginning to doze off, and I've fallen into a bit of a stupor myself, when the clamor starts. At first, I think it's the beginning of the fully drunk stage of the evening, which I can only anticipate will prompt renewed interest in our entertainment potential. But then I see him: Griff Gareson, being welcomed in from a rainy night with shouts and cheers, the hero of Norcia. He shrugs off their delight with bashful enjoyment, letting himself be led into the hall like a welcomed king, his mantle taken, water shaking from him like a shaggy bear. The broken boy I've been tending for weeks is replaced by a man who stands straight again. The Guardians shook him back to life.

Then someone whispers in his ear. His body tenses and goes still. He looks directly at me, where I am seated with the dogs.

For the first time tonight, I would properly like to disappear into the floor.

He approaches, his face twisting as he understands. Sty, stirring, shrinks at the sight of the man towering over us and then recognizes him. "Griff?" he says, rubbing his eyes.

"Who did this, little lordling?"

I answer for Sty. "Stay out of it."

"Like hell I'm staying out of it."

This whole island's been talking, and the one person they forgot to talk to was Griff Gareson. "You don't understand. If you intervene—they said I was your—" Sty and Electra won't know the word, anyway. I force myself to repeat it, unsticking it from my throat.

For a heartbeat longer, he just stares at me.

Then he repeats himself. *"Who did this?"*

I have the feeling that I'm watching a storm cloud swell, for how Griff's rage is crackling. The mingled relief and self-loathing I feel at the sight of it is heady. I know what comes next, and I want it. Never mind the consequences.

I point, imprecisely, to the region of the table under the banner of Turret where the principal perpetrators are deep in their cups.

Griff turns from us, and the storm cloud breaks.

If the Norcians hoped to provide the Callipolans entertainment tonight, they're rewarded. Griff's rage crashes over the offending crew of Norcians. He slams a face headfirst into the table before anyone knows what has happened. Seanan's friends, most from Clan Kraken, a few from Turret, get to their feet shouting, but Griff shouts loudest and they are brought to silence. He doesn't have a dragon with him, but it feels like he does.

"Out," he says, shaking the man whose nose he's broken. "Get out."

They run.

But Seanan, unafraid, speaks from a few seats down from the high table, where he sits among those in honor, his arms folded and smirking. "I had been wondering if we'd see a demonstration of Griff Gareson's love for the dragonborn tonight."

Griff rounds slowly on him with the air of a stormscourge inhaling to fire.

"Say that again to my dragon's face, Seanan," he says.

Seanan lifts his hands, unconcerned. They are burn-scarred from his time serving as target practice in a dragonborn pen. "I don't dare. That's the point, isn't it?"

The clan elders are looking curiously between Seanan and Griff. Griff balls and unballs his fists like he's considering deciding this fists-first, forget the dragon. Fionna, Bran, and the rest of the Woad-riders are exchanging anxious glances. And though I told Fionna I've sworn off Norcian politics, I can't help hoping Griff will, this one time, not be an idiot. For any political rival wishing to paint Griff as brash or a bully with a dragon or maybe just a romantic fool, he's about to hand them a public spectacle as proof.

But thank his Nag and her shrine, Griff seems to sniff the trap. With what looks like an effort of enormous will, he turns from Seanan to the hall at large, and addresses the Callipolans in ringing Dragontongue.

"This is not how Norcia treats her guests or her political prisoners. On behalf of my people, I apologize for this disgrace."

At the high table, Crissa sur Phaedra gives a curt nod.

Griff rotates on a heel to look at us. He's halfway across the hall.

"You lot," he barks, to Electra, Sty, and me. "Come sit."

The last thing I want at this point to do is sit down at a table in this hall, but Griff looks so furious, leaving also seems out of the question, so Electra, Sty, and I make our way to the now-empty seats that Griff has cleared by battery, and he slams three goblets in front of us.

He pours for us without spilling a drop, because even furious, his training as a squire comes through.

"Drink!" he commands, and then stomps off to the high table and the seat that waits for him.

***

Sty doesn't cry until he gets home, and then he doesn't do it until Electra's soft snores fill the room and he thinks we're asleep. I lie awake listening to his misery, weighing the child's need for comfort with the young man's need for courage—and then I remind myself that I can give him neither. The ones he misses are his mother and father, and they're gone.

Long after he's cried himself to sleep, I stare up at the darkness of a roof that hangs too low and creaks too much.

Will it go on like this forever?

The following day I'm summoned not to the lairs but to what was the Greatlord's study. Griff stands in front of a desk overflowing with papers, scowling at it. The last time I was here, I was begging him to spare Phemi. When I enter, he looks up and turns his scowl on me.

"Help me with these," he says in Dragontongue.

No mention of last night. I wonder if he got drunk enough to forget it. But for the first time in weeks, Griff doesn't look hungover. "I thought Duck needed help in the lairs."

"I've found Duck other help. Actually I've found help to replace Duck, too. I need him teaching all those Callipolans Norish."

I approach the table cautiously. The piles are high: They've been accumulating since the Liberation. Few Norcians can read; those of Clan Thornrose who were favored enough to be taught were not the ones spared during the uprising. Griff, who learned on the sly with Antigone as his teacher, is the rare exception. I suspect he is a weak reader at best. At any rate, the number of papers that have been accumulating since the Liberation is daunting even to me.

"How can I . . . help?"

"Tell me which ones are important."

We begin going through the pile. His lips move when he reads, like Astyanax; he goes so slowly it would be faster for me to read the selected correspondence and reports aloud to him, but I know better than to try. Though Griff's ability to follow court politics in conversation is equal to any dragonborn's, he has no fluency with the written formalities of court. He can read figures, but what little he understands of arithmetic he knows from his ten fingers, like a sailor. When he realizes I've caught him counting with them, he goes crimson. I look away.

"It's fine. You don't need to understand the numbers. You find a Callipolan who does and you set them as your accountant."

Griff rubs his forehead with inky thumbs. He's done this so often in the last hour, his forehead's discolored. "Bet you're thinking I'm a real idiot."

No. I'm thinking it's a crime we didn't educate this boy, who is slamming his way through layers of knowledge as if brute force will grant him the education he was deprived of. I'm thinking I should have taught him, not Antigone. "I've seen worse."

Griff looks up. "Who was it, who beat you? The same ones from last night?"

So we're talking about it. *Idiots* must have reminded him. There seems no point denying anything now, not after what he saw happening in the hall. I'm pretty sure I still smell like wet dog. "Seanan's friends? Probably."

Griff's eyes narrow. "What does that mean, probably?"

"It means they put a bag over my head."

Griff whistles. He rubs the ink-stained crease between his brows again.

"Because you're my damsel?"

The translation he's gone for in Dragontongue is so ridiculous, it puts me past cringing to snorting aloud. "That's *not* the right word."

"Did you tell them we take turns?"

"Stop," I say, but now I'm snorting into my hand. "This isn't funny, stop."

Griff, who was grinning, too, sobers suddenly. "You're right. It's not one bit funny. How bad is it?"

I shrug. "You've had worse."

"So?"

I'd imagined his telling me to toughen up at this story, *just a beating, no big deal*. Somehow, his taking it seriously makes the thing worse. I can't look at him, though I can feel him looking at my neck, at that one spot. "You trying to get me to take my shirt off, Griff Gareson?" I joke lightly, because I don't know what happens if I don't joke about this. The room is too small to contain it. Too small, like this island, this future; too trapped.

Griff reaches out. His fingers brush my chin. The place where the oyster bag struck a little too high above the collar. And then I'm looking at him. For a moment, the fact that we're alone, undisturbed, that Griff is sober for the first time in a month and we're no longer fighting, presents itself differently.

"Honestly," he says, dropping his hand and his gaze after just long enough to leave my throat warm, "I'm just glad to find out it wasn't me."

"You?" My voice sounds funny, my head still clearing.

I've missed the feeling of Griff's touch like that.

His voice is rough as he reaches for the next paper. "Yeah, well. I was pretty pissed at you. And I've been drunk a lot. I can't remember a damn thing from the last month."

This is the most insulting thing I've heard yet. "You ass. There was a whole gang of them. I could take *you*."

Griff makes a noncommittal noise, picking up the pen, his lip beginning to pucker in a smile. "Right," he says.

The silence and the work are different after that. Griff is more open about what he finds confusing, and I'm more willing to volunteer the context I suspect he's missing. We find one curious document, a letter from the God-King of Bassilea that must have arrived shortly after Freyda and Ixion departed, asking Rhadamanthus if he had seen his daughter, who was expected home soon to marry his son.

"Yuck," says Griff.

"No. Fascinating. She made Ixion think she was available. Also, I don't think we were aware she'd run off."

I have the dangerous thought that it could go on like this, easily. Picking through paperwork with Griff Gareson. Advising him on courtly etiquette and laughing at his inappropriate jokes. Forgetting the world and forgotten here, as his secretary, his right-hand man. We might, eventually, spend nights again together where both of us were sober and we did more than flirt, and Seanan's goons would lose interest or maybe just be scared off by Griff's tremendous scowl and his stormscourge.

I'm here to serve penance. I'm here to serve my family.

Midday, lunch is called with Crissa sur Phaedra, Cor sur Maurana, and Bran sur Beria in attendance; they bring the trays of food themselves and glance skeptically in my direction as Griff clears the tea table for their repast. This must be some sort of planned council.

"Don't mind Delo," Griff says with a wave of his hand, "he's just sorting papers."

Crissa speaks timidly. "How are you?"

I realize she's addressing me, and then I realize why. "Fine. Thanks for asking."

"Would you like a sandwich?"

I decline with a grimace. Not that I'm not grateful for her

decency, but I'd just as soon pretend the spectacle at the feast last night didn't happen, much less that it happened in front of everyone in this room, two of whom used to be my servants. Bran is suddenly studying his fingers. Griff clears his throat. "Shall we?"

I'd also rather not hear compromising plots involving my family, all else being equal. But not having been dismissed, I end up sorting papers at the desk while they nibble salmon sandwiches made of yesterday's leftovers around the tea table. The talk is of a naval blockade that Ixion is tightening around Sailor's Folly.

"We could take the fight to them," Griff says. "Retake Callipolis, tear down the triarchal banner, all that."

"Griff Gareson wants to attack? How surprising," Bran mutters. A snort I didn't mean to be heard catches the attention of the room, and Bran jabs a thumb my way. "Delo gets me."

"I like the sound of an offensive, too, of course," Crissa says, thumbing her braid over her shoulder. "The sooner we're able to stop imposing on your hospitality, the better, and our combined fleets are evenly matched against the Clovers. But we're lacking our Firstrider, and *she* would say we're lacking legitimacy—"

"*Legitimacy*," says Griff sagely, leaning back to prop an ankle on a knee, "sounds like a fancy word created by someone with a shorter knife to keep themselves from getting stabbed by someone with a longer one."

Crissa translates in an undertone to Cor, who grunts his appreciation. His brows are knitted trying to follow the Dragontongue. Bran and I share another glance of exasperation, and Bran's lip quirks. He swallows his last bite of sandwich. "Griff, the kingsmoot's coming up."

"So?"

"So, do you intend to rule this damn island or not?"

Griff flicks crumbs from his lap and settles more comfortably into what was once the Greatlord's chair. Had I not watched him spending the morning shouldering through the Greatlord's paper-work, rubbing ink on his own face, I'd find this pretense insuffer-able. "Who, me?"

Crissa lifts an eyebrow, like she can't quite tell on what level Griff intends his nonchalance. It's clarified when Bran throws a sandwich at his head. Griff catches it with a bark of laughter. "Yeah, all right," he admits.

"Your main opposition is Seanan," Bran says. "Kraken and Turret—my clan—which Seanan is connected to by marriage. Right now he's done a pretty good job of convincing the elders of most of the clans, save your own, that you're a drunk waylaid with grief and escalating us into a needless conflict with Callipolis. Not to mention . . ." He glances my way.

"Yeah, I picked up on all that last night," Griff says, not fol-lowing Bran's glance. "So what's your point? Hold off bashing Seanan's brains in until after the moot?"

Bran places a palm over his face.

"That, and you should *de*-escalate," says Crissa crisply. "For now. Regardless of your, ah, royal prospects, we don't have a chance against Ixion unless we can figure out the goliathan. As I was going to say, our fleets are more or less matched except for the little matter of Freyda's whalefin."

"Was hoping you Callipolans had some secret tactics up your sleeve. Heroes of the Bassilean Wars, all that."

Crissa shakes her head. "Goliathans haven't been seen on our shores in centuries; the battle lore is considered arcane. I'm sure subduing them is written about in some tome somewhere in the Palace library, but I can't access that anymore."

"Then we shelve the goliathan problem for the time being,"

Griff says. "But how does one de-escalate with Ixion Storm-scourge?" His voice is lifted a little, and he twists to look at me with a show of discovery. "Delo, care to advise?"

I have the suspicion I was kept in the room for this moment, because for all Griff jokes about being an idiot, he isn't one and knows it. Bran watches curiously as I gather my thoughts. My habit of defusing conflict is something my father always regarded as a weakness; I'm unused to being asked to draw upon it as an asset. More because of the document I'm currently skimming than any flash of insight, I say, "The League."

"The what?" says Bran.

"The Medean League. You want your trade partners to join you in opposition of the blockade—Damos, the lesser archipelagos—but none of them wants to risk aggressing against Callipolis and Bassilea. If you want to de-escalate with Ixion"—I lift the paper I've been studying, an invitation to the spring summit in Isca—"you allow everyone to save face by taking the dispute to the League. The blockade can't prevent your attendance if you go on dragonback."

For the remainder of their lunch, I'm kicking myself. How was *that* serving my family, advising Griff on how to counter Ixion? But when the others have left, and Griff and I are alone again, Griff doesn't drop it. He asks all the questions about the League he pretended to know the answers to in front of the Callipolans and then hands me a blank piece of paper and a pen.

"You know how to write," I point out.

"Yeah, chicken scratch. Not well."

"The *Callipolans* know how to write."

"Their Dragontongue's shit. I'm going to say it, and then you're going to make it sound all fancy and official, all right?"

He begins to dictate. It's a letter to the League, requesting arbitration over a maritime dispute with Callipolis. He asks that Ixion dismantle his blockade.

In exchange, Griff will surrender Norcia's dragonborn political hostages.

I'm halfway through writing my own name out when I understand. I look up. "But we're your guarantee."

"You *were* my guarantee. Now my guarantee's ten more dragons. I can send you home."

My heart's racing, and my head's suddenly full of reasons he shouldn't. "I thought you needed someone to help you sort your papers."

"Well. Like you said. The Callipolans can do it just as well as you."

He's right, and I don't think he means the comment to sting. It *shouldn't* sting. And yet it does.

"It would be a way to de-escalate," he says, beginning to sound frustrated, like he can tell this is landing wrong but doesn't know why. "Everyone wants de-escalation. This *de-escalates*. Doesn't it?"

"No, you're right. It—does."

But I find I can't look at him. I write the rest of the note without speaking. And then, though he hasn't dismissed me, I get to my feet.

"I thought you'd be glad," Griff says, his brows knotted.

Truth be told, I'm as confused by my own reaction as Griff is. I should be glad: I'll be reunited with Gephyra at last, able to see my father and the twins again, able to return to the Skyfish Summer Palace after so many years in cold, wet exile. Sty will be raised properly by his cousins in a court where he can hold his head high, Electra will be able to grow old in dignity, and last night's humiliation in the Greatlord's Hall will never be repeated.

This is an act of mercy, and I should be grateful.

But instead of gratitude, I want to shake him. *If I wasn't afraid of a handful of goons, why are you?* And then I know that whatever I'm feeling about this cozy, intimate room, the desk with its stacks of papers and Griff's quiet company, is the greatest betrayal of my family I've made yet.

So I close it down.

"You're right. It's for the best. I am glad."

"Okay," Griff says, and I watch his face close, too. Businesslike, now. "Good. We can make the exchange at the spring summit."

It's a relief when he dismisses me.

24

FARHALL

ANNIE

THE HIGHLANDS

I awake in the vastest, softest bed I've ever slept in. A high canopy overhead frames bedposts as thick as tree trunks. On the far side of the room, floor-length glass doors open onto a balcony and have been cracked to let in the morning breeze and the cries of gulls. I can smell salt. It takes me a minute to realize what I'm *not* feeling: The pain in my back has receded. I roll onto my side, pushing soft bedclothes and bearskins off my body, and discover I've been bathed and the dressings on my burns have been changed. I'm otherwise unclothed.

The mattress is wide enough that it takes a bit of a crawl to reach the edge, where I find a pillow and a blanket on the floor beside it, rumpled as if the person who slept there just arose.

As I rub sleep from my eyes, I try to piece together what happened last night. I remember Lee arriving on the cliffwalk with that gruff, spindly man, whom Aela took a liking to at once and let examine her wings. Were they accompanied by a *bear*? Pallor applying pressure, a love bite on our neck to hold us calm while Lee helped stitch us back together. And then a draft of lovely, all-infusing opiate that had Aela purring her way down to what Lee called *the Trav*, while I giggled my way into the manor. The memories after that have the qualities of dreams: a grand stair-case, the wolf heads as promised, a bath drawn in a ridiculously large tub while—please let me have dreamed this—I asked Lee where all his servants were. His answer, which I found hilarious then and still a little funny now: *It's the off-season.*

I really hope I dreamed that I kept calling him *my lord*, giggling.

As in, *Don't be silly, my lord, this bed's more than large enough for the both of us.* I think I even said it in a serf's brogue.

Dragons above. No wonder he slept on the floor.

I find a loose shift draped over the chair by the bed. I shrug it over my bandaged back and then push open the door into a quiet hall. On one end, the curve of the grand staircase leads down into the main house; at the other, a door is ajar, and I follow it to find a smaller, much more modest stair that leads down into a dark, garden-level kitchen where Lee is frying eggs in a skillet, watched by an enormous dog. When it trots over to greet me, its tail slams the shelves hard enough to rattle them.

I crouch down to rub its ears. "So *you're* the bear. You're a very cute bear."

"That's Argos." Lee's glance flicks to my shift, which ends at the thigh, then back to the skillet with renewed concentration. "Glad you're awake. I was going to bring breakfast up."

I'm still getting happy kisses from Argos. "How old are you, big boy?"

"He's from before. If that's what you're asking."

Lee gestures at the prepping table. I take a seat at one of the stools and Argos rests his giant head on my knee while Lee fin-ishes the eggs. I haven't seen him attempt to cook since we were at Albans Orphanage, but after all the comments I'm pretty sure I made last night, I resist making any crack about his kitchen skills now. Even if the sight of Lee at a stove is endearing. *Didn't your parents teach you?* I'd asked in Albans. *Don't crack it like that, you'll get the shells in.* No shells in today. Lee gives one egg to Argos and plates the other two. They're plain earthenware, not the fancy china I was expecting, but I assume that's because we're in the servants' wing and decide not to comment on that, either.

I need to get it together.

"Sorry about the sleeping arrangements," Lee says, putting a teapot and two mugs in front of us. "Nigel . . . presumed. I'll set up different beds for tonight."

"Oh, but I liked that bed."

Lee grunts. "You mentioned. Last night. A few times."

My lord, do you show all your peasant girls such sumptuous beds?

Lee pours tea into the mugs and I take one, feeling my face heat. The tea is wonderfully warm and my abused feet are blissfully cool on the stone floor. We're close enough to the sea that we can hear the surf through the cracked window. Abruptly, I understand. "It's the master bedroom."

Lee nods into his tea.

I slept in Leon Stormscourge's bed. Really *well* in Leon Stormscourge's bed. And I'm pretty sure I tried to seduce Lee into it, too.

I'm incongruously tempted to giggle again.

Lee stabs at his egg, a perfect over-medium, and shoves some in his mouth. "Like I said, we can move you somewhere else. And me into a—third other place," he adds with uncharacteristic awkwardness. One of his hands goes to Argos's neck and begins to scratch his scruff. The dog's so big, his haunches are level with the countertop. When he leans against it, the table creaks.

I poke at the egg, wondering how to phrase the apology. "So, um, last night—"

Lee's plate is already clear. He shrugs, draining his tea. "Aela was drugged, it was spilling over, don't worry about it. I talked to Nigel, she'll be airworthy in a week, two weeks tops, so . . . I know you're a bit uncomfortable being here, but we don't have to stay that long, okay?"

Uncomfortable isn't wrong exactly, but Lee seems to have decided my giggly hysteria last night was some form of intentional cruelty. I'm not sure I want him to know I was just in awe of a tub. "Okay."

"Do you want to go see the dragons?" He sounds a little stilted.

That's when I realize the low, humming contentment underneath my own contentment is Aela's, close enough to be almost beneath my feet. She's as happy as I was in Leon's bed. I look down at the hemline of my shift. "Yeah. Maybe . . . is my flamesuit around?"

Lee's nose wrinkles. "Trust me, you don't want it. Let me find you something else."

He returns ten minutes later with a well-made but simply cut blue dress, smelling of dust and cedar, which I pull over the shift. He looks at me for a second too long after I've put it on, his expression a little wild, before handing me a jacket to put over it. I don't dare ask which sister's dress I'm wearing. Lee's in a loose shirt and slimming trousers that, I suspect, he found in the armoire of the master bedroom. He looks good in them. With black hair sweeping across his forehead, a little overgrown, and a bit of a shadow on his chin, one more thing I resist saying is *You look dashing, my lord.*

The morning is brisk but not cold, and our feet are so blistered from the trek here that Lee finds me slippers and heads out onto the grounds barefoot. He stumps across the meadow head-down as if hoping that by walking quickly he can keep me from seeing any of it: the vineyard trellises and the orchard rows separated by a trickling black brook; the chickens in their coop behind Nigel's cottage and the horses out to pasture a little beyond that; the high peaks of the mountains rising in escarpments around us on three sides, snowcapped. The gardens immediately surrounding the house are wooded and wild, protecting it from the wind with long cypress arms, and past them is nothing but clusters of yellow gorse, rippling green grass, and the gray sea.

I realize I've seen this picture before: that tapestry on the Lyceum Club landing, the manor on the sea, a green sea-perch amid soaring black walls of stone.

I don't think I've ever seen a place so beautiful.

"It's so *lush*."

"The thermal vents keep the terrace temperate. We call it the Winterless Green."

Argos leads the way in eager bounds toward the cliff edge. We descend a narrow stair that forks from the cliffwalk and leads down to sea level, where it winds into a grotto Lee calls the Travertine, and Trav for short. Terraces of white sediment climb from the surf like a wedding cake, each level a still-steaming pool that overflows into the one below it, and at the base, the hot water hisses where it trickles into the crashing waves. The stairs lead round the Travertine and into a fissure in the rock from which steam billows. Inside, the crash of the surf becomes muffled, and the air grows humid and the stones warm.

"Some of these pools will boil the skin off you. But a few are—perfect bath temperature. As you see here."

In the semidarkness, twined together like a single organism, we find Aela and Pallor lounging in the shallows of a steaming pool. Lee stops short. I have the momentary, very human thought that I've come across something indecent. But neither of the dragons feels shame or even seems to notice us. This, I realize, was the contentment I must have felt pulsing through Aela all morning. This place, she feels, and the feeling courses through me—this place is *perfect*. These wedding-cake-white terraces of steaming water, the fresh breeze off the sea, the safety and the warmth and the cave walls pressing in, perfectly containing her. And Pallor around her, everywhere.

"Well, seems like Aela's feeling better."

Her wings, stitched cleanly along the gashes where Edmund's dragon mauled her, are lifted akimbo out of the steaming water, warm but dry. Pallor's tail is twined with hers in a twisting coil of amber and silver, and as they shift with lazy sighs, it thumps in the shallows and splashes us.

I look up and find Lee's face bright red.

"Usually they make their nests a bit farther in. Where it's dry," he clarifies.

But the thermal springs are where they breed. I have a sudden insight into why I was so determined to get Lee to join me in that bed last night and nearly giggle. My face is hot, too, but evidently enough of Aela's shamelessness is spilling into me that I don't mind.

"Well, they might as well, if we've got a week. Can you feel it?"

Lee's brows draw together. "Can I feel what?"

When I smirk, he rolls his eyes and leads the way back out of the grotto and onto the stairs outside where Argos waits, tail thumping the limestone. Lee splashes cold seawater on his face with his back turned, and while he does, I admire the musculature of his back. There's something very liberating about being able to blame everything on Aela.

"Where to now, Lord of Farhall?" At Lee's stiffening expression, I add, "Sorry."

"Well," he says cautiously, "I had an idea."

His idea, it turns out, is the Stormscourge family library, on the first floor of the manor. I think at first he's joking. Then I wonder, with excitement I also blame on Aela, whether this is the start of a romantic fantasy about libraries I wouldn't be surprised to find Lee had. My amorous hopes are dashed when he shows me the reading table where he's piled a stack of enormous, ancient books.

"These are the old annals my family kept during the Bassilean Wars. The Stormscourge family was responsible for western offensives against the goliathans, and they recorded a lot of the maneuvers in family records. A lot of these aren't even in the libraries at the Great Palace. Dora visited the house only once or twice, and as far as I can tell, she's changed pretty much nothing. My father's old hermeneuta is still here, even—"

"His what?"

Lee points distractedly at a tabletop device I'd assumed was decorative. It looks like a three-dimensional abacus. "It's the way dragonlords trained their sons to read traditional flight notation. They're a bit arcane, wildly outdated by Goran's standards, but the notes from the annals will translate. If I can remember how to do it. Father mostly did the hermeneuta exercises with Laertes, before he was passed over."

I'm pretty sure Aela's steaming brain has me sluggish on the uptake. "You want us to research how to subdue a goliathan."

"Well, yeah. We've got a week, we might as well take advantage of this collection."

The way he says it, I finally hear him. A week before Aela's wings are repaired. A week before we're airworthy. A week before we rejoin the Guardians in Norcia. And, apparently, in Lee's eyes, a week before we rejoin a war.

And all I feel is panic. "I said I didn't want a civil war, Lee. I told Crissa—"

Lee's hands are planted on the table, his eyes widening at my protest. He speaks with the hesitation of someone stating the obvious. "Annie. The Guardians may have a war whether they want one or not. So long as we're powerless against a goliathan, we can't control what conflict we're a part of."

He's right, and I know all of this, but still I'm shaking my head. Suddenly my eyes are hot. *Aela,* I tell myself. *Stupid Aela,* as I rub them.

"*What?*" he says, staring at me. Bewilderment is written across his high cheekbones and narrowed gray eyes.

I want out. I want to be done. I don't want to sit down at one more desk, plan one more campaign, break my heart one more time as I watch my plans fail, or backfire, at the cost of innocent lives and my friends.

I want one week where that life isn't mine.

"Do you think maybe"—I hear my voice shake—"before we sit down to do this, you could give me a tour of the rest of your grounds and pour me tea in the room with all the china and tell me about your family's wolf-head collection? Just, a little bit longer?"

Lee's chin tilts, his brows rippling, like this is the last thing he expected me to say. "You *want* me to tell you about my family's wolf-head collection?"

"I really"—and now I'm crying like a complete idiot, because stupid, stupid Aela—"*really* want you to tell me about your family's wolf-head collection."

LEE

I've never been able to feel Pallor's moods through solid rock the way Annie can feel Aela's, but the sight of him twisted up with Aela in the pools after breakfast did explain a few things.

Like the feeling that Annie in my line of sight clogs my brain with hot water.

"I really, *really* want to hear about your family's wolf-head collection," she says, standing in the middle of my father's library, her auburn hair offset prettily by Penelope's bluebell dress, tears inexplicably squirting from her eyes. I'm not sure which of us is going battier at this point, because even the crying makes me want to cover her face with sloppy kisses like Argos.

Right, then. The wolf heads.

Instead of working on the hermeneuta, I spend the afternoon giving Annie the tour.

I don't think it occurred to me that Annie might see this house and like it. In the convoluted logic of our twisted histories, I thought it would be tainted, as so much between us is always tainted, with knowledge of the dirty underbelly. How did my family build this house, pay for these crystals and china, fill these tables with sumptuous meals and cellars with fine wine? Annie knows. But instead of decrying the corruption beneath, she seems willfully, blissfully enchanted.

I was living in this fairy tale while you starved. This was the home my father returned to after watching yours burn.

But if Annie wants her chance at living in a fairy tale, I'm not going to be the one who stops her.

We pull sheets off furniture and paintings I haven't seen in years, I tell her not only about the wolf heads but the uncles and grandfathers who hunted them and the dragons they rode, and all the terribly austere old family portraits glare down on us as we make our way irreverently through the old life. Then she wants to see the grounds, take a turn on the swing behind the house where Larissa once fell and broke her wrist, visit the pastures to meet the horses, climb the first stairs of Pilgrim's Pass to look out over the fingers of the southern highlands and spy the blue strip of the Medean Sea in the distance.

The sun is setting when I take her down the cliffwalk again. This time, instead of taking the stairs to the Travertine, we climb over the lower rocks to the black sands revealed by a low tide. The oysters we find there are the size of a human foot. Annie holds one up and squints at the rough shell with her nose wrinkled. "Are you sure these are edible?"

"It's cute that you've never had them before."

Her dress is tied round her knees to keep it dry, but when a surprise wave hits our thighs, she yelps. The water so clearly puts her at unease that a thought occurs to me. "Can you swim?"

Annie folds her arms and backs away from me as though I might decide to submerge her on the spot. "We are *not* teaching me how to swim." She is blushing from the cold, her face a bit wet, her hair plastered to her forehead. By this point I've given up caring whether it's Pallor I'm channeling in these moments of blissful appreciation. Argos, who's been paddling around in the shallows happily, chooses this moment to emerge beside Annie and shake. He drenches her in freezing water and she shrieks in a very un-Guardian-like manner. It's adorable.

"It's warm in the Trav."

"No, Lee."

I'll try again tomorrow.

Back in the Big House, Annie disappears to the second floor to run a hot bath in the tub she appreciated so vocally last night, and I make my way down to the cellar to retrieve a bottle of ice wine. The house evokes unexpected memories, and one of them is the way my father talked about our wine. The vineyard's been commercialized under Dora, but much of his personal collection remains untouched in the cellar. His favorite vintage was the one that had a Midwinter frost. The grapes were harvested in the frenzy typical of ice wine harvests, but this one took place amid solstice feasting. *You can taste the joy in it,* he'd say.

For a moment I stand still in the cool cellar, the weight of the memory heavy as the bottle in my hand. I can, just faintly, smell salt and sulfur. Where the cellar ends, the porous tunnels left by eroding thermal springs begin, and you can follow them all the way down to the Travertine grotto below. Perhaps I'm only imagining that I can feel Pallor a little more clearly from here, tired but content.

I make my way back up to the great room and build a fire in the hearth. Annie comes down wrapped in an enormous bathrobe, her skin pink and hair toweled half dry. The house is quiet, empty, and dark except for the flickering fire, but at the sight of her, I feel my nerves go on end as if they were overwhelmed by noise and light. My breath has caught.

"Why are you looking at me like that?"

"Sorry. Here."

I've assembled a truly ramshackle dinner for Annie's fairy tale: ice wine; leftover bread offered by Nigel; and the oysters with their shucking gear. Annie takes a seat beside me, on the floor in front of the fire, as I pour two glasses. She tilts the wine to her lips cautiously. I have seen Annie drink alcohol twice before in her life. This will be the best wine she's ever had.

"Ooh," she says, like she's made a discovery. The fire dances on her face, in her eyes.

"Can you taste the joy in it?"

Her brow lifts. I can feel my pulse in my wrists. I reach for an oyster. Annie watches with evident skepticism as I cover my hand with the cloth, drive the knife into the joining, and twist. "I feel like you should have had servants for this," she says.

"Well, we did. But sometimes we did it ourselves. For fun. Mother didn't let us do it in the house, though." Juice is dripping down my hand as I show her the meaty inside.

"And now you what—roast it?"

"You can, but they're best raw."

Annie bursts out laughing. "No," she says.

I demonstrate. It has been years since I've had an oyster like this. It tastes like Penelope's smile and Laertes's laughter, Larissa's shriek of frustration when she couldn't manage it. *I can do it my ownself.* Penelope always helped me open mine when the others weren't looking.

This house is so empty now. I close my eyes against the blackness as I swallow. The oyster goes down like a lump in my throat.

But Annie's waiting on the other side, smiling and beautiful and a little repulsed, and her face is enough to make the blackness recede. "The best," I promise, washing down the oyster with cool wine.

She's laughing as she shakes her head. "Absolutely not. These things have seaweed growing on them. I'll cook mine, thanks."

She fumbles with the knife, searching for the opening and not finding it. I take it from her, pry the shell open, and cut the flesh free, then hesitate. Annie's looking at me, her knee touching mine beneath that robe. The fire dancing in her eyes is the only thing that moves. I know she knows what I'm thinking of doing.

I lean forward, and she parts her lips. I place the shell against them and upturn it.

Everything slows down after that.

At some point I realize that the hand that was holding the shell has set it down to hold her nape. We are sideways, her still-wet hair tickling my face as she leans her length against me. The taste of oysters and wine is on my tongue and in her mouth.

"Do you think this is the dragons?"

"I don't know. I don't care." It's been an hour since either of us has strung a whole sentence together. "I didn't make the other beds."

"I don't want another bed."

"Another bed for me, then."

Annie lifts her head to look at me. She says, "I don't want another bed for you."

It's the dragons talking, it's the wine talking, and I try to remember the words to articulate this, to remind her that *we* can't have the things we want, the cardinal rule Annie and I live by, our law of gravity. But here in this house, on this night, it feels like gravity has stopped working. I can't remember, with her mouth on my neck and her hand tracing a line down my waist, why we can't have what we want like everyone else. Why we can't just reach out and take it.

So with the last of the wine drunk, the oysters eaten, and the fire down, I hoist Annie into my arms and carry her up the stairs to my parents' bed.

* * *

I wake in the sea of blankets with Annie curled against me, asleep. Her back, still healing from the burns of Edmund's dragon, is an angry red in the half-light. It's barely dawn. She looks so vulnerable, so small, I experience a moment of love for her so fierce it feels like panic.

The alcohol knocked us out last night before anything could happen with significant consequences. But we came close. I knew female Guardians were on some kind of suppressants—a recent medical development touted by the Revolutionary regime—but

Annie indicated from a garbled mutter that she wasn't sure if they'd worn off. "It's . . . probably fine?"

I'd been worried about hurting her anyway. "There are other things we can do."

My face feels pleasantly warm remembering the bit that came after that.

So, maybe we found a way of seizing our moment with no harm done. I still don't intend to ever try it drunk again.

I shift, and Annie rolls onto her other side without stirring. I kiss her forehead, sweaty and warm, and she sleeps on. The sight of her face smoothed in sleep, hair mussed from spending a night in my arms, fills me with such sudden happiness that walls can't contain it. I held Annie, like a lover, and didn't pull the roof down on our heads for daring to be happy.

I need to feel the sunrise.

Outside, a morning mist still lingers, the snowy peaks are dipped in the first rosy hint of sun, and the gray horizon over a gray sea gives the impression of unending sky. An osprey soars level with the cliffs and a mile out, a pod of dolphins breach. I inhale with the feeling that I could breathe in and in and never breathe out. I could gorge myself on this salt air, this bright morning, this fickle, joyridden life.

Far away, mere specks in the distance, ships stud the horizon off Sailor's Folly.

Whose ships?

We're too far to make out the smaller dragon breeds, but a single hovering blot is visible above the stubble, her wings a black line these miles away.

A single goliathan, circling what looks like a blockade.

I think of the annals and the hermeneuta waiting for me in the library. I can't afford to waste another day. I don't know how much time I'll need, not only to read the annals but to parse the flight notation on the hermeneuta. I'll begin after breakfast.

Maybe make that a languorous breakfast in bed with Annie.

"My lord? I've been meaning to speak to you."

I turn to find Nigel trudging his way up the cliffwalk from the Travertine. Argos lopes behind him, scattering sleepy, jabbering puffins.

"Didn't want to alarm you the night you arrived," Nigel says, joining my side. "But there were visitors, the day before you got here. Came on dragonback. Triarchal sigils with that bit from the new government, the clover. Didn't stay long once it became clear I'd had no other guests, but they asked for you."

His equanimous tone brooks no inquiry into the intimidation he certainly received, alone in this isolated place confronted with two dragonriders. "Anyway, I thought it wise to go into town yesterday and ask after what other news might be had."

Town means Harfast, the home of the remotest courthouse in the Far Highlands, where the Garth extended family lives. Nigel himself is a childless widower. He pulls a flyer from his pocket and holds it out. "Found lots of these."

The flyer is illustrated with two roughly drawn faces: mine and Annie's. I am WANTED, DEAD OR ALIVE, charged with the murder of Atreus Athanatos, the First Protector of Callipolis. This, I realize now, must have always been the planned contingency if I proved uncooperative.

Annie is charged with crimes against the people and high treason. Beneath Annie's name, the subheading reads, LET THE BITCH COMMANDER HAVE THE TRIAL SHE DESERVES.

Nigel didn't ask, the night we arrived, who Annie was. If anything, I got the impression he didn't want to know. He seems to be the sort of man who prefers his knowledge of current events outdated; I doubt he can read the flyer he's handed me. But he's clearly guessed enough.

"Thank you for showing me this, Mr. Garth."

He nods. "You'll have my discretion for as long as you need it, my lord. If they come again, we'll send you down the cellar entrance into the Trav."

He lifts his cap, bowing deeply, and makes his stiff way on to his cottage, leaving me to mount the stairs to the Big House. The lungs that felt so full as I stood on the edge of the cliff now feel leaden.

A trial. Ixion has moved past the farce of the Winnowing Tournaments. Annie is no longer invited to fight for the title of Firstrider in the arena; he's realized he can delegitimize his greatest lowborn rival by other means. He wants to string her up and make a spectacle of it.

Which means his hunt for us is far from over.

Inside, I find Annie stirring, as sleepy and happy as I was a half hour ago. The flyer's clutched in my hand, and I'm preparing myself to show it to her when she loops easy hands around my neck.

"I want this week to last forever," she says.

Her face, smoothed of worry, full of smiles, looks like it belongs to another person. A smiling, younger person that I'm only just meeting after all these years of knowing her. I think the sight of it breaks my heart.

I tuck the flyer into my pocket and kiss her hand.

One week. I can give her one week.

"Forever," I promise, and she pulls me back to bed.

25

THE MEDEAN LEAGUE

DELO

NORCIA

In the week leading up to the spring summit, my secretarial work continues. Griff spends most of his days on the Folly, where the blockade has hardened to a standoff; in the evenings, instead of getting drunk and finding me, he locks himself up in a parlor off the provisional palace with Crissa sur Phaedra. I'm tempted to be jealous about this development—even I can't help noticing how pretty Crissa is—until I pass the closed door on my way out and overhear them.

"Right, so I think in this case you'd also be pleading the right to trade—"

They're composing his address to the League. I suppose she does have the diplomatic training, but I still feel a bit snubbed. I'm trained in the language of diplomacy, too. He need only have asked.

Without any supervision to prevent it, I start bringing Astyanax to the Greatlord's study with me. He gets letter lessons as I work. It's a mark of Sty's relief to be off the streets of Norcia that he doesn't complain about a resumption of school. When I ask him about his excitement to go to Callipolis, he looks more uncertain.

"Your cousins will be there," I point out. "You'll be returning to your birthright."

"But Griff isn't coming?"

I don't see how this is relevant. "No. Griff isn't coming."

On the second day, Sty brings a second child with him. "Becca wants to read, too."

I didn't know they knew each other. Now that I think about it, they're close to the same age. Griff's niece stares up at me with wide blue eyes. Her curls are matted. "Hi, Delo."

"Hi, Becca."

Sty's reluctance for school transforms with the presence of a classmate. When I appoint him to teach Becca the alphabet, he puffs himself up like he hasn't in weeks. "Listen closely, Becca, because some of these letters can be really confusing."

Until he speaks to her in it, I hadn't realized he knew any Norish.

The second day Becca joins us in the Greatlord's study, I hold up Lady Electra's hairbrush. Becca makes a face. "You'll pull my hair."

"I promise, I won't. I'm a hair-brushing expert."

Becca's brows knit, unconvinced, but she stands still anyway. I haven't brushed a girl's hair since we were kids, freshly motherless, and I braided Phemi's. It occurs to me, as I press the brush against the bottom of Becca's knots and begin to pick them out, that this place has put more hooks in me than I knew.

So I remind myself that soon I'll see the twins. I'll see Gephyra and fly again on dragonback. I'll see the Skyfish Summer Palace after all these years, bask in the warmth I've missed, and Father will train me as its lord and his heir. *Triarch of the East*. The title waits for me, uncontested: I am the highest-ranked Skyfish dragon-born in the fleet, the only one left of legitimate birth. The title and the Near Lowlands will be mine.

How is it that plucking knots from a child's hair competes with this?

Becca has never had unlimited ink and paper at her disposal before; soon the study is full of her drawings, most of her family, some of Sty's, and occasionally mine. As she gets better at writing, she labels them with chicken-scratch Dragontongue letters, half of them backward, spelling out Norish words. NAG AND TƎH GRAT ᗡRAGON, she shows me, and I'm getting good enough at making sense of her spellings that I read it back to her: "Nag and the Great Dragon?"

She nods and points to a lump under a blue line with wings sticking out. "It's hiding from the Nag under the water."

"I didn't know dragons did that."

"The Great Dragon does," Becca says. "That's how it sneaks up on you."

It's sometimes hard to tell where Norcian oral tradition ends and Becca's imagination begins, but I find it an arresting image all the same, the whalefin dragon hiding beneath the waves like an actual whale. Becca's expression falters, and she lowers the drawing. "Mumma used to tell me this story."

I remember when the twins had these moments, the jolt of a missed stair after they'd forgotten she was gone. "Maybe you can tell it to me, now."

Becca gives me an uncertain smile.

On Sty's and my last day in Norcia, he and Becca conspire in a corner of the study, whispering over a drawing that Becca works on while Sty advises. I don't see it until the following morning, when they present it to me on the balustrade where Griff and Crissa are preparing for our launch. I stare down at four stick figures and two long spiky blobs, one black, one blue. They have been labeled: GRIϤϤ, SPARKER, ᗡELO, GEϤYRA, BECCA, ASTYANAX.

"You can keep it," Becca says generously.

I have to clear my throat to answer her. "Thank you."

Sty and I bade farewell to Electra at the hut this morning, and to the Norcians and Callipolans at breakfast in the Greatlord's Hall; the only person remaining to say goodbye to is Becca, who holds on a lot longer than I expect her to when we hug. I look up to find Griff watching us. He's cleaned up for the Medean League's summit; I find my gaze lingering. His shaved chin and trimmed curls giving him the look of a dragonborn commander. He turns away as soon as our eyes meet. Sty, tugging on his sleeve, has asked to ride with him.

"Of course you can, little lordling."

With a twinge of disappointment, I climb on Phaedra behind Crissa.

As the ground falls away, I find myself twisting to get one last look at the island I spent so long wishing I could leave. Soon we're out over open waters, leaving Norcia behind.

GRIFF

ISCA

Thanks to a lifetime spent listening to Delo's reminiscences about the beauty of the Medean, and a week prepping for the League meeting with Crissa, I'm eager for my first glimpse of the southern sea, dark as wine, and the stony little island archipelago known as Isca that rises, white like bones, out of the center of the sparkling blue. It's so warm and dry this far south—I might say too warm, too dry—that the circular headquarters for the League are built open to the air. External gates of bleached marble lead into private rooms for the delegates and dragons of each nation, and it stirs my heart to see the banners of Free Norcia hang alongside the rest of them.

Less pleasant is the sight of Ixion's Restoration banner, with its black clover in the center of the circling dragons, fluttering beside mine.

But when we take our seats to inaugurate the conference, Ixion's face puckering at the sight of me makes up for it. *That's right, Ixion. How does it feel to look into the face of your former servant and know you'll have to treat him as an equal?* I took Norcia out from under his pasty nose. I smile at him, and he blanches.

The round conference hall of the League, called the Odeon, seats its delegates around a hollow circular table under an open sky. A balcony overlooks it for the interested aides and citizens approved to attend the meeting. The summit begins with a ceremonial dousing, where every nation's dragons are doused and sent back to their nests—except for the dragonless Damos, who disarm their infamous muskets as a substitute. Sparker, bless him, does not fail to give Ixion a dirty look when he lands for his dousing, but he keeps it civil.

The dousing of the other nations' dragons is a delight I don't expect. The lesser archipelagos ride their islands' own native breeds, some clearly cousins of the skyfish and stormscourge; and it's all I can do not to smile at the sight of the tiny teal iscans, who wiggle like little winged dogs at their dousing. Isca's dragons, like Bassilea's, are commanded from the ground—for the opposite reason. They're too small to bear a rider. Crissa, beside me, actually has to mask a small squeal at their cuteness as they flit away.

After that, it gets less cute. The presiding king of Isca begins a mind-numbingly long invocation where he talks about the origin of the League, which I assume everyone here knows, how after the Second Bassilean War, an international institution was called for to prevent a war of such scale ever consuming the Medean states again. Thanks to Crissa, this is a review for me, too. But by the end, if I get the gist of his overly flowery Dragontongue, he's started rumbling about the dangers of expansion.

Ah. That's more promising.

"Shall we discuss the whalefin in the room, then?" the hoary old Damian delegate barks, whose dark skin makes Delo's look wan by comparison. "Bassilea's on the move, and we don't like it."

Crissa sits beside me, behind the sigil of the Revolutionary regime-in-exile—the dragon breathing its four circlets against red. Her arms are folded as she studies the Damian delegate; *bloviating* was how she described their recently elected administration, which refused her request for food aid and has, in general, seemed readier to expound on principles than to act.

The Bassilean delegate rises. His long hair, braided like Freyda's, is oiled and carefully combed, and curls around his shoulder and down his gold-inlaid yellow tunic. "If Damos refers to the situation in Callipolis, Bassilea would like to assure the League that Princess Freyda is acting independently of the God-King."

From the outbreak of whispering this produces, I gather this comes as a shock to them as much as it does to me. The Iscan king leans forward, pulling at his braided beard. "You mean to say, the Bassilean expansion into Callipolis is not authorized by Vask?"

"It was a surprise to all of us."

The Bassilean delegate speaks to Ixion directly. "My lord, where is the princess?"

Ixion's tone is impenetrable; if he's surprised by this news, he's hiding it with his usual scowl. "Her Divine Highness was indisposed. I am here in her stead."

I don't need Crissa's nudge beneath the table to spot my opportunity. At my lifted wrist, Isca nods. "The League recognizes Free Norcia, formerly New Pythos."

"If we're all opposed to Bassilean expansion," I say, rising to my feet, "perhaps the League would agree Freyda has no need for Callipolis and Norcia both."

Ixion's look of vitriol convinces me that I'm hitting exactly where it hurts. His partner at the table is Power sur Eater, Antigone's traitor friend. I recognize his devilish smile from the dunes where he used to chaperone Annie's reading lessons with me, though I can't see what's making him smile at this moment.

"We weren't aware she wanted Norcia," Isca says.

"The blockade she and the Clover fleet have got around our island suggests she does."

More news to the southern delegates, confirming Crissa's suspicion that the bullying of Norcia, on the other side of Callipolis in the North Sea, has gone unobserved. At Isca's grim nod, I step into the center of the round to make the first formal suit of the conference.

I take the stance coached by Crissa, lift an arm, and act like I've done this before. In a way, I have. Blustering is my specialty.

"Norcia's shared history and culture, common allies, and trade partnerships with the members of the League would make her a valuable member state despite her irregular location in the North Sea. She is willing to commit to whatever reciprocal obligations the League asks of her in return for the rights of full membership—including the right to trade."

I make rotating steps as I speak, catching each statesman's gaze in turn. More old men, more stodgy power, but I'm not intimidated by this lot any more than I was by the Triarchy-in-Exile, any more than I am by the Norcian elders and Seanan of Kraken. We have what they need, which is our ore, and if they want it, they'll have to do more than sit there. Isca might host a great conference, but she's a little island, softened by warm sands and bright sun, and she needs our strength.

"In return, we would ask that the League call for an end to Callipolis and Bassilea's blockade of our waters."

My rotation stops when I've come full circle, facing Ixion Stormscourge and Nestor, Delo's father, again. Ixion looks nauseated by the sight of me. Nestor's arms are folded, his lips pressed tight. I remember his voice from the balustrade, barking my name during training. *I don't care that you're burned. Do it again.*

Every time that man made me get back on the dragon, every time he refused me water or breaks or medicine as I trained, he made me stronger.

He prepared me for this day.

I incline my head to my former lords, the polite form of one equal to another in a dragonborn court. Ixion looks like he's considering vaulting over the table and ripping out my throat. It's one of his best expressions. "In exchange, as a gesture of goodwill, Norcia is prepared to release the hostages she took upon her Liberation."

Nestor drums his fingers on the table. "You . . . you have my son?"

He remembers to use the formal address mid-sentence. It looks like it sours his mouth. But I hear something else in his voice: desperation. My smile has widened. I bow a little deeper, teasing them with the bow they think they deserve, and lift an arm to indicate the gallery where Delo watches, frozen like a sighted hare beside Astyanax.

Nestor Skyfish hoped to break me. But intimacy for intimacy in our years of training, I learned his heart. When I told Delo that Phemi was his father's favorite? I lied. Though I knew Delo believed it. The truth is, for all Nestor blusters, for all he rants, when he is most tired, most despairing, the one he asks for is Delo.

Nestor and I seem to have that in common.

"Your son is here, with Astyanax ha'Aurelian, waiting to be taken home. You will forgive that Electra Stormscourge must be held on Norcia a little longer, until we can be sure of your good faith."

Ixion scowls at me. Electra is the one who raised him. He doesn't want Astyanax. But Nestor's glance settles on Delo, above us, and I know I've got the hook in.

I'll save Norcia. I'll free Delo. And I'll say goodbye tonight.

I had really hoped we'd ride the same dragon here.

The Damian delegate chuckles from his belly. "Surely some agreement can be reached," he says, "in time for trading season. I think we in the south agree that this blockade sounds excessive."

The lesser archipelagos are nodding gratefully: He speaks for the general interest. The haggling begins. If dissidents fleeing the Restoration is the problem, then could the blockade not be restricted to Fort Aron and the Callipolan coast, leaving Norcia free to ship her ore south around the cape of Dragon's End to Damos and the southern archipelagos who depend on it?

I'm chuffed with this plan, and Nestor follows along attentively, but Ixion's gaze wanders back to me and he cuts the negotiations off with sudden impatience.

"It's not enough."

Silence falls. Ixion was the one to breach parliamentary protocol, a point I consider with vindication. I feign polite confusion, because there's nothing more satisfying than politely pissing Ixion off. "I'm sorry, Lord Ixion?"

"It's not enough, the hostages. I want *her*."

"Electra?"

"*Antigone.*"

Did I mishear him? Whispering has broken out among the delegates. Crissa straightens in her chair beside me. I do the math. He thinks we have Antigone, which means he *doesn't* have Antigone. Which means she's safe, somewhere that isn't Norcia, and if I tell him we don't have her, then he'll start hunting her in earnest—

I've paused too long.

"Oh. Her. Yeah, sorry. You . . . can't have her."

Crissa has swung round to look at me. In the gallery, Delo's palms creep to the sides of his face. I can practically hear his groan from here. This is that moment when I'm supposed to back down from Ixion and can't.

It's all I can do to keep from groaning myself, but not for the same reason. Dragons above, I was too slow.

Ixion's eyes narrow. "You *have* got her, haven't you?"

I nod, warming up to the performance, hoping to bring it home. I was off to a slow start but Ixion's a slow learner. I can still salvage this. "Yup. We've got her. And you can't have her."

De-escalation. I can practically hear Delo growling it at me. *You're supposed to be de-escalating.* But can you blame me, with a friend in danger, for wanting to help?

"He doesn't have her," Ixion says. "You don't have Leo, either, do you?" He's forgotten to use the formal address.

Both of them on the run? Dragons. I'd thought Leo was marrying that princess. My palms are starting to sweat. "As a matter of fact, we've got him, too."

Ixion turns to whisper to Power sur Eater, Antigone's supposed friend. I always thought the mouth on him was an act not unlike mine, but I'm less sure today, when he leans forward and plants a finger on the table with glittering eyes. "Antigone sur Aela and Leo sur Pallor are wanted for charges of high treason."

"Oh, are they? What did they do?" I'm nearly on full form at this point.

Ixion pushes his chair back with a clatter. "I have had it with this *bullshit*," he says.

The old men are starting to give all of us strange looks, as if they're wondering whether the younger set is quite up to the task of diplomacy. But so far, I have not been the one to break formal register.

Power lays a hand on Ixion's arm. He looks past me to Crissa sur Phaedra. "You want that blockade lifted, you cooperate."

Crissa's face is white. "I'm not cooperating with *you*."

Power points a finger skyward. "It's me or that goliathan, sweetheart. Annie and Lee. You seen them?"

Crissa shoots me a panicked look; I'm guessing she's as anxious about endangering my friends as I am about endangering hers. *And* she's worrying about imposing on my hospitality, to boot. I want to tell her this is a scrape I don't need her to get me out of, but I can't think of a way to signal that without signaling to them, too.

She tells Power, "Our knowledge of their whereabouts has no bearing on this."

Ixion and Power look at each other. Ixion says, "You know what to do."

Power gives him an icy smile.

He gets to his feet, and he's already lifting his summoner to his lips as he walks from the hall.

Crissa lowers her face to her hands. The old men in the room seem more confused than ever. I point a thumb at the door through which Power's gone hunting and lift my chin at Ixion, though my feeling of triumph is ebbing. "There, we cooperated. Can you move your boats?"

When Ixion scowls, Nestor speaks. "A partial dismantling," he grunts. "Callipolis should be able to defend her northern coastline. But we'll allow the Norcian trade ships through, if the League prefers it."

Ixion heaves a sigh, and I smile at him.

Beside me, Crissa sur Phaedra's shoulders tremble.

And all the while, Delo watches from the gallery.

DELO

Griff and I don't find each other until after the feast that night. Or—to put it more accurately—we don't close the distance. I'm aware of his glances across the room as the evening wears on. The banquet hall is lined by slender white pillars that weave like branches into trellises, and that the little dragons of Isca cling to like bats. As night falls, they flit overhead, their bursts of slender flame shooting like stars across the darkening sky.

I'm seated with my father, whose gruffness makes me wonder if I imagined that he looked relieved to see me at the summit meeting this morning. He's not drinking; but then, he doesn't in public. Ixion's in a marginally better mood, nursing his wine and no doubt contemplating Power's hunt for his errant Firstrider. *Parcival*, Ixion corrects, when I call him Power: It turns out he's my ha'cousin and was next in line for the Skyfish Summer Palace if I didn't get traded in.

So maybe that's why Father is relieved to see me.

"We brought your dragon," he says. It's the first time he's directly addressed me since we shook hands for dinner, and it seems to be a substitute for *Good to have you back*. I suppose I did technically exonerate myself by dropping Griff.

"Oh. Thank you."

Neither of us seems able to think of anything else to say.

A Bassilean delegate slides into the space between Ixion and me.

"My lord Ixion, I have a message for your—guest—Freyda Bassileon, from His Divine Majesty the God-King and the crown prince Froydrich, her betrothed."

Ixion turns to him. "I'm sorry, did you just say—*betrothed*?"

The delegate tilts his head in surprise, and nods. "Since birth. The satraps have been told to consider further grain requests no longer in the service of the God-King. If this displeases the princess-heir, her betrothed suggests she return home for clarification."

Despite the warning in the delegate's voice, Ixion's suddenly smiling. "I think Freyda's betrothed and I might have a good deal to discuss. Shall we take this outside?"

They leave together. I linger at the table, trying not to watch Griff. The music has started, the little iscans darting and weaving overhead like a school of fire-breathing fish, and on the ground, the humans begin to dance. To my surprise, Griff makes his way with one of the Iscan princesses to the center of the floor. He picks up the footwork of the waltz so quickly, it probably isn't apparent to most watching that he didn't know it before starting. Soon enough they're both craning their necks to take in the iscans' sky-dance with delight.

Watching him waltz with a foreign princess, mastering each step of the Medean as quickly as she shows it to him, I'm torn between bitter jealousy and pure aesthetic appreciation.

When I've had enough of the woman's smiles and Griff's laughter, I make my way out.

My room is dark, Gephyra no more than a shadow in its center. Her long tail encircles the olive-tree bed. At the sight of me, she rustles to her feet with a purr and twines it round me like a giant serpent. Her delicate snout tickles my face as she sniffs me over.

I wrap my arms around her and let our senses flood together. After weeks apart, it's a relief.

"My Geph."

I lie on the marble floor beside her, running a hand along her smooth scales, and when my thoughts become my own again, they stray to Griff. He's no doubt going to dance the night away with that princess, take breaks on the fragrant balcony to knock back lemon liqueurs, and then who knows where the evening will take him, heady with his own power and newfound status.

You have your whole life to flirt with women. Did it have to start the night we part?

When I've nearly decided to go say it to his face, he appears at my door.

"You left. I looked for you."

I get to my feet, Gephyra's coils falling from me as she perks at the sight of her old caretaker. I want to seize him by those smartly trimmed curls and haul him over the threshold. Instead, I'm frozen. "I thought I should leave you to your diplomacy."

Griff makes a noise. He takes a step closer. "If that's diplomacy, so is this."

Then his mouth is on my mouth and I am home.

***

Much later, sprawled across the olive bed like a dragon coasting on a spring breeze, I descend slowly to earth. Griff's fine clothes are strewn across the floor. His fingers are playing idly with my hair. When I turn to him, he cups the back of my head and the tenderness of it, the familiar feeling of his calloused hand on my neck, makes my breath skip again. Gephyra's lolling on the carpet, as content and relaxed as I am. We've spilled over, but neither Griff nor Geph minds.

How can this be for the last time?

"What happens next?" Griff asks.

My answer is automatic. The future I have wanted and steeled myself for in equal measure for as long as I can remember, the way now cleared by Griff's generous hostage exchange. "I ascend to Triarch of the East, become lord of the Skyfish Summer Palace, and begin the search for a suitable wife. You go back for your kingsmoot."

Griff's fingers pull, more persistently, at my hair. Like the curls are a puzzle he'll solve.

"You'll really have to do that?"

I assume the part he's questioning is the wife. Can he be so surprised? I hum absently. "Just as you should court that Iscan princess to solidify Norcia's standing in the League."

"I'm not Norcia," Griff says.

"Not yet."

Griff's fingers remain twisted in my hair as he rolls onto his back to stare at the ceiling. "Did Uriel and Sebastion take wives?"

It takes me a moment to understand that Griff Gareson is talking about the doomed lovers from the *Aurelian Cycle*. I sit up, and his hand falls away. The wine, the sleepy warmth of Iscan air, the feeling of Griff's fine clothes in my fingers as I pulled them off him make me feel that I am dreaming, and Griff asking about Dragontongue poetry only makes the confusion more total.

"Of course. They were heroes from noble families. They did their duty."

Griff is silent for a second, thinking. Then: "Because their families needed heirs?"

"Yeah, heirs."

"Oh." Griff sounds like he's never thought of this before.

I nearly laugh, but not because I'm amused. This has been the challenge of my life, the idea of women I don't want being contracted into my bed because of the blood in my veins and rules of primogeniture I'm bound to, but Griff, who likes women just fine and doesn't have any inheritance besides his family's shack, hasn't had to spare the thing a single thought. In this one way, he was the fortunate one.

Well, that's about to change, because the kingsmoot will leave him with more than a shack to his family's name, and marriage will start to matter.

I flop onto my back beside him, but we're no longer touching. "At least you'll like it," I tell the ceiling.

Griff lifts his head. "Women? I mean, yeah, in the abstract, maybe."

Somehow this disinterested qualification just makes it worse. "You didn't like that Iscan princess in the abstract. You didn't like—Julia in the abstract."

I almost keep myself from saying her name, but it comes up, like bile. All the old jealousy, revisited tonight. At her mention, Griff sits up. "You got something you're trying to say, Delo?"

It's too dark to see more than the shadows across his face as he stares at me. *I could make you do things you didn't want to do,* he told me drunk, but he didn't have to tell me for me to know. The part of Griff's identity that was shaped by Julia's abuse is still, and perhaps always will be, a little bit raw.

But it turns out, I'm a little raw, too. Seanan's friends and their passive participles helped with that. "I'm just saying, this is going to be easy for you."

Griff is breathing so slowly, I can hear it. I'm preparing myself for the storm, my knees clenching, my fists curling, every muscle in my body tensing. All at once I want to fight him. *Let's see if I'm a match for you, after all.*

But instead of tensing with me, his shoulders sag.

"If you think this is easy for me, you're more full of shit than I realized."

I turn to look at him. He's frozen, vulnerable, beside me. Close enough to touch but I don't, because I've stopped breathing. "I'm full of shit?"

"You're full of shit," he says solemnly.

I've never been so glad of an insult.

I press my palms to my eyes. Geph whimpers. Griff says, "Hush, darling," in the voice he used with her when he was her squire. I feel his voice soothe her, soothe *me.* But that only makes the shuddering in my shoulders worse.

"It doesn't change anything," I tell him, and myself.

"If you say so," Griff murmurs, his lips on my hair, his fingers beginning to explore.

"Duty calls. All that."

"Yeah," says Griff infuriatingly, "you've explained."

I start to explain what I *haven't* explained, something about filial piety, but Griff's done talking at this point, which is really what I've always needed him for, to shut my brain up with his hands and his mouth and his great heart, and I don't have another coherent thought until the morning when, with the earliest birdcalls before dawn, he gets up, pulls on his tunic, scratches Gephyra one last time under her chin—

And leaves me to my duty.

26

—

DRAGON'S END

ANNIE

THE HIGHLANDS

The snow on the mountains is thawing, trickling down the hillsides in glutted streams, and I feel that I am melting, too. Aela's wings heal slowly and all I can think, when I think of them at all, is that I don't want them to. Let the skies be someone else's to rule. Let me stay grounded, blissfully grounded, like this forever. Not a Guardian but a girl in love.

"You're going to have to train them to do these maneuvers," Lee tells me, when he studies the hermeneuta.

Because I'm Firstrider? Because soon we'll be in Norcia, and a fleet will be waiting to be led into war by its commander, *me*? The blockade's cleared. The goliathan's gone. And since the morning we first woke in the same bed, we've stopped saying the word *Norcia* at all.

"You're figuring it out just fine. You can show me, when the time comes."

Lee's exasperation shows in the line between his brows. "I could use your help," he says.

The difference between our abilities at raw computing, in school, was always marginal. Marginal, with me in the lead. But I was never the sort of student to coast on it; I always studied, nose to the books, as many hours as he did. It disorients him that I'm no longer willing to do my homework; I can tell he thinks it's laziness.

The truth is, when I look at flight notation, I feel like hurling my breakfast.

I did what I needed to do. I got the Guardians out. I'm done. Please, let me be done.

The mantra rises like a prayer to the long-dead gods as often as my breath. It visits me in my dreams. Lee brushes off the suggestion that we stay here as a joke, but I don't intend it that way. Aela's wings have healed, but she is heavy and slow and oh-so-content, curled up in the pools of the Travertine, and I feel that I'm curled up in those pools with her.

She has no intention of leaving. In fact, she has business here, and she's about to get to it.

The word that forms as a bubble on the tip of my tongue, the thing I lost and forgot and denied myself and found again in all its sweetness on these cliffs: *home.*

LEE

Aela is healing more slowly than I'd hoped, but Annie seems in no rush to get airborne. Our days are spent in walks and on the shore and by the fire, and she's absorbed with every aspect of it. When I study the hermeneuta and the annals, she keeps me company but doesn't join my work, curling instead on the library window seat to sun herself like a cat and riffle through old poetry. The day our morning walk gives us the sight of a clear skyline—no triangles of sails, no blot of a goliathan over Sailor's Folly—Annie becomes impatient with library work.

"The blockade's gone. We can stay here. You can quit *that*." She's climbing into my lap, rather than to her habitual spot on the window seat, blocking my view of the annals, the notation, and the hermeneuta. I've mapped out at least ten different formations for subduing goliathans, but all of them involve javelins in maneuvers I can barely picture doing a thing against Obizuth's thick hide.

"I'm not sure we can stay here."

I still haven't told her about the wanted poster, the charges of high treason. The blockade's retreat should put me at ease, but it does the opposite. Why did it retreat? What tradeoff was made, or what blow was dealt? Annie *hmphs* and makes a show of rattling open a new poetry scroll. She glances down at it and freezes.

"What is it?"

She reads silently, her eyes growing progressively brighter as they fill. When she's finished, she passes it to me. The fragment's Dragontongue is in the style of a Golden Age epic, but its subject is one usually relegated to folktales for children. The title reads: *The First Exodus.*

> *Sing to me, Muse, of the Skysung Queen*
> *Who before Uriel and Aron and the taking of Old Callia*
> *mourned a warrior-lord sent to the house of the dead*
> *before her, who with the dragon was widowed in anguish,*
> *whose love was so great that she was found worthy*
> *and rode.*
> *North, into death, to gaze upon the Spring beyond the*
> *Stars—*
> *But sing me first her vengeance and her reckoning.*
> *Sing me now your fury-song.*

In the folktales, the Skysung Queen doesn't ride a dragon; her mercy and benevolence bring blessings from the long-dead gods and miracles for her beleaguered people. The vengeance part, the fury part, the dragonriding-into-death part, I've never seen before. Certainly not in epic meter, as if she were an ancient hero.

"What's the Spring beyond the Stars?"

"No idea."

The fragment is signed Vox Draconis, the moniker used to attribute the poems that were collected by Dragontongue scholars into what eventually came to be known as the *Aurelian Cycle*, but none of those were written about a woman. Either this came later, in defiance of epic convention established by the *Cycle*, or those who compiled the canon chose not to include it.

I read the rest, look up, and find Annie wiping her eyes. I'm still not sure what made her cry. "I see why they stuck with the kids' version for all of Freyda's propaganda."

Annie's voice is tiny. "My dad used to call me that."

"Call you—?" It takes me a full second to understand; and then I'm embarrassed by the delay. It shouldn't be so hard for me to imagine a serf comparing his daughter to a mythical queen.

Annie's wiping her eyes with both thumbs now, sniffling audibly. "It fits Freyda better than me, anyway."

I hand the fragment back to her with the sudden feeling that it isn't mine to reread. "Because—what, she's nobly born?"

"Because she's heroic. Full of purpose."

I'm not so convinced of that, but this doesn't seem the moment to argue. "And you're not?"

Annie laughs dully. She doesn't bother answering.

I'm not sure much of the widowed queen's story is anything I'd ever want my own life to parallel, but I sense what Annie's getting at. There was a time when dragonriding was something I imagined being glorious. We were imbued with great and terrible purpose; we were training to make our own legends. It was the feeling that made me yearn to be Firstrider, that Julia tempted me with in our correspondence, and that I turned my back on after our duel.

This fragment strums the old ambition like notes of a forgotten song.

But the song I turned my back on belongs to Annie now. The idea of her handing it over to some foreign princess is galling. I have the feeling this is something important, that I have to make her see it, but the words come out bungled. "Maybe we are like this, and we just don't know it. The Skysung Queen's life probably didn't feel glorious to her, either, while it was happening."

Annie is smiling, pain twisting her face, as she shakes her head. It hurts too much to see such defeat in it. I perch her on the desk and set my hands on her knees. "Do you want to go on a walk?"

She wipes her eyes and nods.

We don't talk about the fragment again. We walk and swim and gather lobster from the traps I set yesterday, which we boil in the fireplace and crack open with pliers. I show Annie how to extract the meaty bits. She has begun making our bread, a skill I didn't know she had. After a week, we have no need of wine to precipitate what happens after dinner. The dragons, who have calmed, can no longer even be blamed for it.

I think, with some satisfaction, that my father would be turning in his grave for what we're doing in that bed.

The following morning, I wake before her and am greeted in the garden by the smell of smoke. Nigel's outside his cottage, too, nose wrinkled. He points to the gray horizon, where a hazy column drifts from farther east.

"A brushfire?"

Nigel frowns. "Bit early in the year for that."

I hike with him up to the first landing of Pilgrim's Pass, muddy with the runoff of melting snow, that leads up the escarpments. From a vantage point a few hundred feet up, we have a view of the rest of the island sloping east. Farhall is one of the highest points of elevation before Dragon's End, so the slopes descend in rolls and crags toward the lowlands from here.

The smoke's coming from past the Riversource. If I had to guess, I'd say it came from Thornham, Rock's hometown in the Near Highlands.

By the time Annie wakes up, the wind's shifted and the smoke has cleared.

A *brushfire,* I tell myself, because she's melted cheese on scrambled eggs and peppered them with wild onion and the look on her face, when she kisses me still in her nightshift, is enough to blow smoke from my mind, too. If the dragon patrols that clutter the skies that day seem a little more frequent than days previous, they're still easy enough to evade in the shadow of the library. It's possible to convince myself that their presence over the highlands is routine security.

The next morning, there's another smoke column. This one from closer, probably within the Far Highlands. And though I can't tell exactly where—the folds of the mountains are too numerous to know for sure—my guess leaves me sick.

"Is that smoke?" Annie asks, smelling it when she wakes.

"Probably a brushfire."

What use is there alarming her with an uncertainty? But the shadow lingers on her face as we make our way down to the Travertine—only to find the dragons absent. The pool they've been lounging in since our arrival is empty.

Annie catches my hand. "Look!"

She leads me back to the open terraces that overlook the surf.

Aela and Pallor are in flight over the waves. Climbing

together—wing to wing, belly to belly—until the moment when they latch talons and fall. They pinwheel lazy, loping loops downward and disappear in the water with a splash. A mating dance. Annie is laughing, enchanted.

"Guess Aela's wings are better. But they shouldn't do that, they'll be seen."

"Oh, *hush*," says Annie. They rise a second time, hook talons, cartwheel down—and a third. It's mesmerizing. A dizziness that I know is Pallor's radiates from the back of my neck to my belly. Rise, cartwheel, splash. They're giddy with delight.

And then they slither back into the Travertine without a glance at us.

I take Annie's hand.

"Did you know today's Springtide?"

She looks surprised, both that I remembered the holiday and that I care. "Oh?"

"It's a good day for a hike."

A Springtide pilgrimage to Dragon's End. We'll hike together, and then I'll tell her about the wanted poster, about the smoke columns, and remind her now that Aela has healed, it's time to leave.

It's time to tell her that the fairy tale is over.

ANNIE

The trail we take today, Lee calls Pilgrim's Pass. It follows the ridgeline of the escarpments from the Winterless Green all the way to Dragon's End. He packs a picnic in a knapsack and includes sprigs of herbs he refers to rather mysteriously as our offering.

The hike takes most of the morning. Argos bounds ahead of us, sniffing the barrow mounds of the dragons of Lee's ancestors, the stone likenesses whose horned stormscourge faces stare out over the sea. As the island narrows to a point, the land gives way to sea on either side. Snowdrifts linger on the northern slope where the southern is already yellow with gorse. The scarf tying my hair blows loose within an hour and is carried away on the wind before I can snatch it. Lee takes my hand, laughing, and leads me on.

It's noon when we reach the standing stones of Dragon's End. They've been exposed to the elements for so many centuries, the wind has rounded their northwest corners. Sheer cliffs end in a point where the North Sea meets the Medean, and behind us lies all of Callipolis. We take seats under the Springtide arch, and I crane my neck to look up at the shrine with a strange shiver. It's unearthly, but also familiar.

"Norcia has these everywhere. But I didn't know any survived in Callipolis."

Lee pulls out the ember box and our offerings. "The rest were taken down during unification under Pytho Aurelian. Stormscourge House got a dispensation for Dragon's End."

We pile stones in a high ring to shelter a fire, nestle the embers inside, and begin feeding it the herbs. Sage, rosemary, heather, for a long summer, long rains, and plentiful harvests.

"Didn't know Stormscourge House was so . . . pagan."

"It's not pagan," says Lee with surprising touchiness. "It's tradition."

"Ohhh."

He scowls at my sarcasm and I smile back at him. I'm privately imagining how nice it would be to do this with him every season's turn. These standing stones, this offering fire, this pilgrimage.

Tradition. Another home-word.

"I've started having those dreams again," I hear myself say.

It isn't how I meant to tell him. It isn't what I *need* to tell him. But now I'm saying it. Lee's got a paper half pulled from his pocket, some sort of flyer, but when I speak, he pauses. "Oh?"

"You know. The ones where they're . . . alive."

"Oh," says Lee, though we've never talked about this before, "those."

He pushes the flyer, whatever it is, back in his pocket and gives the fire a bit of stirring with the poking stick.

Those dreams are the worst kind. At least with the dreams where they die all over again, it gets better when you wake up. But the kind where they're alive? When you wake up, you wish you hadn't. I don't have to ask to know we've spent the last ten years outgrowing the same kinds of nightmares.

"The thing is . . ." I swallow, fixing my gaze on the fire, because I know I shouldn't share this but I've got the self-destructive urge to do it anyway. "Sometimes it's different now. My mum's not there. I'm grown up. And—there's a family."

My face is burning in a way that has nothing to do with the sun or the fire. When I sneak a glance up at Lee's face, it's frozen. I know better than to add the rest. That the house in my new dream is the Big House. That Lee's there, grown up, too. That from this dream, I wake up feeling not gutted but serenely hopeful.

My words feel sticky. "Do you ever . . . do you ever think about what would have happened, if we hadn't become Guardians?"

It's the same question Duck once asked me.

Lee's sitting very still. "Like, if our families hadn't died?"

My face is hot. "No, just if we'd been in Albans together, but there'd been no metals test."

His brows are drawing together, like he doesn't quite understand what I'm getting at. "I don't know if that would have been a great life."

"Maybe it would have been all right. We'd have had each other."

There would have been no Guardian vows, no state demanding we give up everything to serve it. I remember burying my mother better than I remember her, but after so many years thinking of her life as undesirable or even pitiable, I find myself imagining it differently now. I imagine how it must have been, her and Dad against the world, building a home and a life together.

There must have been so much joy. The kind of joy I've tasted, for the first time in my life, this week.

Lee's face softens as he understands. "Oh," he says.

For a moment he seems to struggle with what to say next. "Of course, we'd have had each other. But—we wouldn't have Pallor or Aela. I think I'd miss them, wouldn't you?"

After a week in Farhall, I'm scared to answer that. The dream feels like a betrayal of everything I've struggled to be these last ten years. All at once, I feel colossally stupid for sharing any of this, and Lee's question makes it a hundred times worse.

"Annie, are you . . . is Aela . . . all right?"

I tell my knees, "She's about to lay."

Lee says, "Oh," like this explains everything.

It was what I had intended to tell him in the first place. But his reaction isn't just insulting, it's *wrong*. It's not a one-way conduit. Maybe I am feeling these things because it's her time, but it's her time partly because I'm feeling these things. Grounded, full of joy, this is what I dream of. For the first time in my life, I'm healed enough to imagine a family in the future rather than the past, and he wants to dismiss that as a dragon's spillover? My voice is small, my face still burning. "You don't . . . ever have dreams like that?"

Shut up, says a voice in my head that sounds like Crissa, and I remember most people don't want to be interrogated about their views on having kids. But it's not like Lee and I have ever played by normal people's rules. We have our own.

Lee shakes his head slowly. "I don't want to have a family, Annie."

"I mean, I don't either *now*, but—" I can't believe I'm saying this.

"I mean ever."

The severity in his voice leaves me blinking as if I'd been walloped in the stomach. "Because of our vows?"

As far as I'm concerned, the vows were called off with the Restoration, and at this point I'm inclined to say good riddance. Lee lifts a shoulder, rubbing his forehead, and shakes his head. "It's different for me, the whole . . . family thing. It's always been different for me."

The other morning, I found books left open on the library table that weren't from the Bassilean Wars. They were Lee's father's personal diaries. I didn't ask him about it, but I could tell from the dates he'd left them open to that he'd been searching for mention of Holbin; I looked for myself and found nothing. Lee's father, so loving to his own family, hadn't been bothered to record the horror he inflicted on mine. He was too busy recounting his ice wine harvests and his latest hunting trip.

The thought of family is different for Lee because of me. Because of how my memories have contaminated his. The thought prickles, as I stare at my knees: Leon Stormscourge took so much from us. Even this.

"I mean"—Lee's voice is hesitant—"it's a bit of a moot point right now, isn't it? We can't just hide in Farhall for the rest of our lives, playing house. We're dragonriders."

Couldn't we? is thick in my throat. "I sound like a stupid peasant woman, don't I."

Lee shakes his head, his face pained. "Of course not."

But he doesn't seem to have much more to add to that. He scratches his hair for a moment, staring at the fire, then pushes the silence aside very carefully. "How long does she need?"

He's changing the subject. I hear myself swallow. "A day, two maybe."

Lee pats his knees and gets to his feet. "Okay. We wait for her to lay, we remove the eggs, and then we make the flight to Norcia." He's sounding businesslike again, like he's relieved to have found a way out of the conversation. It leaves me feeling empty.

"Remove them?"

"It's how you control dragon breeding. You return them to the springs when you want hatchlings."

"Aela won't like that."

"Well, we don't ask her." Lee's tone is brusque. "We should be heading back."

He begins to pack our knapsack. Argos, returned from an exploration of the cliffs, bumps his muzzle against my hand, and I rub his shaggy back with unfeeling fingers. I reach for a topic to fight off the feeling of spoiling: "You had something you wanted to show me?"

"Later," Lee says. He begins to stomp out the offering fire, his back turned to me, and the sharp scent of the burning herbs fills my nostrils. I stuff my palms against my eyes to stop the tears. Argos leans harder, tail thumping anxiously against the rock beside me. When we set off up the path, Lee takes my hand and squeezes it. "I'm sorry."

He doesn't say for what.

But as we top the first crest of the high escarpments, I understand at last. On our way here, with our backs turned to the rest of Callipolis, we didn't see it. Now our walk faces the island we left behind, and I can see everything.

Columns of smoke rise from the highlands like a scene of battle. Not brushfires. Blazesites.

I stop dead. My heart flutters like a dragon stalling, about to plummet on a stilled breeze. Has Lee seen this, or part of it? He must have. He's been waking up early and climbing the first stairs of Pilgrim's Pass with Nigel every morning. "This was what you were going to tell me."

Lee makes a noise that's not quite an affirmation. "I only saw two. This is—more than I realized."

I pull my hand from his and set off for the Big House as fast as I can without breaking into a run.

I've been an idiot. I should have seen this coming. Aela's wings have healed, but they haven't healed nearly fast enough. And in the meantime, I managed to entertain, for a fantasy that lasted days, that we could stay here and forget our vows. That I could ever hope for the happiness I'm not allowed.

I forswear all family and the comforts of hearth and progeny, that I be not torn from my purpose.

In the lawn in front of the Big House, a single dragon is waiting for us. A stormscourge, his rider dismounted and lounging against the garden wall with his arms folded, gazing at the setting sun as if hoping it will blind him. When he sees us coming down the trail, he bares a smile.

All that I am belongs to Callipolis. By the wings of my dragon I will keep her. Let my will be her protection. Let my reason guide her to justice.

"Hello, lovebirds," says Power sur Eater.

27

—

THE SUMMONS

LEE

After a week of failing to talk sense into Annie, after a conversation at Dragon's End that took a turn I'm still rattled from, this intrusion is the last thing I want. Power sur Eater stands in my courtyard, the sigil of the Restoration on his Grayrider uniform, a characteristic smirk twisting his lips. His hair has been shaved so close as to make him look bald. Annie marches toward him with her fists balled as if he's what she's come down the hill expecting to find. My hand has gone to my summoner, chained in the old fashion around my neck.

Why does Power *always* show up when he's least wanted?

"How did you find us here?" I ask.

"That implies I haven't known you were here all along." Power sneers at me and speaks to Annie. "Would you mind restraining your, uh, lover? Lord? I have trouble keeping track . . ."

Annie's hand reaches for mine, arresting it on the summoner. "Lee," she murmurs.

"I don't trust him."

"But I do."

For a moment we stand frozen, her hand gripping mine over Pallor's summoner, while Power smiles and watches. It's not that Annie hasn't made a convincing case for Power. It's that I can't stand him. But even I am a little curious what he's about say. I cede to Annie's grip. The summoner falls.

She turns to Power. "Would you like to come in for tea?"

Dragons above, has she lost her mind?

"If tea is a euphemism for something stronger, yes."

Annie turns her back on both of us and leads the way into the house. In the drawing room, Power seats himself in the finest chair—what used to be my father's favorite—and looks around. Most of the windows on the main floor are still shuttered; we risked opening one that looks out over the sea. He curls two palms over the armrests and kicks a heel up over his knee.

"What a lovely little getaway you two have here."

Annie's glance silences my retort. When she moves toward the liquor stand in the corner, Power's lip curls. I close my fingers around her wrist.

"Sit."

I pour Bassilean whiskey into three tumblers, set them on the marble-topped table between us, and take a seat beside Annie. Her knee bumps mine. Power looks down at our touching knees, then back at our faces with a widening smile that looks a little painful. He unfurls the wanted poster I've been attempting to show Annie ever since Nigel handed it to me, and hands it to her.

Annie's shoulders curve over her lap as she reads. LET THE BITCH COMMANDER HAVE THE TRIAL SHE DESERVES. She looks up, pale except for pinpricks of pink on her cheeks.

"You've seen this already."

I nod.

Power takes the poster back from her, sneering in my direction. "I thought there might be a case of . . . interference."

The excuse for my delay sounds paltry in my head. *You told me you didn't want this week to end.* But that's private. Too private to share in front of Power.

"Do you have any idea what's been happening in this country since you went on your vacation?" Power asks.

"We're not on vacation," Annie says. "Aela was injured."

"How unfortunate. Is she *still*?"

At Annie's silence, Power gives a twisted smile. "School closures were just the beginning," he says. "Now it's land. Ixion's been using the debt to Bassilea as an excuse to set fire to all of Atreus's reforms. Serfs who were given land in the Revolution are being reduced to tenants again and charged rent, expensive city work permits are being issued that prevent peasants from leaving the fields—"

Annie has lowered her face into her hands. I summarize the shape of what I was already glimpsing on rounds before we fled. "A return to feudalism by way of economic pressure."

Power nods. "Ixion hasn't redistributed feudal lands to the Three Families yet, but it's only a matter of time. In practice, if not in name, Callipolans are on the verge of being returned to the status of serfs."

It's the shadow that's been over our shoulders since the beginning. The world where someone like Annie belonged to the land she was born to, and that land belonged to someone like me. To tax, to punish, to eliminate as her lord saw fit. With enough legal maneuvering and enough dragonfire to back it up, Ixion can bring all of that back.

I'm chilled at the thought, but I'm guessing it's nothing to how it feels for Annie.

Her voice is muffled through her fingers. "What's your point with all this?"

"Freyda's been cut off." Power sounds oddly breathless now. "We found out at the League's spring summit that her jaunt to Callipolis wasn't authorized. She left her brother at the altar, and now that her private allowance has run out, so has the grain. Ixion's in charge while she's gone to deal with whoever controls her purse strings stateside. But what matters is—"

"She doesn't have backing." Annie's sitting up straighter, her eyes widening.

Power nods. "This is our opening. We're not facing down an empire. We're facing down one girl on the run from her dad, a massive dragon, and a purebred idiot. We need to act before Ixion tightens his grip. I assume you've seen the fires."

Annie moistens her lips. Her glance darts to the window, surely thinking of the columns of smoke we just saw across the horizon. "Blazesites?"

Power nods. "Ixion's, but he's been blaming you. Thanks to an untimely slip from your oaf friend Griff, Ixion knows you're not in Norcia. Officially, the reason he's setting towns on fire is that he suspects their aiding and abetting your escape. Coincidentally, the targeted towns contain those most resistant to paying rent for land they've owned since the Revolution."

Annie's voice is faint. "Where?"

Power flicks an invisible speck of dirt from a fingernail. "Thornham, Holbin—"

Her breath rattles. *"Holbin?"*

"It's where I'd go, too. Those people know how to rebuild. Don't worry"—Power cocks an eyebrow at me with a kind of furious irony—"Ixion didn't lock any doors. Next he'll spread to the lowlands. On and on, smothering dissent and using you and Lee as his excuse."

Argos nudges Annie's knee, tail thumping the tea table, but she doesn't respond to him. She's frozen. Power sees his advantage and leans forward. "You may have been telling yourself that Ixion's Restoration is technically legitimate thanks to some sort of Assembly referendum under threat of dragonfire. But I stand by what our dearly departed First Protector wrote as a young and fiery lad. *When a government ceases to protect its people, it becomes necessary to overthrow it.*"

On the short list of people I wouldn't expect to be able to quote the *Revolutionary Manifesto* from memory, Power is pretty high. Annie's blinking rapidly, and Power only speaks when he's satisfied her eyes have filled.

"The way I see it, you've got two options. One is, haul ass to Norcia and show yourself in the air as soon as possible. It *might* be enough to draw him off his scorched-earth campaign. The dragon's healed now, right?"

Annie nods.

"So that's one option. Of course, Griff's aerial fleet isn't strong enough to retake Callipolis, even with the exiled Guardians thrown in, if Freyda's dragon is a lingering threat. And for all I know, Ixion might keep setting highland towns on fire just for fun. It does make them more likely to pay their rent."

Annie's eyes are fixed on his face. "The other option?"

Power holds her gaze as he reaches for his glass and knocks the whiskey back. "I think you know what the other option is."

For the moment where understanding passes between them that I don't share, I'm uncomfortably reminded of the month this winter when Annie and I barely spoke, and she relied on Power when I failed her. The falling-out they had at the end of that period, she's never discussed with me. But they've always had an understanding I couldn't penetrate.

"To spare the towns and Norcia?" Annie asks now.

"Maybe. I think we can manage more than that."

If they're discussing what I'm beginning to suspect they're discussing, their connection is even nuttier than I realized. "You can't be suggesting—"

Power does not turn his head. "Not talking to you, Lee."

Annie's fingers curl over my knee. She speaks to Power. "Go on."

Power drums his fingers on his knees. "Ixion is all but ascendant. The only thing standing between him and his formal crowning as Triarch Primus is your outstanding claim to the title of Firstridership, a bit of red tape Freyda seems fixated on for her own amusement. You have to be eliminated, and a trial is the easiest method."

Annie is nodding slowly.

"The trial would be a farce," Power says. "A spectacle. That doesn't matter. The point is, executions of the convicted have been taking place in the arena. Publicly. For the highest-profile cases, Ixion delivers the dragon's punishment personally."

Annie hums with sudden understanding. "Ah."

She gets to her feet, presses her hands to her sides, and walks to the window looking out over the sea. Her voice is as distant as the view. "There's still the problem of the girl with the massive dragon, even if the purebred idiot can be accounted for."

"Well, maybe we'll get lucky and she won't come back from Vask."

Annie shakes her head. Her voice is distant, like most of her mind is occupied calculating probabilities. "Not a good enough guarantee. Lee's been studying some family history here. Storm-scourge lore, about goliathans. How to take them out. We were planning to go to Norcia and start training the Guardians and Woad-riders there."

"Fine," says Power. "Option A, you haul ass to Norcia."

"And leave Callipolis to its fate? No. Norcia only needs one of us."

Power looks between me and Annie. Her back is still turned. She stares out the window as if memorizing what she sees. I stare at her, too.

And then I get it.

"No," I say. "You want to defeat Ixion, you fight him; you don't respond to his wanted ad—"

But when Annie turns back to me, she's smiling.

"Don't you get it, Lee? This *is* how I fight him."

ANNIE

I've been marveling, morning after morning, at the feeling of a good dream lingering when it should evaporate. I expected reality to crash in and the fantasy to shatter and it didn't.

But the dreams weren't the fantasy. This was. All of it. This house, these weeks, this stolen time with Lee.

And Power's here to wake me.

I was willfully delusional to think I could retire, could leave Callipolis to its fate with Ixion at the helm, that he would somehow be a commensurate substitute to the regime that came before. Atreus's programs were critically flawed, but Ixion is a blight. The smoking hills he leaves in the highlands make clear he will not stop bullying this country until he gets what he wants.

What he wants is me. And I'm done running.

But I'll throw a little surprise in the mix.

Lee's still catching up. "You've been managing to ignore Ixion's challenges since he started posting them," he says, jabbing a finger at the flyer, "and *this* is the one you're responding to?"

"Yes."

In fact, I look down at the charges listed and feel a serene sense of satisfaction. The mistake Ixion made from the start was that he aimed too high. I have no interest in proving myself as Firstrider. I don't think I deserve that title any more than he does. I let my city fall.

But *crimes against the people*? High treason? These are titles I'm more than willing to let Callipolis give me.

Especially if that's what it takes to save it.

"The trial will draw him off, turn his attention from Norcia, give you the cover you need to train our riders to take down Freyda. And when the time comes, I'll use the spectacle to my advantage."

Lee's eyes are wide. "Annie, forgive me for saying this, but a public trial wouldn't exactly play to your strengths."

For a moment I don't understand what he's getting at. And then I want to laugh.

Sweet Lee, always trying to protect me. He thinks I'm hoping to exonerate myself at Ixion's trial. He's worried about my *public-speaking* abilities. But I know I couldn't win a trial before the Callipolans who hate me; I don't even know if I think I'd deserve to.

Power looks between us, smirking. "Personally, I think she's pretty articulate for a peasant."

I have the urge to hit him. "Not the time, Power. Lee, it isn't about the trial."

"The trial's rigged," Power tells Lee. "A show trial. She'll be found guilty of whatever it is they come up with."

Lee's looking between us like he's sure we're both losing it. "Yeah, *that's my point.* So why would she ever—"

I answer. "Because after I'm found guilty, Ixion takes me into the arena for my execution."

"And then you die—"

"And then I *summon*."

"With what summoner?" Lee shouts.

Power lifts a finger. "In case you've forgotten, your girlfriend's capable of summoning her dragon with her mind, through solid rock."

When Lee's identity was found out, Power and Darius tried to beat us up in the nests after taking our summoners. It turned out Aela and I didn't need a summoner. Judging by Lee's slack jaw, he'd forgotten. I nod in Power's direction and explain to Lee. "And then I publicly defeat Ixion in the arena, and I'm still guilty of whatever they've charged me with, I'm still hated, but who cares, because I've just finished that bastard in front of all of Callipolis."

I don't need their love to do my job.

And this job, I can do. Whether or not I'm Firstrider or deserving. I can do it guilty. All I need is this lowborn blood in my veins, the arena full, and Aela saddled.

I told myself it would be over after I got the Guardians out. I told Crissa I would do what it took to avoid a war we couldn't win. But it's not over until Ixion's finished, and this won't be a war. This won't involve the armies of great empires or the gambled lives of my countrymen.

It will be me and him.

It's time to take this where I should have taken it from the beginning. Dragonback.

For the first time in a long time, when I imagine rising into the air with Aela, I want it.

"And after that," I tell Lee, "you take Freyda's goliathan out with a fleet you've been training in Norcia, and we send her home to Vask with our apologies for the inconvenience."

Understanding flickers at last in his gray eyes.

"We can get them both, Lee. Two heads of the snake at once."

We'd be left with a writhing, headless snake after, and we'd have to make sure nothing terrible grew in its place, but I'm pretty sure Lee and I are a match for the handful of Grayriders and Clovers that will vie for power in the vacuum. They're nothing compared with the weight of an invading empire; and now we know that empire would prefer to go home. The snake will writhe, but its heads won't multiply.

There's one complication that remains with this plan. I turn to Power. "Lee could still pose a problem. This flyer says he's wanted *dead or alive*, but I assume Ixion wants the former?"

Power grins. "As do many of us." I lift my palm, and he rolls his eyes. "Right. Lee's considered too much of a charismatic figure, even with the murder charge. As far as Ixion's concerned, *Leo* needs to be permanently eliminated."

I'm nodding. "So we fake the death. Otherwise, Lee getting away to Norcia will still be a potential destabilizer." My mind is working at a speed it hasn't since we arrived at Farhall. I'd forgotten how it felt to think like this. To *whir*. Parts clicking together, the problem working itself out in my hands. I know on instinct that the relevant variables are this setting, our history, and Ixion's penchant for cruelty—but when they finally lock into place, and I see the solution, it makes my heart constrict in my chest.

"I think I've got a way we could pull it off."

I paint the picture with numb lips. Even Power doesn't seem to be able to think of a snide remark. By the time I'm done explaining, Lee's head is in his hands. I look from him to Power's gray face and feel fleeting uncertainty.

"You don't think Ixion would go for it?"

Power's swallow is thick. "No, he . . . would go for it. If we staged it right, if I suggested it. Especially if you acted . . . upset."

Lee's fingers clutch at his black hair.

I bite my lip to bring the feeling back into it. "I could manage that. And he'd have no reason to block the Travertine exit, not knowing we planned for this. We'd just need someone waiting in the cellar to retrieve Lee—"

"Nigel," Lee murmurs into his lap.

"Right."

"And the dragons?"

"You renounce," Power says. "You'll have to brush up the old training. The Clovers need not suspect conspiracy, so renounce when they arrive. Can you use your mind thing to send Aela in a specific direction?"

"I don't know. I've never tried."

"Practice. They need to fly to Norcia, with a message explaining. Griff sur Sparker can return with Pallor to collect Lee when we're . . . gone. How long do you need, to prepare?"

When I realize Lee's glance in my direction is about Aela and her eggs, my voice finally fails. He answers for me. "At least two days."

He looks away and palms his eyes.

Power acts like he doesn't notice, but even he has gone hoarse. "Right. I can arrange it so the pickup happens on dawn of the third day."

Power studies me for a moment longer, his shoulders ever so slightly sagging. And I realize, for all the bravado he's projected as he and I concocted this plan, it frightens him just as much as it frightens Lee.

But shouldn't it? Power was there the first time I met Ixion. He heard what Ixion said to me. *I own you. And after this war I will make sure you and all your stinking kind remember it.* As far as

Ixion is concerned, I have been and will always be nothing more than a serf who needs to be taught her place.

But as Power has reminded me: The arena's my turf. It's Ixion's turn to learn.

And death has not yet released me.

28

THE TRAVERTINE

ANNIE

Power leaves once we're all able to recite the plan cold, and after that we begin preparations. I expect Mr. Garth to ask more questions when we sit him down to go over the plan, but if he's puzzled, he doesn't show it. He anticipates the role we would ask of him, and volunteers to do it.

"Be best to take Argos into town for the duration," he adds. "Got a niece who's very fond of him."

Next come the dragons. The maneuver we'll need, we haven't practiced since the earliest days of our training. Known as *renunciation*, and usually only taught as a technical exercise, it's the reverse of summoning. A series of sharp whistles blown into the summoner in a specific, staccato rhythm command the dragon to get as far from its rider as it can.

Renunciation is rarely practiced and more rarely needed.

We take the dragons out into the pasture to practice. Aela is grumpy, sluggish, her thoughts only of the hot springs she left behind. When she realizes she's been summoned from the warmth to train, her disgruntlement only grows. Her roosting is a wrench in the plan I'm not ready for.

"Aela looks ready for mutiny."

"Well, we'll go for as long as she'll let us."

We drill renunciations with summoners a few times, refreshing the dragons' memory. After the third time, Aela takes such a long time to return from the Travertine I think she might have quit on us. When she finally returns, she glares at me, as if daring me to keep wasting her time, and I decide to move to the next stage.

Renouncing with minds alone. When Ixion comes, we won't have the luxury of summoning whistles to issue commands the traditional way.

Aela and I are already spilled over, so I tiptoe along our connection, nudging my way, looking for some means to tell her what I want. Aela's thoughts are consumed with the Travertine, its warm pools, how much she wants to return to them—

I let the image of the caves fill my vision, too. *Go on.*

Aela cocks her head, then with a disgruntled snort she launches into the air and flaps her way back across the estate. Mr. Garth, breaking open the spring earth in the vegetable garden behind his cottage, straightens to watch her pass over with a hand to shield his eyes, and Argos lets out a few sonorous barks.

"Can't she go faster?"

Lee's noticed, as I have, how slowly Aela's flying today. At her rate right now, it wouldn't be hard for a well-paced skyfish to catch her.

I say, with more certainty than I feel, "She'll be faster after she lays."

Lee continues to frown up at the dragons.

I add, "It's not the renunciation I'm most worried about."

Lee turns to look at me. "She'll come back to you."

"It's going to be a long separation."

Renunciation can lead to the permanent breaking of a bond

between rider and dragon, if they aren't reunited soon enough after. The dragons drift north, like widowers. I've been suppressing horror at the possibility all day. My arms are folded as if to ward off the thought.

"Annie. Come on. You and Aela are inseparable."

I nod, wishing he'd stop looking at me. For a moment, the mental wall I've been maintaining about what happens after Ixion arrives—when I'm parted from Aela and Lee sur Pallor—threatens to collapse. I shrug it away. "Your turn now. Spillovers."

Even for me, training with Power, spillovers took weeks to master—it was too hard for me to let myself lose control. We had to resort to his calling me names before I got the hang of it. Lee, who keeps himself even more buttoned up, never shares minds with Pallor on principle. But for this plan to work, he'll need to make sure Pallor follows Aela, which means Lee will need to spill over and do it on command.

I study him, standing rigidly beside his dragon, fists clenched, looking more repressed than ever. "So, it helps to have an extremely strong emotion you can tap into. Think of something that makes you feel strongly. Maybe angry, or upset—"

Pallor lets out a sudden growl, and Lee blinks at me. His pupils are dilated.

"Oh. That was—fast."

"Yeah, I wonder what I have to be upset about right now."

Right.

He sends Pallor after Aela, and then tosses his head, clearing it, his pupils shrinking as he extricates. "I think they've got the hang of it."

Back at the Big House, I sit down, for the first time, to look over the annals and the hermeneuta with Lee. The aversion I felt earlier in the week at the sight of work has vanished with the newfound purpose of our plan. Soon the central table of Farhall's library is covered with old, brittle diagrams. There are sketches of goliathan anatomy, of vectors for javelins and soft scale points for entry, of formations for the island breeds opposing her. Last of all, Lee shows me the hermeneuta.

It's so delightful, I can't believe I've waited until now to look at it.

A three-dimensional grid of thin wire and supported by a silver frame, the hermeneuta is designed to stage scale models of aerial battle. Slender rods can be inserted according to coordinates along the vertical, horizontal, and linear planes, each with a small stone dragon affixed at its midpoint. Silver stormscourges, opal skyfish, agate aurelians—even tiny sapphire iscans and great jade damians, not seen since the First Bassilean War—and thrice as large as even the damians: palm-sized onyx goliathans.

I weigh the two goliathan figurines in my hands and wonder whether there's an error. "One of these models is twice as big as the other."

Lee jabs a finger in the direction of anatomy books I haven't read. "Goliathans have pronounced sexual dimorphism. The larger one's the male. The extra horns are for subduing the female."

I inspect the diagram he's pushed my way and shudder. The male looks like a winged sea urchin. "I'm glad Pallor doesn't have those."

Lee's mouth curves. "And I'm glad the goliathan we're dealing with is female."

We stage the female goliathan at the center of the hermeneuta and begin positioning the rods, simulating the formations of aerial battles in the third dimension. As Lee shows me, I let out a laugh of surprise at a sudden memory. "All those years, reminding Rock not to forget the third dimension—"

"He would have benefited from this absolutely. I've worked out some drills based on what I think the formations are supposed to look like, but I want you to check me."

It's work that plays to both our strengths. Remembering the third dimension is a particular knack of mine; and I'd forgotten, until I sit down with these calculations and transpose them onto the hermeneuta, the pure satisfaction I derive from mapping out a formation. Aerial tactics was always one of my favorite subjects. I look up from my work to find Lee watching me, smiling. "There's the Firstrider I've been waiting for."

The title has been a matter of some tension between us in the past, but I hear none of that in his tone now; instead, it mostly makes me feel hot around the collar. "You're not so bad yourself."

Lee's had to make some adjustments to his drills based on how I correct the formations, but for the most part what I notice, as we go over his work, is how instinctively he breaks complex maneuvers into discrete, digestible training segments. I suppose he's had practice, from his years as aurelian squadron leader; but I don't realize, until we sit down like this to collaborate, how much better Lee's instinct for teaching is than our drillmaster's ever was. He's even planned a contingency for the fact that there won't be a real-life goliathan to practice on: Norcia's karsts, which are goliathan-sized, will serve as dummy goliathans.

"Your drills are . . . really good."

"Thanks." Lee rubs his forehead. It's grown late; we had to break to find candles and snacks. "The thing is, I'm still not sure any of these formations will do more than frustrate a dragon of Obizuth's size. Pallor and I had to get past her to find you; she barely felt his fire. Her hide's dense."

That part, I'm as stumped by as Lee is.

"You'll probably have to play it out to know how it works."

The feeling I've gone without for so long I nearly welcome back, of study on the brink of exhaustion with mastery on the horizon, returns in pressure beneath my eyes and an ache in my neck. When we break for sleep, Lee rubs the tendons in my shoulders till I nearly cry with relief.

In the morning of the second day, Lee rises at dawn, kisses me on the forehead, and tells me he's going down into Harfast with Nigel to drop off Argos.

"It shouldn't take the whole day."

Still half asleep, I struggle to remember if this was a part of the plan we discussed with Nigel yesterday. "Both of you? Why?"

The nagging sense that Lee isn't telling me something fades as he pulls me closer. He kisses me, and sleepy as I am, it lights my body with desire. "I've got a bit of unfinished business there. I'll be back in a few hours. You'll do what we discussed with the books?"

Lee and Nigel take the Old Road south on horseback. Lee wears a hooded cloak to hide his face. I stand on the top step, my arms wrapped tight around a borrowed nightgown, and I watch them go. After, while my tea brews, there is a moment where I curl into my knees on the kitchen stool and spill ugly tears into my lap. It's only now that I realize how much I had wanted to spend this day in bed, in Lee's arms.

But there's no use spending this last day—I can't help thinking of it as a last day—weeping. I drink my tea, dress, and carry a large empty saddlebag into the library. The annals from the Bassilean Wars go first; the hermeneuta, disassembled, goes second; and then, in the space left, I pack the scrolls I've read and loved in the last week, the fragments of poetry we've shared. Last of all, I unstick a portrait of Lee's family from its frame and stuff it, rolled up, into the bit of space on top.

Then I take the saddlebag down to the cellar and tuck it in the passageway that leads down into the Travertine, where it will be waiting for Nigel and Lee. I can feel Aela from here. She's not quite ready for me.

So instead of following the porous caves down to her, I leave the Big House and go on the daily walk I had, until today, taken with Lee. The route that takes me from one end of the Winterless Green to the other, along the barrow mounds at the top of the gorse-covered escarpments, through the vineyard and orchard below already beginning to bud with green, and down the stairs off the cliffwalk to the sea. Every breath and sight I take in, I memorize.

When I've completed the loop, I enter the steaming white pools of the Travertine.

There, I find Aela and Pallor with the eggs.

LEE

I haven't ridden horseback in years, since the perfunctory lessons they gave Guardians at the beginning of our training to prepare us for riding dragonback. But after a day on Nigel's gray mare, Tilly, I have a fondness for the gentle, surefooted creature, even if it feels strange to ride so firmly locked to the ground. We return from Harfast late in the afternoon.

The Big House is empty when I come in from the stables. I call Annie's name and my voice echoes on stone. The words I read in a country courthouse seem to whisper in the empty air. *Wife*, *wed*, *widow*, *heir*. Futures that could have been. I told myself it was important to do it alone, without her. That for what's coming, there is only one set of vows that will matter, and she'll need all the strength they can give her. These forms, I told myself, were perfunctory. Not vows but paperwork. Means to an end that, in all likelihood, will never be needed.

Still, there was a moment in the courthouse when my heart constricted to imagine a world in which it could have been more than that. My father be damned, the rot of old memories desiccated by a horizon of blinding light. In that moment, I couldn't remember why I told her it was a future I never wanted. I couldn't remember why she wasn't here, at my side, murmuring the words with me.

Of course I wanted it. Of course I'll always want it.

But Annie and I don't get the things we want.

Alone in this house that has no future, the walls seems to shrink around me, tomblike. I imagine flames, then force the image out.

I go back outside, rubbing my temple. That's when I feel the tug.

Pallor's tug.

It's so rare that it takes me a moment to recognize it; we spent much of our early years together practicing *not* tugging on each other. Then again, the drills yesterday broke that streak. Today, instead of pushing him out, I follow the tug toward the Travertine. He seems to be profoundly pleased about something.

I find him submerged with Aela in the hot spring. Annie is crouched at the edge, knee-deep in the steaming water, arms round her knees. In the center of the burbling fountain and the curled dragons sit three scaly dragon eggs.

The biggest one is amber like Aela; the next, pale silver like Pallor; and the smallest, a mottled combination. They're each roughly the size of a human head. When Pallor sees me, he lifts his snout a fraction, eyes flashing toward the eggs and nostrils flaring proudly.

"Look at you." Aela gives me a haughty snort and I laugh. "No training today, I promise."

The one time my father's dragon laid, she didn't move from the springs for weeks before or after. The worry that presses with this thought, the needs that will come with the morning, I push aside: not now.

Now is a time for rejoicing.

Annie turns around. Her face is wet and ruddy from the steam. "She won't let me take the eggs."

I kick off my boots, roll my trousers, and place bare feet in the hot water beside her. It relaxes all the muscles sore from a day of riding at once. "We don't need to take them just yet."

Water is seeping through Annie's clothes. When I place a hand around the wet fabric at her waist, she takes a shuddering breath. The steam, the muggy happiness of the dragons, is clouding my head, and for once, I don't want it to be clear. I remove my tunic and slide into the water all the way. When I tug Annie's hand, she laughs in surprise, then sinks into the water beside me.

"Hold me?"

I take her into my arms. In the water, she is weightless. Tiny. Too small to let go of, let alone let go. I kiss her hand where Ixion ground shards of glass into it, the tiny spider scars across it, and Annie's breath hitches.

"Annie—"

It's not too late to call this off.

She presses a finger to my lips and kisses them. I swallow the protest and hold her closer.

The crack in the stone overhead lets in trails of vines and a sliver of sky. We bask in the hot water, spilling over with our dragons, watching the sky turn pink over the sea and reflect on the three eggs and the white sediment of the Travertine. I'd meant to tell her about the courthouse and the papers as soon as I got back from Harfast, but in the steaming water with her in my arms, all sense of urgency melts away. A constellation winks into life low on the northern horizon, stars forming the lines of a stick figure pointed north. Between the city smog and the rising peaks of the inner highlands, Annie's probably never seen it.

One last thing I can show her.

"The Skysung Queen." I trace the constellation with her fingers, and I know her shivering against me isn't from cold.

When the sky gives barely any more light, it's time.

We climb from the water, dress, and Annie approaches the eggs, sheltered in the shallows where the water burbles. Aela immediately surges from the water, her hackles rising, and growls. Annie stops.

"Aela, please." Still spilled over, Annie's chest is heaving as she struggles to stare Aela down.

"Pallor," I murmur.

Pallor is twined with Aela, but when we lock eyes, he lets out a low whine of understanding. Sorrow floods down my spine like cool water. He turns from me and places his maw very gently over the back of Aela's neck. Aela whimpers, her hackles softening. Annie sways where she stands.

"Now, Annie."

Tears are running down Annie's face at such a pace, her hands are brushing them away in a frantic, constant motion as she sniffles. She reaches for her basket, kneels beside the eggs, and places them one by one in the blanket lining. Aela begins thrashing under Pallor's grip, her hair-raising shriek reverberating on the white walls, and Annie spins away clutching the basket, sobbing.

"I'm sorry," she says. "I'm so sorry. They can't hatch now. We're going to keep them safe for you, I promise—"

Aela tries to lunge for us, gnashing her fangs. Pallor slams his whole body against hers. His low whine joins hers as she struggles against him.

I take the basket from Annie, seize her arm, and pull her deeper into the nest.

The smooth pools give way to stone stairs, and the stone gradually cools and then dries as we climb to the entrance of the crypt beneath the Big House. There is no light save from the cracked door leading into the cellar. I store the eggs in the stone creche designed to keep dragon eggs in reserve; compared with the warmth of the thermal springs, it feels cold, hard, and unwelcoming. At this temperature, incubation remains suspended for as long as needed.

Before we leave, I make sure Annie shows me where she's stowed my saddlebag. It seems to take the last fight out of us both to look at it.

Up the stairs, in the half-lit house, Annie slumps and retches. I can feel an aching sorrow that starts at the roots of my stomach and extends down into the lairs like an umbilical cord to Pallor.

I knew it was typical to separate the eggs. But I didn't know it felt like this.

Neither of us has the energy to cook, but there's vegetable soup left from the other day, and a drying husk of bread that will soften in it. I heat the soup while Annie slumps at the table, rubbing her forehead.

"Are you extricating?"

"Trying to. It helps that Pallor's comforting her."

Pallor's already faded to a low, sorrowful hum in the back of my head.

I put soup before her. She dips a spoon into it slowly, and then pauses. I know she's thinking, as I am, how little appetite it is possible to have with this kind of sadness clinging in your gut.

But she's going to need more than that for what's to come.

"You need to eat."

At the tension in my voice, Annie looks up. Then she eats the rest of her supper without a word.

We wash up together.

"Do you remember how I had to teach you how to do this, at Albans?"

"I remember. I hated it. And I was terrible at it."

"You still are, a bit."

I flick water at her, and Annie laughs a very soft laugh and swats me with a towel.

After that there's nothing left but to sleep and wait for dawn.

We spread out in my parents' bed. The darkness holds its breath. Annie's fingers find mine, then her lips find my lips, and I am seized by desire that feels like a bottomless hunger. As if I can make her mine, prevent the future pulling us apart, by drowning my body in hers.

At the point of no return, I launch a knee into the mattress to reposition us, but Annie stops me.

"I know it wasn't what you wanted. But I would have had everything in the world with you. All of it. All my days, and all my nights, all my—" She swallows whatever word comes to her. It's a bastard, homemade version of the Callish wedding vows. I know, because this morning I saw them written out when I signed the dotted line alone and told myself it was a question of property and inheritance even as I wished she was there with me and couldn't remember why she wasn't.

I remind myself now: *Because other vows come first.* I set my lips against hers to stop her making new ones and feel her breath hitch. Flames are in my eyes again, and for all I know, flames will be the last thing I see. "I wish I could have given it to you."

I feel her swallow, her throat against my throat. I taste her tears. Annie's lips curve against my cheek in the dark. "You and me, we take what we can get."

When she tugs me closer, I let her.

29
—
RENUNCIATION

ANNIE

I wake from a sleep so profound it feels I'm floating from the depths of the sea. My body is gloriously, triumphantly sore. Lee was careful. It only hurt a little where I expected it to hurt more, and after the pain such tenderness enveloped me that it didn't matter that it hurt. I only wanted to hold him closer.

The thought I have now—the trivial thought that fills me with unexpected regret—is that I would have liked to have had more nights to learn how to enjoy it properly.

I would have liked more than this one night.

His face is smoothed in sleep. The lines of care faded, the shadow dark under his jaw where he needs to shave. Since when, I muse with a tenderness that seems one with the tenderness of my skin touching his, since when did Lee become this man with a stubbled jaw, who holds me with such certainty and kisses me so sweetly—

"Hey."

Gray eyes find me in the gray light. He rolls onto a forearm, and because our bodies are entwined and bare, I feel every shift of him against me.

"Hey."

"How are you feeling?"

"Really good."

I mean it, but Lee groans faintly, as if he has his doubts. He rolls onto his back. "I need more practice."

I rise on my elbow. "I thought you . . . had practice?"

We'd never discussed what he'd got up to with Crissa, but I'd always assumed this was included. Lee pauses, blinking slowly. His eyes have flecks of blue in the silver. How have I never looked into them like this before? "No," he says, like he's unsure whether this should be an apology.

A warmth is spreading inside me, from the knot of my belly upward. In a very small voice, hardly daring to believe my nerve, I tell him, "I'm glad you didn't have practice."

Lee's lip quirks. I kiss it, right at the dimple. He pulls me close, blankets bunching, and groans again. "How long till dawn?"

"Probably another half hour. I laid out some clothes for us."

"Oh?"

Mostly, I laid them out for Lee. One of his father's tunics, its hem embroidered with Stormscourge heather and freshly washed, and a flamesuit I cropped at the shoulder and thigh, so that it could be hidden under plainclothes. "I think they should fit you, well enough."

Lee shaves while I bathe. He grows very quiet as I pull his father's flamesuit on over his shoulders. The clasps are more intricate than those of the uniforms we grew up with; it takes me a moment to figure out how to work them. And then I fasten every one in a room silent, save for Lee's slow breathing. He clasps a belt around the tunic. Last of all I pull the black mantle over his shoulders and affix the Stormscourge brooch.

"There you are. The Lord of Farhall."

Lee swallows. "What will you wear?"

I realize I haven't thought about it.

"I have an idea," he says.

I can hear him rummaging around upstairs as I go down into the kitchen to put on tea. He returns from the children's wing with a simple brown wool dress, a mantle built into its collar, and well-worn riding boots.

"This was Penelope's favorite riding dress. She always talked about the pockets."

By now I've figured out whose clothes Lee's been pilfering for my wardrobe, but this is the first time he's said his sister's name aloud. "Everyone likes a dress with pockets."

They're deep, fitting my fists up to my wrists, and the wool is soft and warm, though it breathes. Lee laces up the back. Then, very gently, he braids my hair and pulls my mother's pendant from the neck of the dress to lay it on my breast. I've returned the Guardian wristband, with its summoner, to my wrist, where the silver and gold glints faintly against the brown wool.

"There," Lee says, turning me to face him. "The Lady of Farhall."

"Ha, ha."

Light is coming in the window through glowing clouds. Lee glances out it. I've begun to feel my heart pattering against my ribs.

"There's something I should tell you," Lee says, "about that."

He takes his tea with one hand and pulls me onto the bench beside him with the other. Every breath we take, the sky grows lighter. "Yesterday I went to the courthouse in Harfast and named you heir to this estate, with Nigel as my witness. Obviously, the house will need some fixing up, after today," he adds, like this only just occurred to him.

I've choked on the tea. "You named me your *heir*?"

"Just in case," Lee says in a rush. "I figured if I'm going to be officially dead, I might as well put my affairs in order. Anyway, highland inheritance laws are tricky, particularly with women, so the language of the paperwork is that you would—in that case—be my . . . widow."

My fingers are curling around the cup. The gray sky is light enough to cast blurred shadows on the wooden table. Lee is looking somewhere south of my elbow, a flush creeping up his neck.

"You put it in writing"—my voice shakes—"that we're wed."

"I'm sorry. I know I shouldn't have. It was just a matter of paperwork—"

"Why didn't you ask me?"

Lee swallows, pinching fingers to his nose, and looks down.

"I would have said yes," I breathe.

Lee breathes in slowly once, then out.

"I know you would have." He finally looks at me. "But I didn't want to be the reason you forswore your vows. Not now, not when you need to—" He breaks off as if this line of thinking hits a brick wall, and I hear him swallow. His hands fold over mine, and close on the silver-and-gold wristband. "I just wanted it to be in writing, somewhere. I wanted it to be in writing that it was you. For me. It's always been you."

He lifts my hand to his lips and kisses it.

"And I know this place could never make up for the home you lost, but I thought maybe . . . You seem to like it, and I thought you might want to . . . come back."

As I understand, my heart grows so full, my eyes burn with it. Lee's steady words belie it, but the careful preparations give it away. He's setting his affairs in order in case he doesn't walk away from this alive. And even as he offers me everything he has to give, he doesn't dare call it what it is.

A home.

I bend to kiss his hair, the spot where the part ends and curls and a half dozen gray hairs already speckle the black, every one of them as familiar as the lines of my own skin.

His eyes close.

From the main floor of the house comes the sound of a rap on the front door.

LEE

Farhall is prettiest in the morning. The dew on the grass, the sunlight creeping down the high peaks from the east, the sky streaked with clouds that reach down to touch the breakers. Annie is prettiest of all, wisps of her auburn hair fleeing its plait, the brown dress hugging her waist, loose at her hips, scalloped across the neck where last night, a blush bloomed as I held her.

These are the thoughts I have, inconsequential, as the script plays out.

They find us, in the hiding place we make in the Big House.

They drag us out.

They surround us in a ring on the drive that loops between the house and the Old Road.

Power and Ixion are there, along with four Grayriders. We are surrounded by six dragons. More soldiers, some on foot and some on horseback, are pouring in from the cliffwalk. A few soldiers are already hammering on the groundkeeper's cottage to see what they'll find, but when they kick the door in, they have no answer: Nigel's already in position.

We're alone on the estate, surrounded.

Somehow, through all of this, I've managed to keep hold of Annie, but at the point where we're led to Ixion, he seizes her by the hair and her hand is ripped from mine. We are forced to our knees at opposite ends of the cobblestone drive, and Annie's wristband is pried from her wrist so that she cannot use it to summon.

"Well done, Parcival."

"Thank you, sire," Power says. "Would have found them earlier, but it turned out they were skulking along the Robber Road. Edmund shredded her wings in their encounter."

Ixion laughs. He shakes Annie by the hair, and she ripples like a rag doll. Her lips remain a line. "Looks like our ha'cousin got a last word in after all. Aren't you going to say hello to your old friend?"

For a moment Annie and Power look at each other. His sneer widens, and Annie turns her face away.

Power tells Ixion, "Always was a close-mouthed bitch."

"Dragons incoming," says the Grayrider holding me.

Pallor and Aela have climbed over on the ridge, drawn to the scene by the noise and the smell and the emotions of their riders.

The renunciation happens now or never.

A ripple goes through Annie, and her eyes snap shut, her lips contorting with effort. Beneath the lids, I know her pupils have dilated. I stare at my hands, focusing on the faint pulse that already bleats from Pallor along my spine.

"Bring them in," Ixion says.

Grayriders launch into the air.

Our connection opens. Pallor is there, frightened for Aela, frightened for me.

It's all right. Just like we practiced.

Aela shrieks and leaps into the air. Pallor follows her. The two of them flutter for a moment, taking in the advancing dragons between them and their riders. Annie's whole face is scrunched with concentration—

Aela lets out a shriek of fury. But compelled by Annie's command, she turns tail. Pallor follows her.

Like we've practiced, that's it—

Like a hood torn from my eyes, Pallor's vision fills them: the ground below, Aela at my wing, the scene of the arrest behind us and the Grayriders hurtling after us in pursuit—

"They're renouncing," someone says.

Ixion clocks Annie on the side of the head, and she gasps, her eyes snapping open. The Grayrider holding me shakes me so hard that my teeth knock together.

As our concentration falters, Aela's wings ripple.

Everything in our instincts, on the ground and in the air, resists the command for separation. For a moment Aela's desire to come to Annie's aid pulses so strongly, Pallor feels it.

I feel it. And Annie whimpers with it.

And then the thing I've been dreading begins: Aela's speed plateaus when it should be gaining. Pallor, who's matching her, feels her reach velocity beside him, like a ceiling they've slammed against.

The eggs. The bloody eggs. She was slow before she laid and she's still barely recovered.

Too slow.

The Grayriders are gaining—

As clearly as if Pallor had asked it, as if we'd been in conversation with each other, I feel the question charge from him to me: an image of what he and I have pondered ever since we began practicing renunciation and noticed her flying slow, heavy.

A wall of fire, and Aela gone.

My answer is forceful as I shove the image out. *No.*

But I see her wings tremble, see Annie's perspiration, and know what Pallor knows, and see what Pallor sees.

Aela won't make it.

She *has* to make it. The plan hinges on it.

But it hinges on Pallor, too: I conjure images of the hermeneuta in the bag. The training that awaits. Annie in Callipolis, drawing them off. Ixion hers to take down, the goliathan ours.

Pallor's answer is made of shapes and sounds, but forms as words.

You can train them from the ground.

The vision I have left is his, because my own eyes are streaming.

Come on, Aela—

The stratus hangs low, its refuge nearly within reach, glowing from the dawn. But the skyfish are gaining faster than the cloud wall approaches.

And Aela needs a few seconds' more time.

In the end, whether it's his choice or mine, I don't know, because in the final moment, the taste of the thought-image-memory-plan is a desire that roots through him and becomes mine.

She is so beautiful.

Our bondmate, our wingrider, our beloved—

Do it.

Pallor makes a jackknife turn.

Reversing his flight, turning on their pursuers. Aela shrieks as she understands, twisting to return to him, but he bellows flames after her and she buffets backward.

We're hovering between Aela and the Grayriders, and the stratus is within her reach.

On the gravel, two meters from me, Annie begins to sob.

"Lee," she says. "No."

"Annie, do it!"

"Someone shut them up!"

The Grayriders bear down on Pallor. Ixion rams his fist into the side of Annie's face.

Annie screams. Aela shrieks. Pallor spreads his wings across the sky and roars.

The sky fills with fire.

Like it did when we sparked. The fire fills our vision, feasts our eyes, sings in our blood. This time, not against the ones we love but for them.

And as with gods, the world quaked.

The Grayriders backpedal in midair, but the two closest skyfish are caught headfirst in the blast. They disappear in it.

When the fire fades, and my blinded vision clears, the blasted skyfish are drifting sideways, listless the way Annie sur Aela was when we sparked. Their riders slump uselessly in the saddle. Dead or nearly dead.

Blood is dripping from Annie's nose and down her chin, mixing with her tears as she sobs.

And Aela's gone.

Ixion curses.

"You two, after her—"

Two more Grayriders mount and take to the air. But they know, as well as I do, that it's a fool's errand.

Aela's lost in the white. Safe.

Pallor's run out. Nothing prevents Power sur Eater and the second stormscourge from surrounding him.

I'm still, like an idiot, grinning. Still spilled over. Tasting Pallor's pride like a drug.

The Grayriders escort Pallor to the ground. They land in the ring formed by the soldiers round me and Annie. Pallor bares his fangs at Ixion, inhales, and bellows again. Only smoke comes out. Still, Ixion takes a step backward.

I laugh aloud.

"The net," says Ixion, turning away.

The chain-link net is thrown, and my laughter dies as it clamps over us. Fear begins to shudder through Pallor, into me. His great black eye finds mine.

"Hey, Pal," I hear myself say, the words coming sluggishly through our fear. "We did good. Really, really good."

His eye blinks slowly. I can feel the net, holding us in, pressing on our wings where they should be free. Pressure is building behind my eyes as my thoughts begin to free from his, as the high of his pride fades, and I feel the protest of my own heart beating. I push my feelings away and reach for Pallor's again. He's afraid, and I have to comfort him.

"You're all right, Pal."

"Get me a knife," Ixion is saying. "I'm not carting it back."

"I thought—breeding?"

"It's clearly pair bonded to the slut's dragon. No point."

Annie lowers her face into her hands as she weeps. The meaning of the conversation feels distant to me. Muffled by the spillover, by the need to hold Pallor's gaze, to keep him close.

"It's all right. I'm here . . ."

Even if I don't hear exactly what they're saying, I know what I'm saying. I recognize it.

This is the final recitation. These are the things you say when it's the end.

"Take her."

Annie is passed from Ixion to Power, who catches her with numb hands, his usual sneer replaced by a clenched jaw. Annie slumps in his arms, her eyes squeezed shut and her lips moving in wordless protest. Ixion walks toward me.

Metal scrapes metal as the dagger is unsheathed. I look up, into the face of my cousin. He looks like Julia, his eyes lit by her same not-quite smile. His knuckles are white on the hilt of a knife.

"Hold the dragon still."

I kneel beside Pallor, touch his scales through the wire, and feel his shudders. Pallor leans into my hand. I wear no gloves; his scales burn beneath my palms, but I only press closer. Looking into the great black eyes as I did the day, when we were small, that he Chose me.

"I'm here."

Ixion raises the knife, and as he sets it under Pallor's chin, the memories course through me.

Memories that are mine, and aren't.

Memories that flood over me like a gift—

There is a little boy that we love. A sad boy, fierce and not quite broken, and we will teach him how to fly. He throws a tentative boot over our wing, reins clutched too tight in a small fist. His thoughts flicker with memories of a father he misses, memories of another life. He blocks them out, just as he blocks us out. He is determined to need no one.

The knife presses, cold iron, against our throat—

We launch into the air. Knees hug us tighter, his arms around our neck, as we spread our wings and rise. Delight leaks from his heart to ours and just for a moment, he lets us in. Just long enough to remind him—

See, little one? There's so much left to live for.

ANNIE

A hush falls over the Winterless Green. The guffaws of the Gray-riders, Power's labored breathing in my ear, the sounds I barely heard myself making all stop. Ixion looks down at the aurelian, frozen for a moment with the knife poised at his throat. Lee, his eyes shot with spillover, is swaying on his knees as he holds Pallor.

I've sagged in Power's arms.

Ixion's lip is twisted. He places a hand on Pallor's crest to steady him.

Then he drives the tip into soft scales and opens the jugular.

Blood begins to pool.

Lee and Pallor slump as one. Lee's fingers curl round Pallor's horned face. He kneels in the blood, holding Pallor's gaze, as it fades.

When Pallor stills, Lee wraps his arms round his knees and folds into a ball like a second corpse.

The thin, straining line that still connects me with Aela pulls taut. Miles away, lost in the white, she shrieks—

Images flash in my head, flickering across my vision in her anguish: Pallor curling round us in the Travertine, coasting beside us as we struggled to spark, dodging and circling us in our first sparring bout when we were ten. Pallor, nuzzling our eggs. Pallor, circling at our wing. Lee's laughter swallowed by the wind as we race to gain height on an updraft, the city spread before us and the sky above. Seamless white for us to conquer—

And now we fly alone.

Aela's shriek splits my head. Ixion and the Grayriders are shouting, covering their ears with their hands, and someone shouts, "Shut her up!" A hand clamps over my lips.

The screaming stops, and that's how I realize it was coming from my own mouth.

All the while, Pallor lies unmoving, and Lee lies curled in his blood like he wishes he were one with it.

"Is he dead?" someone asks, a boot nudging Lee's back.

"Just widowed," says Ixion indifferently. "He'll still drop."

Lee does not seem to be in a place where he hears anything. But I feel the wind that left my screaming lungs come rushing back as I understand.

He'll still drop.

"No—"

Dropping wasn't the plan. After so much gone awry, not this, too—

I've thrashed from Power's arms to the ground. Gravel bites my knees and palms.

"Are we at the part where you start begging?" Ixion says pleasantly. "I've been looking forward to this."

"Power, *please*—" I hear myself say.

A boot connects with my head. Power's boot. The world goes crimson.

Then broken shells crunch as he steps forward.

"By your leave, sire, I've got an idea for an ending that might be more *poignant* for both of them."

It's the line I coached him to say, but in my desperation, I hardly recognize it. I'm doubled over on the gravel, bleeding from the nose onto the sea-bed gravel.

"Oh?"

Power points at the Big House.

"I think," he says, "that Leo and Antigone would be particularly touched by a reenactment."

Ixion looks from me, to Farhall, to Lee curled by the dragon, and as he understands, a smile spreads over his face.

He's taking the bait.

It was supposed to be a performance, this moment. I was supposed to *act upset*.

But as they haul Lee to his feet and Ixion's fingers wind into my hair exactly as Leon's once did, I wouldn't be able to stop the tears flushing blood from my vision if I tried.

"Go on," Ixion tells me, as Leon did. "Make your Plea."

LEE

Hands pull me up, but the world is streaks of color and sound and none of it matters as beat by beat I lose him. The connection dims like lights being extinguished in a vacated house. I feel that I'm racing, room by room, to catch him.

But the lights keep going out. The love that answered me in its first great torrent slows to a trickle. There comes the moment when I wait for the next faint pulse, and it doesn't come.

I'm standing in what was our home, in the darkness, alone.

But I'm also still in this body, trapped in this senseless world, and the shadows around me are moving.

"Go on," Ixion says. "Make your Plea."

Annie kneels in obeisance, the hem of her dress overtaken by the seeping red, palms on the ground. Annie. For a moment she flickers, and I see Aela. Annie, Aela, one. *Our beloved.* She lifts her face to Ixion. Her lips move soundlessly to form the words.

I know what they will be. Though I never had to learn them, I heard my father say them at the end, forced by the ones who hurt us. *Forgive me, Lord, grant us mercy undeserving . . .*

I know they will be the same words Annie once said to my father. Memories to befoul memories in this pool of blood that I would drown in.

In my darkness, her face is a moving source of light.

She gets to her feet.

Callish is the language of the Pleas, but she speaks in

Dragontongue. The poem is not the *Aurelian Cycle* I know but the fragment we found, and the lamentation is the widowed queen's. Tears barely ripple her voice, which has become calm and quiet and strong.

Antigone looks not at Ixion but at me.

> *I was yours when I had nothing, no family or name.*
> *My lord, to me you have been a mother, a father,*
> *A brother, and a flowering husband,*
> *Yet now you go before me to the house of the dead.*

There is silence except for my own labored breath. Annie's eyes hold mine, warmth in the cold, light in the dark.

Ixion breaks the silence with a laugh.

"The whore quotes poetry."

He kicks Annie, who crumples, and then he flicks an arm.

"Tie him up first."

They tie my arms and legs. They seize Annie by the hair, forcing her face up to watch. Then they drag me across the lawn and throw me into the foyer of my home.

The door is locked and bolted.

Outside, the dragons start the fire.

As the ground warms and the flames lick up the high ceilings, paint begins to flutter down like falling leaves. The heat on my skin and the smoke in my lungs are a blessed release as the pain mounts.

When I close my eyes, there are blue skies on Pallor's wing.

PART IV

—

TRIAL

30

—

INTO THE DRAGON'S LAIR

DELO

THE LOWLANDS

The first few days in the Summer Palace are an eerie paradise. In some ways, it's exactly as I remember it: the soaring sun-bleached marble; a glittering azure sea; and breezes warm as a caress wafting through long halls with windows thrown open to welcome them.

On the other hand, the last time I was here, I was a child. The last time I was here, Mother was here, too. Father wasn't a widower in any sense; the twins had not spent years crying themselves to sleep. We were different people. In all those years imagining the Long-Awaited Return, praying the Summer Palace was intact, I didn't stop to consider that whether or not the house would be changed, I would be.

I didn't stop to consider that returning at last, I'd wander these halls thinking of the halls I left; of the one I left behind in them. I even find myself thinking of Sty. When it was time for him to ride with Ixion back to the Great Palace and the ha'Aurelian cousins who awaited him, he didn't want to let go of my hand.

But it's good to see the twins again. Ethelo's joviality finally feels in place, reinstalled in its original sunny halls; Phemi has a gravity I don't remember. I find her chambers cluttered, as always, but instead of her usual arithmetical contraptions, they're filled with books on subjects she didn't previously have interest in: charter writing, political philosophy.

"What's all this?"

"A . . . penance, of sorts. I've been thinking a lot about reconciliation."

At my look, she shrugs, rubbing at her stubbly hair. It's growing back, slowly, since she sheared it off after her widowing. "I think a lot about our explosives in that karst. Griff's family on it."

"Roxana was the one who set them off. Not you."

"No. But I designed them. It's made me think of things I'd rather be responsible for." She flashes me a small, sad smile. "I'm surprised you came back. I don't think it's what you wanted."

I could deny it, but instead hear myself attempt a joke. "When have I ever done what I wanted?"

Father sits me down to strategize on a subject he's free at last to consider in earnest: marriage prospects. I find myself looking at portraits of daughters of wealthy Bassilean satraps, of natural-born sisters of the Grayriders; even of the Iscan princess I told Griff to court. I think of Griff's fingers buried in my hair, the way he looked sprawled next to me the last time I saw him, languorous in my bed. *You think this is easy for me?*

"Whichever union you think brings the best honor to Skyfish House," I tell Father flatly, pushing the pile of portraits toward him, and he looks a little surprised, but mostly relieved.

"I'll look into it," he says.

GRIFF
NORCIA

I thought I'd feel more triumph, coming out of the kingsmoot with crown in hand, but mostly I feel an awful sense of weight. I'm used to navigating the ha'Aurelian citadel as a servant, but the residential wing always seemed too echoing and extravagant then, and the feeling doesn't go away when it becomes mine to live in. This job, it turns out, is conducted mostly by way of letters, and I can't help considering the mountain before me with a thought to Delo, whose absence nags at me like a pulled tooth.

I remind myself he never belonged here. He'll be happier now, *home*. He always spoke of wanting it.

And the first thing I'll do after the coronation is send some of my personal guard after Seanan for a good bashing.

I know Becca's lonely. Shrines, I'm lonely. Even confronting Ixion's sorry face and a battle with my hated former lords would be a welcome change from this stretching solitude. But the blockade has pulled back to the northern Callipolan shore, true to their promise to the League, and the goliathan is nowhere in sight.

I'm itching for a war. And luckily for me, Antigone sur Aela brings me one.

Becca's the one who comes to tell me. She enters the study stinking of the lairs, her hair a bird's nest; she stopped brushing it again after Delo left, and I haven't got the knack myself. "Uncle, Aela's here. Without Antigone."

That doesn't sound good.

I follow Becca down to the lairs at a jog. Along the way, I pass citadel staff—now a mixture of all five clans, one of the things I've been determined to change—who bob in bows and curtsies that I acknowledge with distraction. I'm still not used to it.

Aela's curled in Sparker's stall, half spilling out into the corridor. Sparker, usually a territorial monster, has made room for her without complaint. He nuzzles her like an old friend, and when I scratch beneath her horned chin, she leans into it with a soft snuffle. She's slumping, barely holding her head up, her tail strewn limply across the stones.

But her gaze, when it finds me, focuses well enough, which puts to rest my worst fear: She's not widowed.

"What happened to you, my darling?"

I find the answer tucked inside a canteen clipped to her halter, in which is stuffed a rolled note.

ANNIE
THE HIGHLANDS

The sky above me is latticed with bars, and between the bars and the sky spread branches that have begun to bud. The trees slide slowly past the grid of iron. When the bars jostle, the movement chafes my wrists and hammers along my back and head, inflaming the half-healed burns along my back.

Pain is how I return to earth.

I'm in a cart fitted with a cage, dragon-size, with no dragon to fill it. Shackles allow me to lie down or sit up against the bars. We are on the Aurelian Way, the wagon and its train of soldiers making their way toward the city from the Far Highlands. Occasionally, hunger stabs my stomach, but it's inconsequential.

No covering is offered to the cage. The point of this procession is to be seen. Seen all along the Aurelian Way, from the highlands to the Ferrish Plain, and into the city up to the People's Square before the Palace.

Ixion wants his trophy to be seen by all.

On the first day, Aela still flares in my head. Searching for me. Wanting me.

Every time she reaches out, I push her back.

Norcia. Get to Norcia. Get to Griff sur Sparker.

I slap her away, harder and harder to make the point, hardening my heart to her heartbreak and her pain. Try as I might to make her understand that this is how it must go, all she knows is that when we are both hurting, when we need each other most, I'm pushing her away.

When she finally extricates for good, it's all I can do not to cry out from the loss.

The loneliness that comes after drenches me like cold water.

She'll come back.

I ask to do my toilet and am given a bucket. I ask for water and am given a fistful of melting snow. I lean back against the bars, shove cold hands into the pockets of Penelope's dress, and suck on the ice as my tongue goes numb. When I close my eyes, the vision that paints their lids is fire.

Pallor's blood on the stones. Farhall in flames. Ixion laughing. Lee gone.

He'll be fine. Nigel was in place in the cellar. He got Lee out.

But I have to take that on faith. When we left the Winterless Green, the last I'd seen of Lee was his bound body being hurled through the front door of the Big House before the fire started.

"Firstrider?"

I open my eyes. The voice spoke not with a Bassilean Immortal's accent but rather a highlander's brogue. A young boy trots alongside the cart, dressed in fraying work clothes, ignoring the stares of the soldiers who make up the train.

He shoves a hand through the bars, and I realize he holds in it a handful of wildflowers, heather and golden gorse. The stems brush my hand, and my numb fingers clasp them.

"Is it true," he asks, "that Lee sur Pallor's dead?"

The road is winding. I don't have to twist my head to see what he points to. A column of smoke rising like a black storm cloud from peaks behind us, where Farhall lay. The Big House still burns.

He got out. Please, let him have gotten out.

But even if he got out, even if he survives unscathed, he'll still have lost Pallor.

I feel tears leak unbidden from the corners of my eyes, and the boy lowers his gaze.

"The highlands pray for your fair trial, Firstrider," he says. "Remember the flowers and remember Egan Borisson, at your service."

I hold the flowers slackly in one hand, the name echoing in my memory.

"Boris," I repeat. "From Holbin?"

Boris and his wife, Helga, were among those Holbiners so discomfited by my return as a dragonrider, so many months ago when I made a morale visit on the mandate of the Ministry of Propaganda. This must have been one of the children who hid behind his mother's legs.

Egan nods, bowing.

"Spring's blessings on your house," I manage.

I watch him dwindle round the bend of the Way.

There are more after that. Just Holbiners, at first. Bundles of gorse and heather make a bed on the floor of the cage. Don Macky, eyes watering, kisses my hand through the bars as his wife weeps. Even the widow who once spat on me comes to watch the procession, her arms folded round her black shawl. We pass the smoking husk of Holbin not long after that, its cluster of homes reduced to black skeletons.

I expected the Holbiners to blame me for it. Instead, the furtive whispers that they offer are of loyalty. "Curse the ones who betrayed you," Macky tells me. "I hope it was no highlander."

By afternoon, we have entered the Near Highlands, and the flowers haven't stopped. Not just flowers: I'm given dried fruit, jerky, twists of caramel that melt in my hands. The soldiers mutter to one another, but don't seem to know what to do about the mounting piles of gifts. I can't remember a time when Callipolans felt loyalty to me; that highlanders do now, when I'm dragonless and caged, makes it only stranger.

My fingers reach up often to my necklace to rub the pendant between my fingers. It was my mother's, but it was given to me by Lee. In my hands, it seems to bring both of them close.

The sun is setting when a stormscourge's silhouette grows on the horizon.

Ixion sur Niter lands atop the caged wagon, the dragon's black wings mantling it like a blanket. Fiery eyes examine me in the bed of flowers below.

"Where did these come from?" Ixion demands of the captain of the procession.

The captain waves an arm, vaguely, at the hillside.

"Get them out, get them out—and cover her!"

The captain's accent is harsh with Bassilic vowels. "Apologies, sire, we thought the order was to keep her strictly visible."

The soldiers scrabble to clean the cage of wildflowers. I pull up my skirts to make room for their work, and only look up when boots click directly in front of me.

Ixion has dismounted Niter and entered the cage. For a moment, we stare at each other. The gray eyes, the high cheekbones, the black hair are all similar enough to Lee's to make the hair on the back of my neck stand on end.

"Nice necklace," Ixion says.

Too late, I stuff my mother's pendant back under the collar of my dress. He reaches for it, snaps the rusted chain from my neck, and drops the necklace under the heel of his boot.

The pendant is made of cut glass. It shatters.

"You'll find a less warm welcome in the capital," Ixion says.

***

I'm offered no more water, no more snow, no more food. I don't ask for any, even as my mouth dries and my stomach begins to knot with hunger. I can bear hunger. Thanks to Ixion's family, I'm well practiced. The cage is covered as we make our way out of the Near Highlands and across the Ferrish Plain. The covering is only removed at the city gates.

Ixion was correct in predicting a different reception within the capital. Little though they liked my visits during collections or the fact that I rode a dragon, the highlanders know me as one of their own. The city, on the other hand, has known me as the Guardian willing to crack the whip. The voice who said no to widows begging for a second ration card, who faced them down from the wrong side of a protest line. I was Atreus's enforcer. His bitch commander. The undeserving peasant who was promoted on Leo Stormscourge's recommendation, his whore.

I had a taste of their hatred, of these names, after the Midwinter Attack when the Bunker Riots shook our city and paved the way for the Restoration. I know what to steel myself for.

Still, it takes every ounce of self-possession I can muster not to flinch when I see the placard that they affix to the cage.

THE DRAGONLORD'S WHORE

The expected battery begins. Rotten eggs, expired fruit, excrement. If anyone needs to be reminded of the name to heckle, the placard helps them. I have no way of knowing whether these are actors paid to inspire the rest of the city along the route. But I doubt, in my case, that much encouragement is needed.

Ixion sur Niter leads the procession, and so when I look up, I see the placard and Ixion's back as he sways in the saddle between his stormscourge's silver-tipped wings.

Leading me into the heart of his lair.

I know exactly how long this procession takes because I've done it before: once in Freyda's retinue; and before that as a Guardian, as a member of the Fourth Order, to fanfare on dragonback. I know they are keeping the incrementally slow pace, as is appropriate. I know that at procession speed, the length of the Triumphal Way takes a whole day to cross.

The courage gained from well-wishes in the highlands drains from me mile by mile. By the second hour or so, I feel that my brain has started to float free from my body, and I watch what is happening as if from above. I'm so far away that I'm tempted to laugh. I hear the whispers of the citizens, as they pause in their heckling, their throwing, their laughing:

But where is the girl's dragon?

I do laugh aloud, then. Madly, maniacally. But by then, I'm so far gone that no one thinks anything of it.

There is a moment when the sun blinds my face, a hand is in my hair, the crowd spreads below. Pytho's Keep rises over us, but its crown is bare. The goliathan has not yet returned. We stand on the plinth in the People's Square, and Ixion is shaking me by the back of Penelope's dress like a rag doll.

"Shall we see the bitch put to justice?" he roars.

The people roar their answer back at him.

The Palace Gates. Blackness. Cold stone. Doors slam, then wrench open. The stone seeps its cold through my knees, into my hands. They are stiff with dried egg and excrement.

"Good dragons in the sky above," a woman's voice says.

I blink crusted filth from my eyes and look up into the drawn face of Miranda Hane. She looks thinner than the last time I sat in her office in the Ministry of Propaganda.

"Minister Hane?"

"Antigone," Hane says. "It looks as though a bath is in order."

"What are you—?"

My throat is too parched to finish the question, but Hane answers it.

"What remains of Revolutionary law entitles the accused to legal counsel. I'm yours."

31

—

TRIAL PREP

LEE

THE HIGHLANDS

For a time, pain holds me in its fists, somewhere between sleep and waking, death and dying. It feels like I've been turned inside out. Only slowly, as I return to this shell of a body, finger by finger and limb by limb, do I realize that the loss of Pallor is not where the pain ends. It continues across burns that have torn my skin open and left it dead.

Gradually, the awareness moves from these twitching fingers and mottled skin to the patchwork blanket I lie on, the low thatched roof overhead, and the sound of water wringing from a cloth. When I close my eyes, I see Pallor.

When I open them, a curtain of blond hair catches the light.

"Hey, you."

"Crissa."

I'd forgotten the exiled Guardians were a part of the plan. Her lips brush my forehead with the fondness of a friend and the familiarity of someone who was once more than that. In this weakened state—*amputated* seems the more fitting description of the gaping loss I feel, like a missing fifth limb—it's a relief to be greeted by Crissa and her no-nonsense smile.

"How bad is it?" I ask.

Crissa's voice is bedside-light. "Well, you look like you're in for a sexy scar across your face. Mr. Garth says a falling beam got you. Good thing you'd snuck a cropped flamesuit under that tunic."

"Nigel got out all right?"

"Mm-hmm. Took you out the Travertine as planned, through the cellar. He *was* surprised you'd been able to correctly predict your own manner of execution, I think."

She dips a rag in the bucket at the foot of the bed, then sluices cold water over my shoulder, which is bare. I don't have the courage to look down and inspect the burn myself. I can still feel my arms and legs, which is what matters. Even if most of what they feel is pain.

"Cor's out in the yard with Mr. Garth, preparing the . . . pyre."

It takes me a moment to understand. And then, to remember. For a speck of time, I'd managed to forget. The ache at the nape of my neck begins where previously, I felt *him*.

The fire filling our vision as we told her to go. The blood warm on my hands. Pallor's eyes closing.

Crissa's eyes have filled. "I'm so sorry, Lee."

My voice comes out a croak. "Did Aela—do you know if Aela—"

"She made it safely to Norcia. That's how we got your note."

For a moment, my face is hot with Pallor's feelings. His joy, his relief.

Then they fade.

Emptiness remains, like the echoing silence of an empty room.

A lingering shred of our last spillover, gone. I know, with the certainty of a slammed door, that it was the last. I'll never feel his love for Aela—his love for anything—again.

It's too intolerable to bear sitting still. I force myself up, a palm to the mattress, and Crissa's ministering washcloth falls aside. My surroundings swim into focus. The room's single window, opened for the breeze, provides a view of the still-smoking husk of the Big House. At the foot of the cot where I lie, the saddlebag containing the hermeneuta and the annals waits for flight.

"When do we go to Norcia?"

"As soon as you're ready."

"I'm ready. After the pyre, we should go at once."

The thought of training my friends without wings of my own makes me ill, but I push the horror away. I'll bear it. Compared with what's happening to Annie right now—it's the least I can bear. Pallor bought us time, and I intend to make use of every second of it.

Crissa's tears spill over. The drops trickle down her cheeks, but she doesn't wipe them.

"Lee," she asks, "where is she?"

When I start to say it, my throat closes. I remember Annie on her knees, the sound of a boot connecting with her face as Power kicked her silent. Ixion's laughter. *The whore quotes poetry.* The way he held her by her hair as I was dragged away.

And now she's beyond my help, in the hands of the ones who have hunted her and wanted her to hurt for as long as they've known her name.

Even if she manages to bring down Ixion at the end, she'll suffer first.

"She's in the capital." Crissa lifts her eyes, disbelieving. "She's with Ixion."

ANNIE

After the procession into the capital, I scrub filth from my body in the apartments of Miranda Hane, my legal counsel. It seems an age ago that I sat nervously in her office while she looked over my file and decided to take a gamble on me despite an unpromising track record. I didn't believe I'd won her over until she left a hand-written note for my final match. *Go show them what you're made of.*

We've both come a long way since then. I am no longer a Guardian of the Revolution, vying for Firstrider; and Hane is no longer the Minister of Propaganda. Her crimes against the Triarchy during the Revolution were indirect enough, and her knowledge of the Inner Palace's current bureaucracy valuable enough, to escape charges under the Restoration. But that has not left her without punishment. She has been set with the task of representing high-profile revolutionaries the Restoration saw fit to bring charges against—Guardians, senior civil servants, and Atreus himself, who was tried from the grave.

"How many have you gotten off?" I ask. I'm bathing in Miranda's tiny tub while she waits on the opposite side of the curtain scrubbing Penelope's dress on a washboard. The sight of Miranda Hane engaged in such domestic activity makes me more uncomfortable than the thought of her seeing me undressed, but I've been given no change of clothes.

"So far?" The sound of scrubbing wool stops. "None."

"Do you have a legal background?"

"Mostly academic. The larger problem is that they haven't let the defense participate in selecting witnesses or jury."

A knock sounds from the other end of the apartment, and Miranda inhales as if the noise made her jump. "That will be the physician." She passes a robe through the break in the curtains. "I'll dry your dress while he looks you over."

The physician, it turns out, is Master Welse, whose tenure as Palace physician spanned the entirety of my years as Guardian. At the sight of him, gray hair gone fully white, my eyes prickle.

"Hello, Master Welse."

"There now, Annie," he says, dropping his eyes.

He inspects me cursorily while Miranda stands by the fire, beating the dress dry. Her drawing room has the look of being recently stripped of its furnishings: The walls have faded squares where portraits used to hang, and the single seat I'm instructed to take is positioned as if it had been previously surrounded by a complete set of furniture. Welse diagnoses a concussion, surface-level abrasions, bruised ribs, and dehydration. Nothing that won't be healed with proper meals and time, but I'm not permitted any medication for pain relief. Welse phrases it like this, impersonally, as if there were not a very specific person behind such a needlessly cruel order.

The name hovers unmentioned over the checkup until finally I say it.

"Where's Ixion?"

Welse's quiet, comforting patter stutters to a halt at the question. My voice sounds too small in my own ears. Miranda's eyes drift closed. When she looks at me, I see lines in her face I don't remember.

"He's making a tour of the island. An Ascension tour. Your trial begins when he returns. His hope is to convict you before Freyda returns and to time your execution with the triple coronation. Traditionally the ritual involves a sacrifice."

* * *

I'm kept in a solitary cell for the week that follows, on the windowless side of the Palace stockade, unlit save for the light that filters down the corridor from the guardroom. At night, I dream of Aela and wake straining for her—to feel nothing.

She's hurt. She's far. You'll feel her again.

I push away the fear that I won't and go back to wondering whether Lee's dead.

For one hour every day, I'm escorted to an audience with Hane, who receives me in her stripped apartment, serves me tea, and seats me as close to the fire as my shivering body will allow while she helps me prepare my defense. It feels—if I can block out that I'm hungry, sore, and wearing a dead girl's dress that still smells faintly of urine—as if I'm a Guardian preparing for some sort of official assignment with the Ministry of Propaganda.

We work on elocution, on what to do with my hands and face. It reminds me of countless hours being humiliated in rhetoric class. Of standing on the roof with Crissa, practicing for a morale visit when I was first learning to believe in my ability to speak. We go over breath tricks to calm myself, where to look in the room, and when to break for water. When Hane tells me to *smile more*, I'm incredulous.

"I'm standing trial. I don't think the jury expects me to answer questions smiling."

"You would be surprised."

We practice smiling until my face hurts. We practice smiling as Hane insults me, as she asks every prying, provocative, painful question she can think of. It's a script not unlike the one Power and I practiced when I mastered spillovers, but in reverse. Now my task isn't to feel the pain. It's to inure myself to it.

"Were you sharing Leo Stormscourge's bed at the time of your promotion to Firstrider?"

This, like most of the case Hane is preparing, is based on Megara Roper's original character assassination in the *People's Paper* during the Bunker Riots. In her article, Megara insinuated that I slept my way to the top of the rankings by sharing the bed of my former lord—Lee.

"That is none of their—"

"You stopped smiling. And it's all their business. Again."

We run through the line of questioning again. *No, I wasn't sharing his bed at the time of my promotion. No, I shared no bed. I honored my Guardian vows.* When I point out that technically, the vows are not explicit about the deed itself, only marriage and progeny, Hane purses her lips. "We can't expect the jury to care about such nuance. Have you ever shared Leo's bed?"

The question catches me off guard. For a moment, I remember the feeling of his arms around me. The quiet, the night, the comfort of our held breaths.

And then I see that fire.

Miranda notices my silence.

"The answer," she says delicately, "to that question—whatever the truth may be—is no."

I remember how Lee looked when Pallor sacrificed himself for Aela, his wild, blazing smile, and am tempted to say: *They want to call me his whore? Let them.*

"I think they're going to form opinions about what we were doing on his estate regardless of how I answer that question."

She doesn't look up from her notes. "Doesn't mean you need to help them."

"We were wed. In a deed in Harfast."

Hane looks up at that. "For your safety, I would keep that between us. They will accuse you of breaking your vows, and that would be proof."

I must blink for a second too long, because her voice softens.

"I'm sorry, Antigone."

And then she makes me practice again. Leaving out the mention of any deed in Harfast. Smiling.

Despite never having won a case, Hane seems determined to prepare a defense as if we might. I don't dare tell her that I intend to be found guilty, but she picks up on what she takes to be a defeatist attitude nevertheless.

"You have to *pivot*. Didn't your rhetoric professor teach you anything? When I ask, 'Did you fire on civilians,' you don't just say 'Yes'—"

For a moment, I see the burning Lyceum courtyard and hear the screams. That protesters were stealing grain that the city needed, that I protected on a split-second decision and later regretted. Megara's insinuations about my love life were spurious, but the rest of her article was pretty accurate. "I did fire on civilians."

"You followed laws that you later decided were unjust and helped dismantle. *That's* what you say."

I've got my arms folded. These kinds of arguments, where Hane defends my actions *to me*, are cropping up more and more as we delve into the heart of Megara's article. They feel like unnecessary punishment; the suspicion that Hane's speaking sense only adds to my irritation. "If they're going to sentence me either way, I don't see how it matters what I say. I should just plead guilty and get on with it."

The sooner I'm found guilty, the sooner we get into the arena. I have half a mind to come clean to her right there. But Hane's frustration outstrips mine fastest. She slams the *People's Paper* clipping on the small crate we've been using as a table. "First of all, that's not an option with show trials. Second—even if it were, you should do no such thing."

"Why not? I *am* guilty—"

"You are *guilty* of being trained to use a dragon and groomed by an ideologue to be his enforcer from the age of six. You are *guilty* of trying to do your job as well as you knew how. And when you saw that your job conflicted with your vows to uphold justice, *you learned*. Do you think Ixion and his ilk are in danger of similar improvement?"

"I'm not saying Ixion's better—"

"Then straighten your back."

Burning with a strange fury, I square my shoulders. Hane's on her feet, glaring at me, her eyes glistening. "They may rig it against you. They may try to write you into history as a villain, but I will drink hemlock before I let you accept that without a fight. Do you really want Ixion to have the last word of your story? There's more than one way to win."

That's where she's wrong, I tell myself. There's only one way to win, and it's in the arena after I've been found guilty of everything they charge me with.

"I don't care who has the last word. Words don't matter."

What matters is the dragonfire at the end.

"You know what, Antigone?" says Hane. "Do it for my sake."

32
—
TRADITIONAL PRACTICES

LEE
THE HIGHLANDS

Nigel's the one who remembers the rites of Widowing that accompany the pyre, and finds me once I'm on my feet again with the appropriate equipment. "The sackcloth's a bit impractical, this time of year, but you might still want to do this."

He holds out a pair of sheep shears. My stomach tightens as I understand.

Crissa sits down with me on the back step of his cottage to do it. I lean over my knees, and her deft hands circumnavigate the still-tender burns on my scalp, snipping away clumps of black hair that drift across the garden. The metallic singing of the shears cuts through the quiet evening.

"Who do you want to ride with, to Norcia?" she asks.

It's the first time I've considered how I'll be getting there. As a passenger. Crissa's touch is light on my wrist, bringing me back. The ground feels heavy under my feet. I realize I haven't answered her.

Cor's the obvious choice, because of Maurana's size, but not if I'm like this. Crissa's the one I've always found it easiest to show grief in front of. Even if our romantic history feels like ancient history, the ease borne of it remains.

"Can I ride with you?"

"Of course."

After she's done, we walk together up the hillside to the pyre Cor and Nigel have built among the barrows. For a moment, the sight of Pallor arranged as if he were sleeping, a silhouette against the sunset, makes the reality of it warp. I must have dreamt it. He's right there, he'll turn to look at me, and I'll feel him again—

But he doesn't, and I don't.

Crissa's grip on my arm is tight. When Cor turns to me, his face is contorted and blotchy. There's no sign of the chain-link net the Grayriders threw over Pallor's silver wings, and his great head is turned so that I can't see the cut across his jugular, but it must have been Cor who found this evidence and obscured it. He knows how Pallor died.

What he wouldn't have known, from that evidence, is how proud we were. Of our bondmate, safe. Of our great fire, protecting her. Of our beautiful eggs, of the boy we left behind to stand on his own feet—

The memories of Pallor's emotions refract and separate as I find myself in them.

I press a palm in the same spot on his scaled face where I held him. The scales that have always been so warm to the touch are now cold.

You saved her. But I wasn't able to save you.

And now he's gone, and I'm left grounded on this hard earth, alone.

The Rites of the Fallen Dragon are conducted without words, though the motions are identical to those of the Fallen Dragonlord: Cor sur Maurana lights the pyre and I add the sacrifice, a fat salmon for Pallor's first feast in the afterlife. We forgo the traditional slicing of the dragonkeeper's hand, though Nigel offers to perform it.

The pyre burns down as night falls and the wind drags cool fingers over my scalp. Crissa sniffles quietly beside me; Cor clenches my shoulder with characteristic awkwardness, but I don't shift away. Nigel doesn't need to tell me what happens when the last embers have gone out. I cup Pallor's still-warm ashes in a smarting hand and smear them across my cheeks and along my exposed nape. All that's left besides the ashes is the bones. The barrow mound that will house them remains to be built.

It's dark, the sky glowing with smoky starlight, when I climb on Phaedra's back behind Crissa. As we lift with Cor sur Maurana from the ground, I bury my face in the back of her flamesuit so I don't have to see the ground shrink beneath an unfamiliar wing. Crissa's hair, like my face, smells of funeral ash; her arms are folded tightly over mine. She doesn't try to make conversation.

But I lift my head, a few hours later, when the sun begins to rise.

Norcia spreads before us, surrounded by the karst of Sailor's Folly. It's the first time I've ever seen it up close, and with dawn weaving gold threads through tendrils of mist, lighting the barren crags, it's so beautiful it takes my breath. For the first time since I woke without Pallor, it occurs to me that there are still sights in this world that can do that.

Maybe right now, I can't remember what there is to live for. *But I don't have to*. I just have to do what I promised Annie I'd do. The only way past grief is through it, but on the other side, someone needs me.

I can't afford to keep her waiting.

We land on the highest ramparts of the citadel, where I dismount and shake Griff Gareson's hand. He takes one look at my shorn head and ash-marked face and doesn't have to ask where my dragon is. "Leo. Those bastards."

He learned my dragonborn name from my family and his

former lords. Dressed in a well-cut tunic I suspect was pilfered from a ha'Aurelian armoire, Griff looks little like the scruffy squire who once tended me in secret after a Pythian air strike. This time, I'm careful to use the same respectful register with him that he does with me. "These days, I go by Lee."

When he asks how I've been holding up, I tell him I've been better. But also, here on these ramparts, with the sun bathing this new world in gold, with Annie across the sea on a fighting chance and the wartime lore of Stormscourge House slung over my shoulder, I remind myself I could be worse.

"Heard you might be able to help us with that goliathan," Griff says.

ANNIE
CALLIPOLIS

By the evening before the trial, I can go through every prepped question smiling, hands still, shoulders straight. We've burned every candle down to the nub by the time Hane pronounces us done, but I can tell she's satisfied, even surprised, by my progress.

"For all your poor marks in oration," she says, "you train well."

"Shame I'll lose either way."

Her lips tighten. "Do you *want* to lose?" she asks.

Yes, because our plan depends on it. I lift a shoulder. "Who will be leading the inquisition?"

"I'll find out when you do."

The usual guard has arrived, to escort me back to my cell. Hane tells me she'll see me in the morning, to join my escort to the trial. After rounding the corner that leads away from her apartment, we take an unfamiliar turn. The guard leads me away from the stockade and into the Stormscourge wing. I only understand when we stop outside a door whose filigree of highland heather glimmers in the light of the nearest sconce. At the guard's knock, Ixion opens it.

"Hello, Antigone."

He's in a loose tunic and trousers, backlit by a crackling hearth. He smells of dragonfire. As I stare up at his face and contemplate the chamber beyond, I know this a moment we have both, on some level, been expecting. I knew when I agreed to Power's plan that this was a part of what I would face. After kicking girls out of schools and barring them from the dragonriding fleet, why should this return to tradition come as any surprise? *I own you,* Ixion said once, and he's been waiting ever since to prove it.

The guard releases my arm and walks away without looking back.

I place one numb foot over the threshold, then the other. The door closes behind me. I can feel the blood in my fingertips. But beneath that pulsing blood I feel impatience.

After watching Pallor bleed out, after watching Farhall burn with Lee inside it, Ixion thinks *this* is how he'll break me? I've endured so much worse in this life than this humiliation. I endured worse at the age of six.

"Sit," he says in Dragontongue, gesturing to his bed.

When I do, his lip curves. "They say that when you get them cornered, the struggling stops."

Ixion is Lee's size, head and shoulders taller than me. Built like a dragonlord. Neither of us is under any illusions that this is a fight I can win.

"Animals?" I hear myself answer, in Callish. "Or women?"

Ixion's smile widens. For a moment we are so still, I think we're both waiting for the traditional performance to begin.

But he turns away. He walks to the fire, roaring in the grate, and inspects what appears to be a poker buried in the embers. "Cattle," he says.

For a half breath, I don't understand. Then he pulls the poker from the coals, and I see the Stormscourge cattle brand. The *S*, encircled by heather, that marked the meager herd my father tended for his lord.

I feel myself grow lightheaded.

"I'm curious," Ixion says, "if you'll beg this time, or merely recite more poetry."

* * *

I wake on the floor of my cell, my skirts stuck to the seared flesh on my thigh, and when I shift, I have to bite my tongue against the scream that rises.

I'd steeled myself for violation and for shame, but I had not steeled myself for this—for simple, obliterating pain. His cool dismissal afterward, and my numb walk back to the cell, are a haze. The brand killed all feeling in my leg when it was applied; the pain mounted slowly. And then I lost myself to it.

A guard is at the cell door, which has creaked open. I only realize he's there, and that he's spoken, when he repeats himself. *Get up.* It's the same guard who left me with Ixion last night.

The light has risen. It's time to go to trial.

But when I roll onto my knees, plant my palms on the ground, and try to push to my feet, the fire that redoubles in my leg makes me see white. I bite my lip so hard, I taste blood.

For a moment, I think I won't be able to get up from my knees.

A voice that belongs to another life echoes from a great distance.

They watch us kneel . . . but they don't realize you can think from your knees just as well as from your feet.

The memory of my father restores the breath to my lungs and I feel a fire beneath my lids so hot it brings tears to my eyes. I feel that I am catching fire myself.

And not the way Ixion wanted, when he branded me.

Sing me now your fury-song.

I push to my feet.

Fury powers me through the pain. I favor the injured leg, keeping pace with the stone-faced guard as he leads me through the Inner Palace to the courtyard outside the Hall of Plenty. When I step outside, I force the limp from my stride and cross the lawn to the carriage waiting for me. Green shoots are poking through the dead winter grass, and the sky has broken with spring cumulus that, were I still a Guardian in training, I would spend the morning flying in.

"Good morning, Antigone," Hane says, opening the carriage door.

"Minister."

Hane's expression changes as I take the seat beside her. "What happened?"

It didn't occur to me that even if I masked the limp, my appearance must betray me. The tearstains. My hair. I sweated like a pig after the branding, and I'm sure it's slick with oil. I have just enough presence of mind to know that this rage is fragile. I can't afford to tell Miranda what happened because pity would make it crumble.

Until last night, I didn't care what happened between now and the moment I'm found guilty. But Ixion changed that.

The fight can't wait to begin at the arena. It begins now.

I need them to find me guilty. They *will* find me guilty. But between now and when they do, I will fight to defend my name because I am not the guilty one. The sticky, mottled *S* on my leg will not speak for me.

I grind out the only answer I can manage. "I'm not giving Ixion the last word."

We're moving. The courtyards out the carriage window give way to Palace gardens. Hane's gaze, a little too bright, flicks briefly down, along my body, as if searching for evidence. I dread the question, but Hane doesn't ask it. Her voice is soft, masking emotion, but barely surprised. "Do as we rehearsed, and he won't have it."

She pulls a kerchief and a canteen from her purse and holds them up, a silent offer. I nod. I'm beginning to feel dizzy again; my stomach lurches with the carriage. She wets the kerchief and wipes my cheeks, my forehead, my chin, and my neck. Then she produces a comb, which she picks through my snarled and oily hair.

"Turn your head the other way, now."

I let her braid my hair. The faded impression of my mother's hands swims through my woozy head. When Hane offers me a slice of bread and cheese, I nibble on them. When she passes me the canteen, I empty it in one long swallow and wipe my mouth. I had not realized, until water touched my lips, how thirsty I was.

The carriage comes a little better into focus.

"There she is," Hane murmurs.

"Is there any more water?"

Hane is silent for a moment. "I'll make sure to get you more. But you also shouldn't take the stand on a full bladder."

The crowds begin to gather after we've crossed Highmarket Bridge. Shopfronts that were bombarded during air strikes, ravaged by riots, and finally rebuilt under Freyda are boarded up again on new shortages. Noses press against the carriage windows, palms smack the glass: drawn faces, bared teeth, dirty, bony hands. We can hear everything they shout at me.

My city, I think, with a sorrow unrelated to myself, larger than myself, as the pounding glass reverberates in my aching head—*My city, always frightened, always hungry.*

And it's endured enough.

"They wanted it to be an open-top carriage," Hane says. "I talked that down, on grounds of your safety. But curtains weren't negotiable."

"It's fine. I want to see it."

The crowd chokes our route through the People's Square and mounts on stoops along the Triumphal Way; we cut through Scholars Row, passing the gates of the Lyceum, where I studied as a Guardian; and then we enter the Manufacturing District, still gutted from the Midwinter Attack. The Vault, the city's most ominous administrative building, looms over us as we approach. This was where I interrogated Megara Roper months ago and where, during the Bunker Riots, the Passi protesters based their occupation. They demanded reforms on the streets and in the papers while I quelled the mob.

"There's a courtroom in the Vault?"

Hane nods. "They've been using it for the Clover Tribunal. It's open to the public that can fit, but it's secure against . . . rescues."

The carriage halts in front of gates dwarfed by the windowless fortress they contain. The gathered crowd presses closer. When a guard opens the door on my side, I think the ground two feet below might as well be a leap from dragonback. My skirts have stuck to my thigh again, and the fury that fueled me ebbs as dizziness swells.

"Does the peasant need a hand?"

I do a double take of the guard and find the sneering face of Power. He is dressed in uniform as a Grayrider for Skyfish House, but he wears no battle armor. When I reach out to clutch his arm, he braces it.

I hear the words they're shouting now, but it's nothing new, the things they're saying. Power's arm remains under my elbow as we make our way inside. His lockstep alleviates my desire to limp. To my relief, the main courtroom is on the ground floor.

Power fits my wrists into the shackles waiting for me at the stand. Then he turns, salutes smartly to the judge, and I look up.

Ixion smiles at me from the lead chair of the inquisition.

"Good morning, Antigone."

33

—

THE CLOVER TRIBUNAL

LEE

NORCIA

At my first dinner in the Greatlord's Hall, I take a seat among the Callipolan refugees and see faces I haven't laid eyes on since the coup. Many of them embrace me, weeping; Mrs. Sutter, Cor's mother, kisses my forehead, and Mr. Sutter shakes my hand. After it's gone on long enough, Crissa and Cor insert themselves at the bench on either side of me and attempt to buffer the harder questions, but Duck slips past their defenses.

"How are you handling the sorrow spells?"

That's when I remember he was widowed, too. He's slipped into the seat across from me and leans forward to speak in confidence. Cor's too startled to intervene; I think he must be as surprised as I am by Duck's newfound self-assurance. "If you need to talk, me and Mabalena can help. It's manageable, Lee."

He sounds earnest, even hopeful. As if he wants to make clear life goes on.

It's plain to see that for Duck, it has: He's made a home for his family and the other refugees in a vacant ha'Aurelian manor; he tells me how the ballroom has been converted to a school, where he teaches letters to Norcians, and a girl named Lena—whose relation he doesn't explain, but I gather from Cor's rolled eyes—teaches Norish to Callipolans. The sheepish boy we used to protect from bullies has been replaced by someone who has found his footing in the world.

I suppose I shouldn't be so surprised he's found it on the ground.

I'm installed in a suite with Cor; Crissa sleeps next door. There are empty rooms in the refugees' manor I could have had to myself, but I don't question Cor and Crissa's decision to keep me from being alone. In solitary moments, time seems to stop; the walls tilt sideways, and I find myself staring up at the ceiling with visions of dragonsblood pooling and Annie's tearstained face. I can't shake the feeling that I'm faking being here, being *alive*. That at least until I see Annie again, on the other side and in one piece, living is a performance.

With Pallor gone, will it always be a performance?

It's been a performance before. There were days and weeks and years in my childhood where I felt I was pretending to go on. I got good at it. These muscles at least have the privilege of moving from memory.

The thing that kept me moving then, and now, is work.

"Well, what do you know," Cor says, when I show them the formations favored by my great-great-great-grandfathers, "Lee's family has its uses."

"For a change," I mutter, and Cor lets out his characteristic barking laugh. I realize I've missed it. "The thing is, I'm not sure any of them work."

"Well. No way to know until we try them."

We outline the drills the way we've always done, as if it were a squadron leader meeting back in the Guardian corps, not a last-ditch exercise in exile where one of us will play drillmaster from the ground. Griff tells the Woad-riders to take their orders from me, and that he'll train with us when he has time. He himself is busy preparing for a coronation that will take place, in the old Norcian style, to crown him High King.

Morning dawns with the conditions I need. Enough fog to prevent Clover observation from the mainland, but not so much that we can't train. On the citadel balustrade, at the appointed hour, I find an array of Guardians and Woad-riders waiting in their flamesuits, armed with javelins, their dragons saddled. I'm more surprised when a flash of amber slithers across the flagstones and coils herself beside me. Aela has joined us. Her golden eyes are fixed on me like she's listening, too. I lower my hand, not quite daring to reach for her like I would have reached for Pallor, but her muzzle brushes my palm, closing the rest of the distance. I feel that her touch connects me to Annie—connects me even to Pallor.

And for the briefest instant, an image hovers in my head of eggs, her eyes, his eggs, *our* eggs, and I know I've shared minds with Annie's dragon.

It shouldn't even be possible.

But the mystery of the moment doesn't change its power. For a flashing instant, Aela filled the emptiness left by Pallor's absence. The familiarity of that feeling, of the old connection, penetrates the loneliness and the numbness for the first time in days.

Aela, at least, understands.

I maintain contact with Aela as I speak to the corps. "Let's get started."

It's easier to miss the saddle alongside a dragon missing her rider. Aela remains with me on the balustrade when they leave us behind, and we watch the drills together.

With a karst as a size comparison, I'm able to confirm what I was worried about even in Farhall. Obizuth won't be subdued by the kind of attacks I found in my family's books—at least, not the way I've made sense of them. The riders pepper the karst with javelins that might as well be mosquito bites in the hide of a goliathan, and at the end of the day I tell them good work as they slide sweaty from their dragons' backs, but privately I'm stumped.

What am I missing?

By the time they land, I'm so consumed by the puzzle, I've forgotten to miss flying. I've forgotten I'm even *faking.*

I'm also pretty sure Aela's snorting with my frustration.

When Cor dismounts at my side, his glance goes to the dragon, but whatever he guesses is happening between us, he doesn't comment on. "These formations aren't going to work, are they?"

"Don't tell the others. I'm going to figure it out."

I've got to. Annie doesn't have forever.

ANNIE
CALLIPOLIS

As the trial begins, I'm aware, dimly, of all the ways I'm messing up. I'm not smiling. I stumble through my answers. I fail to pivot. Several times, I have to ask the examiner to repeat his question. When Ixion is the one questioning me, smiling all the while, I dig my fingers into my knees beneath the table to prevent them shaking.

He's not the only one who questions me. But the fact that my examiners rotate, taking breaks, allows them to deny me a break of my own. The Vault's walls are too thick to hear the city bells; the only clock sits behind me, and I'm shackled facing forward. I have no way of knowing how long I'm forced to speak.

The questioning continues until I slump onto the desk and have to be revived.

We adjourn until the next morning and emerge from the Vault

after dark. On the carriage ride back to my cell, free at last to contemplate the ebbing waves of agony in my leg, I decide there is something deliciously ironic about failing so spectacularly and irreversibly in such a setting. Public speaking has always been my bane. I would have failed at this task no matter how much I prepared. The branding only helps accelerate the inevitable.

I went into the Vault telling myself I would not let Ixion speak for me and then sat through twelve hours of him doing exactly that. I'm too tired to even care.

Miranda Hane, seated beside me in the carriage, seems as exhausted as I am.

"Until tomorrow," she says, when the carriage stops before the Hall of Plenty.

Though I sluice the burn with the cold water provided for my supper, there's only so much such treatment can do, and the pain keeps me awake through the night. What fitful dreams I have are of Farhall burning, of Pallor filling the sky with fire, of three beautiful eggs.

But when I wake, I still can't feel Aela at all.

On the second day, my performance does not improve. I have trouble, especially under Ixion's smiling interrogation, following the thread of his questioning. I have trouble focusing my vision at all. I'm enjoying five minutes with my head in my hands during the toilet break Miranda eventually demanded, when it's interrupted by someone kicking open the stall door despite her protests. I jerk upright at the sight of the Grayrider uniform and then realize it's Power. "Do you *mind*?"

"Let me see your leg."

His eyes are bugging. Miranda, who has been leaning against the sink with the heel of her hand pressed to her forehead, straightens slowly. "Power, what—"

But I am feeling something impossibly tight begin to unknot inside me. "Who told you?"

"I got drinks with Ixion last night."

"Oh, so you're drinking buddies?"

"Let me see your leg."

I reach down, seize the hem of my dress, and yank it up. It's the first time I've seen the wound in full daylight; my own stomach turns at the sight of the seared and mottled flesh, the livid trace of an *S* against my skin. Power's clenched fists tighten; Miranda, peeking around his shoulder, lets out an expletive.

"What is that?"

"It's a Stormscourge cattle brand," says Power through gritted teeth, as he bends to inspect it.

"My dad used to put them on our sheep," I add helpfully.

Hane's hand is over her mouth. "She needs to see a physician."

"No," Power says.

"No, *what*—?"

"No, I already suggested that to Ixion and he said it was not necessary." Power's jaw is working. He reaches into a pocket and retrieves gauze, which he hands me to wrap the wound, and a bottle of numbing tincture, which he shoves into Miranda's hand. "No more than three drops every six hours. If anyone asks, I came in here to gloat."

It gets a little better after that. The room stays in focus. I can answer most of the questions with complete sentences. I'm even, with questioners who aren't Ixion, able to force a few smiles.

But the more lucid I become, the more apparent the hostility of this courtroom is.

The audience is full of members of the Passi, the Order of the Black Clover, and the same class-bronzes and -irons who shouted insults at me during the Bunker Riots. When my interrogation finally pauses for witnesses to take the stand, my relief at the break is short-lived. They question Wes Goran, the drillmaster who loathed me; Lucian Orthos, the general's chief of staff who so resented my rank; Jester, the streetlord on whom I fired when I defended the Lyceum granary from a Passi raid.

Megara Roper sits among the journalists admitted, her pen poised on a notebook to record the proceedings for the *People's Paper*, her lip twisted with dispassion. Our brief alliance during my rescue mission does not seem to incline her to be more forgiving toward my earlier track record.

The righteous rage I felt after leaving Ixion's chambers sputters at the sheer and obvious futility of it. What point is there, defending myself to such an audience? Whatever defense I make will be twisted beyond recognition, anyway.

The week goes on, and I slip deeper and deeper into a fugue of disaffection. I see it mirrored in Hane's face.

On the final day, Ixion questions me on a subject that is clearly of great amusement to him.

"Have you ever shared a dragonlord's bed?"

He is smiling. I know the bed that he's thinking of is the one in which he threatened me, branded me, and made me beg for coolant.

I stare into his gray eyes, and the answer Miranda Hane trained me to give fades.

To hell with them. I'm damned anyway. The Guardian program is dead. To hell with these vows, this farce, this boy making a mockery of the sweetest moment of my life.

"I did."

There are ripples of surprise through the audience. Ixion blinks, once.

And for that matter? To hell with the names they call me.

"I shared the bed of the one to whom I was wed, in Farhall."

Miranda Hane, in the front row, lowers her face into her hands. Power arches a brow. Ixion's smile falters, then widens with incredulity. "*You* were wed?"

"Check the deed in Harfast."

I can see Ixion is startled—even, to my surprise, unnerved. Instead of belaboring that I've just confessed to breaking my vows as a Guardian, he twitches a hand toward the scribe. "There will be no need for that. Scratch it from the record."

He asks no more questions about my intimate life. But the whispering continues.

In the carriage that night, Hane is stiff with disapproval.

"You shouldn't be so disappointed," I tell her. "The sooner they sentence me, the better. Add vow-breaking to the list."

"It's not so simple as that," Hane says.

"Oh?"

It turns out the Restoration has been discouraging what they're calling "cross-birth marriages," which saw a rise under Atreus and are in talks now of being outlawed. My revelation was more than distasteful, Miranda explains. In the current political climate, it's incendiary. One more way I'm a peasant forgetting my place.

Good.

"The sentence should be forthcoming over the weekend," she says. "They intend to make a spectacle of the verdict in the Throne Room. But tonight, there will be a feast, and Ixion asked that you serve."

I think of pointing out that the city's starving. But then, that's never stopped the Triarchy. "I'm under arrest."

"I think," Hane sniffs, "the point is more the circus of it. Your claim today made him . . . particularly vindictive."

In the courtyard in front of the Hall of Plenty, light spills from the hall and glints on the thawing pond. The statue of Pytho the Unifier has been restored to his dragon and painted in garish gold. Before I step from the carriage, Miranda passes me Power's numbing tincture for an evening dose.

Outside the hall, also dressed to serve, I find Rock.

With something less than a smile, he pulls up the sleeve of his serving jacket and shows me a forearm marred by a mottled, scabbing S. "I hear we match."

And then I'm in his arms, and he's crunching me into the first embrace I've had since I watched the Big House burn, and I don't want him to let me go.

34

—

FREYDA BASSILEON

ANNIE

Rock was recaptured, he explains, the night the Guardians escaped—and the rider who took him out was Power. At my exclamation of surprise, Rock shrugs. "I thought he was going to kill me, to be honest. Instead he brought me back here for a bit more hell. But we always knew he was a twisted little ass, didn't we?"

I don't think Rock wants to hear my theories about it being a bit more complicated than that.

Like me, Rock's awaiting a death sentence; but Ixion doesn't seem eager to rush it, and in the meantime finds Rock's presence diverting enough to keep around. "They'll mostly leave you alone, if you're quiet enough," he tells me in a lowered voice, as we make our way up the servants' entrance to the back of the Hall of Plenty. He indicates his brand. "Which arm did he do it on?"

"He didn't do it on my arm."

Rock's fists clench. "He did my brand after he burned down Thornham."

Of course he did. Not for the first time, I appreciate the small ways Rock and I share roots. I ask, with dread, "Your family?"

"Safe in Norcia. Thanks to you."

It's the first thing I've had to be relieved about in days.

Not until we set foot in the Hall of Plenty do I realize that when I was told I'd serve at the high table, it would be the same table where I once was seated, at my first feast in this hall, for the Lycean Ball. I sat beside Lee that night, dazzled by the finery. It was the first time I'd ever worn a formal gown.

Tonight, dragonborn swarm the table that was once ours. Only Freyda is absent. Titus Grayheather, the eldest of the Stormscourge Bastards, occupies my former seat; at the head is Ixion, and to his right sits Delo. I stiffen at the sight of them, and Rock nudges me to keep moving.

"It's better if you don't make eye contact."

I know, from the minute tilt of Ixion's head when I first refill his glass, that he knows who serves him. I've done this before, as Abigael of Thornham, but it's different when the point is the humiliation of serving as myself. Ixion's elbow brushes my hip in what seems like an inadvertent gesture, but the touch happens to brush the brand, and for a moment I see white.

"Antigone, you remember Darius, I believe?"

Among the dragonborn sit the forsworn Guardians. Lotus, who avoids looking at Rock; and Darius, the golden-haired golden boy of the Janiculum and a friend of Power's from the years when he bullied me. During the Firstrider tournaments, I won my first public match against him. Darius sits frozen, stricken at the introduction, his marble skin flushing.

"You don't want to say hello?" Ixion asks.

"Hi, Annie." Darius croaks like he has glass in his throat.

"Hello, Darius."

"Darius was telling me a fascinating little story over aperitifs," Ixion goes on. "About a time when he and Parcival cornered you and Leo and something curious happened."

Darius has begun to visibly perspire. I stand frozen, the pitcher clutched uselessly in two shaking hands.

"He claims that you were able to summon your dragon with your mind, without a summoning whistle. Is that true, Antigone?"

I unstick my throat. Darius hunches in his chair. Ixion's glittering eyes are fixed on mine. Titus Grayheather comments from the seat that was mine: "Seems unlikely, for a peasant."

"I agree," Ixion says. "However, that is how the story goes. I wonder, where is Parcival? I would like to hear whether he can corroborate this curious story. You haven't seen him, have you, Delo?"

Delo Skyfish, returned from his stint as a political hostage in Norcia, and summoned from the Skyfish Summer Palace to claim his throne in the triple coronation, has been absorbed in careful conversation with the only child at the table, Astyanax ha'Aurelian, the third ascendant heir. Delo twists around, blinking. "Sorry. Who?"

Ixion's smile is icy. "Parcival. Formerly known as Power, your ha'cousin. Have you seen him? I would speak to him."

Delo's face smooths. "I'm afraid not. Patrol, maybe?"

He returns his attention to Astyanax, who breathlessly resumes whatever story he's been recounting.

I'm turning away myself when Ixion's hand darts out. He twists a finger into my hair to pull my face down, so that his lips are to my ear.

"Is *that* what you're hoping for?" he whispers. "An execution in the arena, a chance to show off your perverted little parlor trick? You think because we haven't killed your dragon yet, you've still got a chance?"

He releases my hair and pushes me back.

"I'll slit your throat in a windowless room."

* * *

It's done. The game's up. Thanks to stupid, callow Darius and a funny story he shared over drinks. I hope he feels better now. I hope he finally feels vindicated after I beat him in the arena in front of his adoring fans and family, for the spot that should have been his.

Ixion's words wash over my numb ears as the hall and the feast fade away. *I'll slit your throat in a windowless room.* I'm dead. I'll never see Aela again, and I'll never know if Lee lived or died.

Power's probably dead, too.

Lee burned, me branded and humiliated, Pallor dead, for *nothing*—

And without the arena to save me, I'll be dead for nothing, too.

"The Clover Court welcomes Her Divine Highness, Freyda Bassileon!"

The whiteness clears. The hall refocuses.

The unexpected announcement and its fanfare silences the dining chatter. Princess Freyda makes her way down the central aisle in dragonriding boots and a flamesuit, unaccompanied and unveiled, as all around the room, courtiers hasten to their feet. She stops in front of Ixion, the black of her eyes slowly fading, the protruding veins shrinking down her neck. She speaks with the lingering many-voices of the goliathan.

"My lord Ixion. So good to see you again."

Ixion has risen, too, but his eyes are narrowed and his smile is forced. "Back from Bassilea so soon? I had thought you would have a great deal of business to attend to, there."

The tone between them is stiffer than it was when last I saw them. As my awareness of the room expands, I realize that the rest of the table strains to listen, too.

"Do you mean parlaying the grain shipments? I've spoken with the accountants in Vask. They are deferring your debt a little longer and sending more aid."

"I mean with your fiancé."

Freyda's chin jerks up. Her eyes flash black. Only now do I notice the scorches that mark her flamesuit. She must have traveled on her goliathan's back this time, and clearly, her journey saw dragonfire. "If you refer to my brother, you mistitle him. I have no intention to honor the betrothal I was committed to before the age of reason. Perhaps he failed to make that clear in your recent . . . correspondence."

"It seems you engender many such misunderstandings about your marital intents."

"Only for those who willfully misunderstand me."

They both seem inclined to keep their voices raised loud enough for the whole table to hear. Ixion's next sally: "I hope your father's health has not further deteriorated?"

"If it has," says Freyda, "it would not change the duty I have to our newest province, Callipolis, and my most cherished viceroy—you." She smiles at him as if this were not a demotion, and offers an ironic curtsy. "I thank you, nevertheless, for your concern with the technicalities of Bassilean succession practices."

She straightens smartly, and ash puffs from her flamesuit.

Finally, I understand. Froydrich has ascension requirements just like Ixion. He needs his sister's hand to take to the throne, and if his father's health is fading, he'll need her hand soon. Ixion took the brother's side after Freyda rebuffed him, sent her home to search for grain, and hoped she'd find herself married on the other side.

But she got out, came back, and now she's here to stay. Callipolis isn't just a project of expansion for Freyda—it's a refuge. Ruling our island keeps a sea between her and her brother's marriage suit.

If it weren't for her dragon holding my country hostage, I might pity her.

Ixion lifts a hand, his lips a line. "A place at table for the princess-heir."

Rock and I scuttle to sandwich a new table setting at Ixion's right, between him and Delo Skyfish. Delo scoots to make room; the lines around his mouth have been plentiful since Ixion asked him about Power, and he seems too lost in thought to notice us. When our bustling is finished, I look up to find Freyda's eyes on me.

The last time we were in each other's presence, I was disguised as her parlor maid and about to run off with the boy she was attempting to marry. Her eyes meet mine in a flash as Rock takes her mantle, and taking her seat, she speaks to Ixion. "Is it appropriate, according to the customs of your people, to ascend to Triarch Primus without first proving your ranking? Just as you take such kind concerns with the technicalities of my brother's ascension, so too I must concern myself with yours."

All pretense of conversation at the high table has, by now, stopped.

Ixion says, "My claim on the Firstridership is unchallenged."

I come to Freyda's side to fill her goblet. I concentrate on minimizing the shaking in my hands. When her fingers lower to my wrist and remain there, I nearly jump. Her touch is slight, but it's enough of a signal that I should not leave her side.

"And conveniently, the one with rank to challenge you is under arrest."

Ixion's goblet settling on polished wood is the only sound at the table. Neither he nor Freyda looks at me, but others do. "If you're referring to that *thing*, Antigone was promoted by Leo's recusal."

"As you were promoted by Julia's death."

Ixion's knuckles are white on his glass. "Setting apart that she is standing trial for treason, I think we can all agree that while patricians and even, perhaps, the occasional lowborn rider might be allowed a chance in a Winnowing Tournament, to allow the competition of a *serf* would be like entering the family's dog."

Rock's hands spasm as he places Freyda's table settings in front of her.

"Oh?" says Freyda. "But I thought it was learned today that she's less your family's dog than your . . . in-law."

This can only be a reference to the trial proceedings. At Ixion's stunned look, Freyda says, "You didn't think I would ask Betsuna to brief me on everything I've missed before I came to dinner?" She waves an uncaring hand in my direction, and adds: "For all we know, the girl is even now carrying Leo's lawful heir."

I have the impression she points this out purely for the enjoyment of watching Ixion twitch.

He looks at me. "Show them."

Heat creeps from my ruffled collar up my neck as I understand.

"Show them, or I will."

I meet Rock's eyes across the table. He has frozen, his face draining of color, but when he shifts his shoulders into the faintest of shrugs, I take strange comfort from it. *We're serving the people who deposed us,* that shrug says, *what's a little more humiliation?*

I gather my skirt into my fist before the high table. A few gasp at the sight of the brand. Freyda, who sits closest, looks at the disfigurement without any change of expression or sound.

"This bitch," Ixion says, "has not married into my family. Whatever some deed in Harfast might say."

My vision is blurring as my fists curl. Freyda says quietly, "Lower your skirt."

I release the hem and take a step backward. One of the Grayriders snickers.

Freyda looks at Ixion. "I'm declaring a mistrial."

Ixion chokes on his wine. "What?"

"A *mistrial*. You will allow that woman, Hane, to participate in the vetting of a new jury without interference. You will allow her to call her own witnesses. And if I hear that you have tampered with the legal proceedings of Antigone's trial in any way again—if I hear that you have so much as laid a finger on her—I will find a different viceroy."

35

—

POWER SUR EATER

DELO

When the time comes to return to the Great Palace and begin preparations for the triple coronation, I find it an unexpected relief to quit the eerie, unchanged Skyfish Summer Palace. Back in the capital, I learn the rest of it: Antigone captured; Leo and his dragon dead; Aela routed. Ixion can't stop gloating.

I can't stop thinking: *Surely this is some mad plot.*

And on the night Freyda returns, I spot the linchpin. My ha'cousin, Parcival Graylily—or as Griff calls him, Power. Who has witnessed Antigone sur Aela perform whatever summoning feat Darius claims she's capable of, and engineered her capture without mention of it. Griff's bewildered words return to me now with new meaning: *But I know Power. Decent fellow. He's friends with Antigone.*

From the look on Ixion's face when he asks me Power's whereabouts at dinner, he's beginning to put the pieces together just as I have.

"I'm declaring a mistrial," Freyda Bassileon tells Ixion.

I watch Antigone sur Aela's crumpled face turn to steel and feel a shiver go down my spine.

This isn't over yet.

After the feast, in the break between dinner and dancing, I do it the way I've always done: too quickly to second-guess myself, before my head has time to catch up with my heart. I return to the Skyfish apartments, and instead of going to mine, I go to my ha'cousin's.

I find Power slumped in a chair, his head in his hands, dressed for a feast he didn't attend. The furnishings of his room are sparer than a servant's; the glass door onto the dragon perch is ajar, cold spring air seeping through. Skyfish balconies are narrower, for a narrower breed of dragon, and I find myself wondering if Power's brutish stormscourge even fits on his. When he looks up and sees I've let myself in, he jumps and lands on his feet.

"What the hell," he says. "*Knock*."

"Whatever you're planning," I tell him, "Ixion either guesses or knows."

Turns out I cannot get this traitor instinct out of my veins. But for once, it's not at odds with my family. For once, this treacherous blood is something I share with kin.

Parcival Graylily, my uncle's son. The Skyfish who rides a stormscourge. For all his posturing, I'm pretty sure he's every bit as much a peasant lover as I am.

Decent fellow.

Power stares at me. He cocks a brow—I can practically see him summoning an ironic retort, maybe to accuse me of the treachery he's guilty of—but instead, he goes to the door and looks both ways down the hall before closing and locking it. "Does he know you're here?"

I shake my head. When I tell him what Darius told Ixion, Power curses. "Petty little sod," he mutters, returning to the single chair and throwing himself back into it. "He never got over Annie beating him in quarterfinals. If Ixion knows Annie's able to summon, she's finished."

I remain standing in front of him, my arms folded against the draft. "She might not be."

"Oh?"

"Freyda just insisted on a fair trial."

Power's brows contort. And then he bursts out laughing. "Well, what do you know."

"I always wondered what side you were playing for."

Power hooks an ankle over a knee and palms his shaved head with a grin. "I wondered the same about you."

For the wrong side, apparently. I'm pretty sure I always have been.

But there's so much *good* on this wrong side. Filial piety, dragon-born duty, the Skyfish Summer Palace and the titles that come with it be damned. I would marry for Father; I would turn my back on my own love and happiness for the sake of my House. But whatever may be said about my heart, I'm done apologizing for following my conscience. I'm not even sure they can be distinguished. I was taught to admire the heroism of my people, to value loyalty and honor— but what is this, what I see in Power, if not the virtues our families claim to laud?

"You should go," says Power, "before they get here."

But it's already too late for that: I hear boots outside and shake my head.

"Then hide on the balcony," Power says.

"I can't just leave you—"

"You have to. I need you to take word to Norcia when it's time."

Neither of us questions that I will.

"When—?"

"The night before the verdict. They'll know what to do."

Power turns to face the door.

I step onto the narrow balcony and close the glass door behind me. My back against the cold stone, my heart hammering, I listen to the sounds of the door breaking in, of voices through the glass. Orthos's, cold and perfunctory. Power's, bored and defiant.

"Lucian Orthos, you traitorous slug, how are you?"

"You stand accused by the Clover Tribunal of conspiring with the—"

Power has no time for it. "Yeah, you got me. I had a plan with Antigone to rustle up her dragon in the arena."

"*Why?*" Ixion's voice this time, rising an octave in confusion.

"Because I'm nuts for her."

This sidelines Ixion completely. "What?"

Power sounds pleased with himself. "Nuts for her. Head over heels, would die to save her, in love with her. It's completely unrequited, she and I both know it, and yet here I am hopelessly, madly in love with Antigone sur freaking Aela."

Standing on the dark balcony outside, my hand over my mouth, I fight a sudden, wild desire to laugh.

"What the hell," Lucian Orthos mutters.

"That's right," says Power. "Waste of my time, wasn't it?"

There are the sounds of a scuffle. I hold my breath, my eyes squeezed shut, though there is only the darkness of the Firemouth to fill them. When I open them, the night is silent and my breath rises in steam. I risk peering through the glass before turning the knob.

The soldiers and Ixion are gone. All that's left of Power is a trail of blood leading out the door.

36

—

THE RETRIAL

LEE

NORCIA

In all my memories of Guardian training, the best part was the moment of launch. Every problem, big or small, faced in your studies, your training, and your life fell away. The world expanded and narrowed and then there was nothing but sky.

I don't realize, until I begin running drills in Norcia, that I can get that feeling from the ground. When I'm watching the dragons surround Turret Karst and tighten, I don't have to worry about Annie or miss Pallor. I barely think about Aela, curled beside me on the balustrade. I'm so absorbed in the exercise, in the needs of the riders, the corrections I'll make for the next run-through that I forget myself. I am, in the purest sense, *alive*.

After so many years dreaming of one future, one great joy, this new one feels like a discovery.

Especially when I see it.

Bran's aurelian squadron attempt to hurl javelins simultaneously, miss the timing by a hair's breadth—and by chance, throw in a quick succession. From my vantage point on the viewing balustrade, I'm able to see the javelins *put-put-put* into the karst, one by one, encircling it in a spiral.

All this time, I've been wondering how javelins could hope to find vital organs on a beast the size of a whale. But now I see it.

The formations won't land a fatal blow because they're not designed to. They're designed to *trap*.

When the riders return to the balustrade, I pull Bran sur Beria aside and indicate his javelin. It's got a slit on the end for a particular form of training rarely used.

"Can those mock up as harpoons, if we get rope?"

Bran's eyes widen, and he nods.

Bind the wings, crash the landing, and finish the job on the ground.

Of course.

With an animal that large, how else would you subdue it?

I'll have to rewrite all the drills, because with rope in hand, the order of every rider's throw will matter—otherwise the lines will be in knots. But the same principles will apply writing these drills as any other. Simplify the task, scaffold the components, recombine into the complex action.

And I've got two dozen riders whose ability I can trust to bring it home.

We'll be ready when Annie needs it.

"Change of plans," I tell them. The muscles in my face are stretched into the first grin I've had in days. "This one's going to be trickier."

"Try us," Cor says.

ANNIE
CALLIPOLIS

Hane is given three days to approve a new jury and find witnesses. Freyda orders Master Welse to treat my injuries. The battery of ointments and medications he prescribes leaves me more clear-headed than I've felt in days but less certain of my future than ever. With Hane's new mandate, the trial's looking better than it ever has—but how am I supposed to get into the arena now that Ixion knows about my *parlor trick*? And where does that put the plan with Lee in Norcia? I sink from these uncertainties into the deepest sleep I've had in a week and jolt awake when the door to my cell clanks open.

"Since you're so in love with her."

Someone rolls across the floor. More figures stand silhouetted in the doorway before the grille slams shut. Labored breathing continues in the darkness and I recognize it from sparring practice.

"Power?"

He lets out a low, wheezing laugh. "Antigone."

"You all right?"

"Yeah, I'm . . . I'll be all right."

But it's clear, even in the dim light, he's not. Something dark and viscous drips down his face; he's leaning against the wall, unmoving. I pour water onto a rag and dab his forehead. The cloth comes away black with blood. He's taken a beating the extent of which I can't tell in this light.

"Are we busted?" I ask.

"Not exactly. I covered for the Norcian operation. They think the conspiracy ends with me."

This isn't a solution I'd have thought of. "How'd you convince them of that?"

"Don't worry about it."

But I'm pretty sure I wasn't imagining Ixion's voice as I was waking. *Since you're so in love with her.* It doesn't take too much extrapolating to guess the narrative Power must have resorted to.

My eyes are welling, and I'm suddenly glad for the dark. I reach for the blanket that came with the cell and pull it over him. He's either in too much pain, or too tired, to comment on the mothering.

"Final stretch, Commander," he murmurs.

Even after he falls asleep, I sit awake beside him, doing the math. Power's busted but not dead, which means Ixion sees a use for him yet. And the fact that he's in here *with me*—

I don't like it.

But for the two days before the retrial, we're left undisturbed. Hane doesn't summon me for further trial prep, so I remain in the cell beside Power, who sleeps most of the time. I slide in and out of dreams that are somewhere far away: windows overlooking the sea, Lee's arms around me, the sound of a sizzling skillet in the morning. I wake and find the arm around me is Power's.

"So how was it?" he asks.

"How was what?"

"Your . . . vacation with Leo." He's slurring, not altogether there, like he's half asleep himself. The physician's tended me, but not him. An ominous sign neither of us has commented on.

"It wasn't a vacation," I correct automatically. I'm tempted to tell him it was terrible, because that seems like the humane option given his failed romantic history with me and the fact that he's lying incapacitated in a cell for my sake. But the wistfulness beneath his slurring words makes me suspect he wants something else.

I once walked through Power's home with him, imagining it was mine. I know how it feels, to reach for a life you can't have and try to fit it over your own body like a borrowed coat.

"It was nice."

He's silent, though fingers reach up to brush his eyes. We're lying side by side beneath the blanket, our sides barely touching. I fill the silence with discomfort, reaching for things I can tell him besides the overwhelming memories of Lee. Mostly, I remember his lips fitting mine in that glorious bed. Power probably guesses that part, anyway. "We went for walks and we ate a lot of shellfish. Aela . . . laid."

Power's face rolls toward mine. I think, for a second, he'll tease. But he just whistles. "First in the fleet, huh? How was that?"

My voice comes out threadbare. "She was really happy."

Now I'm seeing that fire. Imagining Lee lost in it. Suffocating as flames licked up those walls—

He got out. Nigel got him out.

What if I can't feel Aela because I've lost her for good?

"Did the house have a terrific stock of ice wine?" Power asks.

I have the impression he's nudging the conversation in a safer direction. I clear my throat. "Yeah. It did. We had some."

I can feel him nodding beside me. The silence stretches. Something is scratching in the corner, but I know by now not to look. I can't not ask it. "How was it, staying here?"

Power takes so long to answer, I think he's fallen asleep again. He tells the ceiling, "It was Rock or Crissa. I was scared what they'd do to Crissa."

I'm loyal, I can prove I'm loyal, he said, and this is what it came down to. He swallows, wet and thick. I crack the joke lightly, because my breath has caught. "Didn't take you for a gentleman."

"Was that what I was being?"

I kiss him on the cheek, and Power covers his eyes with a hand and rolls away from me.

***

On the third day, the trial resumes, and I leave Power in the cell when I'm summoned. The carriage ride to the Vault finds Miranda positively jubilant after being allowed to vet a fresh jury and find her own witnesses.

"We've got a fighting chance, Annie, I really think we do."

"Even without Aela?"

Now that everyone knows about my mythical summoning abilities, there seems no point in acting like that wasn't what I was aiming for. Miranda's lip curves as she reaches across to tuck a stray strand of hair behind my ears. I braided it myself today. "You dragonriders," she says, "always lack a sense of nuance about these things. The court of public opinion matters most of all."

Without dragonfire to back it up?

Power told me that he tapped Delo Skyfish to relay the relevant information to Norcia in his stead. Originally, the plan was to coincide their fleet's stakeout of the capital with Aela's return and my execution, so that they could attack the goliathan directly after I summoned Aela.

I'm not sure how that plan changes if I get gutted in a window-less room.

But, says a tiny voice in my ear that I hardly dare allow myself to consider, *what if you're found innocent?*

I know Callipolis's hatred too well to hope for that. Even with Freyda's intervention.

All the same, there is new lightness in my step as I descend the carriage at the Vault this morning. The courtroom within has an audience that's almost entirely changed. New faces have been added to the jury from the Upper and Lower Banks and even, if

I'm not mistaken, from the countryside. In the lead chair of the inquisition sits not Ixion, but the patrician judge Samander Eschros. He makes no unwanted asides about my highland hygiene today, as he did on our first meeting at the Lycean Ball; nor does he reference the unexpected moment, at the end of the Bunker Riots, when he said he'd prefer me as Protector-designate to Lee. But he does grace me with a small smile. "Hello, Antigone."

"Hello, Judge Eschros."

Neither Freyda nor Ixion is seen in the courtroom again. But other members of the Clover court watch from the balcony, and I know that the proceedings will not be kept from Ixion. I'm so unused to fair questioning that it takes me a few sallies to habituate to Eschros's method. He doesn't attempt to throw me off or sardonically undercut my answers; instead, he listens and follows up as if willing to give what I say the benefit of the doubt.

We begin with my most notorious interaction with Megara Roper.

"When you questioned Miss Roper during her time of arrest in the Vault, did you threaten her family with the dragon's punishment?"

Megara has looked up from her notetaking in the front row, pen lifted like her brow.

"Yes, I did."

As the whispering breaks out, I add: "It was a hollow threat. Revolutionary law prohibits the dragon's punishment on relatives. But I knew that if I didn't get her cooperation, Megara would face torture. As she told me her mother did—under Atreus."

Eschros nods at this. "Yes. The Clover Tribunal has become all too familiar with the methods of the Reeducation Committee."

"I was not. Revolutionary propaganda was so thorough that even Guardians were not informed of the full history of our regime. I only learned about the Southside Massacre when Megara told me about it."

Megara's pen is twisting in slow circles between her fingers; I'm pretty sure she's stopped writing entirely.

"And at the time of the protests, were you invited to join the Passi?"

"Yes. I refused."

"Why?"

I think I'm needed here, I told Lee, as we stood in the wreckage of the Inner Palace, after an air strike had torn open our city and revealed that the greatest atrocities had been committed not by our enemies but by our superiors. The next day, we were on opposite sides of a barricade.

"Because I believed that if Guardians did not restrain Atreus and the city guard from the inside, we risked a repetition of the Southside Massacre. I repeatedly defied orders from the Inner Palace in order to de-escalate altercations on the streets during the Bunker Riots."

Hane rises.

"That brings me to our first witness, if it's all right with you, Your Honor."

Hane's made good use of her three days' search. The captain of the Southside city guard takes the stand and recounts my orders forbidding lethal force; a civilian describes how I saved his life during the riots, using a doused dragon to stand between him and blows from a guard; and then Lotus himself enters the room, a clover on the lapel of his uniform. Before the questioning begins, he confesses to being a member of both the Passi and the Order of the Black Clover while avoiding my eyes. He looks thinner than I remember, his usually well-groomed hair snarled and overgrown. I have the feeling that whatever decisions he made regarding the Triarchy, he has since regretted.

"Antigone allowed the Passi to start a free press," he says, speaking hoarsely as if he has not used his voice in a long time. "She was the one who refused to retake the Vault, the night we seized the *People's Paper*. The funny thing was—we didn't know, so we used that printing to destroy her reputation."

Megara Roper's pen flies across her notes so hastily, she has to repeatedly shake her hand out. She keeps her head bent over the paper, but I glimpse her free hand wipe inky tears from her cheeks.

Interesting.

That night in the cell, Power rouses himself and pushes a bowl of gruel into my hands. It's tasteless and unsalted, but I have an appetite like I haven't in days and shovel it into my mouth with gusto. I'm most of the way done when I notice what's wrong.

"Where's yours?"

"That was all that was provided." He goes on, before I can react, "I already had some." I'm pretty sure that's a straight-up lie. When I push the remainder toward him, he lifts a hand. "I've just been sitting here. You're the one standing trial."

"You're *injured*."

"What, this? It's a scrape."

We reverse-haggle our way to Power finishing off maybe a fourth of the bowl, neither of us commenting on the fact that they've rationed the cell as if Power weren't here. He cheers up hearing about today's proceedings. "Roper cried? Well done. Bet that felt a long time coming."

He can't see my smile in the dark. "No comment."

In our carriage ride the next morning, Miranda shows me the *People's Paper* with Megara's coverage of the retrial so far. "There's been a tonal shift. Roper has to be careful, of course, because while nominally free since the Bunker Riots, the *Paper*'s been an organ of propaganda for the Restoration as much as it ever was for Atreus under my department. But looking between the lines, she's done justice to the accounts from witnesses that put you in a good light yesterday. I wouldn't be surprised if it starts turning the tide."

This time, when I step from the carriage, none of the people shouting call me a bitch.

I hardly let myself consider it.

Rock takes the stand the second day to talk about grain collections after the Medean Attack, where I gained a reputation for enforcing the law with ready dragonfire. Widowed, facing a death sentence, with family safe in Norcia and his hometown already burned, he seems to have decided he has nothing left to lose by taking the stand.

"Annie and I were the only ones in the Guardian corps who'd experienced collections as kids," he says. "We were both serfs under Stormscourge lords in the old order. So—when the time came, we were the ones called up to do it first. And then we had to train the others."

"And would you say Antigone enjoyed this business?"

Rock lets out a huffing laugh.

"You do know how her family died, right? But if they were going to get Guardians to do it, we knew someone had to do it right. You botch that, people die. Antigone was as careful as you can be. But I watched it gut her.

"Of course, at the time, we thought it was for a good cause. Some sort of heroic effort to save the City. We thought that'd be the end of it. We didn't know then that they'd—start choosing who got to eat more than others, giving Golds more. When we learned that, afterward . . ."

He shakes his head. I can feel my face rippling with the memory: the moment, in the Council Room, when we went from thinking the worst was over to realizing it had only begun. The formula written on the board that would mean certain Callipolans starved because they were deemed less worthy. All of this horror, and our job to enforce it.

Someone in the courtroom blows their nose.

In the cell that evening, Power pushes the gruel into my hands, claiming he was fed lunch. I know it's a lie, but I'm so hungry, I can't bring myself to argue with him. After, I sink into uneasy dreams. There are fires and hatchlings and Lee in the kitchen of the Big House, laughing as he takes my waist with hands soapy from dishwater. Freyda Bassileon points at my belly: *See? I said she was with child.*

When I wake and strain to remember the plan we have with Norcia and challenge I still need to make against Ixion, the reasons I'm in this cell flake like ash.

I could have stayed in Farhall in his arms.

"He's dead." The fear tears out of me, though I intend to hold it in. "I know he's dead."

It's impossible to know from the narrow window above whether it's the middle of the night or near morning. Power's arms are around me, every muscle in his body taut; we lie in the same unforgiving darkness. "What about that plan with the—gardener?"

"Groundskeeper."

"Yeah. So. He's not dead." Power sounds like he's speaking through a lockjaw.

But all I can see is that fire.

The rest of the dream is clinging to me, unwanted, the idea Freyda breathed into life. The Travertine, the eggs, Lee's insisting we be careful until the night I said I wanted everything in the world with him and we weren't.

"What if I'm pregnant?"

I hadn't meant to wonder it aloud. Power sits bolt upright. "Is that—likely?" he splutters.

"I have no idea."

I haven't menstruated since I went on the suppressants years ago. I have no idea when they wore off or what the likelihood is, after a night of indiscretion, that I might be.

What if he's dead and I'm pregnant with his child?

Power rolls onto his knees, facing me. His voice takes the tone of challenge he used when we trained together on the Eyrie and he goaded me to find my anger. "So. What if you are?"

I feel as though I'm untethered from myself, adrift and unable to find the line back. My head is in my hands. "Then I'm just one more stupid peasant woman—"

Just like Ixion and his branding want me to be. Not the sort of girl who rides dragons or defends the Revolution or deserves any better titles than the ones they've given her. I thought I could come here and prove something in the arena with my low birth, the peasant blood in my veins, and yet here I am standing trial before my country as commander of the aerial fleet but dreaming about a kitchen.

Power's voice rises. "Like your mum? Like mine? I'd rather be like them than that excuse for a human being who was my father." His voice is shaking. He's talking about his birth parents. "Some of the bravest women in our lives have been peasant women, Annie. *They're why we're here.* Even if they go unsung."

I lift my head from my hands to find him glaring at me with such fury that I don't blink despite prickling eyes.

"I can't feel Aela."

His eyes widen; his lips part.

"I haven't felt her since I shut her out, after . . . after the fire."

For a moment the cell is so quiet, we hear the ceiling drip. Power says, "I'm sure it's just a fluke. You'll feel her."

But the doubts linger: What if the bond's broken? What if I'm not a dragonrider anymore?

I've never renounced Aela before. I've never been so far from her for so long. I don't know if I'll ever feel her again. And in my darkest moments—when I dream about Lee's arms in the Big House—I'm not sure I want to.

The third and final day, a woman takes the stand whose face I recognize. Her hands shake; her skin is veined and aged beyond its years, her hair frazzled. Her accent is thick with Cheapside and when she speaks, she avoids my eyes.

"When I was in line for my share," she says, "this winter, I'd lost my ration card. There was a long queue, winding round the square, and I told the guard. He looked at *her* for permission. And she shook her head. And I—I lost my head. The babes were so hungry. I shouted at her. Called her all the things we do call her, you know. In her face. She didn't move. Her dragon didn't move. My friends told me to get out of there before it did. Well—round the corner, one of her riders found me, bit of an attitude on him. 'You'd better be glad the Firstrider is more patient with insults than I am.' Then he gave me a new ration card. I hardly believed it at the time. But I've got friends say that happened to them, too. She always did it quiet."

I remember that day. I remember sending Power after her while

I waited in shame under the furious eyes of the square. But I did not know, until now, what he told her when he replaced her ration card.

I want to ride a dragon when I grow up. Like you. I'll be First-rider.

It's not an easy job.

I only realize after the woman's done testifying that tears are coursing down my face.

I'm not scared, Becca says in my memory, and holds out my armor like she's reminding me how to put it on.

At the end of the day, Miranda's arm is the one that folds tightly into mine to help me from the platform; there haven't been shackles since Freyda intervened. A hand reaches out from the aisle we're passing to touch my sleeve. "Take courage, darling," says the elderly juror it belongs to.

"Oh—thanks—"

Miranda smiles at him and steers me on, her smile only growing. "I knew it. I knew we had a chance."

Tomorrow, the jury convenes without me to make their decision; this is, I hope, the last time I'll ever see this courtroom.

We spill out into the yard before the Vault to find a different scene taking place. The city guard is shoving a shouting crowd back from the gates; an unmarked, windowless carriage is hurtling out the drive.

Miranda stops dead.

"That's an arrest," she says. "Who—oh, dragons above, they couldn't possibly—"

She elbows her way to the nearest guard and, after a short conversation, makes her way back to me with the smile wiped from her face.

"They took Megara."

"What? Why?"

"Charges of collusion with the enemy. Her romantic history with Cor Sutter has been a liability from the start."

That doesn't make sense. Cor and his whole family are long gone. "But why *now*—?"

Hane's lips tighten. "Because Ixion is issuing a warning to our jury."

37

—

THE CALLIPOLAN RESISTANCE

GRIFF

NORCIA

I'll admit, I wasn't expecting to see his handsome mug again, and I certainly wasn't expecting to see it like this. Delo bursts into my study spewing rainwater like a drowned otter and shivering to his toes in the dead of night. "I come as a representative of the Callipolan Resistance," he starts, like a prepared recitation, and then stops. "Hello, Becca."

"Hello, Delo," says Becca beside me.

Delo wavers. "Shouldn't you be in bed?"

I find it a little rich that Delo Skyfish came halfway across the sea to criticize Becca's bedtime, but his face is pretty as ever and that's something. "She had a nightmare."

"I drew the Queen and the Star Springs, see?"

She holds the drawing up. I can tell Delo's trying to figure out what's stars and what's water. There are a lot of blobs for dragons, and some extra colors for the auroras, the springs, and the constellation that I'll admit I'm pretty impressed with. She got all the Queen's dots in the right spots. "I've never heard of the Star Springs," Delo says.

"It's where the dragons go," Becca says. "The Queen leads them there."

"Oh?"

Delo doesn't seem about to share what he once told me, that in dragonborn lore, dragons make their exodus north to die. I shift weight, depositing Becca onto her feet. "It's an old Norcian legend. Delo's right. You should be in bed."

When she goes, the air leaves with her. We're alone and there's a very empty sofa between us and it's night and Delo's body is slick with all that rainwater. My mouth's gone dry. "You're here on behalf of the Resistance?"

Delo sounds like he's having trouble keeping track of his sentences, too. "Yeah. Cor brought me in off the perimeter, he's going to round up Leo and Crissa. I was . . . recruited by Power sur Eater."

It seems important to note my victory on this point. "Told you he was decent."

Delo nods like he hardly hears me. Silence festers, and then he barges into it with a kind of violent airiness. "So, you had the kingsmoot?"

"Yeah. They picked, well, they picked me." I fail to sound remotely modest about it.

Delo gestures around the stately apartments I've made such a mess of. "I figured, given . . . this. Congratulations, Your . . . Majesty?"

I can't decide whether I want to jump out the window or tell him to say it again. I could make it an order. "Not crowned yet. Sit."

Delo eases into the chair farthest from me while we wait for Lee and Crissa. He's dripping everywhere. I keep watching the droplets glide down his face. He leans forward and reaches for some of the clutter on the table between us. A few Bassilean crowns lie in a pile, and he begins turning the coins through his fingers, making rather a meal of studying them.

"Your father found you a wife yet?"

Delo shakes his head. "Still searching. These are newly minted, aren't they?"

"The coins? Maybe. We just had a few trade ships in from Vask."

Dragons. What are we even *saying*?

I'm beyond relieved when the door bursts open and Cor stumbles through it, followed by Lee and Crissa, clearly still half asleep. Their mantles are soaked as badly as Delo's, and beneath them, they wear nightclothes. The gale that drenched them lashes the window with abandon.

"Tell me," says Lee. His face is so white, it's practically glowing.

Delo rises, the coins still clutched in his hand. "She's alive. She's fine—"

Lee throws himself into the nearest chair and buries his face in his hands. It's the most emotion I've seen him show since he arrived in Norcia. Crissa sets a hand on his back and rubs slowly while his shoulders shudder.

Delo looks a little unnerved, but at Cor's prompting explains the rest. The retrial, the upcoming verdict, Power's being found out along with Annie's summoning ability. "But it should still be fine," he says, "so long as I help you get Aela in place beforehand. The verdict will be announced in the Throne Room, which opens on the Firemouth. They'll secure the main entrances but won't be expecting any sort of inside support."

He's really turned coat. "Your dad know you're here?" I ask.

Delo pulls at a damp coil of hair and offers an indirect answer. "Power sur Eater made a compelling case for following one's conscience."

I don't think now's the right time to double-check if this affects Delo's plans to let his father marry him off.

"Power?" Cor repeats. "Conscience?" He sounds like he's pretty sure those words can't go together.

Crissa only hums softly, unsurprised.

Lee looks up, dragging a fist across his eyes. "And Obizuth?"

"She's nesting on Pytho's Keep. Ready for you to finish her off." Delo passes the coin across the table. "Something else to be aware of."

A chinless face is printed in profile, encircled by Bassilic script I can't read.

"This is the son," Lee realizes, frowning at the crown. "Freyda's brother."

Delo nods. "Froydrich. The dragon on the reverse is Azuleth, Obizuth's clutchmate."

Lee turns the coin, and a Great Dragon's face—like Obizuth's but horned all over—glares at us.

"The God-King's dead?"

"Not yet. But if they're minting coins in the visage of the crown prince, that means the God-King's dragon must already have submitted to Froydrich's. The transition has begun."

Lee passes me the coin and I turn it back to the prince. The observation comes out before I think to stop it. "Froydrich doesn't have a chin."

I hear at once how idiotic this comment is. Froydrich can't help his chinlessness. But to my surprise, Lee nods like I've noted something significant. "Freyda's family tree is shaped like an hourglass. She doesn't have the Bassileon chin, but her father and brother do. Froydrich is known to have trouble swallowing and his seizures can lead to a fair amount of destruction when they spill into his dragon. Not that any of this is his fault, but his determination to marry his sister is."

As he realizes we're all staring at him, Lee lifts a shoulder and flushes. "Freyda and I talked a lot on our walks."

"Poor Freyda," Crissa murmurs.

"Poor Freyda or not, her dragon's menacing Callipolis," Cor says, "and we've got to take it out."

Lee sets down the coin. "You think Annie will be let off?"

Delo weighs his answer. "It's hard to say. As I left, a stir was created by the arrest of a reporter covering the trial—"

"Not Megara again," says Cor.

"I don't—maybe?"

Cor groans into his hands.

Lee's gaze is fixed on Delo. "But you think public opinion has shifted?"

Delo frowns, hesitates, and lifts a shoulder. "I think she has a chance."

LEE

A chance.

A chance, and I'm grounded, no way of helping her, about to send the fleet I've trained into the night to wait and hear the outcome like a restless child.

A *chance*.

With Cor and Crissa, I help the remaining riders suit up and arm in the lairs. We have a final briefing where I go over the attack plan and the fallback options. "If Obizuth launches before you successfully bind her, target Freyda. You'll know how to time it, depending on the trial verdict."

A *tether-target*, homing in on the goliathan's rider, was historically difficult in the Bassilean Wars, which were mainly conducted at sea—locating the host ship of the tethering rider was a challenge in itself.

But this time around, we'll know exactly where the goliathan's tether is.

I pity Freyda. But if it comes down to it, she can't be spared out of pity.

"How close does Aela need to be, for Antigone to summon her?" Delo asks.

He'll prepare the way for our arrival—*their* arrival, I correct myself. It hits me again: They'll go over, and I'll stay here. Grounded. "Get her into the Firemouth, that should be close enough."

I hardly hear myself.

One by one they leap into the night—giddy for their mission, leaving the lairs empty with a terrible silence in their wake—until the only dragon left is Aela.

"You need to go with them. Go on."

I lay a tentative palm on her burning scales and think of Annie. Probing the connection we shouldn't be able to share. Aela snorts and shudders. Resisting.

"She needs you."

In answer, she gently takes my hand into her mouth and tugs it. Her fangs are retracted, but her breath is still hot enough to burn. I yank my smarting fingers free.

"What—?"

She luxuriates in a stretch backward and then forward, rippling her crest, and lowers herself to mounting height. She cocks her head at me.

"No," I say, as I understand.

She quivers her crest with determination.

"Aela, it's done for me—"

She nips again at my hand, gently with her gums, her amber eye fixed on me, and the sense of it comes as clearly as thoughts once shared with Pallor: *Come with me.*

So I do.

We're not used to each other. I've sat on Aela's back once before, in extraordinary circumstances, when I climbed behind Annie on Aela's back midair to help them. But then, it was only for a minute or so, and Pallor and Annie were there to stabilize us both.

A flight across the sea on someone else's dragon is something else.

Our stuttering connection is no substitute for the true bond between a rider and their dragon. I'm as ill as a green rider on his first flight on dragonback. It doesn't help that Aela has a habit of twitching as if, in moments of forgetfulness, her impulse were to buck this unfamiliar weight off her back.

"The Skysung Queen glossed over these details," I mutter.

When I'm not concentrating on holding in my last meal or reminding Aela not to throw me, my head's full of eggs. Aela's eggs, swimming across my vision. She's jamming them into our faltering connection more rudely and insistently than Pallor ever shared anything. And then I realize we're drifting west, despite my heel in her side nudging us south.

She's taking the opportunity of our flight to steer us back toward Farhall.

"Not the damn eggs. *Annie.* We have to go to Annie."

Aela's anger pulsates like a shock wave: I feel her indignation, her heartbreak, her incomprehension that Annie sent her away.

"She had to do it. It hurt her, too."

We keep drifting toward the highlands, though Aela's slowed. She's completely ignoring the heel I'm digging into her right flank. If I didn't know better, I'd think, at this point, she's toying with me. Finally, I grind out a bargain.

"I'll take care of the eggs, okay? But Annie first."

The images flicker and fade, and Aela's wings soften beneath me. For the first time since I lost Pallor, the tight aching in my chest loosens. I reach down to rub her flank, and when I open my eyes, I find the Ferrish Plain spread below. The storm has cleared, leaving visibility for miles in its wake. We've already passed the blockade, dwindling to toy-size boats along the Callipolan coastline.

Aela allows me to steer her toward the capital.

We follow the other dragons and their riders down to the cedar grove at Parron's Spring, where Delo Skyfish waits by a gated drainage pipe. The Resistance riders will stake out with civilian clothes over their flamesuits to wait for the trial verdict while their dragons wait here for their summons; Aela herself will be snuck into the Firemouth through the drainage tunnel by Delo, bypassing the security they've added to the main entrances. Whispers erupt in the darkness around us as Aela lands and they realize she bears a rider.

"Is that—Lee?"

"Can he *do* that?"

"Looks like he did."

I spot a glint of golden hair and pull Crissa aside. "I'll find you and Cor in a few hours."

"But where are you—?"

"I'm going to try something profoundly stupid."

The plan's been forming as I flew, and now it's as clear as dragonglass even if it might be half mad. The fragment of poetry reverberates in my ears: *Sing me now your fury-song.*

I remember when we thought it'd be like this, Annie said. *Heroic. Full of purpose.*

Maybe we are like this, and we just don't know it.

I set off, as fast as two saddle-sore legs can carry me, for the rain-soaked foothills of Pytho's Keep known as the Janiculum. A half hour later, I'm knocking on the front door of the poet laureate of Callipolis. A skyfish curled on the gravel drive perks up at the sight of me.

"Hello, Lee," says Lotus, opening the door. "What brings you back from the dead?"

I step inside without waiting for the invitation. "I need to speak to your dad."

I got to know Lo Teiran working with him this winter when the secret printing press in his basement was critical to the Passi's reform efforts. But it was poetry, not journalism, that led the Teirans to conspire with the dragonborn. Having never known the same kind of cruelty that the lowborn experienced under triarchal rule, they were seduced with the promise of literary freedom.

Tonight, I find the senior Teiran thinner and grayer than I remember. Though Lotus wears a flamesuit, he has unpinned the clover that should be on his lapel. When I ask about Mrs. Teiran, the men only look at each other. The parlor has the overcluttered look of a bachelor residence. They've seated me between stacks of books on the main sofa.

Lotus hesitates. "Mother's loyalty was—questioned."

Is she imprisoned, or dead? Her confinement issued as a warning, her punishment a threat?

I know this is my opening.

"I think it's time we discuss other horses to back."

Teiran stirs, his eyes lightless, but they lift to mine. "Go on," he says.

"Antigone's jury goes into conclave in the morning. I've heard she has a chance. I want her to have more than that."

Lotus turns away to draw the curtains. Teiran shakes his head. He looks almost pitying. "Lee, there's no point. There's nothing more to say. The people know the truth. With the coverage

Megara's been giving—Antigone's got more sympathy now than I think she's ever had. But there's a difference between knowing the truth and being willing to die for it."

Exactly.

"Then it sounds like we should inspire them."

We've got a poet laureate to advise, a rogue printing press in the basement, and a dragon for distribution. Lo Teiran once complained about a commission to glorify a Revolution he couldn't believe in, but what about a commission for something he can?

Because he's right. Journalism is no longer what's needed.

Teiran snorts, catching my drift. Then he realizes I'm not laughing. "No," he says. "There's no time."

But I'm already smiling. "I thought the Passi did some of its best work on a dawn deadline."

38

—

VOX DRACONIS

ANNIE
CALLIPOLIS

The night they arrest Megara, I have the dream again. I'm an adult. Lee is there. And there is so much life around us. Swimming, dazzling life. I know, in the way you can know your whole alternate history in a dream, that this is a different future that led from a different past. A past where Lee and I met as children, yes, when we were alone and sad; but one in which we are never plucked from that life into something larger. We moved on, small sadness to small joys, until we were grown and our joys overflowed as they entwined. No dragons, only feet on the earth, a life we never had to sacrifice, that no one tried to take from us.

I wake from that dream as the air is smashed from my lungs.

Ixion's fist slams into my gut, his fingers twist my hair. Morning light filters down, diffused, from the cell's high window and glows on his shaking arms as they pin me to the ground.

"It won't change anything," he says.

"I don't know what you're talking about—"

His fingers close around my throat.

"Liar. And you know what I have to say about it? *Wishful thinking.*"

"Let go of her—" Power's voice, somewhere to my left. Ixion ignores him.

"You *wish* you were this. But I saw you. I know what you are—"

The fingers tighten. I'm wheezing. *What is he talking about?*

There is a thump, a rasp, and the air returns suddenly to my lungs. Power and Ixion roll across the floor. Guards spill into the cell. Two pull Power off Ixion, twisting his arms behind his back and hauling him upright. Power is dry-heaving. Ixion holds up a ragged sheet of paper that looks like a Passi printing, then kneels beside me and seizes the back of my head.

"Tell me how you did it."

"I don't know what you're—"

"Liar. Who are you in contact with?"

"No one—"

A boot into my gut, another. I cough onto the stones. Something in my side cracks. Fingers grip my hair and slam my forehead again. Stars explode in my darkened vision.

Power's voice strains behind me. "Freyda told you not to touch her—"

The fists stop raining down; the hands release me. I roll onto all fours and hear boot steps on stone. "Look at me, Antigone."

Ixion's knife is at Power's chest, and Power has frozen. A guard has seized the back of my dress and yanked it to make sure I'm watching. I taste blood.

"Who is responsible for the printing?"

"I swear to the long-dead gods, I don't know!"

"I'll count, Antigone. Three—"

"*Forgive me, my lord, for my indiscretions, which were not intended in faithlessness—*"

I am shouting the Plea, palms on the ground like my father taught me, knowing all the while it *will not be enough*. Ixion's knife remains flush against Power's heart.

I recite it anyway.

"Two—"

"*—grant that my punishment duly owed not be given to my loved ones blameless—*"

"Don't waste your breath, Annie!" Power shouts.

"—one."

The knife slides into Power's chest.

He draws a rattling breath. When the guard releases him, he falls to his knees. Ixion stoops over me, pulls my head back by the hair, and wipes Power's blood across my face.

"They may try to paint you as a hero, but we all know you're just a pleading peasant bitch like your mother before you."

He releases me and I slump.

Lucian Orthos's nasal Palace-standard comes from the doorway. "My lord? You're needed in the Throne Room."

When the cell door slams, for a moment the only sound is my sobs and Power's wheezing breath. I crawl forward, fingers finding the warm pool that grows at Power's knees, fumbling toward him in the dark. My fingers connect with the printing that Ixion has discarded at our feet and I brush it aside. I find Power's wound and press against the opening, but the blood wells, too fast and too thick, seeping down his torso.

"Hey," says Power, reaching out to touch my face, "stop doing that." His old, bantering tone is at odds with his sharp breaths. Faltering fingers fumble for the paper I'd dropped. "Read it," he says.

"What?"

"Read it to me."

The last thing I want to do right now is read the stupid thing. But

Power's fingers are tight on mine, his blood hot on my hands, and so I thrust the printing into the single square of light made by the sun through the high window.

It's a poem. Signed Vox Draconis like the fragment Lee and I found in his manor, and styled, as that one was, like the canonized *Aurelian Cycle*.

But this one is in Callish.

Sing to me, Muse, of the Revolution's Daughter
who after Uriel sur Aron, after Pytho, after the triarchs
of old ages and the corruption of their reign
came lowborn to defy them:
Who was expelled from her home,
fell from all grace,
and rose on a dragon's wings.

It goes on. Barely a hundred lines. Power's breathing is shallow and careful, his fingers tight round my arm as I read it through. By the end, when I look up, I make out his smile.

"That's the kind of poem I can get behind," he says.

Tears are running freely down my face.

Though signed Vox Draconis, it's not enough to hide *him*, peeking through the forceful Callish to render Dragontongue's wordy intricacy, changing his mothertongue to mine like an offering, sending courage across the distance in the one way he has left to meet us on our wing. His voice sends shivers through me like the touch of his fingers on my skin.

Lee is out there, somewhere, alive.

But I am kneeling, holding another boy, whose life is bleeding out.

"Power, please . . ."

I don't know what I'm pleading for, because no help is coming, and his blood soaks us both. I press my hands desperately against the wound. It's no wider than a bootknife's blade, but too close to the heart.

Power lifts his fist to his chest in the Revolutionary salute. And then he reaches out to clasp my hand. Cold metal presses into it. "Time I return this."

I look down at the Firstrider's badge that I left in his keeping, when I went to Norcia.

"It's been an honor, Commander."

At the gesture, I feel as if my heart has been torn open and apart.

And with the force of the rupture, the surge of another heart finding mine across the chasm.

I can feel Aela.

Power's chin lowers to his chest.

The guard finds me curled around him, lips against his forehead, the medal clutched bloody in my hand. When I hear my name, I get to my feet.

39

—

THE VERDICT

ANNIE

Miranda Hane makes a hurried explanation as she escorts me to the Throne Room. The printing was disseminated on dragonback before dawn, the same way the Passi distributed the *People's Paper* when they first took control of it.

Still warm with Power's blood, and my own pulsing with strangled fury, I let her words wash over me, hardly hearing them.

"... I suspect Teiran, though to my knowledge he's never composed in Callish. He must have had a translator. There's a version in Dragontongue, too, distributed on the Janiculum and in Scholars Row—they certainly appealed to both sides of the river, and—*Antigone, why are you covered in blood?*"

As we enter the lantern-lit main corridor leading to the Throne Room, Miranda discerns my appearance at last. I look down at my balled and bloodied fists.

"It's Power's."

She has stopped cold. "Where is he? Is he—?"

Not trusting myself to speak, I shake my head.

We have arrived at the heavy engraved doors. This is where

I leave her. Miranda seizes my arm, heedless of the blood that sticks to her palm, and I look up at her. "Antigone?" Her chin has set, and her brown eyes blaze. "Go show them what you're made of."

I lift a shaking fist to my chest in the Revolutionary salute.

Inside the anteroom, I step in front of a floor-length mirror, tuck my unbrushed hair behind my ears, straighten my shoulders, and lift the sleeve of my dress to wipe the blood from my face and hands. I take in a single breath.

Power is beyond my help. It's time for me to go through that door. It's time to finish what we started.

It's been an honor, Commander.

Sing to me, Muse, of the Revolution's Daughter.

I can feel Aela's blood in my blood, her fire in my lungs. My arms are her wings itching for flight. She's so close. Alive, as I am, with anticipation. How could I ever have imagined a life without her? She and I are one. For the first time in weeks, I feel whole.

I allow the guard to lead me into the room beyond.

Ixion waits on the dais of the triple throne, in the principal chair. To one side sits Delo Skyfish, the ascending Triarch of the East. The third chair, that should be occupied by the Aurelian triarch—in this case, waiting for the underaged Astyanax—is occupied by Freyda. Silhouetted in one of the three glass archways behind them lounges Ixion's stormscourge, Niter.

The court is arrayed on either side of the center aisle I walk down; the front two rows are empty, reserved for the jury in conclave. At the Supplicant's Stone, smoothed from years of obeisance, I kneel to await my fate.

It seems we wait like this for an interminable time.

Then a door creaks open to my right. There is the sound of twenty feet on stone. The jury files into its waiting rows.

"Will the speaker for the jury step forward?" Samander Eschros asks.

The elderly man who told me to take heart rises to his feet.

My heart speeds to twice its rate.

The juror bows low before the Triarchy, then straightens. His voice shakes, thick on vowels of an accent from Southside that stand in high contrast to the court's clipped Palace-standard.

"To the charges of high treason and crimes against the state, the jury finds Antigone sur Aela not guilty."

For a moment, I don't understand what I've heard.

I'm not the only one confused by the verdict. Whispering erupts like wildfire through the hall. Ixion has blanched. Eschros says, "The Clover Tribunal hears its citizen jurors. Antigone sur Aela is cleared of all charges."

I get to my feet.

This isn't how it was supposed to go. I wanted to face Ixion in the arena after being found guilty. But now, on the other side of a verdict I hardly let myself imagine, I realize that there is still one way to face him in the arena. A way I'd written off, too full of guilt to contemplate, but that seems like a possibility for the first time since Callipolis fell.

"I challenge Ixion sur Niter to the title of Firstrider."

The whispering that lit the hall falls silent.

Ixion's teeth bare.

"You and what dragon, Antigone?"

I smile at him. Right on cue, the glass of the central archway shatters.

Aela perches framed by stone, her wings spread.

***

The thing must be done quickly if it is to be done at all. Grayriders, acting as criers, alight on dragon perches throughout the city to announce the tournament, like heralds of old; citizens begin pouring across Highmarket Bridge, into the Palace Gardens, and through the arena gates.

Ixion prepares in his apartments while Aela and I regroup to the Cloister courtyard. There I'm found by Verra and Vicky, caps askew, arms laden with bundles of Guardian armor that look as though they've been gathering dust since the Restoration.

"Abbie! Or, I suppose it's Antigone, not Abigael, now. We found these for you."

I'm startled by their identical beams. "You don't mind that I'm . . . not who I said I was?"

Last time we discussed politics, they were rather ill-disposed toward Atreus's bitch commander. Vicky waves a hand. "When we found out we'd been maids alongside *Antigone sur Aela* on the run—!" She presses a palm to her chest, lifting starstruck eyes to the cloudy sky. "Let us know if there's anything else you need. We were told to outfit you."

I've done a cursory pass over the flamesuit and confirmed what I expected. "I don't suppose coolant is an option?"

Verra and Vicky look at each other, consternated. "We seem to be out of stock."

Sounds like Ixion got there first. I wasn't really expecting it anyway. Just means I'll have to be quick.

For more reasons than one. It's been so long since I had this kind of pain in my abdomen, I didn't at first recognize it. But changing into my flamesuit, I confirm the blood on my thighs and let out what feels like my first full breath in days.

Lee's alive, I'm not pregnant, and I'm going to wipe the floor with Ixion as I bleed.

"I'll get you some of my rags," Verra says at the sight of it, and breaks for the dorms at a run.

Aela's in the center of the courtyard, drinking from the fountain I used to play in with Duck; I won't risk sending her out of my sight, so instead of arming in the nests, we prepare here. I take a moment, before saddling her up, to hold her.

"Never, ever again."

She snorts in agreement and tucks her neck round me, pressing me to her scaly breast.

"You ready for this?"

Sparks flutter from her nostrils as her eyes flash.

"Me too."

I wash Power's blood from my hands and face in the courtyard fountain, steeling myself at the sight. *After. You will feel after.* By the time Verra returns with a fistful of menstrual rags, I've started breaking my time prepping armor to double over the flower bed. I'd forgotten how much I *hate* this.

"Annie, you all right?"

I'm cold-sweating, probably feverish, and only feel intermittently better after dry-heaving. But also I'm pulling on a flame-suit for the first time since returning to Callipolis. I can handle cramps.

"I am *fantastic.*"

Verra holds out a woman's cuirass bearing the entwined silver and gold circlets of the Guardians, and Vicky finds wing pins in the pile that she affixes to my shoulder: the wings of the Fourth Order. I press the bloody Firstrider badge Power saved for me into her hand. It's not quite time to put it back on. "Have that ready for me when we get back."

My breath catches as they pull the Revolutionary armor over my head.

A helmet tucked under one arm, I climb into the saddle. I strap boots into their stirrups, feeling the welcome reassurance of leather cinching tight. Verra pats my calf, and Vicky steps back to take us in and laugh aloud with hands stretched to the sky.

Then I dig my heel into Aela's side and we're in the air at last.

40

—

REVOLUTION'S DAUGHTER

DELO

I'm at Ixion's elbow as we make our way from the Throne Room to the apartments where servants will be waiting with his dragon and his armor. Ever since I got back from Norcia, I've expected to be confronted about going missing for the night. I've steeled myself to come clean and say it just like Power did. *You got me. I'm a peasant-loving traitor.* I think I actually *want* it. But it becomes clear enough Ixion doesn't have an interrogation of me on the agenda. He's shaking with such fury that courtiers clear the corridors at the sight of him.

"I'll show her. I'll show them both."

Them *both*? He's used the feminine plural. I don't understand until we enter Ixion's apartments and find a young man in Bassilean yellow lounging in the parlor. He has a striking lack of chin.

"Sorry to keep you waiting, Your Highness," says Ixion, with a clipped bow. "May I present Delo Skyfish, Triarch-presumptive of the East. I have to take a slight—detour this morning, but I hope we'll be able to reunite you with your dear sister as soon as my business is finished. Please, make yourself comfortable in the meantime."

"Of course," says Froydrich, in a flat and nasal Dragontongue. "I don't intend for us to impose on your hospitality much longer."

He offers a thin-lipped smile. I'm staring at the God-heir, thinking of the coin I held in my palm in Griff's study. On the obverse, the silhouetted likeness of the face that now studies me without expression. And on the reverse—his goliathan.

If Froydrich is here, where is Azuleth?

Ixion turns to me and does not register that I've stopped dead. "Delo, would you and Gephyra be so kind as to join our honor guard?"

"Of course."

Ixion begins to pull on his flamesuit.

LEE

The plan was to get Annie out on Aela's back whether or not she was found guilty, and not take on the goliathan before. When it becomes apparent which way the verdict has gone, and criers begin to summon Callipolans into the arena, I know where to find the Resistance riders who will plant themselves to summon at the end of her match.

In the aisle seats.

Ixion waylaid the Guardians in this arena once; now it's time to return the favor.

I glimpse leaflets poking out of pockets and bags as I join the throng making its way up the stone stairs. Thanks to the scar across my face, no one recognizes me; they've been staring at *it* so much they haven't bothered looking closer at my face. Crissa and Cor, on the other hand, are distinctive for their decision to wear hoods in broad daylight.

"You lot could try to be a bit less conspicuous," I mutter, taking the seat next to Crissa. She adjusts her hood with a huff, but wisps of blond are still spilling out.

Cor leans round Crissa, smirking. "Been sung to by a muse recently, Lee?" He's got one of the leaflets rolled into a fist.

"Careful. I've heard possession of that document is illegal."

Crissa takes the printing from Cor and swats me with it.

I wasn't expecting to enjoy it, sitting in the arena where I'll never fly again. But here with Cor and Crissa, straining eyes for Annie, still high on the creative adrenaline of an all-nighter, I feel more myself than I've felt in a long time.

And then the trumpets sound, and Antigone sur Aela flies over the rim of the arena wall. She sits sure in the saddle, her head high, her auburn hair blowing, the helmet tucked confidently under her arm as Aela descends to the Eyrie.

She's alive. Either unharmed or unharmed enough to fake it.

The crowd begins to cheer and then take up the chant. First a drakonym, and then an epithet: the one I penned, last night, in a frenzy of ink and crumpled parchment in Lo Teiran's study as the words poured out.

Antigone sur Aela, Revolution's Daughter.

ANNIE

The skies billow with cumulus that drift like mountains on a spring wind. As the Palace spreads below our wings, as the blue bowl of the sky lowers to join us and wind whips the hair from my forehead, the beauty of the familiar sight takes my breath. In the arena below, swelling crowds fill the stands with colors and their cheers rise up to greet us.

On the Eyrie, we are joined by Ixion sur Niter.

He glitters in Stormscourge armor like a double of Lee, fury in his gray eyes and a sneer twisting his thin mouth, and juxtaposed, the silver-tipped wings of Niter dwarf Aela by half. But all either of us feel, looking up at them, is anticipation.

We should have done this a long time ago.

Gasps that aren't mine have drawn collectively across the stands. I look up to find Pytho's Keep unfolding. Obizuth spreads her wings to launch. Her shadow darkens the stands as she circles them, and Clover riders scatter from the ramparts like a flock of displaced birds.

And the Great Dragon settles along the wall of the arena with a fold of her wings.

The sun glows through the membranes like a tent roof. Her great head twists, cocks, and a single eye the size of a human head fixes on the scene below.

Fixes on Ixion and me.

She has gone completely still.

The arena has gone completely silent.

Ixion and I turn as one to look up at the Palace Box where Freyda observes. She stands unmoving, the breeze fluttering her short veil. A thin lacing of black veins twist down her neck.

I think of Norcia, of Lee and his books, of the other half of the plan and the fleet I'm banking on. *Are they here?*

If they are, they aren't moving yet.

Ixion and I both dismount. The servant approaches with a bucket to perform the ceremonial dousing. A memory flickers at the sight: Ixion sur Niter above Callipolis, sputtering.

I lift my hand.

The servant sees the gesture and does a double take.

"You refuse the dousing?"

"We do."

To refuse a dousing—to duel with sparked dragonfire—is to duel to the death. In a suit without coolant, this would normally be suicide.

But I know Ixion's secret.

His face glows white under the shadow of Obizuth's wings.

"Lord Ixion, you may accept the terms or surrender your helmet."

Ixion's gloved fingers tighten on his helmet. I'm smiling at him. All the while, Obizuth poises frozen over us.

"We accept the terms," Ixion says through barely moving lips.

The servant lifts the dousing bucket for the crowd to see—and empties it onto the ground.

They are screaming their approval. Screaming—I realize with a flood of surprise—my name.

I make the final preparations as we ready for launch. In the days when Power trained me to spill over, this was the moment when he would have to insult me to provoke high emotion; when Lee and I sparred for Firstrider, I used fury to open the connection. Negative emotions are usually the most readily available.

But today, as I look into Ixion's gray eyes, as I listen to the sound of Callipolans cheering, the feeling that binds me to Aela is less rage than triumph.

I've got my boot in the stirrup when I feel a weight on my shoulder.

Ixion has crossed the neutral space between us. His gloved hand is on my upper arm. His black hair glows red as it blocks the sun.

"I just wanted to thank you."

"Get your hand off me."

"If we were doused," Ixion says, his smiling face in shadow,

"I'd have to stop at the third penalty. But now? I get to keep going for as long as I want."

Aela begins to growl, her crest flaring. On the other side of the Eyrie, Niter's crest rises to meet hers. He looms over her. Ixion makes a point of removing one finger at a time from my shoulder.

Aela's growling rises to a menacing whine as he returns to Niter, her crest slowly lowering. It takes effort to turn my back on them. I throw my leg over Aela's back, trying to shake off the lingering unease from Ixion's touch. *What's his recourse, aside from talk? He's still sparkforsaken.*

Aela and I take to the air, minds locked.

Positions are assumed. The crowd below stills. Roiling spring clouds clog the sky, hanging low over us like a high ceiling, and the wings of the Great Dragon surround us on all sides. But my lowered visor narrows my vision to the stormscourge and the boy opposite us whom we will destroy.

The bell rings. Aela and Niter surge toward each other. Finally, *finally.* This is what I'm here to do. Aela and I don't usually spare time for showmanship, but today we allow ourselves a spiral as we advance, a flourish lightweight aurelians can pull off where Ixion's stormscourge must maintain an unswerving trajectory to reach velocity. I can hear the crowd's admiring gasps below and feel that they're buoying me up.

See, Callipolis? This is how a lowborn rider flies.

Then we're within range, and our filled lungs fire.

The glow of Aela's flames burns my retinas. Ixion sur Niter don't even try to dodge it or to make a shot themselves. They disappear within our blast.

In a doused tournament, that would count as a kill shot. In today's arrangement, we'll keep going for as long as one of us can still get off the ground.

It still surprises me when Ixion sur Niter erupts from my own flames, screaming, and tackles us in a contact charge.

A foul, if this were the kind of match that called them. Contact charges across breeds give unfair advantage to stormscourges. The one time I've dealt with one during a tournament, Power took us into cloud cover to tackle us unobserved. But this charge is in full sight of the arena below, and no whistle from the referee sounds. I don't expect it to.

Ixion wants to make a show of flouting the rules. He wants to show he's above this. All of it.

We'll just have to prove him wrong.

We pinwheel, the weight of them careening us off balance, and the ground rushes toward us. The wings of both dragons beat the air in frantic tandem to maintain altitude. As Aela struggles to free herself from his grasp, Niter slams his maw over the side of her wing and opens it against my leg.

A paltry smattering of ash and sparks showers across my thigh. It would be an embarrassment to Ixion, if anyone below could see it, but Aela's wings provide cover and the sputter has no witness from the crowd below.

It would be hardly enough heat to stop me on a training bout—except it falls on old wounds.

Niter's aimed at my branded thigh.

I hear my own shriek as the heat sets in.

"You see, Antigone? You're not the only one here who knows how to *survive*."

Aela's claws and fangs grow frenzied, and we tear out of Niter's grip and kick away from them. We surge out and upward to reset height. I'm wheezing now, fingers fumbling for coolant valves along my leg in the vain hope that the suit might have some left over. Nothing.

Shake it off.

As Niter resets opposite us, Ixion makes a show of opening every coolant valve on his flamesuit, alleviating the burns he took from Aela's dragonfire. Then he makes time to restock the suit with coolant he has strapped to his saddle. He's got whole canisters of it.

Still, I can see how stiffly he moves. He's in pain.

There's no way he'll face our fire headfirst a second time.

"Ready?"

I move to reset position without answering him. The bell rings again.

We race toward them, letting the fire forge our path, a blazing wall of it, and again—to my disbelief—they barrel through it, enduring the full-heat blast in order to make a second contact charge. This time we perform a flick roll to evade Niter's lunge—

But not quite fast enough. His talons pierce Aela's wings, exactly along the thin white scars from Edmund's mauling and the stitches she's still healing from.

Aela's turn to shriek. She attempts to yank free but only tears the punctures longer—

And then Niter grips her by the neck with his jaws. His fangs are retracted; he's making a show of strength. He shakes her so hard, I rattle in the saddle, and every bounce sends more pain searing through my wounded leg. Aela twists but cannot free herself.

We keep rattling until Niter flings us away.

For a moment before Aela's wings catch on the wind, we freefall. Ixion's voice calls after us. "We don't need anything as crude as *flame*. We already know every way to cause you pain."

"Ignore him—" I'm humming it more to Aela than myself. Her punctured wing beats the air overtime to match the uninjured one and raise us back to the reset height. The pain in my leg and her wing floods between us, clouding our senses. As we spiral on the updraft, her glance wanders down and she lets out a low whine that sends a chill down my neck.

There are officials waiting at the floor of the arena with a chain-link net.

Just like the one they threw over Pallor.

I can feel Aela's thoughts scattering like a thousand fireflies. Flickers of Pallor, of Pallor beneath that net, Pallor's tenderly nursing our shredded wings—Pallor *gone*—

We're sinking toward the earth, her wings forgetting to pound the air.

"Aela, no," I say, though suddenly my eyes are blurring with her loss.

And then the despairing realization slides like sludge from her head to mine.

Ixion will keep ramming us with contact charges, ignoring our flames, and his coolant will last him longer than our shredding wings and waning energy will. His dragon's stamina will outmatch ours over and over because thanks to luck of birth and breeding they are stronger, and bigger, and fitter. In the end it won't matter whether the people cheer my name, or what an inspired jury decides, because this match isn't testing skill anymore. It's a test of brute strength. And in such a test what advantage do we have, a smaller dragon and a scrawny girl, hungry and tired and in pain—?

Small. Scrawny.

The word flickers like a thought on the breeze, fireflies shifting into memory.

A note in my hand from the Ministry, referring to my duties

and suggesting I throw a match against a patrician boy with golden hair. A drillmaster's hand on my shoulder, reminding me of my place. That moment when I decided to hell with them and rose, leaving an iron-gray stormscourge and its golden boy behind. Ramming through a door that had been locked because I was tired of waiting to be handed the keys, tired of being afraid, tired of holding myself in.

When they don't give you the tools to win, you make your own.

Ixion's right. Flames are crude.

The earliest lessons of flying aren't about fire. They're about gravity. The oldest, surest weapon.

I've only got to use it to my advantage.

I slide a hand down Aela's flank as we steady for the reset. She's heaving, poor girl, and I can see the ground through the tiny talon punctures to her wing.

But she feels my excitement.

"Shall we give it one last go?"

She snaps her wings taut.

Then the bell rings a third time, and Aela and I do our favorite thing in the world.

We rise.

Fast as her beating wings will allow, ignoring the pain that shoots through the damaged membranes. Straight into the sky as if we are leaving the earth behind. We clear Obizuth's mantling wings and surge past the circling Clover riders: We are a cannonball that defies gravity, wings that defy the wind, as we rip through the lowest clouds and rise higher.

And because Ixion's no idiot, he tries to keep up with us.

But it won't be enough, it's never enough, with a heavy stormscourge against an aurelian's light frame. They rise, but for every meter they gain, we gain three.

Sprigs of ice creep across my visor. Aela's gasps grow light. I'm holding my breath as we stall in air that is thin and cold enough to drown us. The searing cold offers numbing relief to my throbbing leg.

The city spreads so far below, I could cover it with my palm. Pytho's Keep lies half buried in cumulus. The island of Callipolis radiates from it, lowlands rippling down to the Medean, highlands rising in jagged crags against the North Sea. Their white peaks are all that's left of winter, and green already tints the blackness of tilled fields. The River Fer, swollen and brown, overflows its banks.

Below us, the great curve of Obizuth's wings encircle the arena, the flock of little Clover riders hover above her, and Ixion sur Niter has shrunk to a black insect we will pin to the earth.

We dive.

Pummeling our wings to hasten the force of gravity, transforming our little aurelian into a meteor.

Ixion sur Niter swerves, darts, but our sights are on them.

They assail us with the small, sputtering fire Niter can muster. The heat penetrates my coolant-less flamesuit and scalds my torso and my still-smarting thigh. But it isn't enough.

Not nearly enough.

We barrel through their ash and ram them with a contact charge of our own. This one is so aided by our momentum that they are the ones blown off course. We take them with us toward the earth as if they were a fluttering doll, and they can't get out from beneath us.

Because an aurelian may be smaller, lighter, and weaker than a stormscourge, but not with gravity on her side.

Niter's fangs gnash, fixing on whatever hold they can find. Aela's wings, her side, my legs. Though we scream, we don't let go. And though he splutters, no more fire comes out.

The city enlarges, filling our vision. The curving walls of the arena, draped by Obizuth's wings, rise to surround us like the arms of an old friend—the dusty floor of the arena hurtles toward us—the officials unrolling the chain-link net scatter and run—

Two meters from impact, Aela shoves free of the other dragon with a single sure kick.

Ixion sur Niter collides with the arena floor.

The crack deafens us. The sound of the impact knocks the air from our lungs. When the dust clears, we find a crater.

When I land on the edge of the crater, slice the straps of my stirrups, and dismount, the sound of my boots hitting the ground echoes on stone. I make my way down into the still-sizzling impression. The body of Ixion is thrown on one side, a leg half pinned beneath his dragon.

I think he must be dead until he moves.

A shaking hand lifts the visor. Gray eyes find me. Ixion's body is broken, but the dragon's is still heaving and ready. We stand in front of Niter's maw, at range. Exposed in a flamesuit without coolant, I remove my helmet.

Give it your best shot.

Niter fires, and ash sputters out. A choking cloud of it.

Muttering rumbles through the crowds that watch us.

The word I hear, or maybe just imagine I hear, spreading across the arena like fire: *sparkforsaken.*

After all the dragonborn propaganda about the supremacy of their blood, after all their rigged Winnowing Tournaments to prove who deserves to ride, this is what they have to show for it.

"You want to try that again?"

Ixion screams. The dragon spews ash, billows of it, but no flames come out. The heat passes harmlessly over my unstocked flamesuit.

I'm smiling.

"Go on," he rasps. "Finish it."

Aela stands behind me, poised to fire.

"You called for a tournament undoused," Ixion snarls, weighted beneath his dragon. *"Do it."*

I want it. I can taste it. I can smell his skin crackling, as mine did when he branded me. I can see the light going out of Niter's eyes, just as it did Pallor's. My heart pounds with *wanting it.* I vowed once that I would. Who deserves death, if not this boy, who let the horrors he saw as a child burn him from the inside out and then inflicted those wounds on everyone and everything he touched? On me, on my country—

Aela's breath rattles behind me as she inhales, shallow and long. Building the flames.

But as she does, I feel the cool calm of memories.

I have loved the son of those who killed my blood. I have erected monuments for my fallen oppressors and returned the bodies of my enemies to their kin.

Ixion pounds his fist into Niter's hide, making the dragon wince. But no more fire comes out.

"Antigone, you peasant bitch, finish it—"

I clench my fists, the order coursing into Aela, and she fires.

It streams into the cloud-ridden sky. A pillar of flame for the arena to see, passing harmlessly over Ixion's head. Ixion's protests fall silent as he lifts his head to watch it turn to smoke above us.

I took a vow to guide the City to justice. And justice has always been found by way of my mercy. The only way forward is to look into the face of the one who deserves my hatred and do better. Let Ixion be tried for his crimes as I was by the system I have sworn to serve. A system that—albeit imperfectly—grants power and penalty based on merit.

If that system can find me innocent, then it can find him guilty.

"You won't have legitimacy unless you do it," Ixion says, panting. "What kind of bitch commander can't even finish the job?"

For all I know, he's right. But I also know I've learned the hard way what kind of leader I want to be. And if I can't be that person now—I might as well be back in that cell.

I step forward. "Your helmet." The arena is so quiet, my voice echoes on the stone stands.

Proof of a match won.

Ixion's visor is raised. His eyes are wide with disbelief. He tears off his helmet and for one mad second I think he's going to hand it to me without protest. Instead he tosses it to the ground. He yanks his boots free of their charred stirrups and slams his heels with such force into Niter's side that Niter lurches. *"Fire, you stupid—"*

Before I can say a word, Aela's fury ignites.

In two bounds she leaps forward, knocking Ixion off his broken stormscourge and driving him into rubble-strewn ground. Her rage courses through us. For Pallor before, for Niter now, blazing into a single violent purpose: *This* is the dragon's punishment.

Through her pricked ears I hear the snap of Ixion's spinal cord as his head connects with rock.

Aela lifts her head, her eyes finding mine, and her pupils narrow to slits as she extricates her mind from mine. Her flared nostrils and her glare are enough to make clear: I had my business to settle with Ixion but she has hers, and it follows its own laws. He lies strewn across the stones like a rag doll, a pool of crimson spreading from his head in a terrible halo. Blood spilled in a pool like Pallor's was. Though she's attempting to keep me out, her satisfaction does not fail to trickle into me as she smells it.

A pattering sound is distant in my ears, rising in pitch from the stands. Are they—cheering?

Aela's fangs are poised to sink into Ixion's jugular, to *feast*, when I snap to my senses and step forward, palms lifted. "Aela, that's enough." It takes effort to get the words out through our widening, salivating jaws. The audience's cheering only grows louder, as if her bloodlust is spilling into them, too. But that's their prerogative and this is mine. Ixion's death will have dignity. "It's over—"

The Callipolans' cheering is drowned by Niter's rising howl.

A widow-cry.

Even with his rider's cruelty as a final farewell, the bond's breaking causes him sorrow. He's turned his head, surrounded by his battered, tentlike wings, to take in his fallen master from where he lies broken in the rubble. In the corner of my vision, the officials have hoisted up the chain-link and are carrying it toward us. Their eyes are on Niter.

I lift a hand. The officials and the net pause in their advance.

Niter stretches a trembling, broken wing over the body of his rider, mantling his corpse. For a moment, as Aela and I watch his heaving flank slow in its gasps, the emotion that flits between us is pity. The Callipolans' bloodthirsty cheers have fallen silent as the dragon's keening sorrow fills the arena.

We have had our revolution—but this stormscourge? He had no such liberation.

Niter deserved better than Ixion, too.

The stormscourge lowers his head into the crook of his broken wing as his breath slows.

And then I look around for what feels like the first time.

At the arena, its breath held. At the shadowed wings of the goliathan and the Clover riders circling overhead; at the officials waiting to the side of the crater; and above us, at the Palace Box where Freyda will award the laurel.

I realize that I'm shaking. I can feel, suddenly, the pain of the burns, the flight, the cramps and the blood sticking my flamesuit to my thighs. I'm in desperate need of coolant, a shower, and a meal.

As I sway, I hear a new chant swelling from the stands, soft at first, but growing louder. This time not with an epithet but a title.

Antigone sur Aela, Firstrider.

About bloody time, I think, with strange exasperation, and that's when Obizuth lets out an earthshaking roar and rears.

41

—

THE LEVELING

DELO

I hardly spare eyes for Ixion and Antigone's match, so busy am I searching the horizon for a sign. Not that the duel isn't satisfying; I've had this feeling at a tournament once before, when Ixion competed against his sister, Julia. Then, as now, you had the sense that history was about to be rewritten.

But my chief concern remains the Bassilean prince I was introduced to in Ixion's parlor. Froydrich is here, so where is his dragon? The males are supposed to be even larger than the females.

As Gephyra and I circle with the Clover fleet, we scan the vista below. The Firemouth's empty, Pytho's Keep flattened by Obizuth's nesting, and the wide boulevards of Highmarket are clear. The river is still and engorged. There's no sign of another dragon anywhere below, much less one the size of a whale. Is it possible Froydrich came by sea, not by air?

Aela and Niter rise, plateau, and plummet. Like a twisting, flaming comet, they fall. The sound of their impact on the arena floor reverberates within its walls.

Finish it. Ixion's voice pops distantly in my ears.

Aela fires into the sky—

And then I look again. A river, murky with spring runoff, engorged.

Becca's drawing of the Great Dragon, submerged below a blue line. *That's how it sneaks up on you.*

Titus Grayheather is on my wing, and I yell to him. "Titus, it's the Fer!"

But he's not listening to me. A collective shout of horror, bordering on titillation, has gone up from the Bastards surrounding me. They crane their necks over their dragons' wings. I glance down.

Aela crouches over Ixion, who is spread-eagled. Niter lets out a widow-cry.

Ixion's dead.

I test my feelings and draw a blank. There was a time when Ixion and I were friends. But it was on the other side of a Revolution. I've been mourning that friend for as long as I can remember.

This—just finishes an overdue job.

I'm still looking down at Ixion when the River Fer erupts.

A goliathan twice the size of Freyda's parts the water as it arches upward. A wall of water sloshes over the side of the arena, onto Obizuth. Barges tumble onto the Upper and Lower Banks like little bricks. A horned head turns on the female with fangs bared.

It lunges.

At the same time, from cypress groves at the base of Pytho's Keep stream a fleet of dragons like an erupting flock of birds. The Resistance riders have summoned. Their dragons are already saddled. They weave through the flailing goliathans like sparrows evading hawks and dive into the arena, searching for their riders. When they emerge, it's with Guardians and Woad-riders on their backs.

Just as they—as *we*—planned.

"Delo!" Griff sur Sparker is the first of them to join my wing. "What the hell is this thing?"

Around us, the Bastards from the Clover fleet are staring. "Peasant lover," Titus says, "*still?*"

Whatever way I imagined coming clean, I don't think it was in the air with two wrestling goliathans in between me and the ground. I lift a shoulder, catching Griff's eye, and he grins.

"Yeah," I say. "Still."

Then I explain to Titus and Griff both. "Froydrich's here. I think Azuleth's trying to subdue his mate."

In the arena below, crowds of Callipolans are churning as they scream and push for exits, seeking safety from the Great Dragons. As we watch, the male goliathan seizes the female by the crested neck and gnashes. Her roar of fury shakes the stones. His wing is already mantling hers, his bristly talons sinking into her flank.

"Maybe we should let him?" Griff sounds dubious. "Makes our job easier, if the whole point is to get her out of here!"

Titus splutters. "'*The whole point*'?—what the hell kind of plot is this?"

Before anyone can bother to explain it to him, another voice joins ours. "I've got a better idea."

Antigone sur Aela has risen to Griff's side. Her visor is up, her eyes wide in an ash-blackened face. "Forget the female. Target the male. I'm going to find Freyda."

She wheels Aela round and Griff shouts after her, "To do what?"

Annie calls over her shoulder as she yanks down her visor. "To give her my terms!"

After she's dived into the turmoil below, Griff and I stare at each other. Cor sur Maurana has arrived at his wing, and Titus Gray-heather's still at mine, spluttering. The rest of the Clover riders are facing the Resistance in midair like we're setting up for a melee.

Griff squints down at Azuleth. His horned tail lops the roofs off several manors in the Janiculum as it flails. "Antigone's bonkers. We haven't trained to take on a male goliathan, that thing's beastly."

"Could you do it with backup?"

Griff looks up at me. And then, cottoning on, he glances down the row of glaring Clover riders and flashes his most ingratiating smile. "Hiya, folks," he says to the dragonborn, with a luxurious use of the informal. When we were kids, and he tried this, he was beaten for it.

Titus looks from him to me, his teeth gritted. "You have got to be joking."

I jab a thumb at the girl disappearing into the fires below. "Antigone sur Aela just proved herself Firstrider and Fleet Commander of Callipolis. Unless you or any were thinking of challenging her for that title?" I lift my voice.

The dragonborn look at each other. No one volunteers.

As unchallenged Alternus of the Callipolan fleet, second in command to Antigone, the next order is mine to give. "Then do what Griff says."

Griff looks about as smug as I've ever seen him, and that's saying something. He begins to pair his riders off with mine, passing out the lines to thread through harpoons.

I'm about to take a harpoon myself when I have a better thought.

There's a tether-target to take care of, and I know exactly where to find him.

"Where are you going?" Griff shouts, as I nudge Gephyra into a dive.

"I'm going to neutralize Froydrich."

LEE

The stands vibrate with Obizuth's screams. Horns the length of a human body split the stones and pierce the dragon's hide as

Azuleth bites Obizuth's crested neck. A monstrous, cruel transformation of the same familiarity I watched Pallor perform on
Aela. All around me, Callipolans get to their feet and push for the
exits, screaming. As the tide of terrified citizens pulls me with it, I
realize what's wrong.

The guards, a mixture of Callipolan and Bassilean, are direct-
ing people out the main exits. These will lead into the courtyards
of the Great Palace, the public gardens, and the Janiculum neighborhoods, which are still more exposed.

Overhead, the first harpoon thwacks into the side of Azuleth,
and then the *put-put-put* of the target line follows as the riders
begin their encirclement. The goliathan's furious roar produces
flame as thick as a pillar. The upper floors of the Inner Palace
catch fire. A horned wing slams down and a turret explodes like
chalk. When I lower the arm I've raised to shield my face, I glimpse
a pair of narrow amber wings wheeling under the flames.

Antigone sur Aela lands on the empty stone row above me.

"Lee," she says.

"Annie."

She's raised her visor and is beaming, her ruddy face smeared
with ash and sweat, and she's absolutely gorgeous. "I'm going to
find Freyda. Will you come?" She indicates the space on the saddle
behind her, where I could squeeze in.

But I look at the citizens scrambling down the stairs around me
and find myself shaking my head.

"I think I'm needed here."

Last time, she was the one who said this to me. We're both grinning like idiots now.

"Then I'll find you after," she says, and resets her visor.

Aela kicks off from the ground and I begin to elbow through
the crowd. When I find the nearest guard, I seize him as I point

into the heart of the arena. "You need to evacuate everyone into the Firemouth! The Upper Bank is about to be leveled, it's safer underground!"

The guard wipes a sweating brow. He's barely older than I am—and I recognize him. At a dinner party, long ago, in the War College, he bragged about his brother's feats in the Revolution and toasted my name. "Bad idea," he says, barely glancing at me, "they'd get lost. You do your job, I'll do mine, Citizen—"

"I'm trying to."

That gets his attention. He lifts his cap to squint at me, and his roving gaze travels from the scar across my face to my eyes. "Lee sur Pallor?"

"Gaven. Tell them to make for the Firemouth, and tell them to follow me."

Gaven's eyes are wide. I may as well be a ghost; as far as anyone in this city knows, I'm dead. When he reels in a breath and lifts an arm, his bellow is as loud as a crier's.

"Make for the Firemouth! Follow Lee sur Pallor!"

Though there will be a time to discard the drakonym, it isn't today. The whispers alight through the throngs as they divide before me: *Lee sur Pallor's alive.*

I lead them into the bowels of the Firemouth.

GRIFF

I used to take pride in Sparker's formidable size, but these beasts put that in perspective. It takes all the teams we have, Clovers and Guardians and Woad-riders together, to snare Azuleth. When we start to tighten, and finally his fangs release Obizuth's neck, the female falls gasping on top of a fancy neighborhood at the foot of Pytho's Keep and flattens it.

A lot of rich folks' houses have been knocked out today. Wonder what Delo will think of that.

Where is he? He went to find Froydrich a half hour ago.

Our riders are tightening their ropes, binding Azuleth in place, and now that his wings are restrained, they'll muzzle him to stop the fire. I toss my next harpoon to Bran and dig my heel into Sparker's side.

"Griff, where are you—"

"I'll be right back!"

We head for the high turrets of the Inner Palace as fast as Sparker's big body can go.

As soon as he catches the crackling lightning-over-water scent of a skyfish, we dive. The grille locked across the Inner Palace's entrance to the Firemouth has been torn open by the goliathans' struggles. What's left of the towers is on fire.

We find Gephyra on a balcony three levels down, scampering back and forth as she attempts to squeeze herself through the human-size door. Delo is nowhere to be seen. Sparker tugs Geph aside with a gentle nip of his gums, and as I dismount, I hush her with a quick pat to her flank. "I'll find him, darling."

I step into the smoking darkness. "Delo?"

Silence. Flickering red light comes from the end of the corridor, where a door swings slowly on its hinges. As I make my way toward it, my boots crush broken glass. Somewhere above us, a goliathan thrashes, and the reverberations through the stone of the Palace ripple the ground beneath my feet.

"Delo?"

Inside the parlor, the chandelier hangs sideways, its glimmering crystals strewn across the floor like frozen teardrops. Flames lick up the drapes. In the center of a smoking rug, half covered by a tea table, lies Delo.

Is he wounded? Unconscious from the smoke? Or—surely not—?

It's unthinkable. Panic grips me. I launch forward, shouting his name. After all I've won and lost, not this, *too*—not my Delo—

I'm two steps into the room when something slams me to the ground.

Fingers close around my neck. A chinless face, lost in black veins, fills my vision. I pound a fist into Froydrich's side but the tethering lends him inhuman strength. He catches my fist in his and begins to crush it as if the bones were made of chalk. His teeth are bloody.

"You're that abomination," he growls, in a voice that contains many voices, so deep it vibrates through the ground. "The slave with the dragon."

"Technically a king these days, but yeah, I've got a dragon—"

He spits bloody saliva in my face. And then he's growling, his black eyes squeezing shut. "Come to me. *Come to me*—"

And I realize he's not talking to *me* anymore.

He switches to Bassilic, his voice rising as if chanted by a whole chorus of princes—

With a deafening *crunch*, as stone cracks and metal splinters, the stone ceiling over our heads parts. Sunlight and clouds of mortar pour through. When I look up, blinking, it takes me a moment to understand what's descending into the opening. A glow from within a great maw illuminates fangs the length of my body. I'm staring up at Azuleth's open mouth. Harpoon lines hang off his horns like so many broken threads. Our riders are flitting around him, shouting and panicking as the goliathan seeks its tethering rider. Froydrich throws his head back and laughs—

And from out of sight, Bran's voice calls: "*Heave!*"

The lines dangling from Azuleth's maw tighten as they are

regained, pulled by riders out of sight. The great jaws begin to close. The fiery glow dwindles to fluttering sparks that rain harmlessly down.

From behind Froydrich, a hand appears, holding a brick. It clocks him on the side of the head.

Froydrich slumps sideways, off me.

Behind him crouches Delo, panting, bleeding from the ear, but grinning like an idiot.

Above us, Azuleth blinks as if only now noticing the sunlight, his flared pupils slowly drifting back to their usual slits. His maw is cinched shut. "*Wind up!*" calls Cor's voice, and the ropes begin to circle.

"Were you trying to rescue me?" Delo asks.

I'm grinning a bit, myself. "I mean, you're my damsel."

Still holding the brick, Delo leans forward. For a half second, I wonder if he's going to hit me in the head with it, too. I am pinned under the dead weight of the unconscious Bassilean prince.

"I'm not the one with goliathan slobber on my face," Delo says.

He's smirking. I wipe my face in horror. And then, before I know what's happened, Delo leans forward and kisses me, slobber and all.

I'm so surprised, I nearly forget how to kiss him back. But I remember fast enough.

Bran's voice interrupts. "A little help finishing this up, lads?" He's circling the still-disoriented Azuleth in the haze above us, a chain in hand connecting to a goliathan-sized muzzle.

"Yeah, all right, all right."

Delo pulls the unconscious prince off me, and we go to finish the job we started.

ANNIE

I find Freyda slumped atop Pytho's Keep. Whether she instinctively climbed the winding stair to take refuge in her dragon's nest, or hoped to summon Obizuth from this safe vantage point and flee, she can do neither now.

On the crumbling remains of the bank below, Azuleth struggles vainly as my riders tighten a muzzle round his maw, but he's done enough damage. Obizuth lies across the flattened Janiculum, panting from her wounds. Even if Freyda were to summon her, I'm not sure she'd be able to rise.

But maybe Freyda mounted the steps of Pytho's Keep for a different reason. I find her kneeling on the edge of the Sky Court, surveying the wreckage below as if contemplating the drop. She has a hand to her neck where Obizuth was bitten as if her own body feels it.

Her brother has come for her, and she's lost her one way out. Callipolis has turned on her.

At least part of that feeling, I know.

I slide from Aela's back as soon as her talons hit the ground. "Wait."

Freyda twists. She's torn off her veil; her darkened eyes find me, and the black strings at her neck seem to choke her.

"Antigone," she says, in her many-throated voice.

I approach and curtsy in the way appropriate to equals. The formal address I use is not Bassilea's but Callipolis's.

"Your Highness, I would discuss our terms."

I wait for her black eyes to regain their white rims. Then, I make the proposal in Dragontongue.

"As you see, my fleet has trained to bring down a goliathan. We brought it here today to confront Obizuth. Instead, we protected her from the onslaught of your brother's dragon. If you wish it, we can widow Froydrich now—or we can escort him and his dragon, subdued, back to Vask."

"Why?" Freyda asks. She hasn't gotten up from the edge. "Why do you offer this favor?"

"Because I want something in return."

Not until Azuleth closed his jaws around Obizuth's neck did I see it. Freyda came to Callipolis to back a change of power. But she is not the only one with power to bring to the table now.

What if we did it the other way around?

What if we backed her?

"If you demand a change to the succession practices of Bassilea to claim the throne of the God-King, and your brother and father oppose, we can help. Let us be your guarantee. Let us accompany you to Vask to demand the birthright your sex denies, without the marriage you abhor. As you saw today, we have the fleet to ensure it."

Freyda's chest is heaving. "You would do that?"

I nod. "In exchange, you will remove your ships from our shores, forgive Callipolis's debt, and renounce any right to our vassalage."

I've stretched out a hand. Freyda's slow smile spreads. And then it falters like a hatchling in first flight. "They would never let me have it."

My fingers grasp her wrist. "No. They won't. That's why we have to take it."

She lets me pull her to her feet.

42

—

THE CHARTER

DELO

THREE MONTHS LATER

I've never appreciated how beautiful Norcia is in the summer. The grass glows impossibly green, the sky cracks open with blue, and the karst of Sailor's Folly sparkles over silver waves. A soft wind cajoles you into flight.

Sometimes, I wake and wonder at how close I came to giving it all up.

After the destruction of the Callipolan capital, and the subduing of the two Great Dragons, Griff Gareson prepared to return to Norcia. I'd told myself this was the last goodbye; that duty waited in Norcia for a king who must find a wife. I heard myself wish him well, and I watched him walk away, wishing he'd turn around.

Then I decided it was time I stopped waiting for Griff Gareson to find me first.

I ran after him and said it. All of it. That I'd forsake my duty for him, but I couldn't ask that of him for me. That he was, as Mabalena had put it, *the sunlight in my darkness*, that I would remember him always, my king across the sea, and I hoped he'd find happiness with whomever he made his queen. I embarrassed myself soundly, and Griff let me go on like this for far too long, a bit of a smirk on his face, before he finally put me out of my misery.

"Delo, you idiot," he said, "it's elective."

I couldn't believe he'd interrupt my declaration with politics. "What?"

"The *crown*."

When still I didn't get it, he pointed a finger at his own head and twisted it in a circle. "There's no need," he said, "for heirs."

I saddled Gephyra immediately after that. And when Astyanax found us about to launch and asked to be brought *home*, I pulled him onto the saddle with me. I left the twins with the letter to my father, formally recusing myself as his heir. I've yet to hear his reply. But I've heard from Phemi, and she tells me to be patient. *You're still his favorite, you know. He'll come round.*

I can't spend my life waiting for that.

Especially not today.

Griff Gareson wakes crankily and slowly, sprawled across more than his share of the bed, and when he remembers what's coming, he groans and tells me he'd rather I rejoin him under those covers, so I tear them off. Becca lets me brush her hair, Sty shovels down porridge, and on another day I'd send them down to school and let myself into Griff's study to organize his correspondence before, a little after dawn, we take the dragons out.

But today, we have other plans.

Becca and Sty lead the way, with skipping bare feet, up the winding stairs of the citadel and into the Garden of Folly, where the next High King of Norcia will begin his coronation vigil. Griff walks alone to the center of the standing stones, and when his eye catches Becca's, he winks. For the next twenty-four hours, and the last time in his life, he'll kneel.

And after that, we'll be here to see him rise.

I once worried that reading about heroes of the old Houses

made me unsuited to the life of one. Now I know it does. In this corner of the earth that is mine, I will read poetry and grow old in love.

Let them sing of others.

GRIFF

Kneeling in the Garden of Folly, fasting for one day and night, I look out upon the home that has been freed and the people who have become mine to care for.

I once told myself it was for nothing, our revolution that cost so much. Now I know it was for everything. The citadel has been rebuilt, with the old ha'Aurelian trappings gone for good. The clans' banners hang from the ramparts, all five. And down at what was Conqueror's Mound—now the Moot Hill again—we find a place to meet in counsel. The harbor, repaired, welcomes trade ships from Callipolis and Bassilea, barges from the karst mines newly opened in the Folly, and trawlers bringing in heavy hauls. Queen Freyda, the first female sovereign of Bassilea, is visiting soon with gifts of grain, and Delo and I will welcome her with a feast.

The summer's plenty overflows.

I would have had Agga see it, her daughter's belly full, her lips moving as her fingers trace the first words of Norish, her smile as she climbs on my dragon's back. I would have had Granda see me kneeling here, on my coronation vigil, before my anointing.

But maybe they do see it.

The sunset bleeds over the garden as the shadows of the clan-karsts grow long. A lone charter snakes its way through the Folly and I wonder, as I watch it, what Norcian returns from a northern passage. As the night passes, my shivering grows violent and dreams seem to come to me waking. I remember Antigone, sobbing on the stone. Becca, her hair flopping like seaweed as she was dropped into my arms. A future, if I could only see it past the grief that pulled like muck underfoot.

Truth be told, Agga says, *I knew this was coming since the day they gave you a dragon.*

With the dawn, the Folly blesses me with rain. It drips down my head, down my face, and into my mouth. My blackened vision clears, enough for me to see my palms on the stones, the skies roiling over karst, and Sparker riding the storm with joy. Lightning flares and thunder crackles. The shrines have found me worthy.

The sun rises, the storm clears, and the elders cover my shoulders with a flowing anointing robe and bid me rise. I walk barefoot with them through the citadel gates and down to the Moot Hill, where the clans spread below to hear the vows.

"He has been found worthy and would be your king, the one you have chosen among your elders. Will you follow him?"

The elders answer, and then the clans. "We will."

"And will you serve your people?"

"I will."

"Then bear the crown of the five clan stars."

The five circlets are clasped into one, and set upon my brow.

"Rise, High King of Norcia," says Bran.

And then it's over, and Becca and Sty and Delo are there, surrounding me, and Delo's smiling so wide his eyes are creasing at the corners. He gestures to the harbor, where a storm-beaten ha'Aurelian charter has come into a port. It's the same one I saw snaking its way through the Folly and now, for the first time, I recognize it. The last time I saw it, the paint was fresh where now it's faded, the wood had not yet turned gray with age, and I was only a boy.

A lone figure has disembarked from the charter and makes his way up the hill.

"There's someone here to see you."

ANNIE

When Aela and I finally return from Vask, the city we find in Callipolis little resembles the one we left in shambles after the Great Leveling. The rubble of the Palace has been cleared, the foundations of new government buildings have been laid, and the Janiculum Hill has been vacated. The patrician families who were rendered homeless in the Leveling must decide whether to rebuild or to move on. Reconstruction was directed in its initial stages by Lee, but he's gone by the time I arrive, leaving the upcoming protectorship elections to be managed by Miranda Hane. In the meantime, the Lyceum Club serves as our provisional seat of government.

I remember being intimidated by this place, in the past, when I was invited into it; but today, in the private, wood-paneled room on the upper floor of the Lyceum Club where I sit down opposite Phemi Skyfish, I know I'm not the nervous one.

Before the Leveling, Delo's sister and I had never spoken. The most I knew about her was that she and her twin were the ones who rigged the Norcian clan-karsts with explosives, and that during Griff's uprising, she was widowed. Today, she holds out a scroll with trembling fingers. She's written a document in both languages, Dragontongue and Callish, and tells me she's been working on it since she left Norcia.

It's a charter.

Phemi proposes that the feudal leases on the freeholds be voided in perpetuity and schools reopened under the Revolutionary guidelines. The triarchal estates should have permanently circum-scribed territory, and the dragonborn families who have reclaimed them should be given a choice: remain as custodians of their ances-tral properties on behalf of the state, and give up dragonriding; or continue as riders, and give up claim to their inheritance.

"A balance of power. A safeguard against corruption, the estates separated from the riders." I like the sound of this, but the details seem sticky. "How would the riders give up their dragons? By Widowing?"

No rider in their right mind would make such a choice. Phemi bites her lip, her fingers drifting up to rub the nape of her neck, and holds out a letter written in the looping Dragontongue of an aristocratic hand. "My brother writes of a discovery in the north, made by a Norcian mariner. Griff Gareson's father, actually. There's a place—a kind of haven, where dragons fly wild, the Nor-cians have stories about it—and Griff's father claims to have seen it. The Norcians call it the Star Springs."

I didn't realize Griff's father was alive. A line of poetry returns to me from the epic of the Skysung Queen: *North, into death, to gaze upon the Spring beyond the Stars* . . . "I thought the dragons go north to die."

Phemi shrugs: maybe not. "It's worth looking into."

I remember the fear I had, in that cell, that the separation I'd made with Aela would be permanent. But if Griff's father is right about a haven in the north, then such a lasting renunciation might be less a punishment than a solution—especially for riders who chose this life when they were too young to understand what they were giving up when they took their vows.

For all we know, the dragons might like it better to fly wild, too.

Phemi proposes that those who choose to remain with their dragons—be they dragonborn, bastard, or lowborn—take the title

of Guardian and form a Council of Riders to serve the democrati-
cally elected Protector.

"This seems fitting. Are any opposed?"

Phemi's brows knit. "You agree, then, that the policy of Guardians forswearing marriage and children should continue?"

I'm surprised by the question. "Of course." Atreus's vision
was flawed in many ways, but the desire to keep dragonriders
from building aristocratic dynasties is one I've never questioned.
"Why?"

"Well," says Phemi, a finger massaging her unbraided hair, "the
person that policy affects most is—you. By some accounts, you
are wed."

It's the last thing I'm expecting, and all I can say is, "Oh."

Phemi explains with evident hesitation. "The paper trail is
slight and inconclusive. Witnesses in the room at the time of your
trial say you claimed it, but Ixion had that claim scratched from
the official minutes. A property deed has been found in Harfast
with you named as a widow-heir to Farhall, but no marriage
record has been found to corroborate it. So, depending on the
interpretation . . . Farhall is yours and you are married to Leo
Stormscourge, who turns out to have survived—or it isn't yours
and you aren't. Whether you remain a Guardian is . . . up to you."

My breathing has turned shallow.

"We have the deed," Phemi goes on. "Depending on what you
decide, we can authenticate it or—destroy it. Naturally I'd understand if you wished to think it over, before telling me what you'd
like to do."

What I'd like to do. It sounds blasphemous.

After so many years of living the life that chose me—now,
finally, it's my turn. I can decide whether I choose it in return.

I reach for an answer and instead, for the first time since

leaving for Vask, find myself remembering the dream from the prison cell. Lee holding me and spinning me where we are nothing and no one. He told me once family wasn't something he wanted, but I remember the way he looked at me when he said that Farhall was mine to come back to, if I wanted it. That he'd wanted it in writing that *it was always me*.

I would have had everything in the world with you.

I wish I could have given it to you.

What if it's still something we can have?

Once, in conversation with Duck, I wondered if I had the chance to make the vows again, whether I would. *You're allowed to be happy, too,* Duck said, and I didn't believe him then but now, suddenly, miraculously, he's right and I am.

I'm allowed to have it. I'm allowed to have that house, and Lee, the joy my mother might have had that I have only glimpsed. I can reach out and take it. I can descend to earth as I fantasized, in Farhall, of doing, and join Lee on the ground.

All I'd need to give up is Aela and the city spread beneath our wing.

But at the thought, I feel I'm being shaken awake.

A protest rises up in me, incredulous, and it sounds a little like Pallor's growl. *Sing to me, Muse, of the Revolution's Daughter.*

I remember the relief I felt at the sight of blood on my legs. I remember Power pressing a badge into my hands as he told me it had been an honor. I remember Aela's fire as she laid our enemy low, her amber wings glowing in the sun, the rightness we felt at our connection restored.

I was at my lowest, as far from *happiness* as it was possible to be, in that prison cell. But it was there that I remembered who I was and what I'd come here to do. And if I had to choose between this fantasy of a carefree life and the moment I rose to my feet with a poem clutched in my hand and Power's last salute lingering as goose bumps on my skin—

My stomach is in knots, but not, I think, from indecision.

"Would you mind if I took a few days? There's someone I need to discuss this with."

"Of course," says Phemi at once. "Take your time."

After our meeting is done, I pack a saddlebag for a long weekend. I leave the city in able hands, who can handle it while we're gone, but who will need us when we return.

Then Aela and I set off for the closest thing we have to home.

LEE

When I first came back to Farhall, it was only to build the barrow mound. I imagined it would be a kind of burying of myself. I had no plans for what would happen next. Annie was leagues away, managing affairs of state in a foreign empire, and the Guardians who hadn't joined her were at work rebuilding a city I was ready to leave. I longed for fresher air.

Though it wasn't for lack of options in the capital.

"The people and the High Council would welcome you," Miranda Hane told me, "and the charter Phemi Skyfish is drawing up would allow it."

She was talking about the upcoming protectorate elections. I'd heard about Phemi's charter by now. A strict division between politics and dragons: I liked it in principle, and Rock, similarly freed from his vows, had told me he was considering it. It turned out that my Widowing opened the door to politics in a way that life as a Guardian hadn't. Pallor's sacrifice set me free of the blood in my veins, the curse I couldn't get out, in ways I was only now beginning to understand.

"I don't think I'm ready yet."

"Well, give it a decade or two," Hane said drily.

A *decade*. It seemed like imagining a lifetime with two feet on the ground. What I itched for was the barrow-mound, and I couldn't imagine what would come after, much less what would come after in ten years.

So I returned to Farhall. I dug the barrow. I laid the bones. I closed the door.

And I wondered what would happen next, until Nigel Garth asked about plans to rebuild the Big House, and I found myself looking them over. I was struck by how large it was, *obscenely grand* for a single family, as I once told Annie, but not by other standards. In size and shape, it was not unlike Albans Orphanage or the Cloisters. The rooms need only be divided and increased in number, and you'd have a different kind of home entirely.

I found myself imagining other futures for this green square of land at the edge of the world.

When Annie sur Aela arrives, our first reunion since they departed for Vask, I have the thought bubbling in my head like steam off the Travertine. Annie brings herbs for a pilgrimage to Dragon's End and the marble headstone she's had commissioned in the likeness of Pallor's brooding features, to be set over the door to the barrow. Tilly, the gray mare I've grown fond of, hauls a cart bearing the headstone up the escarpments for us, and with Aela's help, we set it over the barrow-mound door. In Dragontongue, it reads:

HERE LIES PALLOR AURELIAN, WHO CHOSE A STORMSCOURGE.

Aela curls at the base, and for a time, Annie and I busy ourselves grooming the heather that grows around the door, listening to the gulls fuss on the waves.

When the sun is low on the horizon, we make our way back down to the Green. From the cliffs beside the partially reconstructed Big House, we watch Aela coasting level with us on the sea breeze as the setting sun spreads rosy fingers. I wonder if the dragon's remembering, as I am, that she once spun pinwheels over these waves with Pallor. Her thoughts no longer mingle with mine, as they did for that strange spell in Norcia where grief bound us. She's all Annie's again. Still, when she looks at me, our gaze locks the way it used to do with Pallor. I lift a brow at her, and she flicks her tail in return. I resist a smile.

So Aela hasn't forgotten, either.

I'm about to share the idea that's been percolating, half mad, since I dug the barrow, when Annie speaks. "The estate papers declaring us wed conflict with the new charter. I need to choose. This, or—that."

It takes me a moment to understand what she's referring to. I'd had the papers drawn up in case I didn't make it out of a burning building; but only now do I realize what their implications are for us if I'm officially alive again. I feel a fluttering in my heart and my fingertips. The blinding horizon that I once imagined in a courthouse bleeds into the sunset warming our faces; for a moment it's startlingly vivid.

But also, it already feels like a memory.

Annie's mouth is rippling, unable to produce words, but I know whatever she needs to say, she needs to say herself. "Oh?" I feel like I'm attempting not to startle a skittish bird.

"I—do you still—you told me once you never wanted it. Was that true?"

When she finally turns to look at me, what she sees in my face makes her eyes grow bright.

"And you?" I ask. "Do you still want it?"

Annie blinks rapidly. "Yeah, I still want it," she says, her shoulders drawn together, and looks away.

I've got the seagrass gripped in my knuckles as the words pierce and twist. Like a deep stretch to the muscles, the pain mounts as it does its healing work, though I know this moment can't be endured much longer. She seems unable to produce the *but* that hangs over her answer, and for a moment, she looks so much like the shrinking classmate I remember that I'm tempted to smile.

"But," I prompt.

She speaks slowly and carefully into her knees. "But—I have work to do."

I feel a rush of pride mingled with a little bit more of that twisting pain.

"I know." Could she think I don't know that? After what happened, after *Pallor*—? Annie looks up, surprised. "That's why we . . . We wanted you, we *want* you, to do that work."

She hears his name in it, and rubs her eyes with a sudden, jerking gesture. Aela veers from her coasting position and reattaches to the cliff face with a soft crunch. Her tail coils round us, nestlike, as she settles to the ground, and Annie's hand unconsciously finds her crest and squeezes. Her chin is rippling almost too hard for speech, but she gets it out.

"I figured I could still visit. Holidays, like this. If you—wanted. I mean, you might want to see other people. I'd understand—"

This nearly makes me laugh. "Annie."

She sits rigidly beside me, her eyes on the dragon. But when I slip an arm around her, she curls closer, and for a moment, she lets me hold her. The pain ebbs, leaving me feeling drained, but my heart and head strangely clear. I feel a familiar scalding heat under my bare palm and find Aela nudging it, seeking my attention exactly the way Pallor used to. Surprise catches at my throat as I begin to scratch her beneath her crest, where Pallor used to itch.

"What will you do?" Annie asks in a wobbling voice.

"I think . . . I have work to do, too."

Our sides separate as she tilts back to look at me. Aela's head tilts as she cocks an ear in my direction. Now it's Annie's turn to cajole my words out. "Oh?"

I find my way toward it haltingly. "You know how the Cloister was destroyed, in the Leveling?"

Annie nods.

"I've been wondering if there might be a better place to rebuild it."

It began with remembering how Annie looked, when she first saw the Winterless Green. The way her face smoothed and found peace in a way I'd never seen before. It made me wonder if other young Guardians might find peace here, too. Far from the temptations of politics and power, in a place better suited to study and contemplation.

In a Big House with lots of rooms, and windows that look out over the sea.

Annie listens, her fingers tracing my palm, her eyes on the horizon. "Who would run it?" she asks softly.

"Well . . . I was thinking . . . I could. Maybe not yet. But when it's time, when we're ready."

When I'm ready.

Callipolis begins again. In the best, fairest version of herself, I think we would renounce dragons altogether. And maybe one day, we will. But in the meantime, so long as she depends on their protection, dragons are her best defense and dragonriders must be trained.

Atreus once told me I was his greatest mistake, and the more I think about it, the more I'd like to make a career of it.

"I'd have to get more of a staff," I add, "though Nigel's a decent start. And I could get the other Guardians to help for semesters at a time—Crissa, Cor, the ones who'd be suited to it. Duck and Lena maybe, which would also strengthen ties with Norcia. And . . . you, when you got time off from your military duties. If you wanted."

Annie's breath is slow and soft, her arms tight around her knees, and her silence makes me unexpectedly nervous, so I go on. "I was also thinking . . . it's no longer about political leadership, with the new charter. We don't have to worry about test scores or whatever else Atreus wanted. And in that case—preference for children to be brought for the Choosing could be given to found-lings, orphans."

"So this could be their home," Annie murmurs. "A better life for those who had no futures."

She doesn't have to say *for kids like us.*

I nod, swallowing. "And . . . I've already got three eggs to start with."

Ours.

She's still watching that sunset, her face bathed in red, wisps of her auburn hair glowing. I can't read her expression. But when she speaks, her voice is thick. "I think . . . Aela would really like that."

The dragon's already purring beside us.

After that I lead Annie through it, her hand in mine, the foun-dations of the home being rebuilt, mostly roofless and slightly wall-less. In the room that will be mine—smaller and more mod-est than the one that was my father's—I close the door, pull Annie onto my bed, and remove her flamesuit. Her lips trace the burn scars down my face, and mine trace the brand on her thigh.

"You came back to me."

"And you came back to me."

Her lip curves against mine. "Now, my lord," she says, "wasn't there something you wanted to practice?"

A little later, we make our way down to the Travertine, with Aela leading the way and Argos loping at a lazy trot behind, and in the wedding-white sediment as the sun goes down, we bring the three dragon eggs to the steaming water, and Aela curls round them to wait for her hatchlings.

ACKNOWLEDGMENTS

Danielle Burby, my agent, has looked after this project from beginning to end with unwavering attention to its welfare and mine. Gretchen Durning and Arianne Lewin, my editors, have guided the writing: Ari's stamp on the book and trilogy was characteristically invaluable; Gretchen's dedication was inspiring and her insight a guiding light. The formidable forces of G. P. Putnam's Sons Books for Young Readers and Penguin Teen have overseen its production: Jen Klonsky, Natalie Vielkind, Cindy Howle, Anne Heausler, Laurel Robinson, Misha Kydd, Elise LeMassena, Tessa Meischeid, cover designer Kristie Radwilowicz, and illustrator Steve Stone.

I am grateful to the talented writers and friends who have followed this trilogy through two books and kept me on track for the third: Eloise Andry, Paul Baker, Elayne Becker, Kristen Ciccarelli, Lizzie Cooke and Michael Johnson, Phil Dershwitz, Marcy Flanagan and Michelle Mirecki, Kaitlin Gladney, Joanna Hathaway, June Huang, Sam Lee, David Molina, Laura Brooke Robson, Alissa Spera, Bridget Tyler, Leslie Vedder, and Sandra Vasquez Ventimilla.

My mother set me up in my childhood bedroom to write the

end of Part III (I'm sorry, Mom), and Erin McDonough drove us down the Pacific Coast Highway while I revised in the passenger seat. Reese Eschmann convinced me to take the chance on a writing retreat I needed, and James Persichetti sat across from me in the Bertrand Café while I drafted the last chapter. Nora and Vera have been a daily ray of sunlight through Chicago winters and pandemic blues, and I'm grateful to their parents, Ingrid and Arvind, for their encouragement and understanding.

I first remember talking about what would become the The Aurelian Cycle late at night in a college dorm room with Robert Stone, who said Plato's *Republic* with dragons sounded like a cool idea. Eight years of marriage and countless drafts later, he apologized for reading *Furysong* only twice. Thank you for helping with the dragons, my dear. It's been a joy building this life with you.